"It is time," said Fistandantilus, excitement turning his voice painfully dissonant. "Get ready to light the candle, human."

Tanis held the mirror in one hand and groped for Brandella's hand with the other. When he found it, she pulled away. Her hand was cold as death.

The chant began so low it was almost inaudible. Slowly, the sound grew louder, the words unknown and unknowable.

The chanting grew still louder. The cabin began to quiver as if the wind outside were trying to pick the little shack off the ground and hurl it off the foothills, down to the valley below. Water and mud dripped between growing cracks in the ceiling. The dead branches crisscrossed over one section of the roof began to break apart and tumble into the room. A moan escaped the terrified weaver, but Tanis dared not comfort her.

Fistandantilus continued his chant, his own voice howling even louder than the wind.

Tanis didn't know what was breaking the cabin apart—the spell or Death trying to hold on to its victim. The forces of magic and nature were clearly at war. . . .

## DRAGONLANCE® Preludes

Before the War of the Lance . . .

Before they became heroes . . .

*Darkness and Light*
Paul B. Thompson &
Tonya C. Cook

*Kendermore*
Mary Kirchoff

*Brothers Majere*
Kevin Stein

*Riverwind the Plainsman*
Paul B. Thompson &
Tonya C. Cook

*Flint the King*
Mary Kirchoff &
Douglas Niles

*Tanis, the Shadow Years*
Scott Siegel &
Barbara Siegel

PRELUDES VOLUME SIX

# TANIS,
## THE SHADOW YEARS

### BARBARA SIEGEL
### & SCOTT SIEGEL

**For David Luhn—**

In our world, beset by dragons, a poet takes the field. Protected by the gleaming armor of his intellect, and with Henry James as his stalwart ally, he enters the fray with an army of eloquent works and carefully considered thoughts at his command. Whether the battles are won or lost, at night we sit around the telephone campfire listening to his war stories til nearly daybreak. Such is the way of warriors. Such is also the way of friends. Such is not the way to toast marshmallows.

We will always be a part of each other's memories . . . and phone bills.

## ACKNOWLEDGMENTS

The authors wish to offer their deeply felt appreciation to Mary Kirchoff for her stalwart support and generous spirit. She is someone who can be counted upon during difficult times. Thanks are also due to Pat McGilligan, who is easy to work with and who has a sharp editorial eye.

In addition, we are grateful to Ellen Porath for sharing her invaluable knowledge of the DRAGONLANCE® world, and to Bill Larson, who skillfully shepherded our manuscript through to its final form.

# Tanis, the Shadow Years
©1990 TSR, Inc.
©2000 Wizards of the Coast, Inc.

Distributed in the United States by Holtzbrinck Publishing. Distributed in Canada by Fenn Ltd.

Distributed to the hobby, toy, and comic trade in the United States and Canada by regional distributors.

Distributed worldwide by Wizards of the Coast, Inc. and regional distributors.

Cover art by Matt Stawicki
First Printing: November 1990
Library of Congress Catalog Card Number: 200310084

9

US ISBN: 0-7869-3039-X
UK ISBN: 0-7869-3040-3
620-17995-001-EN

U.S., CANADA,
ASIA, PACIFIC, & LATIN AMERICA
Wizards of the Coast, Inc.
P.O. Box 707
Renton, WA 98057-0707
+1-800-324-6496

EUROPEAN HEADQUARTERS
Wizards of the Coast, Belgium
T Hofveld 6d
1702 Groot-Bijgaarden
Belgium
+322 467 3360

Visit our web site at **www.wizards.com**

# PART I

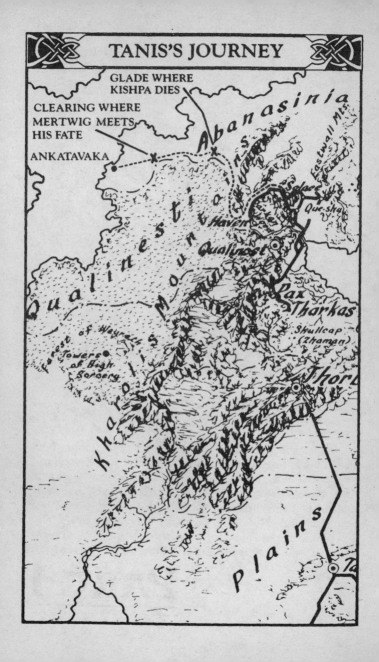

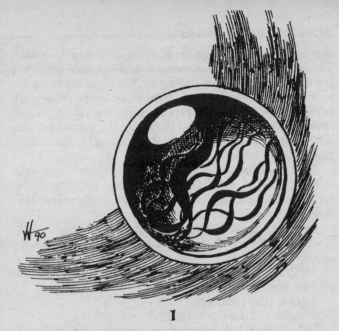

# I

# Juggling Choices

"ANOTHER MUG OF ALE FOR MY FRIEND," CRIED THE homely dwarf.

Tika, the young barmaid, sighed. It was late. Very late. And the red-haired teen-ager was tired. Even Tanis, who had come back to the Inn of the Last Home after all his friends had gone, looked drained. He sat there alone, save for the exuberant dwarf with the funny nose and drooping ears who had suddenly befriended him.

Tanis, almond-shaped eyes thoughtful in his tanned face, shook his head at Tika. "No more ale," he said. "At least not for me."

The barmaid planted her feet sturdily before the dwarven stranger and flung the bar rag over one shoulder. The bean-shaped common room in the Solace inn, once the site of hours of storytelling by Tanis and his companions, now stretched emptily behind her to the stonework fireplace. No flames flickered against the stonework to cheer the lonely room, and the dying embers added precious little warmth. All in all, Tanis thought, the atmosphere suited his mood just fine.

Tika, freckles standing out from her skinny face even in this failing light, challenged the stranger. "And you, sir?" she demanded. "You're finished for the night, isn't that so?"

The dwarf smiled at the barmaid and gave her a wink. "I wouldn't dream of drinking alone. Perhaps you'll have one with me?"

"Hmphh." The skinny teen-ager raised her chin and pressed her lips into a thin line.

"I guess that means no?"

"Hmphh!" Tika's eyes flashed.

"What a vocabulary you have," the dwarf said, mock-seriously, his ears drooping a notch lower. "Myself, I love words. May I teach you the phrase, 'I'd be delighted to have a drink with you, Clotnik, you beguiling wretch?' " He grinned in a manner obviously intended to be charming.

She fought it, but just a bit of a smile creased her mouth.

Clotnik crowed. "I saw that!"

"Hmphh!" Tika ran off to the kitchen.

Tanis's tired eyes sparkled at Clotnik's playfulness, at Tika's shyness—which Tanis now saw would ripen into allure when she reached womanhood. Tanis remembered a time when he had been equally innocent. Laurana. Yes, he had felt the heady pleasure of a girl's meaningful gaze, and had it been possible, he might have answered that look with his heart. More recently there had been Kitiara. He had ended it with the hot-headed swordswoman just hours before, and for his honesty he had received a slap in the face that jarred his teeth loose. But even now he was wondering if he hadn't been a fool. It was too late to do anything about it; Kit had already left on her journey with Sturm. Tanis knew, with a black certainty, that he would not see Kit—or any of any of his companions—for five long years. And maybe not even then.

Tanis unknowingly clenched his hands. Whether from long ago or from mere moments past, his memories stabbed him deeply with a painful sense of loss . . . and the shine in his eyes vanished.

Clotnik laughed as Tika disappeared into the kitchen, but his expression quickly darkened when Otik, the inn-keeper, emerged through those same doors with a tally sheet in his hands.

"I don't know how you managed to drink all that ale," Otik said with a trace of awe in his voice as he placed the tally sheet down on the table in front of Clotnik. "You must make a good living to build up such a bill," he added pointedly.

Clotnik squirmed for a moment and then brightened. "You've had such a busy night," he exclaimed, grabbing the innkeeper's hand and shaking it. "You must have made a small fortune. What is money, then, to such a successful businessman?" He hurried on, not giving Otik a chance to utter as much as a syllable. "Why, you don't need money. Money would be wasted on you!"

The rotund innkeeper glanced warily at Tanis. The half-elf merely shrugged.

"Money you could extract from anyone," the dwarf rambled on without bothering to draw breath, "but a demonstration of nearly unimaginable juggling skills . . . well, only Clotnik can give you that. And for this special performance," he quickly added in a kindly voice as he pulled a large traveling bag from beneath the table, "I won't ask for any payment at all except the money to cover this bill, plus two more mugs of ale. No, make that three—one for Tanis, one for me, and one for yourself."

Otik appeared uncertain, as though he didn't know

what to do first: strangle the bamboozling little dwarf or simply tear out his tongue. After a moment's thought, the decision was firmly made. He'd strangle him and *then* tear out his tongue.

By then, Clotnik had opened his traveling bag and had extracted five intricately detailed, glistening balls, one of gold, one of silver, one of brass, one of iron, and the last one of delicate glass.

"Shall I juggle for you?" Clotnik asked the mesmerized innkeeper.

Otik didn't answer. He just stared at the obviously valuable balls grasped in the juggler's hands. His eyes protruded slightly in his round face.

"I think you've got his attention," Tanis said dryly. "In fact, you've got mine, as well. Not to mention young Tika's," he went on, gesturing toward the kitchen where the barmaid could be spied peeking through the doorway.

Clotnik looked back at the red-haired barmaid. "I love an audience," he said with a satisfied smile. "I live for this." And then he began to juggle. The balls of gold, silver, and glass shimmered in the candlelight as they flew up and down, creating a stark contrast with the heavy iron and brass balls that cut through the air around them.

"Juggling comes naturally to everyone," Clotnik said easily as he deftly plucked the glass ball out of the air and then threw it up again, this time from behind his back. "We juggle our friends, keeping one in the air while we squeeze attention from another. We juggle our work with our pleasure, our needs with our shame, and even our love with our hate. Everyone juggles, all of us trying to keep as many balls in the air as possible, trying to grab at each opportunity before it comes crashing down at our feet."

Now Clotnik juggled all five balls in a fast, tight circle, the round objects blurring from the speed with which he whipped them through the air.

"Take Tanis, for instance," the dwarf continued effortlessly. "Although he says little that is personal—after all, we've only just met—he talks of leaving Solace at dawn. Yet he doesn't sleep. Why? Perhaps he has yet to decide where he will go, come the morning sun. It must be so, because he will not speak of his destination. Ah, what mystery and intrigue! Don't tell me *he* is not juggling!"

The juggler continued. "Where are his friends? Scattered to the four corners of Krynn for five years, he tells me. So Tanis tosses up a ball of loneliness"—and Clotnik used a deft movement to single out the gold ball for a heartbeat before returning the glittering orb to the flashing circle.

"Meanwhile," the juggler commented, "Tanis tells me he plans to make his journey alone. Ah, toss up a ball of danger, for no one should travel alone in these troubled times. And even as those two balls travel in their circular arc, Tanis must keep the ball of his birth in the air, as well. Because, of course, his ultimate juggling act is between his elven and human halves."

Otik, arrested in the act of wiping his hands on a streaked white apron, drew a sharp breath and gave a troubled glance at Tanis. He didn't know how the half-elf would react to Clotnik's indelicate remark.

The half-elf, betraying no emotion in his voice, carefully said, "Tell me, my friend, what do you juggle besides those balls? Do you juggle your life's breath somewhere between impertinence and honesty?" His hand shifted casually to the sword at his left side, although like most creatures of elven blood, he never would have taken a life unnecessarily—and certainly not out of annoyance alone. Still, it might not hurt to caution the young dwarf that not everyone would be so forgiving. "I wonder how many times you have misjudged your audience and said the wrong thing to the wrong person." Tanis moved his hand back to the table top.

"Many times," Clotnik cheerfully conceded, his eyes flashing green in the candlelight. "I have often been cut down to size. You know," he added with a mischievous grin, "I used to be much taller."

"Besides free drinks," asked Tanis, narrowing his eyes, "what is it that you want?"

"Want?"

"He hears well, Otik, don't you think?"

The innkeeper nodded, his eyes drawn again to the whirling balls that Clotnik now juggled in yet another pattern, this time using his right hand to juggle three in a circle and his left hand to juggle the other two in the traditional up and down method.

"I'd like to travel with you," Clotnik said guardedly.

Tanis laughed shortly. "Even though you don't know where we'd be going?"

"I didn't say *I* didn't know where you were going," Clotnik corrected. "I said *you* didn't know."

Tanis cocked his head to one side and considered the juggler.

Clotnik began tossing the balls high into the air from behind his back, each ball nearly touching the ceiling of the inn as he juggled all five in a huge ellipse.

"Your father must be very proud of you!" said Otik suddenly, overcome by the juggler's performance.

At those words, Clotnik's head whipped around to look at the innkeeper. And in that instant, the juggler lost his concentration. He tried to recover, but it was too late. The iron and brass balls thudded to the floor, one just missing Otik's foot. Clotnik managed to grab the gold and the silver spheres, and then he lunged for the swiftly falling, fragile glass ball. Unfortunately, it had sailed out of his reach. "No!" he cried.

Tanis, swift and graceful, dove out of his chair and, landing on the floor with arms outstretched, plucked the delicate glass ball out of the air.

Tika burst into applause from her vantage point at the kitchen door. Otik cheered. And Clotnik let out a sigh of relief that sounded like the *whoosh* of a metalsmith's bellows. "I can't replace that if it breaks," explained the juggler, wiping the sweat from his slanted forehead with a sleeve.

"Then why do you risk it?" Tanis replied, examining the intricate blue and green design on the otherwise clear glass ball before handing it back to Clotnik.

"Why bother juggling at all if there isn't some risk involved?" Clotnik asked nonchalantly, returning the five balls to his traveling bag. "After all, who would go see a man fight a hatori to the death if the hatori had no teeth?"

"Good point, but why fight a sand crocodile in the first place?" Tanis retorted.

Clotnik gave a short laugh. "I'm going to enjoy traveling with you," he said. "You have a lively mind—not to mention a quick hand."

Tanis kept his tone urbane. "It seems you've accepted an invitation that I have yet to offer."

"You will offer."

"Why?"

"Because," Clotnik said, leaning over to whisper, "I can take you to a man who knew your father."

Tanis felt the color drain from his face. A hand, cold and inexorable as death, clenched his ribcage with killing force. The half-elf sat in stunned silence, his heart thumping wildly.

His father.

All his life he had wanted to learn something, anything, about the man who had spawned him. All he knew was that once, during a warring time between humans and elves, a human soldier had had his way with an elven maiden, Tanis's mother, leaving her broken, battered, and with child. What kind of man would do that? Tanis questioned yet again. What kind of blood did the half-elf have running in his veins? Tanis's mother had died only months after Tanis's birth, leaving him to the care of distant elven relatives—and part of neither world, human nor elven. After ninety-seven years of life, Tanis still wondered about that human warrior. But how could this juggling dwarf know anything about the stranger, no doubt long dead, who was his father?

Clotnik seemed well satisfied with the reaction his comment had had on Tanis. So he turned to Otik and declared, "As for you, my fine innkeeper, have I paid my bill?"

This time it was Otik's turn to squirm; he hated giving away his hard-brewed ale. Yet the juggler had truly put on a magnificent show. "Don't you have anything you can give me toward the settlement of this debt?" Otik pleaded.

"Not a thing," admitted Clotnik, "except my showmanship. Come now, isn't that worth more than any metal coin?"

"Well—"

"So it's settled," he announced triumphantly. "Now, where are the three mugs of ale that are part of our bargain?"

To Otik's surprise, Tika was already carrying them out of the kitchen.

*　　*　　*　　*　　*

Tanis stood on a rise looking back at Solace in the valley below. He and Clotnik had left before dawn, and just then, as the sun's first rays flooded across the top of the valley, they illuminated the village's majestic treetops like a crown of jewels. Lower down, radiant golden shadows traced the homes and businesses in the vallenwood limbs in which they were perched. By far the dominant feature in the landscape was the Inn of the Last Home, nestled in tree branches atop a staircase that spiraled around the trunk of the huge tree. Tanis resolutely shoved aside the memories of convivial times at the Inn; the future beckoned now. If only it were as predictable, as illuminated, as the staircase to Otik's establishment.

"How long before we meet this man you spoke of?" Tanis asked.

Clotnik, his ears drooping still farther in the throes of what appeared to be a minotaur-sized hangover, winced at Tanis's brisk tone. "Several days," he said quietly. "Maybe longer. You must be patient."

"Did this man know my father personally?"

"He'll tell you everything when you meet him."

"Were they good friends?" Tanis persisted.

The dwarf sighed and clutched his head. "Just wait," he begged. "What's your hurry? You've waited ninety-seven years to learn more of your father. What matters a few more days?"

"Every day matters," Tanis replied, noting that Clotnik somehow knew exactly how old he was. Very few knew his total years. Any doubts he harbored about the juggler's genuine knowledge about his father were muted by that one offhand remark. "I have something to do as soon as I finish meeting with your friend," the half-elf added vaguely.

"And what might that be?" the dwarf casually asked as they trudged along a sun-dappled road to the west.

Tanis did not answer. The real reason he had suggested that the companions separate for five years was not entirely noble. He wanted to strike out on his own, alone, to find something to believe in, something in which he could take some pride.

He had watched others grab at life while he stopped and considered, balanced his options. Some might have said that as a half-elf, his options and possibilities were limited by virtue of his birth. He didn't want to believe that. Those he knew and loved best had a purpose in their lives. He had none.

Kit, much as he thought her mercenary ways immoral, reveled in her military skills. Then there was Raistlin; he wanted to be a great wizard, and he was willing to sacrifice anything for that. Caramon, Raistlin's warrior twin, had a purpose, too—to care for his brother. Sturm Brightblade believed in his knighthood, in his Code, and it gave him strength and dignity. Flint Fireforge had his metalsmithing, a trade and art that gave the dwarf pleasure as well as pride. And Tasslehoff Burrfoot . . . well,

Tas was a kender, and that didn't count.

Tanis fell into a dark mood. What had his ambition been? To sit around the Inn of the Last Home and listen to his friends tell tales of their exploits while he slowly grew old and did nothing?

He had had an idea, a thought, a wild dream. But he had told no one. It had been his secret, something he dared not share with his companions for fear that if he failed, he would, in his own mind, further lose their respect. But Clotnik was a stranger. Why not tell him?

"I am going to become a sculptor," he blurted, realizing he had been nearly bursting to share his ambition.

"In wood? Stone? Clay?" asked Clotnik, seemingly pleased to find the half-elf finally willing to talk.

"Stone, I think. Something that will last."

The juggler gave Tanis a long, thoughtful stare.

## 2

# Fire in the Night

"It's cold and it's wet, but it's not nearly as satisfying as Otik's ale," said Clotnik as he drank deeply from the clear, clean little lake they'd found at the edge of a wood. It was nearly dark, but they still could see beyond the trees to where the land opened into rolling meadows and fields.

Tanis dunked his head into the water. Then, like a dog, he shook his wet mane of reddish-brown hair; droplets rained around him on the sand. Refreshed, he sat down and leaned back against a tree, comfortable in his soft leather traveling gear and cloak.

He closed his eyes and, in a habit he had begun after

leaving Solace three days earlier, tried to picture what his father must have looked like. It made some sense that there would be a family resemblance—at least in regard to his human features. He imagined a tall, broad-shouldered man with deep-set eyes, a dimpled chin, and a mouth with a slight downward turn of the lips. He liked to think that his father was handsome, strong, and intelligent. All he knew for certain, though, was that his father was a man who would take brazen advantage of a defenseless woman. The half-elf wanted desperately to discover something good about the man who had done so much harm to his mother. And soon he would know. The juggler had promised.

A worrisome scent suddenly caught his attention. Tanis opened his eyes and asked, "Do you smell something?"

The dwarf looked offended. "Look, I *intend* to bathe," he blustered.

Tanis smiled humorlessly, his eyes somber slits. Clotnik caught the half-elf's concern and sniffed audibly. Then he shook his head. "I smell nothing out of the ordinary," the dwarf said.

The half-elf, however, continued to scan the horizon—what little of it could be seen through the trees. "Smoke," he said brusquely, staring into the tree line.

"Oh!" said Clotnik, alarmed. He scrambled to his feet, ready to run but apparently uncertain which direction was best. Ignoring the panicky dwarf, the half-elf stood and walked calmly to the edge of the wood.

Clotnik dogged his steps. "Elves have such good vision. Do you see anything?"

"I'm not sure . . . " Tanis replied slowly. "The sky beyond those hills to the north seems a little brighter, but the twilight can fool the eyes. We'll know better when the sun goes down."

The juggler alternately wrung his hands and tugged at his brown beard. Around them, the breeze began to pick up. When he spoke, his voice was pitched half an octave higher than normal. "You don't think the fire is behind us, do you? I mean, the forest isn't burning, is it?"

Tanis hesitated, still gazing into the trees and wishing he could hasten nightfall. "I don't think so," he answered slowly. "The wind is blowing from the north, and there's the smell of cinders on it." At that moment, the wind briefly shifted and Tanis lost the scent, causing him a moment's doubt. "Maybe it's nothing," he added, unconvinced.

They waited and watched the northern sky. The twilight slowly faded, bringing darkness everywhere—except to the north. To their horror, the sky before their eyes danced with an ever-brightening light. They could see no flames, but there was no doubt that behind the hills, a great grass fire blazed. And if the wind continued to blow in their direction, the fire certainly would overtake them.

Clotnik's fidgeting had increased; seemingly unaware of his actions, he pulled small tufts from his brown beard. "We've got to run!" he blurted.

But Tanis shook his head and stopped the dwarf from edging away with a curt wave of one hand. "Impossible," the half-elf replied. "You can't outrun a grass fire. Besides, it could be miles wide. We'd never outflank it. Our best chance is right here; we've got the lake to protect us."

"We could go back the way we came. The fire wouldn't burn through the woods as fast as it will sweep down the meadows."

"That's true," conceded Tanis.

"Then let's go!"

"No."

The small dwarven body nearly vibrated with frustration. "Why not?" he demanded.

Tanis, sympathizing with his companion's fear, tried to keep his voice soothing. "This wood is small. We came through meadows to get here. This is like an island of trees, and we could get trapped in an inferno. No, this is the safest place to make our stand." The half-elf smiled reassuringly as the dwarf made a visible attempt to control his nerves, shoving his fists deep into the pockets of his dark brown trousers and acting as though witnessing killer grass fires were as everyday an event as juggling for travelers in far-flung inns.

"What do we do?" asked Clotnik.

"There's a fallen tree back by the edge of the lake," Tanis recalled. "Let's shove it into the water. At least we'll have something to hold on to."

Clotnik began to turn and run, but Tanis grabbed him by the edge of his green tunic. "Fill the water pouches. When this is over, the lake may be full of soot and ash."

The juggler nodded and hurried toward the lake.

Tanis's elven vision allowed him to see well in the darkness, and he busied himself with digging a shallow hole in the ground, where he tossed their packs and the carefully crafted silver-inlaid broadsword that Flint had forged and given him as a gift during their last night at the Inn of the Last Home. The broadsword reminded him vividly of the differences between the two dwarves—irascible old Flint Fireforge, tough and true as the metal he forged, and the excitable Clotnik, as changeable as the whirling designs he created with his juggling balls. Of course, a difference of nearly a century in their ages could account for some of that, Tanis thought.

No more than six or seven minutes had passed while Tanis buried everything, yet in that short time, the sky had gone vermilion and smoke had begun to choke the air. Tanis glanced at the closest hill to the north and saw the blaze sweep over its crest. Plants exploded into red, orange, and yellow from the heat of the blaze. Small animals dashed, panic-stricken, from the grasslands to the lake. The inferno was moving fast in the wind, gobbling up the tall grass in the meadow with insatiable hunger.

"Quick!" ordered Tanis. "Help me push that log into the water!"

"Where is it?" cried Clotnik in a panic. He suddenly broke into a coughing fit from the smoke. "I can't see it!"

he finally managed to sputter.

Acrid smoke and ash flew in clouds through the air. Fortunately, Tanis's elvensight allowed him to see the warm red glow cast by every living thing, although the aura that outlined Clotnik's stocky body blended increasingly with the growing heat. The half-elf hurried to his companion, who stood at the edge of the lake. Tanis ripped a piece of cloth from his tunic, dipped it into the water, then held it over Clotnik's mouth and nose. "Tie it around your face," he called over the roar of the encroaching fire. "It'll help you breathe."

Clotnik tied the wet cloth over his face while Tanis created his own mask from another piece of cloth. Then Tanis led the juggler to the nearby log, and they put their shoulders to the heavy fallen tree and heaved.

It didn't move.

"Again!" Tanis commanded.

They threw their shoulders against it.

Nothing.

Tanis turned to look behind him. The fire was halfway down the hill.

"Push or die!" shouted Tanis.

They pushed. With a loud sucking noise, the log came free of the mud at the lake's edge.

"It's moving!" Clotnik cried.

"Keep pushing!"

They planted their feet as best they could in the slippery muck and shoved one more time. The log suddenly swung free and eased into the water, rolled several times, and then floated slowly out toward the center of the lake.

Clotnik fell to his hands and knees, his lumpy face pale with exhaustion under the dirt and ash.

"Catch your breath," Tanis said—somewhat needlessly, he realized; Clotnik could do little else but gulp for air. "We'll need long, sturdy sticks to push away any burning debris that falls near us. I'll find them. You wait here."

The half-elf searched the ground nearby, doing his best

to ignore the flames rushing down the hill toward the woods, until a terrible cry reached his ears.

His head shot up, and he squinted into the bright, leaping flames that stretched from east to west along the northern sky as far as he could see.

At first he saw nothing except a blaze of bright yellow and red. Then a shadow, standing out from the background scarlet, leaped across his line of vision.

Tanis shielded his eyes from the blinding light and the heavy smoke that was sweeping in ahead of the flames.

The shadow was a figure, and it was moving. But was it a man? Instinctively, without hesitation, Tanis took long strides away from the safety of the lake, toward the edge of the woods, hoping for a better look.

"Where are you going?" demanded Clotnik.

"I think someone's out there."

"Oh, no!" The horror in the dwarf's tone outpaced any panic the little man had shown until now. To Tanis's surprise, the juggler raced to join him. The half-elf reacted with a panic of his own. What if the man out there was the one who had known his father?

By this time, the front edge of the grass fire was no more than a hundred yards from the tree line.

"Help . . . " came a ragged cry.

"Over there! To the right!" Clotnik shrieked. "Did you hear it?"

Tanis didn't bother answering. He saw the movement, captured the image of a man's silhouette against the nearly blinding flames, and ran as fast as he could toward the conflagration.

The roar of the fire and the choking wind that swept before it were nearly as overwhelming as the blistering heat. Still, Tanis fought his way forward. Someone was running toward him; a figure in a long robe stumbled just barely ahead of the leaping flames of the grass fire.

"This way!" shouted Tanis, waving his arms.

The man looked up; fire had scorched the rear hem of his dark robe. The man and the half-elf were no more than ten yards apart when the man held out his arms, called out something unintelligible, and collapsed in a heap. His robe smoldered; the fire raced to consume him.

Tanis was faster.

He practically vaulted the last ten yards and scooped the man into his arms. The leading edge of the grass fire nipped at the edge of Tanis's leather tunic as he moved as fast as he could away from the flames. He was running downhill with the powerful hot wind at his back, so despite the weight in his arms, Tanis was able to stay ahead of the fast-moving fire, but not by much. Soon the swirling smoke enveloped him. Breathing heavily, his eyes burning, Tanis lost sight of the woods. He stopped, confused, the man a dead weight in his arms.

"Where . . . ?" the half-elf stammered. He didn't know which way to run. The sound of the fire seemed to surround him, and there was no hope of catching a glimpse of Clotnik, elvensight or no elvensight. He wondered, for the first time, what it would feel like to burn to death.

Just then a hand reached out and grabbed his arm. "This way!" said a choked voice only barely recognizable as Clotnik's. "You got turned around. The trees are over here. Hurry!"

Relief showered over Tanis like a spring rain. Once again the juggler had surprised him. The half-elf followed Clotnik's lead, and a few seconds later they emerged from the cloud of smoke into the temporary shelter of the trees. The fire leaped bare yards behind them.

They ran toward the lake as the tree line at the edge of the meadow exploded into flames. Tongues of fire shot up along the bark and ignited the limbs above. The heat was so intense that leaves began to burn even before the flames had reached them.

"Is he alive?" Clotnik asked worriedly as they began wading into the lake.

Tanis looked down and saw that he held an old man, his iron-gray hair streaked with ash and his thin face seamed with age. "I think he's still breathing," said the

half-elf, "but he's badly burned." As if to give credence to
Tanis's words, the old man's skin sizzled and smoked as it
came in contact with the cold water of the lake.

When the water became too deep for wading, Clotnik
and Tanis, with the old man in tow, swam toward the
log, about twelve yards away. The grass, bushes, and
trees all around the lake burned orange, red, and blue,
with flaming branches raining down around Tanis and
Clotnik as if there'd been a cloudburst of fire.

Then, finally, Tanis asked the question that burned as
hotly in his heart as the flames that surrounded them: "Is
he the one who knew my father?"

The juggler nodded.

Tanis clenched his teeth until his jaws ached. He
wanted to scream, to slash at fate with his sword so that
it could never tease him so cruelly again. Somehow, he
kept his silence.

As the night wore on, Tanis and Clotnik clung to the
log, taking turns keeping the old man's head above the
water. They had no sticks to push away burning debris,
so they had to use their feet to shove away anything dangerous that came crashing down near them. More worrisome, though, were the hot cinders that filled the air
above the lake, hissing as they splattered into the water.
Any one of the cinders could burn out an eye or disfigure
a face. They had to be on constant guard, not only for
themselves, but for the old man. More than once, they
had to pull him under the water to keep him from getting
burned. He coughed and choked, letting them know that
he was still among the living, although just barely.

And the fire raged on.

## 3

# The Bargain

---

It was nearly morning when the fire finally
burned itself out. The wood was a smoking relic, and ash
swirled above the lake on desultory breezes.

Clotnik lay half in and half out of the water, one leg
wrapped around the stub of a branch sticking out of the
log on which he was sprawled. The other leg, as well as
one arm, dangled in the cold water.

Tanis, who had just awakened from a short and troubled sleep, gazed at the juggler with sympathy. Clotnik
looked like an abandoned child who had run out of
everything, including hope. But Clotnik would be fine
with a little rest. The half-elf's gaze passed to the thin, old

---

man, propped in the crevice between the partially submerged tree trunk and one of its sturdy limbs. Tanis watched, frozen, until the man's chest rose again. He still lived, then. At least the cold water soothed the old man's badly burned skin; it was a small blessing.

Tanis pushed away the dirty surface water with a few flicks of his hand and then splashed his face. Although stiff from being in the water all night, the half-elf began to kick his legs and stroke with one arm, slowly maneuvering the log toward the shore.

He had nearly reached an open patch of land when a hoarse voice croaked, "You."

The half-elf immediately glanced at Clotnik, thinking the juggler had revived. But the dwarf snored on.

"Here," said the voice. "It's me."

Tanis adjusted his gaze to the crook of the tree limb and was surprised to see that the old man's blue eyes were open. He stopped swimming.

"Keep going," ordered the ancient one. "Get me out of this water before I shrivel up."

"You're badly burned, old one," Tanis said softly. "The pain is going to be very bad when I lay you down on the ground."

"What do you know of pain?" the old man asked sarcastically. "Just do as I say."

Clotnik finally stirred. He lifted his arm to stretch and promptly slid off the log and into the water. Flailing for a handhold on the tree trunk, the juggler splashed and screamed for help, not realizing that he was a mere dozen yards from land.

Gliding easily through the ash covered water, Tanis grabbed Clotnik around the neck and pulled his head high above the surface of the lake. Dirty water streamed from the dwarf's brown beard. "Easy," Tanis said firmly. "You're okay. Take hold of the log," he said, gesturing with his head. "We're almost on dry ground."

"Good!" gasped Clotnik, grasping the log.

While Tanis pushed the log closer to the shoreline,

Clotnik glanced over at the old one, who was smiling— or maybe grimacing. The ancient's face was badly burned. And despite the best efforts of Tanis and Clotnik, cinders had burned away portions of the old man's iron-gray hair.

"I didn't think you'd live till morning," Clotnik said solemnly.

The man's voice carried the hoarseness of pain and exhaustion. "I had no choice."

\*　\*　\*　\*　\*

Tanis dug up their meager belongings, then took a blanket from his pack and dunked it into the lake, spreading it out on a flat piece of ground.

"Help me," Tanis said to Clotnik, indicating the old man.

Clotnik swallowed and came to stand knee-deep in the water on the other side of the ancient.

"Gently now," said Tanis.

As they lifted the old one, the stench of his dying flesh assailed them. Clotnik made a point of not looking at the poor man—at least not until they put him down. That's when the juggler saw that his own hands and arms were covered with burnt loose skin and congealed blood— and it was not his own. His stomach revolting, he shot a look at the ancient. "By Reorx!" said Clotnik. He quickly turned away from the sight, staggered a few steps away, and vomited into the lake.

"It seems I'm rather overcooked," the old one said.

"You accept your fate with surprising calm," said Tanis respectfully.

"It was my own fault," the man rejoined, blue eyes filming over with tears, doubtless from the pain of his burns.

Tanis frowned. "You can't blame yourself for not outrunning a grass fire," he said gently.

"I don't." The blue eyes cleared again and studied the half-elf. "I blame myself for starting it."

Tanis raised his eyebrows. "Why did you set it?"

"Sligs were after me," the old one explained. "Quite a lot of them, in fact. I thought the fire would stop them or kill them."

Tanis looked around. Nearby, Clotnik was recovering from his bout of nausea. Steam and smoke still rose from blackened trunks and boughs. Any animals in the area had long since disappeared. Sligs, huge, intelligent cousins of the hobgoblins, would have a hard time hiding in the lake's blaze-scarred surroundings.

"It seems to have worked," Tanis agreed. He paused, then resumed as if talking to himself. "I've never known sligs to travel in this part of the world. They must have been after something valuable." The old man averted his eyes but didn't reply, and Tanis went on. "The fire stretched from one horizon to the other. You must have set the fire some distance from here."

The old one tried to shake his head and winced. The numbness from his overnight stay in the cold water appeared to be wearing off, and the terrible pain was only just beginning, Tanis saw. The blue eyes seemed to go out of focus again, and the man sighed and closed them.

"No," he whispered. "It was not very far away, at all. It was my magic that spread it so wide."

"You're a mage?"

"What's left of one," he replied with a dull laugh.

Something didn't add up, Tanis thought. "If you saved yourself from the sligs with magic, why didn't you cast another spell to save yourself from the fire?"

"I couldn't . . . "—and his voice trailed off before he visibly pulled himself together—"I couldn't cast another spell so soon after the first. My strength is not what it used to be." He shook his head, remembering. "Once the fire was started, I had no way of controlling it. I got a good head start, but when the wind changed direction and it came after me, I didn't think I'd make it."

Clotnik heard the last of this as he returned from the lake. He was pale and trembling, one hand held at his stomach as if to keep it calm, the other wrapped tightly around his chest as if to ward off a chill despite the rapidly rising sun.

"The only reason you live is Tanis," the juggler said. "He saved your life."

"I remember," whispered the pain-wracked mage. "When I saw him, at first I thought he was his father."

Tanis felt himself go lightheaded. His mind was a jumble of questions, yet he couldn't find his voice. Please, he thought, let him live long enough to tell me what he knows.

Clotnik reached out and carefully drew a waterlogged twig from the old man's grizzled hair. "You should rest," he gently advised the wizard.

The mage responded by tightening his lips. The old man must have shown a mulish streak in healthier days, Tanis thought. "You know better," the wizard objected. "There is too little time. I must talk to the half-elf while I can."

The mage tried to turn to look at Tanis, but the effort brought him only unendurable pain. He groaned down deep in his soul as his eyes rolled up into his head.

Tanis hastened to speak. "We'll stay with you until—" The half-elf couldn't finish.

"Until I die?" the mage told Tanis through clenched teeth. "No. Not you."

Tanis did not know what to say.

"We must strike a bargain," the old mage said slowly, with increasing difficulty. "A deal. Knowledge of your father . . . in return for a favor."

"Of course," Tanis said without a moment's delay. "Tell me what you want, and if I can do it, it is yours."

The blue eyes suddenly turned steely in his ash-smeared face. "I want you to find someone for me . . . someone who will perish without your help." He cried out the final words, and his hands shot up and grabbed Tanis's tunic. His fire-blackened fingers curled, and he used his handhold both to pull Tanis closer and to raise himself up off the ground. In a strangled voice, he exclaimed, "She must be saved! I need your word!"

"Was the woman you speak of out there on the plains with you when the fire struck?" Tanis asked in alarm, preparing to rise and search for what, at best, would be a charred corpse.

The mage shook his head, however, and pulled Tanis closer with strength born of desperation. "She's very far away," the old wizard said sadly.

Tanis eased the man back down onto the blanket. "Who is she?"

"She is Brandella," he said simply. "There is no other like her. And you must find her, save her, so that she can live on after I die."

Clotnik finally interjected, "Kishpa, you haven't explained it to him."

"Give me water," demanded the mage. Once he had sipped from Clotnik's water bag, he gave a deep sigh and continued. "Three years ago I cast a search spell, hoping that my magic would tell me whom I should seek. My magic told me to find you, Tanthalas," he said, using Tanis's elven name. Kishpa coughed, and Clotnik offered him more water. The old wizard refused it and went on. "I have sought you ever since. My hold on you is simple. Your father came to my village ninety-eight years ago. I will lead you to him if you will give me Brandella."

The old man rested a moment, catching his breath.

Tanis was having nearly as much trouble breathing as the old mage. His father. Was it possible? Ninety-eight years were but a short time to an elf, but Tanis's father was human. He couldn't still be alive. Tanis wondered if his doubts showed in his face.

"How am I to find this woman, this Brandella?" Tanis asked hurriedly.

Kishpa's blistered lips cracked into a bleeding smile. "The same way you will find your father. You will look for both of them in my past. They live in my memory."

## 4

# The Mage's Plea

Tanis felt his hopes crash around him like one of
the burned-out tree trunks that now marred the landscape. Kishpa's blue eyes gleamed with an intensity that
doubly alarmed the half-elf.

"The old man is delirious," Tanis said. "Clotnik, help
me set up the other blankets to form a tent around him.
We ought to protect—"

But Clotnik continued to kneel impassively on the
sandy dirt next to the mage. "He isn't delirious," the
dwarf said firmly.

Tanis glanced from the juggler to the mage, thinking,
Maybe *I'm* the one who's delirious.

"Brandella is living and breathing inside me," said Kishpa hoarsely. "So is your father. Or at least they will be for as long as I live. That's why I need you, Tanis." The mage suddenly coughed up blood. He wiped it off his fire-scarred face, breathlessly forging on. "While I'm still conscious, I'm going to cast a spell. I will send you deep into my memory, back to the time when I knew my Brandella best and when your father came to my village." He stopped and Clotnik gave him a worried look.

Few sounds broke the morning calm; pieces of charred wood occasionally thumped against each other in the lake, and a branch broke with a crack and dropped to the littered ground only yards away. The smell of smoke was still strong. The half-elf and the dwarf were silent as they waited for the aging wizard to overcome the latest spasm of pain. Tanis watched the mage's shallow breath barely move the charred robes that once, he knew, had been red and velvety.

A fierce expression crossed the mage's face; he refused to let the pain stand in his way. "Learn what you will about your father," he said, "but find my Brandella and escape from my mind with her so that when I die, she will live on. I don't want her memory to die with me, Tanis. Do you understand? I love her too much to see her perish with me. Find her. Free her."

The old man slumped back, watching Tanis with a stare that now waned from demanding to hopeful. "Will you do it?" Kishpa asked weakly.

To actually see his father? To meet him? "Yes," he replied. There could be no other answer.

The mage managed a smile. "There is much you should know," he said, "but I must concentrate now and build my strength for the spell. Clotnik," he called, "tell Tanis what to expect. And be quick. Time is short."

Clotnik took Tanis by the arm and led him a short distance away. They seated themselves on the log, now wedged on the bank, that had sustained them during the night. Clotnik looked out over the lake, his thoughtful green eyes soft as moss agates. Wrinkles creased the dwarf's skin around his eyes, and Tanis realized that his companion might not be as young as he'd thought. Clotnik began speaking as if from a long distance.

"Kishpa knew Brandella long ago, during a time of war," explained the juggler. "There was disease, and humans were in flight, sending their armies westward to untainted lands. They marched against scattered elven villages north of Qualinesti, vowing to drive those in their path into the Straits of Algoni."

Tanis knew of the wars between the humans and elves, of course. Those invasions were yet another reason the two races remained suspicious of each other—and another reason members of both sides considered Tanis, a product of those violent years, an outcast.

"And my father?" he prompted.

Clotnik looked at him for the first time, his eyes sympathetic. "Your father was among those soldiers. I tell you this so that you are prepared for what lies ahead. Violence and bloodshed will surround you, and you could become their victim. It is possible that you could die in Kishpa's memory."

"I will be careful," Tanis promised.

Clotnik shook his head, however, and put one hand on Tanis's muscular forearm. "Death is only one of the dangers," he warned.

Tanis looked aside at the old mage, lying a few yards away on the sandy ground and marshaling his strength for the ordeal ahead. The half-elf replied, "I must take the risks." Then, when the dwarf remained silent, Tanis looked back at him. "All right. Explain them."

Clotnik removed his hand from Tanis's arm and ventured on. "Kishpa doesn't know what will happen if a stranger enters his past. You may change the whole direction of his life, you may change only his memories, or you may change nothing at all. He is willing to risk any consequences just as long as you find Brandella and return with her before he dies. If he should breathe no more, neither will you." The dwarvish gaze grew as sharp as one of Flint's forged swords. "At least not in his memory," Clotnik went on. "What will happen to you—whether you will ever be able to return to this life—he does not know, either."

Tanis sat silently, assessing the situation. All his companions, from huge Caramon to tiny Tas, were off on their own adventures. But he'd be willing to wager they were keeping their booted feet in the present, at least. The half-elf started to speak, but Clotnik hurried on. "All I can tell you," the dwarf said, "is that you *must* find her and get out of Kishpa's memory before he dies."

"How?" Tanis asked.

Clotnik looked surprised. "With magic, of course."

Tanis felt that somehow the juggler was hedging. "And Kishpa will get us out?" Tanis pressed.

Clotnik smiled oddly before saying, "If all goes well." When moments stretched long without comment from the half-elf, Clotnik chewed briefly on his lower lip, leaned back, and asked, "What is it?"

"Kishpa looks human," Tanis said, his face hard. "How could he have been a young man in love with a woman nearly one hundred years ago?"

Clotnik allowed himself a brief laugh before sobering and responding. "He looks human under all those burns? Reorx's beard, no!" he replied. "His grandfather was elven." Clotnik's voice took on a gossipy tone. "As best as I can figure, he's one-quarter elf and three-quarters human. The elven features, admittedly, are rather hidden. His longevity, though, is obvious proof of his heritage."

Tanis nodded once, slowly. There were other questions to ask. "How will I find my father? And Brandella? What do they look like?"

"You will find them both in a village named Ankatavaka, on the northeast shore of the Straits of Algoni. You will recognize your father because, as Kishpa described him to me, he looks a little like you—in the eyes and in the mouth. There are differences, though. Kishpa told me that, unlike you, your father had long, black hair, a badly broken nose, and, during the short time he was in Ankatavaka, a slash wound in the right leg from a broadsword."

"What of my mother? Did she live in Kishpa's village, too?" Tanis held his breath. To also meet his mother, who had died shortly after his birth, would be worth all the dangers the old mage's plan could present.

"No," Clotnik said, his face averted. "Kishpa did not know her. On this question, I cannot help you."

Tanis sighed deeply. "All right. Then tell me about Brandella."

"She was a weaver when Kishpa knew her. You will recognize her when you see her, Tanis. Of this there is no doubt."

"But how?" Out in the lake, a pair of waterfowl tried to land on the scummy surface. Squawking in apparent dismay, they took off immediately and flew west. Tanis's gaze followed them.

"You will know her because Kishpa loved her, and you will be in his memory." The dwarf tried to look reassuring. "You will come to understand."

Tanis wasn't so sure. Nonetheless, he did not pursue the matter.

The dwarf made motions as if to return to Kishpa, and the half-elf asked, "What about you, Clotnik? Why have you done this for the old man?"

"This? This is nothing," the juggler said sorrowfully. "I wanted to make the journey instead of you. Kishpa wouldn't let me. It had to be you, he said; the search spell had been specific." He took a deep breath, glanced back at Kishpa over his shoulder, and said in a low voice, "But I don't believe him. He just didn't want me to go."

"Why?"

"For the same reason I *wanted* to go," he said obliquely, toying with a bit of sodden bark from the log on which they sat. He tossed the bark away and looked Tanis full in the face. "Should you survive your journey, I will tell you. And you will have things to tell me. But enough now. The time for talk is over. Kishpa is ready." The dwarf rose, cutting off further questions, and hurried back to the wizard. Tanis followed more deliberately.

The mage looked up at them with eyes suddenly malignant, and Tanis fought back second thoughts. He'd always been cautious—too cautious, his companions sometimes told him. This time he would push ahead without continual second-guessing, he vowed.

With some effort, the ancient wizard plucked two objects from a small, charred, watertight pouch that hung from his belt; he held them up. The first was a tattered piece of cloth that Tanis could see had once been bright and colorful, full of shades of red, yellow, and purple. The second object was a simple wooden writing instrument. The wizard handed Tanis the quill but kept the fragment of fabric.

"The cloth is all I have left from her," the mage said sadly. "It is the last remaining shred of a scarf she once made for me. Take it and give it to her as a token of my love."

"And the quill?" asked Tanis.

"Take it with you, also, and leave it in the past. It was for this that the sligs were after me. This plan is the safest way of keeping it out of their reach."

Sligs, known for their sharp teeth, ugliness, and generally antisocial attitudes, were rare near Solace. "Why would these sligs want your quill?" questioned Tanis. "It looks ordinary."

"The quill foretells danger," the mage replied. "Whoever possesses it will never be caught by surprise. You can see how valuable it would be to an army of such creatures intent upon conquest." Kishpa's lips tightened in resolve. "They must not have it, Tanthalas!"

Tanis was about to ask another question when Clotnik interceded. "Kishpa is weak. We must hurry."

The mage stroked the faded piece of cloth and handed

it reluctantly to Tanis. The half-elf carefully concealed the cloth and the quill inside his tunic.

The wizard nodded his thanks and then closed his eyes.

But suddenly, just before he began his spell-casting, the relic of a being that once was full of life lifted his raw, bleeding hands, seemingly oblivious to pain, and pointed at the half-elf. "There is one more thing you must know," Kishpa whispered. "Someone will try to stop you from freeing my Brandella."

"Who?" asked Tanis, leaning lower to hear better.

"Me."

As Tanis recovered from his surprise, the mage intoned words that Tanis had never heard before. The otherworldly sounds were musical, not so much language as an intricate series of notes. Kishpa repeated them again, then a third time. Tanis glanced at Clotnik.

"It's not working," the half-elf said softly.

Clotnik glared. "Shhh!"

But then the mage closed his hands into two fists, shook them, and then opened them again. Dead skin dropped from his fingers in ribbons, but the mage didn't appear to notice. He closed his fists a second time. Shook them. Opened them. Closed them a third time. Shook them . . . and then Tanis disappeared.

# PART II

# 5

# The Dark Pit

Tanis was still looking down, but instead of seeing Kishpa lying on the ground, he saw the black leather boots of a soldier, toes pointed in his direction  Tanis immediately lifted his eyes, catching a glint of sunlight on the blade of a broadsword swooping straight down toward his head!

Elves revere life. Before a battle, elven troops and leaders gather to ask forgiveness for the lives they will take in the coming dispute. But this time, there was no time to move, think, or feel. Suddenly, another sword came from out of nowhere to block the downward sweep of the first. There was a loud clang as steel struck steel, and a voice shouted, "Draw your blade!"

Tanis didn't need to be told twice. Instinct from a lifetime of battle experience took over. He threw his right shoulder into his attacker, knocking him down, then pulled his own silver-inlaid broadsword from its scabbard. He intended to protect himself while getting away from whatever madness he had been plunged into. Standing at the ready, he quickly realized that he was in the midst of a small group of elven and human soldiers engaged in deadly hand-to-hand combat in an opening in a forest.

The half-elf had but one problem. He didn't know which side he was on.

A human soldier, his long, brown hair greasy, settled the issue when he lunged at the half-elf, his sword's point aimed at Tanis's heart. Tanis parried deftly. The human countered by swinging his sword in a wide arc, trying to slash the half-elf's left arm. Tanis sidestepped the flashing blade, kicking the human in the stomach. The soldier clutched his belly and doubled over in pain, his groans mingling with the cries of other humans and elves in the glade.

An elven soldier, seeing the human down and defenseless, stepped in front of Tanis and brought his saber down hard across the back of his enemy's exposed neck. A life ended.

Tanis wanted to look at the faces of the soldiers and search for his father. But with the air heavy with the stench of blood and sweat, with death at every turn, he didn't have the luxury of studying the features of all these potential killers. Better to get away, he decided. Before he could manage it, though, another human attacked, slamming his shield into Tanis's back. The half-elf went down face first. Leaping onto Tanis's prostrate body, the soldier threw away his shield and pinned the half-elf under his greater weight. From the corner of his eye, Tanis saw a huge, slablike hand scoop up a heavy rock. The half-elf fought for survival, wrapping his arm around one of the human's legs and then heaving with all his might.

The rock went flying out of the soldier's hands as he fell over onto his back and spun halfway around. Tanis didn't kill this one, either. Instead, he swiftly rolled in the other direction, grabbed the human's shield, and used it and his sword to hold back the surging skirmish line of enemy soldiers.

But not for long.

"More humans!" cried an elven voice in warning. Tanis instinctively knew exactly where to look. He felt the ground shaking, and he knew it was cavalry. The horsemen could only be coming from the open field to the east. In the strong light of late morning, they thundered across the meadow and swooped down on the small elven defense force with cries of vengeance. Lances impaled the elves, and swords cut them to pieces.

It was a rout. Tanis managed to knock one rider off his horse and break the lance of another, but there were too many.

"Retreat!" cried an elven leader. Then, more to the point, he yelled, "Run!"

Tanis fled, pursued by two humans on horseback. It was a hopeless race, and Tanis knew it. He needed protection fast. Off to his left, he saw a tree stump. It wasn't much, but it would have to do. He veered, the horsemen gaining on him with every step.

He reached the stump and circled behind it just moments before the pair of horsemen closed in on him. Delaying the inevitable, Tanis swung his sword and hacked off the point of one lance before ducking below the point of the second spear, which whooshed past his ear.

The horsemen galloped by him, kicking up a cloud of dust that blinded and choked Tanis. He tried to breathe, to clear his eyes, knowing that he had to be ready for the horsemen when they turned to make another pass at him.

He heard the horses rear and neigh, and then came

their pounding hooves, drawing closer yet remaining unseen somewhere beyond the slowly settling cloud of dust. He heard the screams of other elves, unseen beyond the cloud, as they suffered death blows from the humans. Tanis steeled himself, hoping he would see the horsemen before it was too late. Then, just a short distance away, he saw the horses. The riders leaned forward to get a better look at their victim as they charged in for the kill. . . .

That's when the two hands reached up out of what proved to be a hollow tree trunk and grabbed Tanis from behind, pulling him down into the darkness.

\* \* \* \* \*

Tanis lay stunned on the damp ground, his face caught in a dim shaft of light from the killing field up above. He felt something—A sword? No, too blunt. A stick?—poking him in the side. He stirred.

"Life is wonderful. Without it, you'd be dead," a voice whispered. A laugh followed from the darkness.

"Who are you?" Tanis asked, dazed from the fall.

The voice was harsh, gravelly, and deep, despite its current hush. "I'm called many things, very few of them complimentary, but my name is Little Shoulders Scowarr. And I'm not sure that's so complimentary, either."

"You're a human?" Tanis said, searching the ground for his sword.

"Your sword is just a little to the right of your hand. Be careful of the blade," Scowarr said. "Your eyes will get used to the darkness soon."

The voice may have come from a human, but its owner *had* rescued him from the other humans. And enemies tend not to help their foes find a lost weapon, Tanis conceded. He grasped the sword and eased it into his scabbard. He could just make out a figure in the shadows.

The voice rose to a tenor now but remained whispery. "Come with me, but keep your head down. This is a very narrow tunnel."

The half-elf followed the shadow into the gloom until there was no shadow, only a voice: "Before those soldiers showed up, the village was so healthy they had to kill one of its citizens just to start a cemetery."

Tanis was only half listening. "Is this village called Ankatavaka?" he asked.

He felt, rather than heard, his companion come to a dead stop before him. The voice sank deep again, with a new, irritated rasp. "That's a joke, boy. Where's your sense of humor?"

Under the current circumstance, the half-elf thought, a sense of humor paled next to traits necessary for survival. "Please . . . is it Ankatavaka?" he persisted.

"Yes," the voice said, obviously annoyed, "and while I'm still willing to talk to you, I guess I should tell you to stay to your left when the tunnel divides." The human resumed walking.

A few moments later, Tanis fought to keep from getting pinned between the narrowing tunnel walls. "I'm not sure I can squeeze through," he called out.

The voice seemed to have lost its irritation. "Keep going. If I could, I would happily give you my little shoulders, nickname and all. It's just this sort of activity that they're great for."

Who cares? Tanis wondered. Actually, the voice was beginning to sound more like a kender than a human; Tas wandered conversationally, too, but the owner of this voice had displayed an unkenderlike tendency toward irritability. Tanis resolved to humor his rescuer. "Does this cave widen eventually?" he asked.

"The other advantage," the voice prattled on hollowly, "is that I make a rather thin target. As you can see, I like to look on the bright side. If only there were some light. By the way, what is *your* name?"

"Tanis Half-Elven."

"Well, Tanis—may I call you that, or do you prefer the entire title?"

---

Tanis puffed with the effort of inching along a passageway designed more for a dwarf or kender than someone of human blood. "Anyone who saves my life can call me anything he wants. And if you don't mind my asking, why *did* you save my life?"

The voice, ranging up into the alto register now as its owner became winded, reverted to an earlier question.

"First of all, Tanis, the tunnel widens again soon and then cuts to the right before there's a sudden drop. You'll fit through just fine. And . . . " Tanis heard several deep breaths, and the voice dipped back to baritone. "And as for why I pulled you down here into this miserable dark pit, the answer is simple. I need protection. And now you owe me your life."

Tanis grimaced in the darkness. Certainly the old mage, breathing out his life on some lakeshore a century in the future, did not have the time left for Tanis to let himself get diverted from the quest for Brandella. And Tanis definitely had priorities of his own. In his mind, however, he could hear Sturm Brightblade quoting the Solamnic oath, "My honor is my life," and he suspected that his former companion would find the time to help Scowarr, regardless of the consequences.

Scowarr paused—for dramatic effect, Tanis was beginning to realize—then said, "You know, some people pay their debts when they're due, some pay them when they're overdue, and some never do."

"That's clever," Tanis conceded.

"But you didn't laugh," Scowarr complained.

"I smiled. You just couldn't see me because it's so dark."

"Not good enough. Anyway," the man persisted, "the question is, Are you going to pay me back?"

Tanis made one last effort to escape from the responsibility that now pressed about him like the tunnel's narrow walls. "I didn't ask you to save my life," he pointed out.

The voice balanced annoyance with an equally irritating note of reasonableness. "True, but I'm asking *you* to save mine. And it comes out the same in the end. Let's not quibble, Tanis. Can I count on you?" Tanis could almost hear his companion hold his breath for the answer.

Tanis had to be honest—or as honest as he could be. If he tried to explain the whole story, the human never would believe him. "I'm here to find two people," he said. "I must find them as fast as I can, and then, after I find them, I must leave immediately. I have no choice in this. If I can protect you in the meantime, I will. You have my word."

The gravelly tone dropped from the voice. "Good," Scowarr said. "And you can have my whole sentence."

Tanis groaned.

# 6

# The Rising Tide

"SOME PEOPLE FARM. SOME tan hides. There are tinkers, smiths, teachers, clerics, soldiers. Everybody does something. Me," said Scowarr, "I tell jokes."

"To earn your daily bread?" asked Tanis doubtfully as he inspected his broadsword for damage.

The thin-framed human, whose otherwise youthful face was deeply etched with laugh lines around the eyes and mouth, did not answer. Instead, he picked at the small, smokeless campfire that burned in their seacliff wall cave.

Tanis thought he had embarrassed his new friend into silence. "I'm sorry," he said softly.

"I'm the one who's sorry," Scowarr replied mournfully. "Of all the jackanapes I could have saved today, I had to pick one who doesn't laugh at my jokes, who doesn't smile at my cleverisms, *who hasn't even heard of me!*"

"Shhh! There's no telling who else is in these tunnels," said Tanis, pointing toward the last hole through which they'd crawled. Scowarr had led Tanis through a honeycomb of tunnels, depositing them in a cave that lay just north of Ankatavaka, facing west. The noon sun beat down on the sea, but the cave remained damp and chilly.

The human glanced nervously over his shoulder, took a deep breath, and closed his eyes for a moment. "Don't scare me like that," he said. "I was sick once and went to a healer. I told him that I was afraid to die. He said, 'Don't worry. That's the last thing you'll do.'"

Tanis smiled.

"That's it?" Scowarr demanded. "One of my best jokes, and all you can do is lift one-half of one lip?"

Tanis hastened to conciliate the man. "I guess my thoughts are elsewhere. Sorry."

"'Sorry,'" Scowarr mimicked. He pouted and sat, wordless, until the moments stretched uncomfortably long. Finally, he spoke. "I was dragged from my home because of my fame as a funny man and forced to tell my jokes to this idiot army of humans." He spat out the word "humans" with sarcasm.

"But *you're* a . . ." Tanis began, then, thinking better of it, leaned closer to inspect his sword as though he'd just found a nick in the blade.

Scowarr continued heedlessly. "'Entertain them,' the officer told me. 'Make them laugh; they're far from home, and their morale is low. You always make people laugh, Little Shoulders. That's what your neighbors say. Make my men laugh. Make them laugh, or I'll change your name to Broken Shoulders. Or worse.'"

"That's why you're here?" Tanis interjected.

Scowarr nodded. "And I've begun to think that my neighbors were trying to get rid of me."

Tanis wasn't sure if that was a joke or not. Luckily, Scowarr didn't explode when the half-elf neglected to laugh.

"We were just a few miles from here," Scowarr went on. "It was yesterday. There must have been three hundred soldiers sitting on a hillside while their commander waited for orders.

" 'Make them laugh,' he said. 'Now.'

" 'But it's the middle of the afternoon,' I told him. 'It's hot. They're tired. They're in a bad mood. This isn't a good time.'

" 'They're hot, they're tired, and in a foul mood,' their commander said. 'And that's just why they need a good laugh to keep their spirits up.'

" 'It's not the right time,' I complained again. So he put a knife to my throat . . . and I told my jokes."

Tanis leaned forward, suffering for the poor, frail soul who sat across the fire from him. "What happened?" he asked, knowing that Scowarr needed to tell it.

Scowarr looked out the cave entrance at the Straits of Algoni. The waves danced in the distance, but Tanis knew the funny man wasn't seeing the beauty of the natural world. He was back in time, suffering humiliation in front of hundreds of soldiers.

"They laughed," Scowarr conceded. "They laughed a lot. I was overjoyed. Such a big audience." His voice began to rise again, and he poked once more at the fire. "Such gales of laughter; it was enough to make you feel like a god. Except they weren't laughing *with* me, Tanis. After I'd told maybe eight or ten jokes, one of them—one of my own kind!—shot an arrow at me."

Tanis sat up, shocked, against the dank cave wall, and Scowarr hastened to add, "Oh, he didn't intend to hit me with it. And he didn't. But he inspired dozens, then scores, of them to do the same. Can you imagine it?" Scowarr's face glowed hotly with the memory of his fear and shame. "They didn't like my jokes, so they decided to kill me. They thought *that* was funny!"

"How did you get away?" the half-elf asked, astonished at the casual cruelty of the human race.

"I dove underneath a nearby wagon. If it hadn't been there, I'm sure they would have murdered me. One good thing came out of it, though," he said, brightening.

"What was that?"

"I came up with a joke. Do you want to hear it?" he asked. His thin face was dark with wariness.

"You sure you want to tell it to me?"

"If you promise not to slay me if you don't like it."

Tanis nodded. Scowarr sat up. His voice dropped an octave. Tanis could almost see him on a stage somewhere. "Did you hear about the funny man who told the same jokes three days running?"

"No," Tanis replied encouragingly.

"He wouldn't dare tell them standing still."

Tanis smiled. "That's good," the half-elf said kindly.

Scowarr, obviously frustrated, ran one hand through his short, tufted, light brown hair. Close-shorn hair was rare among humans, except for children and some warriors. Tanis could almost believe Scowarr favored the style because it would bring an immediate smile to people's lips. Then again, maybe he cut it himself. The human's face showed anything but a smile now, though. "What do you mean, 'That's good'? You didn't laugh!"

"But I can see that it's funny," Tanis protested.

"You have to *feel* that it's funny, not *see* that it's funny." Scowarr turned back toward the sea, reminding Tanis suddenly of an out-of-temper sparrow with its feathers in a fluff.

Despite himself, Tanis was beginning to like Scowarr. He was about to say so when a wave broke high against the seacliff wall and sent salty spray into the cave.

The campfire sizzled. Another wave brought a small flood sloshing across the floor, washing out the fire. In an instant, Tanis and Scowarr were up on their feet, the water at ankle depth.

"The tide is rising," said Tanis, venturing near the cave

mouth and looking out into the strait. "We have to get out of here."

That's when he spotted a ship anchored just down the coast in the harbor of the elven village. Small fishing vessels, lying heavy in the water, ferried boatloads of citizens to the waiting ship.

"They're evacuating," Tanis said sadly. "The humans must be massing a huge army to make elves flee their homes."

Scowarr joined the half-elf at the cave mouth. The human was a full head shorter than he. "Yes," Scowarr said, "that skirmish you were involved in was only the beginning of the battle. The humans want all the land north of Qualinesti, and they make no secret about their wish to either drive the elves south or into the sea. And they've just about done it, too."

Another wave broke high on the cliff and covered them with green foam. Scowarr, thin clothes clinging to his spare frame, shivered.

Tanis feared that the tunnels might flood before the two could get to higher ground. There were only two choices. One was to jump out of the cave and swim to safety. The rising tide was pounding against the side of the cliff, however; one unlucky move and the pair could be crushed or drowned. The other possibility was somehow to climb the sheer cliff face to the top. The obvious problem with that choice, Tanis thought, leaning carefully out the cave mouth, was that it looked all but impossible. But not thoroughly impossible. . . .

"Can you climb?" asked Tanis.

Scowarr recklessly stuck his head out of the cave and looked up. Tanis lunged for a fistful of the human's shirt to keep him from tumbling into the sea and hauled the man back in. Scowarr appeared unaware of his close call, although his eyes were round with Tanis's suggested escape route. "Now I know why you don't laugh at my jokes," Scowarr said. "You're mad."

"It's not as far as it looks. Maybe thirty feet," said

Tanis. "Besides, there are tree roots sticking out of the rock face," he added. "We can use them for handholds."

"You go first," insisted the funny man.

It hadn't occurred to Tanis to do anything except go first, so he carefully dug his foot into the rock ledge at the side of the cave mouth and began to climb. He found a crevice for his right foot, a small outcropping to grab with his left hand, then a bush growing out of the rock face in which to steady his left foot, then another crevice for his right hand, and so it went until he was halfway to the top. The sea continued to rise, the deadly waves beating against the cliff until Tanis feared for the safety of the man waiting below.

"The water is up to my waist!" cried Scowarr, his voice drifting up to Tanis on the surf-soaked wind. "I'm coming! Don't fall, or you'll knock me in, too!"

"At least he's managed that announcement without telling a joke," Tanis muttered.

" . . . which could certainly put a damper on things!" the human sang triumphantly.

Tanis stifled a groan.

The half-elf continued to climb, his hands cut from grabbing the sharp-edged rocks, the blood mixing with his sweat to make everything he touched slick and slippery. Still, he worked his way closer to the top, hand over hand, foot over foot, edging toward safety. He settled his left foot on a tree root. His right foot rested on a protruding rock. He held on to a fossilized piece of driftwood with his left hand, and then reached for a grayish bush with dying flowers with his right.

The bush didn't hold.

The plant came out of the sea cliff wall in a rush of broken clods of rock, dirt, and rotten roots. The dirt flew in Tanis's face. He lost his balance, and both feet slipped off their moorings. . . .

# 7

# Multicolored Hope

"NO!" SHOUTED SCOWARR FROM BELOW AS THE TINY avalanche reached him, pelting him with stones and a shower of dirt. Luckily, the bush itself didn't hit him. And neither did Tanis, who clung to the fossilized driftwood with one hand while desperately trying to reclaim his toeholds.

"Hang on!"

Tanis's heart leaped with hope; the new voice came from the top of the cliff!

"I don't have a rope," the female voice, pitched low, volunteered, "but I have something else. Please! Hang on!"

Tanis's arm felt as if it were going to rip right out of the socket. If only he could find some halfway solid footing. But the more he struggled to find a place for his feet, the greater was the strain on his arm.

"I'm lowering it," the woman called out. "It's coming down on your right. See it?"

He saw it—a thin, pink shawl dangling in the wind.

He grabbed it with his free hand. The shawl, and other shawls of red, blue, purple, and yellow to which it was tied, went taut.

Breathlessly, Tanis called out, "What's your end tied to?"

"A cart," came the reply. "I put stones under the wheels, but it's sliding toward the edge of the cliff. The cart's too light, and I can't hold it. Hurry!"

Tanis heaved himself up the multicolored rope of shawls as if he were climbing a vine in the forest.

"Hurry!" the woman pleaded. "The cart's sliding faster!"

Hand over hand, Tanis struggled. His arms ached, and his mouth was as dry as the loose dirt that kept breaking away from the rock face.

But he was getting close to the top. Just a few more heaves up the makeshift rope . . .

The half-elf looked up, hoping to see a hand stretched out to help him. Instead, he heard a scream and saw the cart coming over the top of the cliff. He wasn't going to make it!

The cart tumbled over the edge, smacking into Tanis, who had been a mere few feet below it when it fell.

Stunned by the blow, Tanis knew only that something terrible had happened. He flailed helplessly as the churning sea rushed up to meet him—until a wind like no other Tanis had experienced blew up from beneath him with such force that it stopped his fall and sent him flying upward. At the same instant, the cart crashed into the sea-cliff, breaking apart in the wind. Splintered wood whipped all around him, its lighter weight sending it careening skyward far faster than Tanis's own flight.

Unable to breathe, Tanis tried to turn over on his back as he soared ever higher on an invisible carpet of air. All he could manage, though, was to roll over and over as the wind caught his arms, turning him in ever-faster circles. On one of his revolutions, he caught sight of Scowarr surging skyward, catching up with him.

By the time Tanis reached the lip of the seacliff wall, Little Shoulders was within easy reach. His face a portrait in terror, Scowarr reached out with both hands and gripped Tanis's left shin so hard that the half-elf thought the human might snap it.

They floated up over the top of the cliff, where the calmer air sucked them out of the gale. They hit the ground in a sprawl, tearing up meadow flowers as they rolled over the bumpy ground.

Confused, gasping for air, Tanis lay still for a moment. Then he remembered the woman. He struggled to his knees and, sensing a presence behind him, turned.

The woman, a matronly dwarf with eyes like green chips of malachite, ran toward him. Walking slowly behind her was a young man who also looked vaguely familiar. Tanis's senses were still reeling, and he had trouble focusing.

The woman reached him first and took his bloody hands in her own. "I heard a cry and that's when I saw you," she said in a comforting, motherly voice—the same voice that had signaled rescue from the top of the cliff. "I thought you'd be killed for certain when my cart went over the cliff." Her hand moved to his forehead. "I'm so sorry I couldn't stop it."

Her hands were soft and warm. Instinctively, he leaned close and breathed in her scent. It was a fragrance of spring flowers tinged with the clean aroma of fresh cotton. He felt comforted by her presence.

"I'm sorry about your cart," he said finally, feeling a deep pang of guilt. "You lost everything, didn't you?"

"It was nothing compared to the loss of a life." She

glanced at Scowarr, who was finally stirring. "Two lives."

"I . . . we . . . thank you most sincerely for what you tried to do," Tanis said with humility.

"What about me?" boomed the man, who swaggered up behind the woman. "Don't I get any thanks? After all, it was my magic that actually saved you."

Tanis blinked. The face was thinner, the hair thick and black, and the robes clean and crimson. Was it Kishpa? The man was so young, so healthy, so full of vigor. His blue eyes gleamed in a young face. It seemed impossible. Yet . . .

"You will speak to Yeblidod, but not to me?" questioned the man good-humoredly. He turned to the woman and kidded her, saying, "Mertwig will be jealous." Then, more seriously, he added, "Don't be concerned about your loss. I'll talk to Mertwig about replacing what went over the cliff."

She looked up at the wizard and nodded humbly.

Meanwhile, in his mind's eye, Tanis tried to picture him as an ancient man with charred skin, lying on a blanket, begging for help. They were so much the same, yet so markedly different.

Although still dazed, Tanis knew that he had to be careful. He remembered Kishpa's warning: *There will be many who will try to stop you. I can warn you about one of them . . . me.*

When the mage turned back to him, Tanis awkwardly tried to rise to his feet. "I'm sorry for my lack of good manners," said Tanis. "Let me thank you now." He swayed but remained erect; even though he still heard the wind howling in his ears, only a light, early afternoon breeze ruffled the flowers and grasses at the top of the cliff. "May your magic always be a blessing to you," he added with an unsteady bow.

The woman reached out and took his arm to keep him from falling.

The magic-user bowed in return, saying, "Your words do you credit. But I must say," he added, narrowing his eyes, "you are not of my village, and your blood lines appear to be, let us say, betwixt and between. One might ask where your loyalties lie."

Accustomed to such queries, Tanis was able to reply evenly, although annoyance, as usual, burned just below the surface. He pretended to be unaware of Kishpa's elven bloodlines. "My loyalties lie with those who call me friend," Tanis said steadily. "And you? To my eye, you appear to be a human and potentially an enemy to Ankatavaka yourself. Where are *your* loyalties?"

The dwarf pulled at Tanis's sleeve. "You know not of what you speak," she said, apparently embarrassed to be overheard by the wizard. "This is Kishpa, grandson of Tokandi, who was a much-revered elder of Ankatavaka."

"Who was also a notorious lover of human females," the young Kishpa chimed in with a hearty laugh. "My father was like you," he said, gesturing at Tanis. "He was a half-elf. He married a human woman—it seems to be a family weakness—and they gave birth to me. You ask me of my loyalties. I answer: This is my home. These are my people, and the humans who have gathered to attack it are my enemies. Enemies," he added with sudden harshness, "like this one." He pointed at Scowarr.

Little Shoulders seemed to shrivel with fear. He was not only speechless, but for once, jokeless. Kishpa's lifesaving magic had left him awestruck.

"Scowarr is no enemy of yours," Tanis intervened. "The humans tried to kill him, and he fled. And when I was about to be killed by this same enemy, he saved my life. Let a man's actions speak for him, rather than the accident of his birth."

Kishpa studied Tanis. "Ah, a philosopher, too?"

"Hardly."

The wizard smiled. "And modest. But tell me this—what is your name?"

"Tanthalas, or Tanis, as you please."

"Tell me, Tanis, what brings you to this place?"

Kishpa's voice lowered. "Why are you here, and why now?"

The intensity of the man's tone startled Tanis. It was as if this young Kishpa suspected something. Lying was not in the half-elf's nature; on the other hand, he feared telling the young mage the real reason he had come. Yet he had to say something, something that was true, so he blurted, "A dying man asked me to find someone for him. I came as soon as I could, and I will leave for home, I think, very soon. At least I hope so."

Kishpa seemed unconvinced. Tanis wondered if he had blundered already.

8

# At the Barricades

In the hope of diverting Kishpa's thoughts, Tanis quickly gave his attention to the quivering Scowarr. "Where is your good humor, my friend? Isn't laughter born out of fear?"

The funny man looked at Tanis balefully before replying, "I'm getting so used to being scared that when I feel safe it scares me."

Yeblidod giggled.

Scowarr brightened at the woman's reaction. "But now I'm starting to feel better," he added.

"Where are the two of you going?" asked Yeblidod, a plump, sweet-looking dwarf. She gestured around her at the meadow, flowers waving in the light breeze, the rising sea crashing in the background, the shouts of elven residents of Ankatavaka thin in the distance.

"We're going nowhere in particular right now," Tanis answered evasively, "but what of you? Where were you going with your cart before you tried to rescue us?"

The woman pointed out over the cliff to the ship anchored in the village harbor to the south. "Mertwig is delivering our son and many of our belongings to that boat. I was to bring the rest. You see, we live outside the village, and we can't protect our house. Mostly, we just want our boy to be safe from the fighting."

"You should be going, too," scolded Kishpa. "It isn't going to be safe here when the humans mount their attack. You're setting a bad example for Brandella."

Tanis nearly jumped at the sound of the woman's name. She *was* here. But was she leaving on that ship in the harbor? Kishpa had noted the half-elf's sudden movement, Tanis could see; the wizard was giving him a curious glance. But Yeblidod rattled on, drawing the mage back into conversation with her when she said, "Oh, Brandella makes up her own mind. You know that. Nothing I do, one way or the other, will have any effect on her."

"Nor anything I do, either, it seems," complained the wizard. "You know it will go hard with her if the village falls. A human woman living among elves . . ." He let the thought remain unspoken. "By the gods," he went on, frustrated, "I wish both of you would take that boat out of Ankatavaka so Mertwig and I could fight with clear minds. As it is, the odds are much against us."

Correctly interpreting Tanis's raised eyebrow as a question, Kishpa continued to the half-elf and Scowarr, "Since the winter of sickness, I am the only magic-user left in the village, and I am still not fully trained. Worse, our scouts say the human army outnumbers our fighters by at least six to one. Isn't it better that the women, the children, and the very old ones should be safe at sea when the siege begins in earnest?" he pleaded.

Yeblidod countered, "Those who want to go should go. But Canpho says I can help him with the healing. You know that the healer will need all the help he can get." She continued, her mild alto growing strident for the first time, "As for Brandella, she is good with a longbow—better than most. She will do the village far more good fighting here than she will marooned on a ship out in the sea. Besides," the dwarf concluded simply, "she and I are willing to take the risk."

Kishpa looked put out, but Tanis was relieved. Brandella intended to stay. But where was his father? He wouldn't leave until he'd found the man. His father most likely was with the massing human army. It wouldn't be until the battle was joined that the half-elf would have a chance of spotting him—and how easy was that going to be?

Tanis felt himself slipping into melancholy.

"You seem unhappy," said the dwarf, her small, delicate mouth creased into a frown. "Just moments ago you were saved from certain death. You even chided your human friend about his somber face. And now, for no reason that I can see, your face crumbles into sadness."

Tanis tried to marshal a smile, but Yeblidod seemed unconvinced. "Kishpa!" she called out, a sudden grin crinkling her emerald eyes. "Perhaps one of those spells you've collected will cheer him. Why don't you try the one that makes his toes sticky?"

Kishpa laughed. "You like that one?"

"Oh, yes," she cried, an eye on the half-elf. "When you used it on Mertwig, I had him dust the floor with his bare feet."

Kishpa adopted a jovial tone. "You see? I keep telling you my spells aren't completely useless."

Tanis didn't know what to make of this. "A spell to make someone's toes sticky?" he asked. "What's the point?"

"None," Kishpa replied, a broad smile creasing his thin

face. "I just collect spells that are stupid, foolish, and—
so Yeblidod often says—useless. I've got one," he said,
warming to his subject, "that takes the white out of
snow. Another will provide a black mustache to everyone within a one-mile radius, be they man, woman,
child, or even animal." He gestured from horizon to horizon and turned the sweeping gesture into a bow.

Tanis chuckled despite himself. Scowarr, on the other
hand, appeared unwilling to encourage anyone's humor
but his own. Instead, the humorist studied the ship riding
the waves in the harbor to the south.

"Have you ever used the mustache spell?" asked Tanis.

"What? And gotten run out of Ankatavaka?" Kishpa
threw his head back and roared with laughter at the
thought of the entire elven village wearing mustaches.
Facial hair was a rarity among elves.

Yeblidod and Tanis joined the laughter, while Little
Shoulders Scowarr waited for the right moment to
spring a joke of his own. When the others finally quieted,
he said, "There was this farmer who had a daughter—"

"Quiet!" ordered Kishpa, cutting Scowarr off in mid-
sentence. "Listen!"

Over the sound of the thrashing sea came the thunder
of drumbeats. The four grew somber.

"The human army is advancing," said Tanis.

"I shouldn't have spent so much time here," Kishpa
spat out angrily, his mood instantly dark. "I'm needed on
the battlements, and I waste my time here saving two
who care nothing for my village."

"That's not true," Tanis said defiantly. He had to get
into the village if he was going to find Brandella and his
father. If it meant taking sides in the war, then that's what
he'd do. "I've fought humans before, and I will fight
them again," he declared. "I told you I'm loyal to those
who call me friend. You saved my life. I will fight by your
side to protect you and those you care about. And so will
my friend. Isn't that right, Scowarr?"

"Me?" The slender human looked shocked. His voice

squeaked. "Fight?" He grew pale.

Tanis nodded sharply. Scowarr hastened to recover, casting nervous glances at the wizard whose magic had rescued him from a deadly tumble into the sea—and whose magic, presumably, could reverse the process just as easily. "Yes, of course, without question," he gibbered. "Just give me a sword. A stick. Anything you say."

"Very convincing," said Kishpa, his voice dripping sarcasm. He turned partially away from the half-elf and the funny man, speaking to an obviously embarrassed Yeblidod. "Of course, all our elven allies will be delighted to have a human they do not know fighting side by side with them." The mage whirled and began to stomp off through the wildflowers.

Tanis sidestepped to intercept Kishpa's passage; the mage glowered. "A matter easily addressed," the half-elf said. "We'll bandage his head as if he were badly wounded."

"You can cut up my last shawl for the bandages," volunteered Yeblidod in a soothing voice, seemingly anxious to resolve the dispute.

"Scowarr's clothes are already so tattered that they could just as easily be elven as human," Tanis continued, ignoring Scowarr's wounded look. "Besides, his stature is such that, once his head is covered, no one will doubt that he is elven—just as long as he keeps his jokes to himself," he added pointedly, glancing in Little Shoulders's direction.

The mage looked at Yeblidod, out to sea, and back at the village, where the sounds of a populace preparing for defense shivered through the moist air. Then he shrugged. "We'll need anyone who will fight. Bandage him on the way," Kishpa said. "Come now. We'll be needed on the barricades."

The truth of his words could hardly be doubted. A mere fraction of an instant passed between the utterance and the moment when Tanis, Kishpa, and Scowarr found themselves on the battlements surrounding the village of Ankatavaka. The dwarven woman was no-where to be seen.

Neither Kishpa nor Scowarr nor any of the elven de-fenders who surrounded them seemed either surprised or perplexed by the newcomers' sudden appearance. Tanis's first thought was that Kishpa had cast a spell that had sped them to this place. Yet the half-elf had heard no ut-tered words of magic nor any mention of a spell. His head spinning, Tanis finally realized that the old mage, fighting for his life on a sandy beach three days west of Solace, probably had forgotten his frantic rush from the seacliff to the village nearly one hundred years earlier. Once forgotten, it was as if the journey had never oc-curred, at least to the mage.

There was no time, however, to dwell on such riddles. The drums of the massed human army sounded insis-tently. From his vantage point atop an overturned wagon blocking the main street of the village, Tanis saw them coming. Thousands stormed out of the woods and into the open meadow that led to the village. From their ragtag uniforms and undisciplined charge, they seemed more like a huge mob than a well-trained army. Unfortu-nately, the elven defenders who manned the barricades were no better trained than their human enemy.

Tanis quickly studied the village defenses. He was ap-palled. No water brigades stood by in case of fire. No re-inforcements waited in reserve in case a section of the barricade was breached. No one was assigned to gather arrows shot over the barricades by the enemy.

Even as Tanis scanned the barricades, so did Kishpa. But unlike the half-elf, the mage searched for a single face. "Where is Mertwig?" he exclaimed. "Has anyone seen him? Is he all right?"

"The old dwarf said not to start the fight without him," an elf by the main gate called back with a nervous laugh.

"Old?" bellowed a craggy-faced dwarf who lumbered down the street toward the main barricade. "Who said I'm old?"

When the dwarf reached the barricade, he stopped and stared at the strangers. He looked questioningly at Kishpa, who glanced at Tanis and Scowarr and nodded his head as if to say, "I know them; don't worry."

Mertwig shrugged. "I'm coming up," he said.

While the dwarf climbed the battlement, Kishpa turned and stared at the oncoming human army. He stood atop the barricade like a red-robed beacon of inde-structible hope. The elves behind him looked to him as their savior; the humans who were fast approaching looked to him as their principal target. Despite Kishpa's one-quarter-elven blood, it was obvious which side held his sympathies, his loyalty, even his love.

"I hope your magic is strong," Tanis called up to Kishpa. "This village isn't prepared to withstand a long siege."

The mage didn't appear to have heard him. Kishpa was mumbling dark words. The conjuring had begun.

Tanis waited for something dramatic to happen. The only thing that changed was the proximity of the attack-ing hordes. The humans, in need of new lands and weaned on distrust and hatred of everything and every-one unlike themselves, surged forward. Soon they would be in longbow range.

Kishpa continued to chant, his eyes closed, his arms in constant motion, his skin seeming to glow with a faint silver aura, perhaps caused by the changing light of the early afternoon sun. A fast-moving dark cloud hung low in the sky.

The front ranks of the human army stopped their charge, knelt with their longbows, nocked their arrows, and sent them flying at the barricades . . . and at Kishpa.

Tanis immediately leaped from behind his cover and grabbed the mage around the knees, knocking him off his feet as a storm of arrows ripped through the air above them. The two of them rolled heavily down the side of the wagon and thudded to the ground on the inside of the barricade, landing in a heap of dust.

More than a dozen elves, led by the dwarf, Mertwig, rushed to help Kishpa up off the ground. He shooed them away, telling them to get back to their posts. "I suppose you think this settles your debt with me," said the mage to Tanis.

Tanis felt his lips tighten in the face of the mage's implacable air. "In time of war, there is no such thing as a debt for saving a life," he said with dignity. "It is one of the duties of a warrior to save the lives of his fellow soldiers; one should not keep score of such things."

"You have character," said the mage, mollified.

Tanis decided candidness was his best tactic. "It will do me little good if your magic doesn't work," he said, keeping his gaze locked on Kishpa's. "And I fear your spellcasting has had little effect except to draw several hundred arrows in your direction."

Kishpa barely suppressed a laugh.

"Do I sound like Scowarr?" Tanis asked.

"No," the mage said. "But you are unintentionally funny. Look over the barricade, and judge my magic anew."

Tanis scrambled up the side of the overturned wagon and gazed out over a marsh of mud and slime. The sky above the open field had turned black with heavy rain clouds, which poured down a deluge that was blinding in its intensity. In a matter of minutes, the field had turned into a swamp.

The elves cheered. Many left their positions on the north and south sides of the village perimeter to congregate on the eastern barricade and enjoy the spectacle of Kishpa's magic and to create their own special brand of rainfall: arrows that sprayed down upon the helpless humans in a deadly shower.

The human army was being decimated, and the charge from the east had been stopped cold. But while the larger human force was mired in mud and blood, a second force attacked virtually unseen from the south. The cries for help from the beleaguered elven defenders who had stayed at their posts went largely unheard over the roar of seeming victory on the east.

Without thinking, hundreds of elves watched the enemy become mired ever deeper in the east while others raced to do hand-to-hand battle with the humans who had breached the eastern wall and were entering the village. Tanis knew that the greatest danger wasn't from those humans. "Follow me!" he shouted to any elf who was within earshot. "We must take back the southern barricade. Whoever controls that wall will control your fate."

They were a small band of elves against an ever-growing number of humans. Tanis saw that Scowarr, bandages flapping around his head, was silently running to the attack alongside him.

"I know what you're thinking," Little Shoulders rasped as he ran. "You're thinking, 'Why isn't he making jokes now?' Well, I'll tell you why: When you're in deep water," he said, "the best thing to do is shut your mouth."

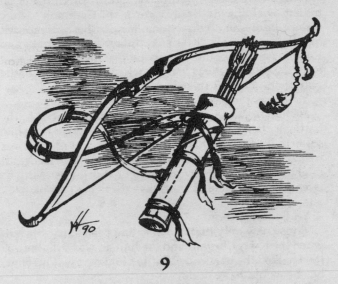

## 9

# The Sacrifice

The human soldiers flowed over the southern barricade like water rushing over a falls. But there was a dam up ahead that sought to stop the onrushing tide, a dam not of earth and wood, but of a small phalanx of elven villagers led by Tanis.

As Tanis raced into the fray, he felt a fear that was new to him. He was confident enough fighting several enemies at once; he'd done it many times. But he had never taken on so many foes without his good and true companions at his side.

Yet he charged on.

He was used to having Flint Fireforge on his right,

waving his fearsome battle-axe, Sturm Brightblade on his left, wielding his deadly sword, and Caramon Majere tossing bodies in all directions, making his presence felt in a thousand ways. Kit's swordplay, Tas's hoopak, and Raistlin's magic could always be counted upon to help even the odds. He was fearless when he went into battle with them. He was full of fear without them.

Yet he charged on.

He had no idea if the elven villagers who raced to the battlements with him could be counted upon to fight like soldiers. In fact, he had no idea how many of the elves had actually heeded his call to storm the barricades. It might have been as few as three or four or as many as twenty or thirty. He did not have the nerve to look back and count.

Yet he charged on.

Tanis knew only that Scowarr had been alongside him when the charge began, and the human was still there as they neared the barricades. Little Shoulders was no Flint, but he would have to do.

*　*　*　*　*

A woman stood on a balcony. Directly below her she saw humans fighting with elves in the streets. To the east, she could see the main army of the humans struggling in the unrelenting downpour that rained only on them. It was the sight to the south, however, that filled her with dread. The barricades had been breached. A small branch of the human army had broken through, and all of Kishpa's warnings to leave Ankatavaka came home to her. But she dismissed them now as she had dismissed them then. She would not flee her home, not while she still had the power to fight back.

The woman appeared fragile, but she was not; a great heart beat in her chest. Her exquisite face, however, belied the woman's fighting spirit. She seemed eternally, mysteriously feminine, with shining brown eyes so dark they appeared almost black, fringed by improbably thick lashes. Her glistening eyes, which mesmerized almost like Kishpa's magic, contrasted sharply with her delicately pale skin. She had a strong, proud nose, a delicate, sensuous mouth, and thick, curly hair that spilled nearly to her waist. Each of her features, alone, was startling in its perfection. All her features, together, were breathtaking.

She was Brandella.

With a longbow in her hands and a pile of arrows beside her, Brandella took aim at a human climbing over the barricade and let loose of the bowstring. She didn't see her target as a fellow human, but rather as an enemy. She had qualms about killing, certainly, but not about defending her home, her friends, and her life with Kishpa. Her arrow struck its mark, lodging deep in the human soldier's left thigh. He fell backward, clutching his leg, then tumbled off the outer edge of the barricade and out of sight.

It was then that Brandella saw the elven charge to retake the battlement. She estimated nearly one hundred humans were swarming over the barricades, yet only a force of a dozen or so villagers were attempting to retake it.

With controlled fury, she began shooting her arrows at the enemy atop the barricades, trying desperately to buy a few moments more for the handful of elven martyrs.

Despite her barrage of arrows, she expected the charging elves to be quickly slaughtered by the far-superior human forces. Although some elves did fall, the rest still managed to fight on, driving the humans, step by step, back up toward the top of the battlements. Brandella looked closely and saw someone she'd never seen before. He was taller than the other elves, and he fought with a ferocity she'd never witnessed. He ranged in front of the others, muscular body lithe in tooled leather, urging the elven soldiers on, battling like a brave warrior she had dreamed about as a little girl, a man who would come to her from a mythical world and take her on a grand journey to eternity.

With all her heart, she hoped he would not die.

\* \* \* \* \*

Tanis had no idea how many humans he had slain. He was drenched with blood and his own sweat. His broadsword slashed through his enemies, cutting a swath of red for the rest of his small and ever-diminishing contingent to follow.

Unknown to Tanis, the group had a secret weapon in its midst. It was Scowarr. With his head wrapped thoroughly in bandages, except for small slits for his eyes, nose, mouth, and ears, he was a fearsome sight. He had the appearance of a creature risen from the dead, a ghostlike apparition that could kill but could not be killed in turn. The horrible screams and cries that spewed from his mask of bandages sounded unearthly and terrible. The humans had no way of knowing that those screams were the hysterical ravings of a terrified man who had no idea what he was shouting in his abject fear. Neither did his fellow fighters, who pushed themselves faster and fiercer, following his example.

Wherever he charged, the humans fell away, stumbling back in dread of his wildly swinging sword. Soon Tanis and many of the remaining elven fighters took advantage of the effect Scowarr had on the enemy and attacked those who were already stumbling backward in fear.

The desperate tactic worked, and the line of humans began to falter and break. Tanis plunged forward, parrying the blow from a battle-axe, then kicking his foe in the stomach and knocking him backward from the top of the barricade. Another human dove at Tanis, attempting to wrap his arms around the half-elf's legs and wrestle him to the ground.

What the human hadn't counted on was the arrow that came out of nowhere to lodge in the back of his neck. His arms went slack as his limp body slammed into Tanis.

The half-elf recovered his balance, wondering who had shot the arrow that had saved his life.

Brandella smiled grimly as she plucked another arrow from her rapidly diminishing pile.

\* \* \* \* \*

The battle for the barricade was hardly over. Although Tanis and the others had gained the top of the battlement, now they had to hold it until the village reinforced them. The twilight made their situation that much more difficult.

Only eight of the elves who had joined him in the charge remained on their feet, and several were badly wounded. They couldn't hold out for long. Brandella nocked another arrow for her longbow, and let the deadly missile fly. Then a frantic voice challenged her from below the balcony.

"Brandella! You're still here!" Kishpa cried in anguish. "I hoped you were on that ship in the harbor."

Brandella saw the mage below her on the street. "Never mind me," she called back. "You must use your magic to save our people on the southern barricade."

Kishpa shook his head. "I can't," he intoned with a groan. "I exhausted myself with the storm spell; I won't have enough strength for another spell until morning. Mertwig says—"

Brandella slung another arrow onto her bow. She took aim on the distant barricade as she shot sharp words at her lover. "Never mind what Mertwig says. Have you seen what our people have done, how they have fought?" she insisted.

"I have," he admitted. "They are brave indeed, but you should have been on that ship!"

She let loose with the arrow and watched with satisfaction as another human soldier plummeted from the barricade. Her tone remained impatient. "Please, Kishpa, say no more about my leaving. Say only that you'll help those poor creatures on the battlement!"

Brandella didn't immediately notice the pause that followed her words. "I'll try," Kishpa finally said solemnly. "I'll do it because you ask it of me."

His tone penetrated her concentration, frightening her, and with a shock, Brandella realized what he risked for her. She leaned over the edge of the balcony, far out over the street, crying, "Wait! Don't sacrifice yourself! I didn't mean . . ."

It was too late. Kishpa already had entered a trance and was muttering the sacred, long-forgotten words that would create an enchantment. His mage's robes stood out against the gray of the cobblestones like a splash of red blood.

When he finished, he collapsed on the street.

# 10

# The Enchantment

The silver-inlaid broadsword in Tanis's hand might as well have been a boulder with a handle. His arm was so weary he could hardly lift it. As twilight descended, after more than four hours of intense fighting, Tanis and the others stood atop the barricade as yet another wave of human soldiers stormed the battlement.

They were eight bloodied defenders against nearly fifty fresh troops. Tanis looked apprehensively over his shoulder. He was shocked, yet unsurprised, by the sight of the empty streets behind him. No one was coming to help them. The villagers had gone after the humans who had already breached the barricade. Busy fighting little battles and small skirmishes from door to door, they were oblivious to the doom that awaited them if Tanis and his small band were destroyed. He drooped with fatigue, staying on his feet only by an act of will. Was it only a day ago, the half-elf wondered, that he was caught in the fire with Clotnik, or was the fire still scores of years in the future?

Scowarr stood next to Tanis, his bandaged head splattered with human blood. He had killed no one, but his presence in their ranks surely had been key to the brave elven stand. He had long since stopped screaming in total terror, principally, Tanis thought, because the man could no longer speak above a raspy whisper, and even that seemed to pain him. The human—Had Tanis once thought him frail?—was long past fear now, his fevered mind awash in the battles he had fought and survived. No matter that his throat felt as if he had swallowed hot coals, nothing alive or dead on Krynn could have stopped him from talking now. . . .

"I think—yes, I know—I should have become a Knight of Solamnia," he sputtered painfully.

Tanis looked over at the man and fought a smile as he compared Little Shoulders Scowarr with the muscular Sturm Brightblade.

"Imagine," Scowarr rasped, "fighting all those soldiers for so long, and I'm still alive! Not even a scratch!" He grabbed Tanis by the arm and exclaimed, "They see me coming, and they run! Imagine it! Ah, but you don't have to imagine it. You can see it with your own eyes! They fear me and my sword, shrinking from my every step. Let them come!" he screeched.

With Scowarr's exuberant movements, tufts of his light brown hair poked through gaps in his bandages, but he appeared unaware. Instead, he struck a defiant pose in the dying light. "Let them come!" he proclaimed. "Let them see what they get at the hands of Little Shoulders Scowarr! I'm not afraid of any of them. No more! Never! I say, let them come!"

Tanis wanted to hug this put-upon creature, who was willing to die with the dignity of a giant. If anyone, friend or enemy, dared to tell Little Shoulders the truth, Tanis swore he'd slay the offender. Scowarr's delusion was the ultimate blessing from the gods. Tanis hoped that when his time came, he could die as full of pride.

The front line of human soldiers, swords and battle-axes at the ready, clambered up the barricade toward Tanis and the others, yelling oaths and battle cries.

Tanis stood his ground stoically, but not Scowarr. Little Shoulders taunted them in return, shouting through his pain, "I'll give you death by the bellyful! You think you have an advantage in numbers, but all it means is that more of you will die by my sword! Come! Die!"

If Scowarr had frightened the enemy before with his incoherent screams, he unnerved them now with his unreserved boldness. The humans appeared unwilling to take on a blood-streaked warrior who was so obviously in the throes of insanity. The humans split their ranks and climbed the ramparts on either side of Scowarr, choosing to attack any of the others rather than the figure with the blood-covered, bandaged head.

Tanis held a shield that he had picked up earlier from a fallen human. He threw it at one onrushing soldier, deciding that his fighting arm was too weak to hold the broadsword with one hand. He gripped the handle of his blade with both hands for what he knew would be his final fight.

Without any warning, a strange tingling shot through his fingers and up his arms. In the fading light of sunset, his sword appeared to glow red and, to his astonishment, became extraordinarily light. He wondered if he, like Scowarr, was experiencing a delusion. If he was, he intended to enjoy it.

He brought his sword to bear on a charging soldier. With a swiftness more often seen with a knife than with a sword, he swung his blade in a wide arc, slicing off the soldier's hand in one quick, clean stroke.

Catching Tanis off balance, another human tried to stab him in the side. With the speed of lightning, the half-elf recovered, his broadsword flashing back to block his enemy's lunge. A moment later, the human lay bleeding on the barricade, a victim of Tanis's glowing red sword.

Off to his right, Tanis heard Scowarr shout, "Afraid to fight me, eh? Then I'll bring the battle to you!"

Oh, no, thought Tanis. Don't do it, Scowarr!

Waving his sword over his head, Scowarr did exactly what Tanis feared he would do: He charged down the barricade alone into the oncoming enemy troops.

Tanis couldn't let Little Shoulders die without trying to help him. It was suicide for both, but if Tanis was going to die, too, he would do it with the same flair as Scowarr. "Bring me more victims!" Tanis cried wildly, mimicking Little Shoulders's choleric tantrum as he raced down the front of the barricade after his friend, cutting down everyone who stood in his path. "Death to those who block my way! Who will fight me? Who wants to die?"

Tanis stabbed a human who was about to bring a battle-axe down on Scowarr's head. He cut open another soldier who tried to impale Little Shoulders with a lance. For his part, Scowarr didn't seem to have the slightest notion that he was in danger. He kept waving his sword and shouting, a man possessed by his own sense of immortality.

As for Tanis, he knew that death had to come soon. Yet his sword arm refused to grow weary, and his blade flew everywhere. Another soldier went down, then another. But Tanis's battle sense told him that there were too many of the enemy, crowding too close. He couldn't fight them all. Behind him, Tanis heard the wild shouts of the remaining elves with whom he had fought to regain the barricade.

Then the humans broke and ran!

"What on Krynn . . . ?" Tanis burst out as he watched the soldiers leave their dead and flee, leaping, down the barricade.

Another elven shout broke the twilight air. Scowarr's wrathful outburst had spread to his fellow warriors, inspiring them to a level of courage that went far beyond bravery. Seeing Scowarr and Tanis charge down the battlement, they had thrown caution to the wind and joined madly, wildly, almost joyously, into the fray.

The humans had had enough. Fighting eight such mad creatures was too much to contemplate. Instead, they turned and fled.

"Come on back, you cowards!" Scowarr taunted, apparently unwilling to end what was, no doubt, the shining hour of his life. He began running after the enemy.

Tanis was quick to grab him by the flapping edge of his bandages, which were finally coming undone.

"It's over!" the half-elf told Scowarr firmly. "You can rest now."

The funny man stared at Tanis through the slits in his bandages. His eyes seemed to cloud over . . . and then he passed out.

*　*　*　*　*

Torches burned that night in every street and alley of the village. Human soldiers roamed within Ankatavaka, and they had to be found. That wasn't all. New defense plans had to be devised in case the human army attacked again at daybreak—which was all but certain.

Tanis, his strangely glowing sword safely ensconced in his scabbard, prepared to leave Scowarr in the care of his comrades-in-arms. The elves had repaired to the front of a nearby hall and were busily unwinding Scowarr's bandage by torchlight, eager to see the brave soul who had helped spur the victory. Tanis watched from the back.

Finally, the last bandage fell away, revealing a thin man with tufts of short, light brown hair.

"A human?" cried one elven soldier.

"What?" "Human?" came the responses from the other elves, who stared at Scowarr in shock. "He's not elven!" cried an injured elf. "Not elven?" replied still others.

Silence fell over the group as nearly a dozen pairs of almond-shaped eyes studied Scowarr's distinctly non-elven features. A piece of bandage still clung to one rounded ear, and Scowarr's smile grew crooked as he gazed back at his companions of only a few minutes before. Finally, he cleared his throat. "Have you heard the one about the cleric, the mage, and the tinker?" he asked hopefully.

Tanis froze, hoping he wouldn't have to defend the human against the elves whom Scowarr had helped save. The silence stretched longer as Scowarr's smile faded and the elves continued to exchange dumbfounded glances. One old elf chortled, then drew in his breath sharply and looked sideways at his colleagues. "A human!" he muttered wonderingly.

Another elf, streaked with dirt and sweat, let loose with a chuckle. "I'll be a slig!" he commented, then reached over and clapped Scowarr on the back. Another elven mouth stretched into a smile and opened into guffaws.

As laughter spread from elf to elf, Tanis relaxed and slipped out the door. As he slipped into the street, he overheard talk of raising a monument to honor Scowarr's heroics . . . if Ankatavaka survived, of course.

The light from more than five hundred torches bathed the seacoast village in a flickering orange glow as Tanis searched the streets for clues that might lead him to Brandella or deliver him to his father.

"Do you know a woman named Brandella?" he asked many a scurrying elf.

"Yes," replied everyone he questioned.

"Where can I find her?" he immediately countered.

They all answered, "With Kishpa, of course."

"And where is he?"

None knew.

No one had seen the mage since late afternoon. The wizard apparently had vanished. Teams of elves had been sent out to search for him. Without his magic, the villagers couldn't hope to hold the human army at bay.

Tanis tried another way of finding Kishpa's lover. He remembered Clotnik had said Brandella was a weaver. "Where does Brandella work at her loom?" he asked a rotund elven smith.

"Works and lives in the same place, m'boy," said the smith as he sharpened one of countless swords and knives that had been left with him overnight. "Y'know, my wife is rather fond of the shawls Brandella makes; wears them all the time. Costs me a fortune. But it's worth it. Keeps the wife happy, y'know."

"That's important," agreed Tanis, trying to remain patient. Perhaps ordinary chitchat helped the smith remain calm, maintaining the illusion that life as usual was still possible. "But can you tell me where she lives?" Tanis pressed.

"Try the second floor over that way," the smith said, using a worn hammer to point down the cobbled street. "See that overhang?"

Tanis nodded.

"That's her place. My wife . . ."

Tanis thanked the smith, ran directly to the overhang, and looked up at dark windows. He hurried through the doorway and took the stairs three at a time.

Knocking loudly on the door at the top of the stairs, he stood and waited, wondering what Brandella would look like, how she would act.

To his dismay, no one answered the door.

Tanis glanced down the stairway. When he saw no one lurking in the shadows, he put his shoulder to the door. It got away from him and swung open with a crash. Tanis grimaced.

Lighting a candle he found near the doorway, Tanis scanned the large room. A loom stood in one corner with baskets of bright red, yellow, and purple yarn beside it. Near the back was an unmade bed, the scent from the sheets aromatic and exotic, and there, too, were several baskets of yarn. Then he saw what he should have seen from the very beginning: All four walls were covered with a huge mural; even the ceiling was part of the enveloping painting.

Despite the meager light from the single candle, the images were bright and lively. Tanis couldn't figure out where the mural began or where it ended, and the more he peered at it, the less it mattered. The pictures told a story that needed no beginning, middle, or end. There were scenes of Kishpa, his physique perfect, his face flawless, his inner essence shining through his blue eyes with regal purity. It wasn't the mage's magic that shone, but the painter's art.

There were also scenes of children playing games. One of the children—a girl with black, unruly curls—always seemed to have her back turned to the viewer. Exquisitely dressed elven dancers leaped to music one could almost hear. Here, too, was an older girl, her hair flowing in thick, black curls down her back; her face also was hidden. There were scenes of merry festivals, viewed, it was clear, from the terrace overhang off to Tanis's right.

All of the scenes, wherever he looked, were joyous and happy, save one. On the ceiling, over her bed, Tanis noticed the woman with dark curls, her face obscured this time by the shoulder of a man, running toward a light that seemed to be a great distance away. The man was sweeping her into his arms, carrying her forward, and her body seemed to say, "I will go with you to the very source of light itself."

Trying to make out more detail of the woman's face, Tanis held the candle up close to the ceiling. The painter had hidden her features well. As he pulled the candle away, he saw something. The candle came loose from its holder and fell into a basket of yarn that sat on the floor near the bed. He quickly grabbed the candle and snuffed out the beginnings of a fire, only to find a piece of paper, now slightly burned, in the basket.

He steadied the candle back in its holder, held the note up to the flame, and read:

*Dearest of my Heart,*

*Please do as I beg you, and think only of your safety.
A home is just a place to live; it isn't worth risking your
life to save. I know what you're thinking: I'm a hypocrite
because I'm staying behind to fight. I stay because it is
my duty; my ancestors would be shamed if I left the children of their friends when my magic was needed most. I
do not stay out of pride or desire. My only desire is to be
with you. I keep you in my heart, in my mind, every moment of every day. Please, your life is too short as a human to risk it here. Go to Qualinesti. Our people know
you, and you will be safe among them despite your race.
Save yourself so that I may love you later. I will find you
there when the battle is over. Go to the fisherman called
Reehsha. He has promised me that he will ferry you to a
ship in the harbor that sails for Qualinesti. You can trust
him to save you a place on his boat. Don't delay. Do this
for me, and know that I love you always.*

*Yours Ever Faithful,*

*Kishpa*

"Reehsha," whispered Tanis.

He was about to rush out the door and make his way
to the harbor when he remembered that there had been
something about the picture over the bed that had startled him, making him drop the candle. He hurriedly
raised the flame for a quick look—and saw that the man
carrying the girl with the black curly hair toward the
light . . . *was he!*

Or was it?

The features of the man on the ceiling seemed too perfect, too handsome, too majestic. No, he decided. There
was just a passing resemblance in the face, but nothing
more. Nothing more at all.

## 11

# A Cry in the Night

"Reehsha? Yes, everyone knows old Reehsha," said a sinewy elf who was patching his small skiff at the edge of the water. "Keeps to himself a lot these days. Didn't even help ferry the women and children to the ship," he added, gesturing out to the open sea.

Although he hadn't asked the question, Tanis now knew that Brandella had not done as Kishpa had begged; she had not left for Qualinesti.

"It could be the old man is smarter than most," the elf went on. "It was probably a good thing he didn't take his boat out there. I'm kind of sorry I did, myself."

Tanis was taken aback. "What about the women and

children?" he asked. "They had to be taken out of the village, didn't they?"

"Sure," agreed the fisherman, his face a map of wrinkles, "but the waves were something treacherous, and there were too many boats out there. Half kept banging into the other half. That's how I got this hole in my bow. We lost four women and six children to drowning; they'd have been safer in the village, taking their chances with the humans than with those rough seas. Yes, Reehsha is a wise old man."

"I want to meet Reehsha," said Tanis. "Where can I find him?"

The elf laughed harshly, his teeth showing whitely against his deep tan. "You may want to meet him, but he may not want to meet you. Reehsha doesn't have many visitors. And that's the way he likes it."

"He can always turn me away. Just tell me where to find him."

The elf spat into the sand and pointed across the beach. "At the far end, way past the piers. There's a shack back up in the rocks a bit. Maybe you'll see a light. Maybe you won't. But he's there."

\* \* \* \* \*

It was cool, dark, and peaceful by the edge of the sea, and being away from the village light was soothing to the eyes. Heavy waves crashed upon the sand, leaving a white foam tinged pink by the red light of Lunitari. Tanis breathed in the damp night air as he walked along the sand; the smell of the sea revived him, helping him forget the soreness in his arms and legs. The scent of salt and seaweed was a welcome change from the stench of battle, although elves in general preferred living in wooded areas inland to spending their lives by the sea.

Passing a rickety wooden pier that jutted into the thrashing surf, Tanis suddenly stopped. Without quite knowing why, he turned and stared at the old wooden structure. He thought he'd heard something odd, a sound that somehow didn't belong. At the same instant, a flock of birds skittered off the pier and into the wind, flying on a strong sea breeze.

His elvensight revealed nothing out of the ordinary. Tanis relaxed. It must have been the birds, he reasoned.

He started walking again, debating what he would say if he found Brandella and Kishpa together. How would the half-elf explain his presence? Perhaps he could say, "The whole village is looking for you, Kishpa. Please hurry. The elders are making new plans for the defense of the village. You must be there!" Once the mage was gone, Tanis reasoned, he could get Brandella alone and tell her why he had come for her. And then, he thought sourly, she'd think I'm a dimwitted fool.

Like a child, he kicked at the sand. Then he stopped. There was that sound again. He turned and looked back at the pier, staring intently into the dark shadows beneath the wooden structure, holding his breath, listening. What he heard had sounded like a muffled cry. Or maybe it was the flapping of wings—except this time there were no birds to be seen. And wasn't that a faint red glow he saw under the pier? Perhaps his elvensight, which caught the aura of living things even in little light, had focused on a shore animal.

His pulse quickened. It wasn't the birds he'd heard before at all. The birds flew away when they were startled by a sound, the same sound he'd heard. And now he heard it again. It *was* a cry.

As swiftly as his legs could carry him through the soft sand, Tanis dashed toward the pier. He could hear nothing over the sound of his own deep breaths and pounding legs, but the memory of that cry kept him running.

No light shone beneath the warped and rotting wooden boards of the pier. Tanis couldn't see details of who was there, but his elvensight revealed something large, shaped like a man. And surely, with the light of Lunitari behind Tanis, whoever or whatever was there could plainly see him.

In the darkness, a tall, powerfully built man with a barrel chest crouched over the bruised body of a terrified woman. He held a long, thin-bladed knife in one hand and an ornate, heavy shield in the other. The human jammed his knee into the woman's throat to keep her from crying out as he watched the intruder approach. He could tell by the interloper's forthright stride that they would do battle. He smiled at the thought.

The human had killed twelve elves after he'd scaled the barricade. He had thought that his fellow soldiers were going to overrun the village, but for some reason, few troops had followed him. Trapped inside the elven stronghold, he had killed seven more villagers since nightfall, weaving in and out of back alleys, using the shadows for cover. But elven patrols were getting closer all the time. He needed a hostage to keep them at bay until his fellow soldiers attacked again on the morrow.

Providence provided one.

She had been walking alone along the beach when he saw her. He'd leaped out from his cover, grabbed her around the mouth and throat, and dragged her, kicking and thrashing, back into the darkness beneath the rotting old pier.

Barely able to breathe, the woman lay near unconsciousness, no longer struggling. As he heard someone approaching, the human paid her no mind, lifting out of his crouch and edging toward an outer wooden pillar. He didn't need a hostage to protect him from a single elf. Hiding, the human waited.

As Tanis reached the pier, he slowed, not out of fear, but out of caution. He didn't want to walk into a trap. Before he went any farther, he called out, "Is anyone there? Are you all right?"

No answer.

That troubled him.

Someone was there. Someone had cried out. Of this, Tanis was certain.

Wisely, the half-elf stepped just inside the blackness

under the pier and then dropped silently to the sand, no longer silhouetted against the moonlight.

Tanis strained to hear any telltale sounds. All he heard were waves breaking against the front of the pier and the water roiling against the pillars that stretched out into the sea. He heard no voices, saw no movement. The only smell was that of the sea and shoreline.

The human was startled. Where had the interloper gone? He'd disappeared. The human, unused to fear, didn't panic now. He realized that his enemy was smart. It would be a good battle, he thought, one to savor in tales told over the crackling coals of a fire.

Tanis inched his way deeper into the darkness.

The human didn't move. He knew the game well. The first one to show himself would likely be the one to die.

Despite the sound of the sea, it was as if the darkness under the pier was deathly quiet. It was its own world of silent treachery and stealth.

Tanis, his face pressed into the cold sand, began berating himself for having strayed from his duty. Finding Brandella had been the task at hand. He had no reason to be under this pier, searching for the gods knew what. Soon, he began thinking, he should give this up; he was losing valuable time. What he did here would make no difference to the world, or even to Kishpa.

He had almost convinced himself to get up and take his leave when he heard the faint sound of someone breathing off to his right. He had called out before, and the person had not answered. That might mean that an enemy hid here in the dark.

The half-elf moved closer, his hand on the grip of his broadsword. From the sound of the breathing, Tanis gauged that he was just a few feet away from his foe. His enemy had given himself away, and he would die for that mistake.

In one fluid motion, Tanis rolled to his feet, pulled his broadsword from its scabbard, and swung its deadly blade in the direction of the sound.

# 12

# The Confrontation

As soon as Tanis unsheathed his sword, the blade gave off its shimmering red glow, casting a dim, otherworldly light on the underbelly of the pier. Only then did Tanis see his terrible mistake. The sharp edge of his broadsword was swooping down on the neck of an unmoving, defenseless dwarf.

Tanis's blade was in full motion; he couldn't stop it. All he could do was throw his body to the left, away from the woman, and hope that he somehow missed.

The blade whooshed through the damp night air and came down hard, burying itself deep in the sand just above the woman's head.

The human heard the sound of the broadsword coming free of its scabbard and readied himself for the kill. The red glow of the sword surprised him, but the light it threw off made his attack that much simpler. He saw his enemy clearly and dove at him with his knife pointing directly at the middle of Tanis's back. But the human did not expect his enemy to spin away from him at the last possible moment.

Tanis felt the impact of a glancing blow to the shoulder when the human hurtled past. The half-elf rolled over and came to his feet in one easy motion, his glowing sword held high. The human recovered just as quickly, squaring off with his knife and shield. The creaky pier stood an arm's length above them.

The two men locked eyes. The human saw a half-elf who looked physically formidable, yet confused and unsure of himself: an easy kill.

Tanis saw himself.

They had the same eyes, the same mouth, the same shaped face. The man had the badly broken nose and long black hair that Clotnik had described. The only thing missing from the juggler's description of his father was the slash wound on his right leg.

This was the man Tanis so much wanted to discover, to meet, to learn about, but now that he had come face to face with him, Tanis didn't know what to do. Perhaps a gesture, he thought. What if he showed the man he meant no harm?

Tanis lowered his sword, hoping that his father would be struck by their resemblance and do the same.

The human saw his chance. He lunged forward with his knife hand to slit the throat of the half-elf.

A cry, not of surprise or fear but of infinite sadness, escaped Tanis's lips as he stumbled back out of the way, instinctively raising his enchanted sword to block the blade. With knife locked against sword, the two men's faces were mere inches apart, and Tanis could stand it no more. "Look at me!" he shouted at the distorted image of his own reflection. "Can't you see? I'm—"

"—the next to die!" the human swore as he slung one leg behind Tanis's feet and shoved.

Tanis tripped and fell heavily onto his back. His head hit the ground hard, stunning him momentarily. The human had the advantage, and he pressed it. Leaping on top of Tanis, he rammed his shield into the half-elf's face—to hurt him and to blind him to his next move, Tanis knew, a move that would involve slitting the half-elf's belly open with one long rip of his knife.

His father was bigger, heavier, and stronger than Tanis. But such experts as Kitiara, Sturm, and Flint had taught the half-elf to defend himself in ways no ordinary soldier would know. Just as the human's knife twisted down toward his stomach, Tanis executed a flip and roll that sent his father tumbling sideways. The knife missed its mark.

Both scrambled to their feet, Tanis faster than the human. With any other enemy who was obviously out to kill him, Tanis would have met deadly violence with lethal force. But this man was his father. Would Tanis cease to exist if he killed the man, or would his position in Kishpa's memory protect him? Was it fair to spare the man who would go on to rape Tanis's mother? Or had the heinous act already taken place? Tanis made a quick decision and, with a whip of his broadsword, slashed a deep cut in his father's right leg. The man yelled and hobbled backward, his leg spurting blood.

"Surrender!" offered Tanis. "No more harm will come to you. I swear it!"

The human ignored him. He had seen enough of this half-elf; he wanted no part of him. The soldier retreated to the prostrate dwarf woman who lay helpless in the red-hued shadows. He dropped his shield and picked her up around the waist, putting his knife to her throat.

"Drop your sword, or she dies," he said.

Tanis stared at this man who was his father. "You would kill a helpless woman?" he asked, his voice quivering.

The soldier laughed bitterly. "You doubt me?"

The wild, animal look in the human's eyes told Tanis that his father was telling the truth. He would kill her.

The woman stirred, opening her eyes. Tanis looked at her closely for the first time and gasped. It was Yeblidod, the dwarf who had tried to save his life on the seacliff with her rope of shawls.

Tanis dropped his sword.

"You fight well for someone half-elvish," offered the human.

"I had hoped that you were a better man," Tanis said, his voice barely above a whisper. "I should have known better after what you did to my mother."

But maybe his father hadn't met his mother yet. Maybe this brigand hadn't yet had his way with her, destroying her life. Suddenly, Tanis neither knew nor cared if killing this human would mean that he, himself, would never be born. If it meant that his mother would be spared the cruelty of this man's attack, perhaps it was worth his own sacrifice. Disgusted and repulsed by the man who had fathered him, Tanis could take no pride in his own blood.

As the human backed away from Tanis, moving out from beneath the pier and dragging Yeblidod with him, the fishermen who had been caring for their boats marched across the beach. The human saw them and ducked back behind a pillar, forgetting Tanis for an instant.

The half-elf charged his father. Yeblidod saw him coming and bit the thumb on the hand holding the knife at her throat. The human yelped and let her go. As she slumped to the ground, Tanis plowed into the soldier's midsection with his head, bashing him into the wooden pillar.

The impact knocked the knife from the soldier's hand, but the man was more startled than hurt. He struck Tanis on the back of the head with his balled fists, once, twice, three times, until the half-elf faltered and fell to his knees. The human kicked him in the head, and Tanis fell backward, rolling over twice.

Desperately, the soldier tried to find his knife in the sand. But Tanis had fallen close to his broadsword, and he reached for it.

The human saw the half-elf pick up the glowing red sword. He ran.

Tanis would have chased after him until they reached the edge of the world, but Yeblidod cried out, "Help me!"

Without even thinking, Tanis stopped to aid the bruised and battered woman. He swore under his breath as he watched his father disappear into the night.

## 13

# Brandella

*Yeblidod's face was cut from a cuffing to the tem-*ple, and blood ran down her cheek, dripping off her chin. Bruised around the throat, she had difficulty breathing.

Tanis looked at the pain in the beaten woman's eyes and thought of his mother. How much worse it must have been for her! A churning in the pit of his stomach made him grab two handfuls of sand and squeeze them, waiting for the pain to subside. But it didn't. Sweat beaded his face, and he slowly began pounding the ground with his fists, over and over again, harder and harder. He had met his father and was appalled. How much of that human animal was inside him? Worse, he'd had it within his power to rid the world of the beast, and he had failed.

Tanis could take no more.

With a wail of pain that startled a frightened whimper out of Yeblidod, Tanis abruptly sheathed his glowing broadsword. Then, under the cloak of darkness, he stormed to his feet, lifting the bruised woman in his arms. "I will take you to safety now," he said through clenched teeth, fighting back his tears. "And then I will see to it that the man who did this to you dies." He looked down at her and in a hoarse whisper, added, "I swear it on my mother's life."

She nodded, sighed, and closed her eyes.

She was as light as a child in his arms as he ran across the beach, the lightweight cotton of her long skirt whispering in the sea breeze. He took her to the wooden shack of Reehsha, the closest place he knew of. No light burned, but he pounded at the door anyway.

"Go away!" someone called out in an angry voice.

"I will not!" Tanis shouted with a fury that he hadn't known he possessed. "Open this door. A woman needs help. Open it now!"

The door opened tentatively, and Tanis kicked it the rest of the way, pushing into the dark room.

"Light a candle!" Tanis ordered.

A brief moment later, a dim light flared in the room. Frantic to find a place to lay Yeblidod down, he turned and spotted a ramshackle bed under the window but was dismayed to find that someone was already in it.

Kishpa lay unconscious on the pallet. Red robes outlined the thinness of the mage's body. His chest barely moved with his shallow breathing.

"Move him!" Tanis ordered, whirling around to face a haggard-looking old elf who, nonetheless, possessed sinewy muscles in his arms and legs.

"He's sick," said the old one. "I will not move him."

"If you don't move him, I'll kick him out of that bed. I

swear it," the half-elf warned. Yeblidod, no doubt awakened by the stridence in his tone, moved fretfully in his arms.

The candlelight exacerbated the fisherman's spent look. "You don't understand," the old man protested. "That's—"

"Kishpa," Tanis finished, lowering his voice as Yeblidod stirred again. "Yes, I know. He'll be all right. I know it. He'll live to a ripe old age. Don't worry about him. But this woman needs care right now."

The old man was reluctant to move Kishpa until he recognized the woman in the half-elf's arms. "Yeblidod? Tell me what happened," he commanded, moving close. Tanis caught a faint whiff of fish.

Tanis was rapidly losing what little control he had left. "Never mind that now. Just make room for her."

Reehsha did as he was told, easing the mage off the bed and onto an animal skin rug. Kishpa stirred but did not awaken.

"Bring me hot water and bandages," said Tanis. "And a blanket."

The old man did as he was ordered. Tanis was awkward and clumsy as he tried to tend to Yeblidod's cuts and bruises. Then a husky feminine voice sounded from the doorway behind him.

"What happened? Who's hurt?" the new voice demanded.

Tanis turned and beheld the image of a woman like none he had ever seen. Her pale skin fairly glowed against her dark, curly tresses, and every delicate feature of her face looked as if it had been painted in perfect fleshtones by a master. Her figure was accentuated by a thin, black, woven top, cinched tight around her narrow waist with a cord, setting off long, shapely legs. She wore brown leather shoes with silver buckles, and a woven skirt the color of new leaves.

There was no doubt in Tanis's mind that he was looking at Brandella. And in her own right, she could have sparked the shock that coursed through him now. But the resemblance to another woman, the echo of an earlier love, sent a pang through the half-elf like a fiery bolt from a longbow. Brandella's black hair was long, practically waist-length; Kitiara's short, black curls had framed her face. But the brown eyes could have been those of sisters. Brandella was a softer, more feminine version of Kitiara. Kit had been his—as much as any man could dare to claim the tempestuous swordswoman—only short days before. And now she was traveling, the gods knew where, with Sturm Brightblade.

Kitiara would have laughed at Tanis's current pain, he knew. "What, Tanthalas? Not . . . not regrets?" she would have sneered, flashing him her crooked smile and probing the wounds caused by their parting. Yet there would've been an undertone of passion that would have left him breathless.

He couldn't imagine this woman, Brandella, sneering at anyone. He realized he was staring and forced his gaze to the woman's companion. Behind Brandella stood the dwarf, Mertwig. When the dwarf saw who lay on the pallet, he bolted across the room, crying, "Yebbie! Yebbie!"

Yeblidod raised her arms weakly to her husband as Tanis stepped out of the way. The dwarf wept at her bedside as she patted his head. "I'm all right," she reassured him in a thin whisper, a raspy imitation of her formerly warm alto. "Some rest, a little soup, and I'll be just fine."

"What happened? Who did this to you?" Mertwig asked, weak chin wobbly in his craggy face. He wiped his eyes with the tail of his dark brown shirt.

"A human. But he," she said, indicating Tanis, who stood quietly in a dark corner, "he fought him and drove him away."

Mertwig nodded at Tanis in gratitude, clearly unable to say what was in his heart. The half-elf understood; the dwarf Flint was much the same way.

Hurt though she was, Yeblidod appeared mostly frightened and shaken by her ordeal. Brandella shooed Mertwig away and looked after the matronly dwarf.

"Where is Canpho?" asked the old fisherman in a low rumble.

"I couldn't find the healer, Reehsha," Brandella answered softly, without looking up from her seat on a low, three-legged stool next to the rickety bed. "There are many who are sick and dying. He could be anywhere." She cast a distracted look at Kishpa, lying without movement on a fur pallet on the floor.

"But Canpho would come if he knew it was Kishpa," insisted the frustrated fisherman. His gestures made wild shadows on the bare walls of the candlelit shack. "They would find him for you and send him."

"We couldn't risk it," Brandella said plaintively. "If everyone knew that Kishpa was ill and unable to cast his magic to defend the village, there would be panic. As it is, many are worried that our mage is nowhere to be found. If they hadn't discovered a distraction, Ankatavaka would be awash in fear."

"A distraction?" Tanis asked.

Brandella nodded without glancing his way. "A funny little human they have dubbed a hero," she explained, wiping Yeblidod's forehead gently with a moistened fragment of one of her shawls. Brandella glanced over her shoulder at the old fisherman. "I'm afraid that we alone must fear for the village. And I with guilt," she added, her eyes suddenly filling with tears, "because it was my fault that he has come to this state."

The old elf stepped forward, quickly flaring to anger. "You're at fault? How?"

She turned back to her nursing of Yeblidod, ignoring Reehsha's implicit threat. "I asked too much of him," she tried to say evenly, though Tanis could clearly see the hurt in her eyes. "The humans were about to break through the south wall," she said. "There were only a handful of defenders left, and I begged him to use his magic to save them because they had been so valiant. He told me that it was too soon for him to use his magic again, but I insisted."

Brandella faltered, then took a deep breath and steadied herself by covering Yeblidod with a blanket, her ministrations completed. The dwarven woman, soothed by her friend's calming hands, slipped quickly into sleep.

Tears glittered on the weaver's thick lashes. "He cast his spell," she continued. "I don't know what it was or even if it worked, but he collapsed right after that. He hasn't regained consciousness." It was a statement, not a question. A tear trickled down her face. She didn't wipe it away.

"He warned you!" bellowed the old fisherman. "If he dies, it's on your head! And if he dies, by the gods, I'll have your head, too! I'll feed it to the fish!" Reehsha stomped about the room, clearly forgetting the two invalids lying a short distance away.

"Enough!" Tanis shouted. In the same instant, he drew his broadsword, its ominous red glow filling the small shack. He now knew full well the source of his blade's power. It had been Kishpa who had enchanted the sword, saving his life and, quite possibly, the village of Ankatavaka. "I told you," the half-elf growled. "Kishpa will survive. Be a good friend to your mage, and swallow your oaths."

Mertwig, shaking with the strain of the evening, shouted, "Don't kill him!" Brandella tried to shush him, glancing repeatedly at the motionless Yeblidod and Kishpa.

"A warrior wizard!" Reehsha exclaimed. "I have never seen one!"

"I am no wizard," said Tanis harshly, lowering his sword so that its point tilted toward the old elf's face and lowering his voice to please Brandella. "I am just a friend to Kishpa and a servant of his lady."

"You lie!" Reehsha shot back, undeterred by the blade's proximity to his nose. "You must be a warrior wizard. You have a magic broadsword, and you have now twice foretold the future. How do you know that Kishpa will live?"

Before Tanis could answer, Brandella grabbed his hand and squeezed it. "Is it true? Will Kishpa be all right?" she begged softly, dark brown eyes aflame with hope.

Although well aware that he would be hard-pressed to explain how he knew it, Tanis couldn't deny her the peace she so desperately needed. "Yes," he said. "He will live."

A sob escaped Brandella's throat. Then she looked at Tanis again, more closely, and a sudden, strange flash of recognition leaped in her eyes. She gasped.

"I . . . I don't know how . . . how soon Kishpa will revive," Tanis offered, embarrassed by her reaction to him. He swallowed and took control of himself, adding, "I don't know if he will be able to help Ankatavaka when the sun rises and the humans renew their attack. I know only that he will have a long life."

"Then you *are* a mage," Reehsha intoned, self-satisfied. "*You* could help Ankatavaka!"

"I told you I am no mage. But I know *this* mage," Tanis said cryptically, pointing at the unconscious Kishpa. "And you need not worry for his health."

"What of Yeblidod?" begged Mertwig. "Do you also know how she will fare?"

"She will be fine," the half-elf said, deciding there was no reason to say otherwise. "You need not worry about her."

Mertwig and Reehsha finally appeared at a loss for words. For the first time in long moments, silence fell on the fisherman's ramshackle quarters. Reehsha's face still showed suspicion, Mertwig's face, only relief. Brandella had dried her tears and watched the half-elf intently.

"Who are you?" the dark-eyed weaver finally asked, quietly and kindly. Her voice was steady. "You are a stranger to Ankatavaka, yet you claim to know my

Kishpa. You call him friend and declare yourself my protector. Why is this? And by what magic do you possess such a sword?"

"All good questions, Brandella." Tanis dared to gaze into her eyes. Her tears had made her appear that much more pallid, yet the half-elf realized there was a cord of steel beneath the soft demeanor that was as strong as the broadsword he now sheathed.

"You know my name?" she asked.

"I know it well."

"Then use it well and tell me both what I wish to know and what I need to know."

"My name is Tanis," he began slowly, trying to decide how much he should tell her. The candle sputtered. Mertwig resumed his vigil by his wife's side, and the fisherman slumped onto a wooden bench by the door.

Tanis's problem, he knew, was that at some point he would have to escape the elder Kishpa's memory. He had been told that Kishpa would help him. But how? And when? Without that knowledge, he was reluctant to tell Brandella too much of the truth for fear that she would laugh at him. And he didn't know yet whether she would confide immediately in her lover—the man who would try to prevent her from leaving this time and place.

"I come from somewhere far away," he began, not quite sure of what he was going to say. "And I possess no magic except for what has been given to me by Kishpa. It is he who brought me here. And it is he who enchanted my sword. You see, I was on the south wall of the village when your mage cast his spell. . . . "

Brandella heard nothing else that he said. She simply stared at Tanis, remembering how he had looked from afar on the battlement. Yes, she thought, it was him . . . the man from the dream.

## 14

# At Last, A Hero

*Scowarr stood on a heavy wooden table,* surrounded by a sea of happy, hero-worshiping elven faces. He had them just where he wanted them: listening . . .

The funny man's patter was coming fast and sure tonight. He ran one hand through his short hair—the elves seemed to find the cut of his hair especially amusing—and launched into a new joke. "I once asked an elderly elf, 'To what do you attribute your old age?' His answer? 'The fact that I was born a long time ago!' " He widened his amber eyes and nodded significantly at the crowd.

The elves roared with laughter. Scowarr glanced down modestly, taking the opportunity to steal a glimpse of the elves' gift to him; they'd provided the slender human with a new set of clothes, the forest-green slacks and jerkins that Ankatavakan men preferred, to replace the filthy rags he'd worn while fighting the human soldiers.

After a day of carnage and death, Scowarr's jokes were a welcome release, a way to forget and to ignore what would come on the fast-approaching morn.

"And talk about the weather," he rambled on, "the only good thing about rain is that you don't have to shovel it."

In the back row, a middle-aged elven woman, one of several women who'd chosen to stay and fight beside brothers and husbands, yelped and poked her mate; again the crowd erupted with guffaws and applause.

Scowarr had been at it for more than two hours. He'd dredged up just about every joke he knew and more than a few that he'd made up on the spot.

"It's a miracle," he murmured, adding mentally, *Or maybe it's magic.* In the back of his mind, he wondered if that young mage, Kishpa, had cast a spell making him genuinely funny or had conjured up a village full of laughing elves. The very fact that the elves were giggling at his jokes seemed even more amazing to him than their hailing him as a great warrior. Elves did not have the greatest sense of humor on Krynn—at least from a human point of view, he thought charitably. Elven folks tended to be rather sober and serious.

But they were anything but serious tonight. Scowarr drank in their laughter until he reeled with it.

It might have gone on like that until dawn, had not a village elder rushed into the hall, calling out, "To the streets! Everyone! We must find Kishpa!"

Scowarr frowned; his audience was distracted. "What is it?" he asked the intruder. "Is there trouble?"

"Magic-users!" cried the elder, blue eyes flashing under a shock of white-blond hair. "One of our spies has come back from the human encampment. He says they have wizards to aid them tomorrow. We must find Kishpa!"

Unwilling to yield his place of honor, Scowarr boldly shouted, "If the mage must be found, then I will help you find him!" Then he knelt and softly asked, "Does anybody know where he could be? Any idea at all?"

"Some say he used his magic to turn into a field of shimmerweeds," a young, wide-eyed villager said.

Scowarr hated to show his ignorance, but he asked the question anyway. "Why would he do that?"

Another villager laughed. "Is this another joke?"

"No. Really," Scowarr protested, keeping his voice low. The elves closest to the table were beginning to exchange amazed glances, and the comedian was loath to tarnish the newfound shine on his reputation.

"You don't know what a shimmerweed is?" the same villager asked, surprised. When Scowarr shook his head, the elf went on. "It blooms only at night, getting the only light it needs from the moonlight. But when the petals catch the light just so, the shimmerweed blinds anyone nearby and causes him great confusion."

"Oh," said Scowarr, sagely nodding his head. "*That* shimmerweed. I knew that. So Kishpa is surrounding the human encampment, keeping them from attacking us during the night? Is that what you're trying to say?"

"That's what I heard."

Another villager interjected, "That's not what *I* heard." He edged in front of the first speaker and said, "My uncle told me that someone saw Kishpa become invisible so that he could walk among the humans, undetected, and learn their plans of war." Other elves murmured and added their conjectures.

"We're wasting time," complained the village elder who had sounded the warning. He forced his way toward the center of the room where Scowarr held sway. "These are just rumors, idle talk, foolish gossip. It isn't like Kishpa to disappear without a trace. Even his human lover, Brandella, has vanished. But Kishpa must be found and told of this new threat. Without his help, the humans will drive us into the Straits of Algoni."

"Brandella didn't vanish," piped up an elf from the back of the room. "I saw her just a short while ago, hurrying down toward the fishing boats."

"She was alone?" asked the elder.

"No, she was with the dwarf, Mertwig, but it was odd. They seemed to be hiding in the shadows."

"To the fishing boats!" ordered Scowarr, relishing the ring of his commanding baritone. Even more pleasing to him was the reaction of the elves. They did as he said!

\* \* \* \* \*

"Do you hear something?" Mertwig asked from his perch near his wife's bed.

"Someone's out there," Tanis agreed from the back of the room, hearing the faint sound of a voice on the wind. He turned to Reehsha, who had moved from the bench to the window and pulled aside the fishnets that served as curtains. "Can you see anything?"

"It's a mob!" the old fisherman replied, visibly startled. "I can't tell how big, but there look to be at least fifty torches lighting the far side of the pier, where the fishing boats are moored."

"What are they doing?" Brandella asked in a whisper.

Tanis went to the window to see for himself. He grimaced. "They seem to have a purpose. It looks like they're looking for something—"

"Or someone," Brandella interrupted, staring down at Kishpa, who lay unaware beside her. One hand continued to stroke the wizard's brow.

"Trouble!" Reehsha suddenly blurted.

"What is it?" Mertwig and Brandella asked together.

"They're coming this way," said Tanis, trying not to alarm the woman who cared so deeply for her mage.

Her hand went to her throat. "They must not know!" she protested. "They'll lose hope. Don't let them inside!"

"We may not have a choice," said Tanis.

Brandella rose and lunged across the room toward the half-elf. She took his hands in hers and squeezed them.

Her closeness nearly unnerved him. Kit was a beauty, and Laurana the epitome of young, elven loveliness, but Brandella's very essence was heart-shattering. At her touch, he felt himself go as red as his glowing sword.

"You said he'd recover," she said. "You said he'd live. Think now of all those who will die if Ankatavaka's people panic."

Brandella's skin was as delicate as porcelain above the black shirt and the loose green skirt, both obvious products of her loom. Tanis felt his blushing creep inexorably to his hairline. The young weaver appeared unaware of the effect she was having on him, however. "There's no place to run," she continued. "A few may survive by taking to the fishing boats, but the rest will be slaughtered if our defenses crumble. I beg you; stall for time! Don't let them know the truth. If the villagers fight, they have a chance. If they run, they'll die. You're a warrior. You know what I say is true."

The woman's beauty was almost more than he could bear. The warmth of her hands, the scent of her hair and skin, the perfection of every feature, all made Tanis's mouth go dry. Yet there was more to her than the appeal of her flesh. There was the same energy and passion that had drawn him to Kitiara. Without, he hoped, the all-too-human yearning for power.

"I will do what I can," Tanis promised.

"You are a worthy man," she said simply, looking up into his blushing face.

He wanted to ask her if he was worthy of *her*, but he refrained. Nonetheless, he found himself unwilling to let go of her hands. A moment passed. Was it his imagination, or did she seem reluctant to let go, too?

"They're getting closer," Reehsha announced.

Tanis freed her hands. Brandella gave him a shy smile.

A moment later, Tanis opened the door, stepped outside, and with fingers gripping the handle of his sword in its scabbard, he faced the oncoming mob.

## 15

# IN SEARCH OF THE MAGE

*"LOOK!" CRIED AN ELF, APPARENTLY TIRED OF TROMP-*
ing around in the wet sand near the fishing boats.
"There's a light in Reehsha's window!"

"Maybe he's seen Brandella and Mertwig," suggested
another elf. "Let's go ask him."

A murmur of assent went up among the elves, who
numbered almost one hundred, and Scowarr was quick
to jump out in front of the crowd, shouting, "We won't
rest until we find Kishpa!"

It wasn't all bravado on Scowarr's part. He enjoyed
the role, playing the hero to the hilt, but he also was worried about the mage. After all, Kishpa had saved his life

on the seacliff, and the human was not unmindful of his debt. If Kishpa needed rescuing, Scowarr was willing to do his part. He even thought he was capable of it.

The torches blazed, lighting the way across the beach for the anxious elves and their temporary leader. The waves crashed at their feet, reflecting the torches' glow.

When the searchers climbed the rocks toward Reeh-sha's shack, Scowarr felt his legs and arms aching. Exhaustion was catching up with him, but he refused to give in to it. He wanted to be a hero again—and that meant finding Kishpa.

As Scowarr led the crowd toward the shack, the door to the crumbling old building suddenly swung ajar. Golden light illuminated the darkness, and the silhouette of a fighting man, strong and straight, walked into the shimmering aura and waited.

\* \* \* \* \*

Tanis decided to keep the door to Reehsha's shack open. Closing it behind him would have suggested that he was trying to keep the crowd from entering. Rather, he reasoned, let it appear as if he had nothing to hide from them.

As they got closer, Tanis stared in disbelief at the sight before his eyes. "Is that you, Little Shoulders?" he called out.

"It isn't Huma of the Lance."

There was some appreciative laughter from the elves behind the funny man. Tanis, however, said nothing.

"Well," said Scowarr with gentle sarcasm, "based upon your hearty laughter at my little joke, I now know for certain that the image before my eyes is that of my dear, ever-so-humorless friend, Tanis." At this, the half-elf proffered a small grin.

"Of course, I could be mistaken," Scowarr went on, hope playing on his thin features.

"You were right the first time," said Tanis with a hint of playfulness. Yet when the torches from the mob had come close enough, Scowarr could see the hard expression on the half-elf's face.

"I was worried about you," said Scowarr, the elves behind him suddenly quiet and patient. "I haven't seen you since the battle. I feared something had happened to you."

"Not to me. You passed out, and I left you with friends. Or should I say admirers?"

"Good friends," the funny man said emphatically, waving an arm at the elves crowding close behind him.

"So I see," Tanis said. "But what are you all doing here when you should be resting for the battle that is sure to come at daybreak?"

"We've come in search of Kishpa," said Scowarr.

"If I see him," Tanis said shortly, "I'll tell him."

"Where's Reehsha?" demanded someone from the back of the mob. "What are you doing in his house?"

"A woman was attacked under the pier," explained Tanis. "A human soldier did it. I brought her here."

"Did he kill her?" a shrill voice asked.

"No. But she was hurt."

"Yes, but where's Reehsha?" insisted the elf at the back of the mob.

"I am here," the old fisherman called gruffly from the window. "Now leave us be."

"Who is she? Who got hurt?" several curious elves asked at once.

Tanis didn't answer them. Instead, he reached out and touched Scowarr's shoulder, noticing the new clothes but saying only, "Remember the dwarven woman who tried to help us at the seacliff?"

"Of course . . . oh . . . *not her?*"

Tanis nodded.

Scowarr wearily rubbed his eyes. "I feel terrible," he said to no one in particular. "Just terrible."

"She'll be all right," said Tanis.

"What's her name?" someone called out.

"Yeblidod," Tanis answered without thinking, and then

a moment later realized the enormity of his mistake.

"She's Mertwig's wife!" several elves exclaimed at once.

A stocky elf, holding a torch and standing behind Scowarr, shouted, "This must have been where Mertwig was going with Brandella. And if Brandella is in there, I'll wager Kishpa's there, too!" The elf rushed forward, trying to push past Tanis and into the shack. The half-elf grabbed him, accidentally knocking the burning torch out of the elf's hand. The torch soared over the rocks onto the beach, and the damp sand extinguished it with a sizzle.

"You can't go in there," Tanis said sternly.

"Who are you to stop me?" The speaker displayed a belligerence more typical of humans than elves, Tanis thought.

"Someone who cares for Yeblidod," he said simply. "She's sleeping now and should not be disturbed."

"I don't know you," the villager shot back. "For all I know, *you* attacked the poor woman and—"

Before he could finish the thought, Tanis leaped at the elf with a savage cry. He went straight for the elf's throat with his bare hands. In a mad scramble to try to stop him, it took six elves to pull Tanis away from his nearly strangled victim.

The elves had thrown Tanis to the ground and were preparing to beat him into senselessness when Scowarr shouted, "Stop! He's my friend!"

Reluctantly, the elves did as their hero commanded. Tanis stared at Scowarr as the half-elf rose to a sitting position on the hard ground.

The funny man gave him a crooked smile in return. "What can I say? They like me."

Tanis smiled in return. He was glad they did.

"You know," said Scowarr, "the one thing you can get without a lot of trouble is a lot of trouble."

Many of the elves laughed at his cleverness. Tanis merely nodded. For his part, Scowarr shook his head with resignation. He leaned down close to Tanis and complained, "You are the most difficult audience I've ever had."

"What about all those arrows?" Tanis reminded him.

"Second most difficult audience," the funny man amended.

While they were still close, Tanis took his chance. In a low but insistent voice, the half-elf whispered, "Get them away from here."

Scowarr looked at his friend with a questioning glance. He didn't know who or what Tanis was really hiding in that shack, but there was no question in the funny man's mind that something strange was going on.

He was very curious about the game the half-elf was playing. Scowarr pursed his lips as he stepped away from Tanis and considered his options. He wondered if the villagers would heap still more glory on his little shoulders if he discovered whatever Tanis didn't want found. He also wondered what Tanis would do to him if he betrayed the half elf's trust. The lure of glory was strong, but Scowarr didn't want to be a dead hero. Besides, he had done rather well for himself by following Tanis's lead. He decided to do it again and hope for the best.

"Come, fellow soldiers," Scowarr announced. "We're wasting our time here. The dawn will break soon, and let us not break with it. We must be ready to fight the humans with or without Kishpa. Are we not brave?"

"We are brave!" the mob cried out, stoking their own courage.

"Are we not strong?" His voice rose several notes.

"We are strong!"

"Are we not ready?" Scowarr raised a fist on the last word.

"We are ready!"

"Then let us prepare to fight." He paused, then, "To the barricades!"

"To the barricades!"

A great cheer went up, and the mob quickly scrambled down the rocky path toward the beach. Scowarr marveled at the effect he'd had on these elves. He almost— but not quite—hoped that he would die this day so that he would never have to face his ordinary life again when the praise and honor stopped. He lingered behind as his followers hurried away.

"You did well," said Tanis gratefully when they were alone. "You have my thanks."

Little Shoulders bowed his head in acknowledgment. "It was my pleasure to help you. But there's just one thing."

"Yes?"

"You must tell me what's going on," Scowarr pleaded. "Why wouldn't you let anyone in the shack?"

Tanis was about to tell him when a figure crossed in front of the doorway behind them, blocking the light. Scowarr squinted to see who stood there as Tanis turned to look, too.

"I'm glad I saved your lives," Kishpa said weakly from the doorway, the light streaming out into the night from behind him. "I seem to have made the right choice."

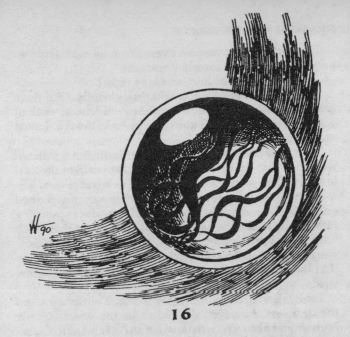

# 16

# To Keep a Promise

A beautiful woman appeared next to Kishpa, the light throwing mysterious shadows across her magnificent face, partially hidden by her cloud of black curls. She held one of the mage's arms to keep him from teetering on his unsteady legs. Scowarr was delighted to have found Kishpa, but he was overwhelmed by Brandella.

"Who is she?" he whispered to Tanis.

"A woman who will not be forgotten," the half-elf replied.

"Huh?"

"Never mind." Then, aloud to the mage, Tanis said, "I assured Reehsha and Brandella that you would recover."

The wizard narrowed his eyes. "So they said. Did you know, or were you merely guessing?"

"Does it matter, as long as I was right?"

"Perhaps it does," Kishpa said thoughtfully. "But there is no time now to ponder the question. Come in, both of you, and tell me what is going on in Ankatavaka. I must know everything."

Tanis and Scowarr started for the door, but a shouted warning from the direction of the village caught their attention. They all turned to see what the trouble was. The mob that had followed Scowarr had apparently flushed one of the human soldiers out of hiding and was pursuing him. Kishpa, like the half-elf, could make out that much with elvensight, although they both doubted that Scowarr and Brandella could catch much detail. Tanis saw that the soldier was big, his long legs giving him a loping stride.

Tanis tried to focus on the man's face. The distance and the darkness, however, proved to be too great. Yet the human was the right size, and he had been spotted near the beach. It might be him, Tanis thought. It might be my father. Without another thought, the half-elf bolted in the direction of the human.

Brandella would have to wait. Old Kishpa would have to wait. Everything would have to wait until Tanis kept the promise that he had made to Yeblidod—and to himself.

"Where are you going?" shouted Scowarr.

Tanis didn't answer.

The others at Reehsha's shack shrugged and headed into the cabin. All, that is, except Brandella, who lingered in the night air watching Tanis recede into the darkness.

*   *   *   *   *

While Reehsha went to tend his boat and Scowarr slept huddled on the floor, Mertwig paced, trying to decide how to ask Kishpa for help. He wanted to give his wife a beautiful, delicate glass ball that the famous Piklaker had created. Unfortunately, the price was far beyond his means. But if Kishpa would merely vouch for him, the artist would be honor-bound to let him buy it.

Mertwig was a proud dwarf. Asking favors did not come easily. Finally, though, he managed to ask, "How long have you known me, Kishpa?"

Kishpa, resting on the wooden bench by the door, his red robes pulled around him against the cabin's chill, raised an eyebrow. "My whole life," conceded the mage. "You know that. Why do you ask me such a question?"

Mertwig drew a breath, made a decision, and plunged on. "Because I need you to speak on my behalf."

"To whom?" the mage asked warily.

"To Piklaker." The dwarf tried to look resolved, but his weak chin failed him. It wobbled with his nervousness.

"I heard you were eyeing his wares," said the wizard dubiously. "You really shouldn't—"

"No lectures!" interrupted the dwarf with sudden temper. "I simply want you to tell the artist that I'm good for the price of a certain glass trinket." He spun away from the mage, crossing his short arms before his chest. "There, I said it."

"That 'trinket,' " the mage said sarcastically, "is worth more than what you earn in a year."

Mertwig turned back. "So what? It has value. I can always sell it later if I can't pay for it. Besides, I'm not asking you to buy it for me, I'm just asking you to tell Piklaker that you vouch for me." His voice took on a pleading tone. "If you do that, old friend, he'll let me have it."

Mertwig saw Kishpa glance at Brandella, looking for her guidance. She nodded. Mertwig knew that Brandella didn't consider it her business, or Kishpa's, to decide what was right or wrong. The mage's duty, the weaver would feel, wasn't to judge his friends but to give them what he could and let them make their own choices; if Mertwig wanted to put himself into debt for his wife, then that was his decision. As long as he wasn't asking Kishpa to foot the bill, she would see no harm in what Mertwig was suggesting, the dwarf knew. But Kishpa would likely have a different view, Mertwig worried. He wished he'd never embarked on this conversation.

Kishpa frowned at Brandella's reaction.

"I don't know . . ." he said slowly. "This is a matter of honor. If I vouch for you and you can't pay, it will make me look like a fool to Piklaker—to the whole village. Don't you see that? Don't you see that you're asking me to risk my own reputation? I would do it if you needed food, a roof over your head—something serious. But you want to buy a foolish, useless bauble."

Mertwig stamped his foot, then looked over to where his wife still slept. "Don't tell me about foolish and useless," the dwarf countered heatedly, keeping his voice to a hissing whisper. "What about your collection of ridiculous spells? How much have they cost you?"

Kishpa's face showed his fatigue, and the long sleeve of his red robe shook as he drew his hand across his eyes, tangling his shock of black hair. Obviously, he didn't wish to argue. He simply sighed and tactlessly replied, "The difference is, I didn't buy anything I couldn't afford."

The two, facing what could be death in battle on the morrow, stared across a widening chasm in their long-time friendship. Mertwig barely held his temper. "I'm telling you, I have to get that glass ball for Yebbie, especially after what she's been through tonight. She deserves it! Besides," he added plaintively, "I told everyone I was going to get it."

Kishpa appeared to be battling between his head and his heart. His gaze didn't meet Mertwig's. "I . . . I wish I could help you."

"By the gods, if anything goes wrong, I'm the one who's going to look like a fool! Not you!" said the dwarf, his voice suddenly stone cold. "Just tell Piklaker that I'm good for the debt. I'm not going to beg."

Rising wearily from the bench to put his arm around Mertwig's shoulder, the mage tried to break the tension. Kishpa's red robes seemed almost garish against the earth tones of Mertwig's stained clothes. "Please. You're making too much of this," the wizard said, his pained face a sudden portent of the old man he would become. "There's no reason for you to get angry with me. We simply have a different way of looking at things. I can cast a spell for you and create the—"

"No," the dwarf said petulantly, throwing Kishpa's arm off his shoulder. "I said *I* would buy the glass ball for her. *That* glass ball. I promised her. I keep my promises. Will you help me or not?"

"No."

*　*　*　*　*

Tanis saw the human soldier make a sharp turn into a narrow street. The mob of elves saw him, too, and followed, screaming for his blood. Tanis, behind the elves, feared they would reach the human before he did.

"He ducked into the stable!" came a cry from ahead.

The stable was right next to the smithy, and Tanis knew where that was. Rather than follow the elves, he circled behind the stable, hoping to catch the human as he tried to slip out the back way.

He wasn't the only one who had that thought, however. A small band of elves broke off from the mob and rushed to the rear of the stable. They got there before Tanis, and it was they who came face to face with the human.

Three of them were carrying weapons, while the fourth held the torch, which cast dancing waves of light on the determined faces of the angry elves. The human's face remained shrouded in shadow. Tanis heard the rapid breathing of the combatants and the crackling of the torch as he rounded a corner. He sprinted to join the group.

The fourth elf was the first to fall, the human's sword

impaling him in the chest. The torch and the elf fell as one to the ground, the light quickly extinguished in a pool of blood, dying along with the one who had held it.

In the sudden near-darkness, the red moon casting a weird glow over all, another elf charged the human, swinging a battle-axe. The human sidestepped and slashed with his blade, cutting a deep wound in the elven fighter's side. The elf screamed, dropped his weapon, and fell in a heap.

The remaining two elves held back warily, seemingly hoping to keep the human at bay until the rest of the elves could join them. The human rushed the two villagers who stood in his way.

Despite the blackness behind the stable, Tanis's elven-sight showed him the back of a tall, powerful human bringing his broadsword to bear on a young elf who was clearly overmatched. Next to him, another elf crumpled to the ground, his right leg nearly cut in two.

The main contingent of elves had heard the sounds of battle and would join their fellow villagers soon. The human had to be aware of that. He intended to quickly dispatch the remaining elf who blocked his path.

Except Tanis was there to stop him. The half-elf left his feet and dove at the human as the soldier's sword came down at the hapless young elf. Tanis hit the human behind the knees with his shoulders, knocking him off his feet. The human's sword skittered out of his hand as they both went down, rolling over each other several times in the dirt.

The human ended up on top, quickly pinning Tanis's shoulders to the ground. The soldier reached for his belt and pulled a long, thin-bladed knife from a sheath. Tanis looked up at the man who was about to kill him.

At the same moment, blood began to spurt from the human's mouth. The tip of a sword protruded from the front of the man's throat as he dropped the knife and fell, dead, on top of Tanis.

The young elf whom Tanis had saved only a moment

before stood over the pair, retrieved his knife from the human and wiped it on the back of the dead man's shirt. Then he shoved the corpse off Tanis with one push of his leg and extended a friendly hand to the half-elf.

Tanis was grateful on two counts: He was alive, and he had not been denied the chance of killing his father.

The dead human was a stranger.

*     *     *     *     *

The inky gray light of the false dawn was diminished even further by a fog that began to blow in from the Straits of Algoni. In the murky light, the tense citizenry of Ankatavaka watched and waited. The villagers who had survived the battle of the day before stood on the ramparts on the east, south, and north sides of the town, fear their constant companion. The day before, they had been emboldened by Kishpa's presence. If that hadn't been enough, two brave strangers—the bold human, Scowarr, and his enigmatic half-elf companion—had joined their ranks. The pair had made a difference in turning yesterday's battle.

As the new day broke, however, the elves discovered that Kishpa had disappeared and that neither Scowarr nor Tanis had taken positions on the barricades. They feared they had been abandoned. Worse, they feared that their cause was hopeless. Word had spread that the humans now had magic-users on their side. It seemed as if the beleaguered defenders of Ankatavaka had little chance of surviving. The humans were likely, indeed, to drive them into the sea, just as they had promised they would. Many of the elves were privately considering taking fishing boats and fleeing while they still had the chance. The closer it came to sunrise, the less private the talk became. When they plainly heard the humans breaking camp and preparing to attack, the elven defense began falling into disarray, with loud arguments and occasional fistfights.

At first, a few elves on the eastern barricade climbed

down to the street and hurried toward the sea amid angry shouts from some of those who stayed behind. Soon, though, the example of those who'd fled inspired others, and scores upon scores of elves on all three sides of the village threw down their weapons and ran down the main street of Ankatavaka toward the boats.

Halfway to the waterfront, however, they came upon a dwarf, a young mage, and a funny-looking man with little shoulders. The trio stood in the narrow cobbled road, blocking their way. Shops loomed closely on each side.

"You shall not pass!" proclaimed the mage.

Flanking the wizard, the little man and the dwarf drew their swords in warning to those who might disobey the command.

This was no phalanx of intimidating soldiers blocking the path of the fleeing elves. It was just three men, alone, one with magic and the other two with swords, standing against neighbors in the murky morning air. The mage was pale and weak, and his companions didn't appear to be skilled warriors, from their looks. Yet the fleeing elves stopped. They would not dishonor their wizard, his old, dear friend, their hero—or themselves.

"I am returning to the barricades," announced the mage, blue eyes flashing. "I shall not be defeated. I'll protect our village, our homes, our way of life. I am going back. Come with me."

Then the dwarf with the craggy face and slanting forehead pointedly growled, "I'm going back to the barricades because friendship and loyalty are not mere words to me. Come with me."

Before anyone else could speak, the funny man with the tufted hair and little shoulders said, "I'm going back, too. Your battle is my battle. Today, like yesterday, your village is my village. And today, like tomorrow, my blood is your blood. I'm going back. Come with me." After he spoke, Scowarr felt his skin prickle. Maybe, he thought, he should forget about being funny and concentrate on being heroic.

The crowd muttered with uncertainty. "I'm going back, too," one wizened villager finally said. He turned, and two friends followed. Either shamed or inspired, an ever-growing column of villagers turned and marched back toward the barricades, their hope renewed, their heads held high.

The elves who had stayed behind on the barricades to defend their village were waiting grimly for the human attack when a cacophony erupted behind them. There were whistles, cheers, and voices raised in song. The deserters returned as if they were a fresh new army of reinforcements. But the most heartening sight of all was Kishpa and Scowarr, marching at their head.

Scowarr had promised that he would find the mage and bring him back. He had kept his word.

When the mage and the previous day's hero finally climbed the barricades, Ankatavaka was a village that felt fear no more.

But then, the battle had not yet begun.

## 17

# AN Apparition

THE FOG ON THE BEACH WAS SO THICK THAT TANIS couldn't tell if the sun had come up or not. He walked back to Reehsha's shack in a murky gloom that mirrored his inner thoughts. He realized now that the chances of finding his father were more remote than ever. There were too many humans and too little time. Once the battle for Ankatavaka began again in the morning, many would die—possibly Tanis himself. And when one side won the battle, the other would be slaughtered. He had vowed to Yeblidod that he would wreak vengeance on her attacker. His mind was numb with shame; he wasn't likely to fulfill his oath.

With a heavy heart, he climbed the rocks that led to Reehsha's home. It wasn't until he neared the shack that Tanis noticed, with a start, that no candles burned there as they had when he had left. Had something happened? He rushed to the door and anxiously flung it open, not bothering to knock.

Brandella looked up in startled surprise. She was sitting next to Yeblidod, swabbing the sleeping dwarf's head with a cool, damp cloth. The woman put a finger to her lips, indicating for Tanis to be quiet.

Tanis nodded meekly, letting the tension drain from his neck and shoulders. He glanced around the inside of the dingy one-room cabin and saw that Brandella and Yeblidod were the only ones there. "Where did the others go?" he whispered.

"Wait," she silently mouthed, getting up and coming toward him. When she reached him, she took his arm and led him out the door. They walked a short distance in silence, the gray fog enveloping them as they strolled through the rocks to the beach. They could see each other, but little else, the shack merely a dark image that floated in the distance.

"Kishpa, Mertwig, and Scowarr have gone back to the barricades," explained Brandella. "They left just a short while ago." She'd thrown a shawl over her head, but droplets of moisture clung to the curls above her brow.

"And Reehsha?"

"He's gone to tend to his boat. When he returns, he will look after Yeblidod." Brandella glanced at him curiously. "And what of you? Will you stay here, or will you go to fight the humans?"

"Perhaps neither," he answered truthfully. "I came here for a reason."

"I know," she commented matter-of-factly.

Tanis did a double-take and took her by the shoulders. "You *know?*" he asked.

"Yes," she replied, her face puzzled, pulling slightly away from him. "Scowarr explained it to us last night after you ran off. He said you came to Ankatavaka to find two people."

"Oh. I see." Tanis took a deep breath. He could hear the waves in the distance, but they were lost in the grayness. The fog seemed to be suffocating him. Or maybe it was Brandella. The mist played around her face, softening her features and giving her an aura that seemed altogether fitting for a woman who was a memory.

"The human you were chasing? Was he one of those you came for?" she asked, gently extricating herself from Tanis's grip.

"No," said the half-elf, not quite knowing now what to do with his hands. He finally pretended he was cold by blowing on his fingers and rubbing them together.

"Then why did you run after him?" Brandella persisted.

"It doesn't matter now," he said, face downcast. He felt the damp of the fog clinging to his leather clothing. Seagulls cried, somewhere out at sea.

"It seems to matter still to you," she said, reaching out and tenderly touching his cheek, "or you wouldn't seem so sad." She surprised him with her gentle gesture, and she seemed more than a little surprised herself that she had been so bold.

"You're very kind," he whispered hoarsely.

"And you are very brave." It was a statement, not a compliment. Her eyes were frank, not coquettish. "I saw you on the southern barricade yesterday. I hoped that you would live."

"I hoped so, too," he said with a smile.

She laughed, a warm and infectious sound that came easily. "Scowarr's sense of humor must have rubbed off on you," she said.

Tanis raised an eyebrow. "You find Scowarr funny?"

She nodded, dark eyes quietly amused. "I don't know if it's what he says or how he says it, but, yes, he makes me laugh. Isn't he remarkable?"

"It would certainly seem so."

"He's more than just funny, though," the woman went on. "He also tells the most amazing stories. Truth to tell, I found them a little hard to believe. He told several, for instance, about you."

"Oh?" Tanis turned toward the sea.

"He said you appeared out of thin air, right in the middle of a skirmish. He was watching from a hollow tree trunk, and one moment there was nothing and the next moment you were standing there." Out of the corner of an eye, the half-elf could see the weaver eyeing him, watching for his reaction.

Tanis shifted his feet on the seaweed-strewn sand. He didn't know if he'd have another chance to speak with Brandella alone. If he was going to tell her why he had come to Ankatavaka, this had to be the time. She had given him the opening; he only hoped he could convince her that he was telling the truth.

"I did appear out of thin air," he said softly.

She took an involuntary step backward, clutching the knot of shawl at her throat. "Then you aren't real!" she breathed, eyes wide. "You're an image, an apparition!"

Tanis threw back his head and laughed. Her words struck him with such ironic force that he couldn't help himself. "*I'm* unreal?" he said, choking on his words, taking a few steps away from Brandella and then turning back and facing her. He threw aside both hands. "*I'm* an apparition? Oh, how I wish Scowarr could hear this," he added with a broad grin. "He thinks I lack a sense of humor. If only he knew!"

"Only knew what?" Brandella asked, confused by Tanis's strange behavior.

"That I'm the only one here who *is* actually real. You, Yeblidod, Kishpa, Scowarr, Ankatavaka, the humans outside the barricades—you're all only images living in the memory of a dying old mage. When he dies, you all will disappear. This isn't your life the way you lived it; it's the life you lived *as he remembers it*. I'm real flesh and blood. I'm the living being walking among the ghosts of one man's past. He cast a spell and sent me here."

"You're mad!"

"You don't believe that," Tanis said. "You know that Scowarr was telling the truth. You know I've come here for a reason."

Her confusion seemed to be turning to anger. A pink spot appeared on each high cheekbone. "You can't just stand there and tell me I don't exist," she protested. In her annoyance, she let go of the shawl and it fell back from her glorious hair. Tanis caught his breath.

"You do exist—in memory," he said. "You are real—in memory. You do live and breathe—but it's not your own life. I've come to change that."

A sob suddenly rose in her throat, and Tanis felt a pang for what he was putting her through. "No," she cried, turning away from him and becoming nearly lost in the mist. Like the ethereal figure she was, she called out to him from the enshrouding fog, her words a painful cry: "I've dreamed of you—but with fear!"

Tanis moved quickly through the mist and reached out. He snared Brandella by the arm and pulled her in close to him. "Don't fear me," he pleaded. "The old mage sent me here for you, Brandella. To free you."

She stood her ground, curls flying free in anger. "Free me from what?" she demanded. "From my happy life? From the man I love? This is not possible. I refuse to go!"

Tanis shook his head. "You don't understand. This is *Kishpa's* dying wish."

She straightened defensively and flounced back a step. "He's not dying. You said so yourself. You said he would live to a ripe old age."

"So I did. And so he has. Listen to me. Where I come from, ninety-eight years have passed since you cared for Kishpa here in Reehsha's shack. Where I come from, he is old now, dying in a burnt-out glade, lying against the side of a blackened tree, imagining you, remembering you in your glorious youth. And it is he—the old mage, the old Kishpa—who has sent me here to take you from his memory before you cease to be."

"It's a lie!" Brandella cried, eyes aflame. "It's a trick. Kishpa suspected that you were not to be trusted. He told me so. And now I see that you have come to destroy us. I won't let you!"

To Tanis's utter astonishment, Brandella drew a short-bladed knife from a hiding place inside her shawl. She was fast, and Tanis was too dumbfounded to move. But she stumbled as she jabbed the blade at Tanis's side, drawing blood with a cut above the hip.

Before she could stab him again, he grabbed her wrist and squeezed it until she let go of the blade's handle.

"You're hurting me," she protested.

"I could say the same of you." As he spoke, he picked up the knife and threw it into the rocks at the edge of the beach.

A small but steady stream of blood oozed from what was luckily a minor wound. He stanched the flow with his thumb, jamming it over the cut.

"You do me an injustice," he said with more calm than she might have imagined possible from someone who had just been attacked. "I mean you no harm. I only wish to do what Kishpa has asked of me. And I'm afraid there isn't much time. He could die at any moment, and that would be the end of all of us."

She started to turn her back but appeared to think better of it. "Your brain must be addled," she objected.

"Please," he begged. "Think a moment. Imagine yourself in his place. You are part elven. You have lived another ninety-eight years, and the human you once loved has long since died. But you remember her well, thinking of her always. And now you lie near death. Except she, in your memory, is still young and full of life, just as you always pictured her, no matter how the years might have changed her. Wouldn't you, if you could, want that image to exist even if the mind that remembered it no longer lived? Wouldn't that, in your moment of passing, be a gift of love beyond anything you could ever imagine?"

Brandella did not answer at once. Tears filled her eyes. "Yes," she finally said. "It would be a great act of love." Then she wiped her eyes and composed herself, saying, "It's a lovely thought, but it doesn't mean that what you're saying is true. You're asking me to leave the man I cherish for a string of pretty words."

"Not for a string of pretty words," Tanis countered. "For love. Brandella," he whispered, finding it hard to say these words, "I yearn for the ideal that Kishpa has found. All my life I have craved what he once had with you. He grieves for its loss. I never had it, and I grieve even more that I may never know it."

Brandella stared at him with luminescent eyes.

Tanis drew from the inner pocket of his tunic a piece of once-colorful cloth that still held faded shades of red, yellow, and purple. He held it out to her.

Brandella slowly took it from him and examined it.

"It's my weave," she said shakily.

Tanis nodded.

She turned it over, hands unsteady, face ashen. "It's a remnant of the same scarf I've been weaving for Kishpa these past few days. How can it be home, unfinished, and here, ancient and tattered?" One hand went to her mouth, lips trembling.

Tanis only watched her closely. His heart went out to her in her confusion.

"Kishpa gave this to you?" she asked, looking up.

"As a token of his love." Tanis saw her eyes shift, and he knew.

She believed.

## 18

# The Final Attack

BRANDELLA BROKE AWAY FROM TANIS AND RAN BACK
toward the shack. The half-elf didn't know what to make
of her reaction. Was she reeling with joy or despair?

Inside the cabin, Brandella stood with her longbow in
hand and a quiver of arrows slung over her shoulder. "As
soon as Reehsha returns, I am going to the barricades,"
she announced quietly but firmly.

Yeblidod stirred in her bed at the sound but did not
awaken.

"But what of Kishpa's wish?" Tanis demanded from
from the doorway. "Don't you understand? He may die
any moment."

"I *do* understand," she fiercely countered. "But I will not go with you. Not now. It is this Kishpa that I love: the one on the barricades, fighting for his village. It is this Kishpa who made me, a human, feel at home in an elven village that I now love."

Sadness and anger vied for dominance on the weaver's face. Brandella had changed to an outfit more suitable for battle than the previous night's skirt and woven blouse—brown leggings the color of a doe's eyes, with an overshirt of deepest green. The costume added to her air of calm assurance. Once again, her self-confidence reminded Tanis of Kitiara.

"Understand me, Tanis," Brandella said firmly. "I was a mere girl floating in the wreckage of a slaveship that foundered in the Straits. The chains were still on my feet, their weight destined to pull me off the piece of hull that I clung to for life. If Kishpa had not had a vision of me during the storm, I would have perished. On rough seas, he sailed out to find me. To save me."

She looked away from Tanis, visibly embarrassed at what she was about to say. "At first I loved him out of gratitude. He treated me with kindness, taking pains to make sure his elven friends—and dwarves like Mertwig and Yeblidod—did not snub me because of my race. Then," she said boldly, gazing once again directly into Tanis's eyes, "he taught me how to learn so that I could teach myself. I learned to weave, to paint, to use a longbow . . . and finally, when I grew up, I learned to love him. And he loved me back.

"Now you ask me to abandon my mage," she continued in disbelief, shaking her head, "to abandon the Kishpa I know so well, because you say the old Kishpa has a wish. But I don't know the old Kishpa. I don't know how the years have changed him. I only know that *my* Kishpa would be terribly hurt if I left him now."

She shook her head as Tanis made a dissenting move.

"Listen to me," she said. "He is weak from enchanting your sword. He would never admit it, but he is afraid for himself, for me, and for the village. If I desert him now, it will break his heart. How can I deserve the love of the Kishpa of the future if I abandon the Kishpa of the present?"

"You are eloquent in your devotion," Tanis said softly. "Still—"

She cut off his words with a commanding gesture. "Speak no more!" she ordered. "I will go with you when the battle is over. Not before. I will not let *my* Kishpa down when he needs me most. If what you say is true, and I am nothing more than a memory, I would not have my disappearance in his moment of need be his last remembrance of me."

"Then you will go with me when the battle is over?" Tanis asked.

She still hesitated. Then—"Yes." Decision was suddenly clear on her delicate features.

"Then I will accompany you to the barricades," he insisted. "I will fight alongside you and make sure—as best I can—that no harm befalls you. But whether the battle is won or lost, when it is over, I will take you with me."

"I will make sure—as best I can—that no harm befalls you, either," she said, flashing a sudden warm grin.

\*   \*   \*   \*   \*

Fog hugged the shore, but most of the village basked in brilliant early-morning sunshine. Stone-fronted shops appeared deserted on each side. Tanis and Brandella hurriedly stepped down the empty streets, marking the sounds of battle from up ahead.

"It has begun," she said grimly.

They ran to the barricades, only to find the elven defenders panicking along the eastern wall. Hundreds shouted at Kishpa from every direction, begging him to do something before it was too late.

Clearly something terrible was happening. Tanis and Brandella climbed the ramparts, clambering their way toward Kishpa, who stood in plain view atop the barricade. When they reached the top, they saw what was driving the elves into a state of abject fear.

"By the gods!" Tanis exclaimed.

The human army had swelled to immense proportions, gaining reinforcements that easily numbered more than five thousand and perhaps as many as ten thousand.

"Where did they all come from?" Brandella wondered, squinting against the sun.

The enemy troops were virtually uncountable, charging toward Ankatavaka like an endless sea of humanity. Their numbers stretched in every direction, entering the open meadows on all three sides of the village. And they kept streaming out of the woods.

The elves didn't have enough arrows to kill this many humans, even if they hit their mark with every one let loose. The odds, they all realized, had become impossible. They were about to be overrun by an army that outnumbered them at least thirty to one.

Yet Tanis was surprised to find Kishpa, a figure in red robes boldly silhouetted against the eastern sky, calmly surveying the oncoming human horde. Tanis looked around for Scowarr and Mertwig, surprised that they were nowhere in sight.

Kishpa, having given Tanis a suspicious stare when the half-elf showed up with Brandella, finally answered his lover's question. "They came," he said matter-of-factly, "from a spell, and that's how they shall perish."

"Are we imagining them?" asked Tanis.

Kishpa straightened his red robes, fluttering in the morning breezes. "No, it's a duplication spell," he explained. "Most of them are phantom reflections of a much smaller number of real soldiers."

"See there," Kishpa said, and indicated a young, blond human carrying a distinctive quiver tooled in blue and yellow. "Now look there, wading across the stream. And there." Tanis and Brandella followed his pointing finger. A blond warrior carried the same quiver across a creek;

not 30 yards from that soldier, a duplicate warrior hurried past a tree.

Kishpa looked pleased with himself, his relaxed smile contrasting . "They might have fooled me," he admitted, "but they overdid it, duplicating far too many soldiers. It made me suspicious, and so I looked more closely. That's when I noticed that too many of them are dressed exactly the same, are holding their bows in the same way, and are running in perfect step with each other. That's when I knew.

"The spell, by the way, is rudimentary," he added, "but I've never seen it done on such a grand scale. There must be at least a half-dozen magic-users in the human camp. If this spell is any indication of their power, none of them are terribly advanced, but, combined, they can come up with very powerful magic."

"Are you strong enough to stop them?" Brandella asked worriedly, putting her arm around the mage. Her brown eyes gazed warmly into his blue ones; Tanis looked away.

"I don't know," the mage replied candidly. "I need to husband my magic, so I must counterattack with a spell that is relatively simple."

"I hope you have something in mind," Tanis said irritably, "because, reflections or not, they're getting awfully close."

"If either Scowarr or Mertwig does his job, then we just might—ah, just in time!" the mage exclaimed, pointing down to just inside the village gate. Little Shoulders skidded to a halt below, holding a small metal box in his hands.

"Open the gate!" Kishpa ordered.

"No!" cried a chorus of elven defenders. The ones who didn't reply looked fearfully at the dissenters but did not move.

"Do as I say!" the mage commanded angrily.

No one moved.

Tanis, Kishpa, and Brandella looked into a sea of recalcitrant, almond-eyed faces. With an oath, Tanis jumped down off the barricade and raced across the cobblestones to the gate. He reached for the pulley rope and was about to yank down on it when, just above him on the battlement, a fearful elf with a knife tried to cut the rope. Instead, Brandella sent an arrow flying through the elf's sleeve, pinning it to the battlement wall.

Tanis hauled on the pulley rope; then, as the gate swung open, the half-elf bowed to the weaver up above. She inclined her head and winked.

Once the gate was open, the mage shouted to Scowarr, "Open your box and empty it onto the ground just outside. Then get back in. And you, Tanis, close the gate!"

Scowarr and Tanis did as they were told.

The human horde was fast closing in, covering the open field between the woods and the village. The sound of their charge was deafening, but Kishpa concentrated on his spell, repeating the same strange words over and over again.

Nothing seemed to be happening—until a terrified cry howled from the front lines of the human army.

## 19

# A Spell Upon You

THERE WERE MORE SCREAMS FROM THE HUMANS AS Tanis scrambled back to the top of the barricade.

The half-elf recoiled from the scene below. A giant spider, with scabrous, long legs and an eager mandible, was turning the humans in its path into masses of slashed and bleeding flesh. The human reflections of those who were killed or injured took on the same bloody countenance as the originals, so scores seemed to fall in agony. The creature killed silently, but the din of the victims was deafening. Brandella turned from the sight with a horrified cry; many of the elves reacted in the same way.

It wasn't long before the very sight of the hideous creature sent the real soldiers into a headlong retreat, their duplicates instantly following. Those humans who were farther away, however, nocked their arrows and sent them flying in the direction of the gigantic spider.

A rain of wildly aimed arrows filled the air, and, perhaps fearing that they might kill the creature, Kishpa continued jabbering away in a long-forgotten tongue, murmuring sounds that Tanis suspected only Raistlin would have known and understood.

Kishpa, with what Tanis realized was a fine sense of justice, used the same duplication spell as had his human counterparts. As the mage's words became more intense, the screams from below grew to a soul-shattering extreme as the humans suddenly found themselves facing a growing army of giant spiders.

Spiders will avoid a fight unless they feel threatened and sense that they have no choice. With the barricades behind them, they had only one direction in which they could easily go. And from that direction came painful arrows and thousands of swarming humans.

With the spiders constantly churning their scaly legs in a field of men, it became virtually impossible to tell which of the spiders was the original and which were the magic duplicates. Slaying the right spider might have ended the humans' ordeal, but they had to fight all of them at the same time. Arrows from the elven barricades made the trial that more hellish for the soldiers.

The human army, both real and unreal, fled as one. They turned like ships on a stormy sea, twisting in one wave and then tacking as if with the wind. Feasting on human blood, the real spider followed after them, hungry for more. And the rest of the duplicate monsters followed in a macabre dance of dozens of thin, long, sharp-edged legs that skittered across the open meadow like so many nightmares. The humans were routed.

The elves on the barricades cried with joy at their deliverance. The chant of "Kishpa!" went up among them, echoing into the morning sky.

For his own part, the mage stood slumped against Brandella's shoulder, exhausted. Supporting her lover, the weaver sent Tanis a look that seemed to say, "See? I told you he would need me," and Tanis nodded shortly. A handful of grateful villagers rushed up to their mage and carried him down on their shoulders, Brandella following. The rest of the elves danced on the barricades, showing little of their notorious elven reserve.

"We must have a feast!" cried Canpho, the healer, rushing around the main square on his stubby legs.

"Yes, a feast!" echoed the elves, rushing down from the battlements.

"We must send for the women to come home to us!" shouted Canpho. "We have been saved by great magic!"

The cheering thundered, and Kishpa, his face etched with weariness, nonetheless glowed in their praise. No wonder, Tanis thought, that the mage would remember this moment in all its detail years later.

"Come, we will build bonfires on the beach!" declared Canpho. "Let everyone find whatever food they can spare. We will share our meager stores in victory."

The barricades emptied, and the elves of the village carried Kishpa along in a daze of happiness.

Scowarr stayed behind with Tanis. The slender human had switched back into yesterday's rags—minus the bandages—no doubt to preserve his new finery.

"Why aren't you going with them?" the half-elf asked.

"Yesterday *I* was their hero," he complained, sulking.

Tanis smiled at his all-too-human friend. "Elves are not as fickle as humans, Scowarr. They won't forget what you did. But right now Kishpa deserves his praise. Don't be jealous of him."

"Who said I was jealous?" Little Shoulders demanded defiantly.

Tanis didn't answer. A strange, loud scratching had captured his attention. It seemed to be coming from somewhere behind him. He looked over his shoulder and staggered back in horror at the sight. A long, thin, bloody spider's leg was looping over the barricade wall!

"I'm not jealous at all," Scowarr went on petulantly. "I'm surprised you would actually think—"

Tanis reached out and grabbed Little Shoulders by the collar and spun him around.

Scowarr paled as he watched another leg appear. "It's not possible," said the human in tremulous disbelief.

Another leg came over the wall. Then another. The barricade shifted under the weight, groaning as if in anticipation of the horror to come, as the spider pressed down on its forward legs. The grotesque body of the creature suddenly came into view, its back legs swinging forward, as it steadied itself on the top of the battlement.

A moment later, long, bloodsoaked, razor-sharp spider legs began appearing all along the barricade walls. On every side, the legs appeared, clawing, reaching, climbing. Up they came, the duplicate spiders following their master, a vision of death that moved inexorably down the barricades.

"I feel like a fly," Scowarr mumbled.

"You'll taste like one, too," Tanis answered.

"*Now* he makes jokes."

The half-elf drew his enchanted sword, the blade glowing red. Scowarr began to follow suit, pulling his own broadsword from its scabbard. "No," said Tanis, stopping the human before the sword was free of its sheath. "Go for help. I have my eye on the real spider, and if I can keep it at bay, the duplicates will not go forward."

"You can't fight it alone," Scowarr insisted.

Tanis was moved, even as he prepared to fight. "You have broad shoulders, my friend," he said. "Don't ever let anyone tell you otherwise. But you can help me best by doing as I ask. Get Kishpa now. The spider will not wait while we debate."

Still Scowarr wavered. "I don't know if I should go."

Tanis swung around, putting the tip of his blade at Scowarr's throat. "*Now* do you know?"

Scowarr blinked. "Uh . . . yes."

"Then go!"

The human did as Tanis ordered, scampering as fast as his legs would carry him in the direction in which the villagers had gone.

The massive spider, touched by magic, sensed the presence of Kishpa's magic in the glowing red metal of Tanis's sword; this was danger. The spider rubbed its horrific legs, and a screeching, scratching sound pierced the air. It was a call, Tanis realized, to its duplicates to form a protective circle around it. They rushed toward their master in a flurry of skittering legs.

Tanis, trying desperately not to lose sight of the only real spider in this army of gigantic grotesques, charged among them, his sword raised and ready.

Racing into this web of monsters, Tanis's first thought was that he was committing suicide. The spiders towered over him and he questioned what good even an enchanted sword would do when all he could attack were the creatures' legs. Still, he hacked at the limb of the first monster that blocked his way. He sliced off a hunk of one leg; the beast sprayed blood, proving that while it was a duplicate, it was no mirage. It could kill and be killed. And what happened to one duplicate happened to all: blood spewed from numerous severed legs.

Wounded, the creatures flew into a killing rage. Those closest to Tanis tried to slash him with their sharp-edged legs. However, Tanis had a faster, sharper blade. His glowing broadsword, an extension of his arm, was a blur of color, whipping first left, then right, cutting off pieces of spider leg as if he were a mad woodchopper.

Blood ran in the street like water from a spring mountain thaw. But the runoff was neither cool nor refreshing for Tanis; his battle gear was splatterd with the hot liquid that made the cobblestones slippery underfoot.

He had to get to higher ground, he thought, as he fought to keep his balance in the streams of flowing blood. As he slashed with every step, the spiders moved fearfully out of his way until he reached the barricades. It was here that the real spider waited, its army of protectors decimated and bleeding. The real spider suffered none of the wounds of the others.

Tanis rubbed his face to wipe off the blood that had nearly blinded him. The seemingly endless attack of the spiders had eased, many of the creatures hobbling away from him on uneven stumps.

But from off to his left, a huge spider, massive and untouched, began spinning a web. With a jerky movement of one thin leg, it threw the mass toward the half-elf, who tried unsuccessfully to outrun the sticky substance. The glutinous webbing caught the warrior, who fought uselessly to free himself, beating back the panic that he felt rising in his chest. With two of its forelegs, the spider pulled, knocking Tanis down. The half-elf tumbled off the barricade and fell into the bloody street below, his sword slipping out of his hand and becoming tangled in the spider's web near his feet.

The spider drew the thin, white cocoon closer. The half-elf, stunned from the fall and disoriented, rolled over onto his back. The behemoth, seemingly sure of its kill, brought yet another leg to bear in dragging Tanis closer. When Tanis was nearly underneath it, the beast began lowering its massive body, its maw dripping.

A dark shadow blotted out the sun. A horrible smell made Tanis want to wretch. A scent like rotting meat shocked him out of his state of semi-consciousness.

Tanis opened his eyes and saw through a hazy white webbing the dripping mandible of the spider.

He began to lift his hand, but the broadsword was not in his grip. He reached around frantically, trying to find the blade. But it was no use.

Time had run out for him. With no sword, he could not defend himself. Trapped in the webbing, he watched in silent terror as the spider prepared to devour him.

**20**

# Fight to the Death

*The beast screamed. The roar, so close to Tanis,* echoed painfully. Then the spider suddenly turned away from him, releasing its hold. Struggling against the sticky webbing, Tanis twisted to see what had happened.

Looking through the spider's spindly legs, Tanis saw a most unlikely looking savior. It was Mertwig! The old dwarf had come up behind the creature and had crushed the bottom of one of its legs with his battle-axe. And now the monster focused its hate on a new enemy.

\* \* \* \* \*

Mertwig cursed himself for a fool. What good could he do except get himself killed along with the half-elf? Yet he had to do something to help the noble soul who had saved his Yeblidod.

The dwarf had mindlessly dropped the heavy leather bag that he had carried out of the alley, attacking the monster with the hope that he could divert its attention away from Tanis. In this he had been successful. But now who was going to save *him* from the deadly creature's wrath?

Mertwig cursed again, loud and richly profane. There was much battle experience in his aged heart, and Mertwig knew that one did not enter a contest of war with the expectation of getting help from anything except the weapons carried in one's hands. Those weapons—his axe and a knife with a long, curved blade—were not going to be enough against this hovering monstrosity. Nonetheless, Mertwig stood his ground, spinning his axe in a wide arc over his head. He intended to throw it at the spot where the spider's legs joined, hoping to strike one of its bulging eyes, blinding it. Perhaps then he would have a chance to pick up the heavy bag and run. It was his only chance.

The spider appeared to see no threat from the axe whipping in a tight circle around the dwarf's head. It lunged forward with three legs, its body dipping low. Just then the dwarf let go of his axe. The weapon soared upward, cutting through the air on an angle that took it high over the spider's head. It struck nothing except the barricade behind the behemoth.

"Reorx!" Mertwig bellowed, and dove to the ground behind the massive, leather bag.

*  *  *  *  *

As soon as Mertwig had distracted the spider, Tanis tried once again to find his broadsword by feeling his way along the edges of the imprisoning web. He couldn't locate it. He wanted to raise his head, but the restraining cocoon around his body made that impossible. Frustrated, he kicked at the lower end of the webbing with his boots, hoping to tear it.

It did not tear or rip. His leg motion, however, caused something caught in the webbing near his right foot to rattle and scrape against the ground. Tanis heard the sound and rejoiced. He had found his sword.

Tanis quickly rolled over on to his right side. Curling up as much as the glutinous webbing would allow, he used his right foot to push the blade higher while he bent downward to reach with his right hand.

His fingertips touched the edge of the broadsword's handle.

Tanis stretched as far as he could. He gained another inch but could not quite grip the sword. His muscles felt as if they were going to snap from the strain, but he pushed them even farther. This time, his fingers were able to wrap around the end of the handle. Then he gave the handle a little tug, and it jumped up into his palm.

The sword glowed crimson.

Tanis lifted the blade, and it easily sliced through the webbing. He was free.

Scrambling to his feet, the half-elf saw Mertwig's danger as the dwarf dove behind the sack. Even as Mertwig leaped through the air, Tanis was dashing up the side of the nearby battlement with long, loping strides. At the top, he saw that the dwarf had briefly avoided the spider's sharp-edged legs. The monster would not miss the next time.

The half-elf had to kill it outright, or die in the attempt. Gauging the distance, Tanis ran along the top of the barricade toward the spider's body, and then jumped out into open space. He flew through the air until he landed on the monster's back, his sword his anchor, digging it deep into the spider's body.

The spider reared up in shock and pain, trying frantically to throw Tanis off its back. Tanis slid off to the right but kept both hands firmly wrapped round the handle of his broadsword. The sheer weight of the half-elf's body caused the blade to slowly slice downward, gutting the creature.

The spider tried to get at Tanis with its flailing legs, but the angle was impossible. Then it rammed its side against the barricade, nearly crushing Tanis. The half-elf anticipated the impact and jumped free, pulling the sword out of the spider. But before the monster could right itself, Tanis leaped up yet again. With one swift and powerful stroke, the sword came down on the center of the creature's body, where its nerves and all its senses met. In that moment, all the wounded duplicates vanished. And the one, lone, vanquished spider curled and crumpled heavily to the ground, dead.

Tanis fell with the creature, landing at the foot of the barricade.

Mertwig hurried to the half-elf, kneeling at his side. "Are you hurt?" The dwarf shook uncontrollably, his face ashen.

Tanis, breathless from the fall, could not answer at first. He pulled himself into a seated position, but his head whirled.

Mertwig shoved the half-elf's swimming head down between his knees. "Yeblidod makes people do this when they feel faint. Stay there, and breathe slowly. I'll fetch the healer," the dwarf ordered. But Tanis reached out for Mertwig's arm and held him there. After a few moments, Tanis was able to speak. He lifted his head. "I'm all right," he wheezed. "Help me up."

With the dwarf's assistance, Tanis got to his feet. Despite some wooziness, he was relieved to find that he was still in one piece. Which was more than could be said of the spider.

"I've never seen anything like it—" Mertwig began.

Tanis would not let him finish. Instead, the half-elf said, "If not for you . . . " He fought back another wave of dizziness, then continued. "I owe you my life, Mertwig. If there is anything I can ever do—"

This time Mertwig cut *him* off, looking up with an insulted expression. "It is I who owed you a great debt for saving my Yebbie." But then he paused as the two heard the distant sound of people storming up the street. "But now that you mention it," Mertwig hurriedly amended, "there is something you can do. I beg of you, tell no one I was here. You never saw me. Never. What you did, you did alone. May I have your word?"

Tanis was bewildered. "But why . . . ?"

"Please. I must have your word!" insisted the dwarf.

"Of course, but—"

"Then it's a solemn oath," said Mertwig. With that, he dashed over to the heavy sack he had dropped earlier, hoisted it over his shoulder, and then ran down a dark alley. He was already out of sight when Scowarr, Kishpa, and Brandella turned a corner, leading hundreds of elves in the half-elf's direction.

\* \* \* \* \*

Scowarr and the others slowed and then stopped. The sight of Tanis standing alone near the fallen spider filled them all with a sense of awe.

Kishpa studied the half-elf.

"I feared to find you dead and the spiders rampaging through the village," said the mage, visibly relieved.

Brandella's reaction surprised everyone—especially Kishpa, it seemed. After stopping and taking in the scene, she suddenly dashed ahead of them all and wrapped her arms around the half-elf, hugging him close.

Eyebrows were raised over numerous pairs of almond-shaped eyes, but no one spoke except Kishpa, who, when he reached Tanis, said with considerable restraint, "We are grateful for what you have done for Anka-tavaka." And then he gently but inexorably pulled Brandella away from the bloodstained half-elf.

"Tell us how you did it," Scowarr asked excitedly, mindless of Kishpa's jealousy and the embarrassment of the rest of the elves.

Tanis, taken aback by Brandella's uninhibited approval, tried to minimize his actions, saying, "I could not have survived if not for the spell Kishpa cast over my sword. Beyond that, I simply had much luck."

"And much bravery," added Scowarr, proud of his friend.

Kishpa's eyes narrowed. He seemed to be battling several emotions—discomfiture with Brandella's reaction to Tanis, respect for his bravery, and perhaps jealousy over sharing the spotlight with a half-elf who increasingly appeared to be his rival. Tanis, watching, wondered which sentiment would emerge victorious.

He got his answer when the red-robed mage turned to face the crowd. "We have yet another victory to celebrate today," the wizard cried. "To the feast!"

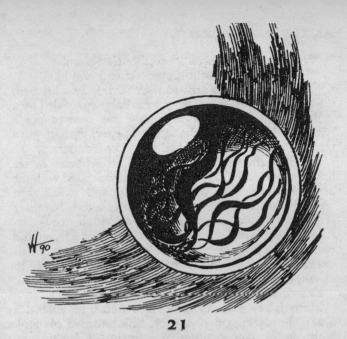

## 21

# The Challenge of Truth

It was a feast that would be remembered for years ever after.

The bonfires burned along the beach, and there was much rejoicing. Scowarr was pleased that Tanis had been right. Throughout late morning and early afternoon, the human was besieged by well-wishers who praised him for his heroism. He had not been forgotten, after all. He beamed.

Later, when Scowarr finally sought out Tanis, he found the half-elf sitting by himself on a rock ledge at the fringe of the merriment, watching the soothing monotony of the waves.

"Where have you been?" asked Little Shoulders.

"Sleeping. I'd almost forgotten what it was like."

Just then, Mertwig arrived with Yeblidod on his arm, the bandaged cut on her temple partially concealed by a wide-brimmed hat. She was pale but seemed much stronger. The shock of the attack apparently had worn off, and a good, long rest had done her wonders.

Canpho, the healer, rushed over to Yeblidod to see how she was feeling. He was obviously pleased with the answer because he smiled broadly and called out, "Friends, we have cheered many heroes today, but there is one here now who remains unsung. With her considerable healing skills, she helped to save many of you and your friends from certain death after the first day of battle. Herself nearly killed last night, she has come back to us whole and happy! I give you Yeblidod!"

Everyone cheered.

Mertwig's face was blissful. He looked at his wife with a gaze bordering on reverence. She returned his look with one of awkward embarrassment. "I don't know what to say," she whispered to her husband.

"Just say thank you," he replied sweetly.

She lowered her head humbly, unable to speak. Kishpa and Brandella applauded lustily along with everyone else.

Mertwig quieted the crowd and proclaimed, "Canpho, you and all of our friends know how much my wife and son mean to me. Like yourselves, I wanted to send my family away before the attack. But Yeblidod, like several of the women"—and Kishpa sent a barbed look in Brandella's direction—"would not go. She sent our boy away for his safety, but she stayed behind to add her healing powers to those of the wondrous Canpho."

One elf, obviously a bit worse for wear after imbibing a few tankards of victory ale, stood on the sand and burst into another hearty cheer—although it was uncertain whether he applauded Yeblidod, Canpho, the victory, or the ale. His compatriots, giggling, pulled him back down on the sand. Mertwig cast a patient look at the sky and waited for silence.

"For my own part, like all of you I did what I could on the barricades," he said, the sun casting strange shadows on his craggy face. "With the danger we all faced, many of you, I'm sure, made promises to your loved ones that you would do this or do that for them if all went well with the battle. I, too, made such a promise."

Yeblidod looked surprised as her husband continued, "And before all of you, I now keep that vow."

Mertwig opened a small box and took from it a fragile, delicately detailed glass ball that shimmered like a huge diamond in the sunlight. "This, before all of you, I give to my beloved Yeblidod."

The glass globe, which rested comfortably in Mertwig's hand, was mostly clear, with subtle traces of azure and moss. Mertwig used two hands to pass it gently to Yeblidod. "The clearness of the glass is for the purity of my wife's love," he proclaimed, looking steadily at Yeblidod. "The strands of blue celebrate the sky that witnesses this moment. The green threads in the glass . . . well, they simply reminded me of the gentle green eyes of my own true love," he concluded.

The crowd heeved a collective sigh as Yeblidod, oblivious to two huge tears creeping down her cheek, stroked the glass bauble and held it up to the sun. Even Tanis was moved. There were thunderous applause and cheers from everyone—except Kishpa. The mage frowned with dismay and looked at Brandella. She, too, had a worried expression. It did not stop her, however, from clapping her hands in appreciation of the old dwarf's romantic gesture.

After his speech, Mertwig proudly shepherded his wife through the crowd, yet kept his distance from Kishpa. He also stayed away from Tanis. The half-elf was perplexed by Mertwig's strange behavior.

Suddenly, everything went black. The sun disappeared. The beach was no more. There were no sounds from the crowd. All was emptiness, except for the loud, irregular beating of a heart. There was no up or down. No east or west. Tanis found himself trapped in a void, neither rising nor falling. He groped ahead of him, reaching for whatever he might find in the darkness. But there was nothing. Only the thudding that seemed to grow weaker with each passing moment.

The half-elf reached for his sword. It was an empty gesture; there was no enemy to fight. Helpless, not knowing what he should do, Tanis cried out, "You must live! I will save your Brandella. Keep fighting!"

Did Kishpa hear him? Tanis would never know. But a moment later the sun reappeared. He was back on the beach, still perched on the rock, and the celebration was still on. But it was much later in the day than it had been just a moment ago. The sun was low in the sky, sending long, amber shadows across the sand. Lunitari, the red moon, could be spied on the horizon.

More worrisome yet was that the happy idyl of mere seconds before had turned into a confrontation between Mertwig and a pasty-faced elf whom Tanis did not know. The faces of the observers were somber.

"I saw you sneak out of my uncle's house," declared the elf, whose honey-brown hair just brushed his shoulders. "I could not imagine what you were doing there. I knew you and he had been friends once, but that ended long ago. My uncle had no use for you and your dwarvish ways."

Mertwig opened his mouth, but Canpho, his brown eyes crinkled with worry, interrupted.

"This is a joyous time," the healer said, coming between the young, angry elf and the distressed Mertwig. Canpho faced the elf. "There is no need for these hard words. You're upset by your uncle's death. We understand—"

"You understand nothing!" shouted the elf, unmollified. "This dwarf, knowing that Azurakee was dead, broke into his home and looted it while the rest of us were at the barricades!"

At the heinous charge, the assembled elves fell silent. The waves breaking on the shore and the crackling of the dimming bonfires were all that could be heard. The faint smell of roast venison mingled with the usual scents of the seashore.

Finally, Canpho spoke cautiously. "Think a moment, young one. Be sure of what you are saying. Mertwig will forgive you, I'm sure, if you retract your terrible accusation."

"I will not retract," the elf said resolutely.

"Then I will not forgive!" Mertwig erupted. "How dare you slander me in this way? And here, in front of my wife, my friends—"

"You have no friends, thief!"

Mertwig lunged at the young elf, who dodged back against his assembled kin. Canpho and several other elves grabbed the dwarf and held him back. "Dwarves!" muttered one old elf, his icy blue eyes reflecting the belief in elven superiority that was one of the least attractive attributes of the race. Tanis, himself the frequent target of hatred by both humans and elves, felt his heart go out to the brave dwarf who dared to live among elves.

"I saw him!" insisted the youth, his soft, pallid cheeks quivering with indignation. "He came out of Azurakee's house with a bag over his shoulder. I went in after he left, and all the valuables were gone. Stolen! He robbed the dead!"

"Lies!" countered Mertwig, sweat slick on his slanting brow. "Don't listen to him!"

"What proof have you?" Canpho demanded of the young elf.

The accuser lifted his round chin proudly. "Only what I saw with my own eyes."

"There!" the dwarf exploded. "He hasn't a shred of evidence to back up his outrageous charges."

The elf began to struggle against the hands that still held him, his feet scuffling gouges in the sand. "I am *not* lying! Ask the dwarf how he managed to buy the glass ball for his wife. You all know he is poor. Ask him that!"

Tanis had listened to all of this as he searched the crowd for Brandella. At the mention of the bag that Mertwig had supposedly carried, the half-elf gave pause. He had seen the dwarf hiding behind such a bag during the battle with the spider. Yet Mertwig had saved his life in that same battle. All he had asked for in return was Tanis's silence, and so the promise had been given. The half-elf hoped he would not be called upon to break that vow. But mostly he hoped that Mertwig was innocent.

Then Tanis spotted Brandella. She was sitting next to Kishpa, both with grim expressions. The half-elf slipped off the rock and sidled close enough to overhear their conversation.

"You must speak up for Mertwig," Brandella told the mage in a low voice, squeezing his hand.

"And say what?" he asked in quiet, yet desperate frustration.

"That you believe in him. Tell them that you stand by him. It will carry much weight." Her eyes glowed dark against the deep green of her woven shirt.

Kishpa looked unconvinced. "But what if he's guilty?"

"Then," Brandella argued, "you will have been wrong in one thing but right in the other."

"The other?" The mage raised his brows.

"Loyalty to your friend," the weaver said simply.

He paused, obviously torn. "My loyalty is to the truth," he finally said fiercely.

Brandella cocked her head and stroked the velvety sleeve of his red robe. "Would you not defend me if I lied or stole?"

"That's different," Kishpa replied, looking away.

"No."

"It is," he insisted.

"Not to me."

"Please," he said, shaking his head. "No more of this. Let me listen."

She let go of his hand.

Tanis moved through the tense and ever-angrier crowd.

"I bartered for that glass ball in good faith," Mertwig said indignantly.

"With what?" demanded the elf.

"Uh . . . it's of no matter to you."

The crowd rumbled at the dwarf's evasive answer.

"From whom did you purchase the ball?" asked Canpho cautiously.

"I'd rather not say," said Mertwig.

"He'd rather not say," the young elf taunted, "because if he did, you would know that my uncle's treasures had paid for that glass ball."

"Where *was* Mertwig when the humans began their attack?" questioned a thoughtful elf who had patiently attended to all of the charges.

"He had gone off with Little Shoulders Scowarr to find a spider for Kishpa," replied another elf, pointed ears peeking from ash-blond hair.

"Yes, but he never came back," noted yet another elf.

Mertwig grew uneasy with the direction of the comments. "I didn't want to return without a spider," offered the dwarf. "And I didn't know that Scowarr had found one so quickly."

"Very convenient," the accusing elf said snidely.

"It's true," insisted Mertwig.

Scowarr pushed forward to defend the hapless dwarf. "What he says is so," Little Shoulders offered. "We separated early on so that we'd have a better chance of finding what Kishpa needed."

"Where did you leave him?" persisted Canpho.

"I don't know the village that well," conceded the human. "I believe it was in front of a large white hut with lots of light-blue flowers in front."

"That's my uncle's house!" declared the young elf.

The rumble among the villagers grew more ominous. The accuser's friends had released their hold on him.

Canpho ran one hand over his hairless head as he surveyed the dwarf. "You had better tell us from whom you bought the glass ball," he said. Tanis heard Yeblidod gasp.

"This is not to be believed," stammered Mertwig. "Are you giving credence to this slander?"

Canpho did not answer. Instead, he said, "It would just be best to tell us the name of your seller. That way, we can put these charges to rest."

Mertwig blustered, and Tanis saw Yeblidod's eyes, so recently filled with happy tears, begin to glisten again. "Well, I don't see what good it will do," the dwarf said. "And it's terribly unfair. I want to keep the price I paid private. This ball was a present, and my wife need not know how much I paid for it." He cast the crowd a beseeching glance, but the tide seemed to have turned against him. Only a few elves nodded encouragingly at the beleaguered dwarf.

Yeblidod moved to her husband and tenderly threaded her arm underneath his elbow. Mertwig gave her a quick, embarrassed glance and then looked away.

"So, you'll tell us who sold it to you?" asked Canpho, acting relieved.

"It was the artist, Piklaker," said Mertwig.

"Is Piklaker here?" Canpho called out.

When there was no answer, the healer asked, "Has anyone seen him?"

Loud buzzing filled the air as everyone talked among themselves, asking who might have seen the well-known elven artist last. Finally, someone standing near Kishpa shouted, "My brother said he left the village right after the human retreat."

"Another convenient answer," snarled the angry elf who had leveled the thievery charge against Mertwig.

"I didn't know he had left," countered the dwarf.

"Then tell us how you paid him. What did you barter?" insisted the youth.

Mertwig hesitated. He caught Kishpa's eye and, in that

moment, gave him a look that begged him to say something.

The mage remained silent, his eyes blank.

"I . . . I gave him . . . gave him a promise," stammered Mertwig. "I told him that . . . that I would pay him with my work."

"You're lying!" declared the young elf. "You couldn't pay Piklaker's prices with a year of your work. Maybe not even two!"

"Tell this uncouth vermin to mind his tongue when he speaks to his elders," Mertwig told Canpho, mustering all of his dignity.

"I do mind my tongue," shot back the youth, "when I speak to honest elders!"

Mertwig tried to grab the youth, but restraining hands held the dwarf tight. The elf stood aside, hands on his hips and a knowing look on his face.

Meanwhile, Canpho turned his gaze to Kishpa, expecting that the mage would settle the issue by coming to the dwarf's defense. Kishpa, however, sat nearly still, his only motion the black hair ruffling with the breeze. He did not meet the healer's eye. That spoke volumes to Canpho.

"This is not the proper forum to debate these charges," the healer intoned. "Tomorrow, the village elders will convene to hear the evidence and make their pronouncement. Let us speak no more of this today."

Mertwig was stunned. "No!" he shouted, struggling against the hands of those he'd once called friends. "I will not be put on trial for giving my wife a gift! I would rather leave Ankatavaka than be subjected to such humiliation."

Canpho said nothing.

Kishpa said nothing.

Tanis, however, could not stay silent.

## 22

# RENDEZVOUS

MERTWIG STARED IN ANGUISH AS THE HALF-ELF PUSHED
his way to the clearing at the center of the crowd.

"I know not the merit of these charges brought against
the dwarf," Tanis said loudly, "but I have something to
say that no one else has knowledge of."

Mertwig flushed. He wanted to cry out, "Traitor!" but
he knew if he did so it would go badly with him. Instead,
he hunched his shoulders and lowered his head as if to
ward off a cold, hard wind.

"You know little of me," Tanis conceded to the villagers
of Ankatavaka. "And, to be honest, I know little of you.
I do know sacrifice and bravery, though, and I saw it—

and live to describe it—thanks to the dwarf who is now under suspicion."

Several elves murmured and shifted their weight. "The dwarf has lived here a long time," said an elf who had remained silent up until now. "Let's not be hasty." Several other villagers nodded their support.

Tanis waited for them to be silent. The late-afternoon sun bathed his hair in a reddish glow. His tooled leather also picked up an auburn warmth. Mertwig realized that Tanis would be far more comfortable tracking deer through the forest than addressing several hundred elves. Unlike Scowarr, Mertwig thought, the half-elf speaks out of duty, not love of attention.

Tanis plunged on. "Let it be known that Mertwig, the dwarf, came to my aid when I fought the giant spider. He saved my life at great risk to his own. For reasons he did not explain to me—modesty, perhaps?—he asked that I not give him his due."

Yeblidod glared around the group, daring them to criticize her beloved Mertwig.

"I break my word by saying this, for how can I remain silent?" Tanis continued. "I speak up for him now because such heroism seems hardly to match the picture of a thief that has been painted. I ask you all, would a thief risk his ill-gotten treasure—let alone his own life—to save a stranger from certain death?"

While the elves chattered among themselves, impressed by Tanis's argument, Mertwig heard Brandella say to Kishpa, "He speaks eloquently for your friend. Should you not do the same while you still have the chance?"

Mertwig moved his head slightly to catch the mage's response. Kishpa was crimson. "I warned Mertwig," the mage said sullenly. "He made his own choice."

"Then you think he's lying? You think he's guilty?"

"I . . . I don't know. I just—"

The dwarf and Kishpa saw a change in Brandella's expression. The mage stopped speaking; Mertwig also felt his interest quicken. Something had agitated Brandella. He scanned the crowd and saw Tanis weaving his way in the pair's direction.

"What's wrong?" Kishpa asked his lover.

"Nothing." Brandella averted her face from Kishpa, unwittingly giving Mertwig a clear view of the heartache in her soft eyes.

"I know better," the mage insisted. "Please, what troubles you?"

She shivered. "I'll be fine. Just be still." Brandella made a gallant effort to control her emotions, calmly singing out, "Look, here comes Tanis," as the half-elf approached her on her other side. Tanis nodded pleasantly at Kishpa and then said something in Brandella's ear. Trembling ever so slightly, she nodded her approval, said a few words that the mage and the dwarf could not hear, and the half-elf quickly moved on.

Mertwig could see that all thoughts of his own dilemma had flown from Kishpa's mind. Something was happening between the half-elf and Brandella. And judging from Kishpa's set expression, the mage had vowed to find out exactly what it was.

\* \* \* \* \*

"I've come to remind you of your promise," Tanis had whispered to Brandella. "The battle is over. It is time for you to leave this place before you—and everything else here—vanishes. Meet me behind Reehsha's shack."

The weaver clung for a moment to the thought of staying behind, of disappearing when the old wizard could dream of her no more. There was something appealing in the notion of dying together in that way. But who would remember *Kishpa* if she were to die? Who would keep *his* memory alive? She agreed to meet Tanis.

\* \* \* \* \*

Before the half-elf began pacing the garden, he had looked inside Reehsha's house, pleased and relieved to see that the fisherman was away.

From where he stood, Tanis could not view the celebration on the beach, but he could see the shimmering waves of the Straits of Algoni. The sun soon would set in its depths, and the golden fire on the water's surface would disappear. He hoped he would vanish with Brandella just as quickly and easily.

The half-elf suddenly felt his heart beating fast. Now that he was so close to fulfilling his promise to the old mage, he realized with a start, he had no idea how he was going to get back to his own time! Clotnik had told him that Kishpa would do it. But how? And when?

Tanis was deep in thought when he heard a voice softly say, "I am here." She stood at the far side of the garden near the house. The setting sun's slanting rays caught her hair, giving her dark curls a becoming reddish glow— and setting Tanis's heart to an even greater pounding.

He hurried to her.

*　*　*　*　*

Brandella had told Kishpa that she was tired and going home. If there was one thing he knew about the woman, it was that lies did not come naturally to her lips. Distrust, however, came rather easily to him.

The mage had begun trailing her at a safe distance. But Scowarr saw Kishpa leaving the celebration and rushed to join him.

"I've got one for you," the funny man chimed. "Have you heard about the mage who always says no?"

"No."

"Caught you!" the human declared.

Kishpa saw Brandella making a sharp turn away from the path that led to her home, and he frowned.

"Don't like that one, huh?" asked Scowarr.

Kishpa didn't answer. He quickened his pace, making a sharp right turn and following after Brandella.

"Here's another one, " Little Shoulders persisted, keeping pace with the mage.

"Not now," Kishpa snapped, waving Scowarr away.

"What did I do?" Scowarr asked, his countenance a study in injured innocence. The little human could have had kender blood, the mage thought.

"I'm sorry," Kishpa sighed. "I have something personal to attend to. Go back to the beach, and enjoy yourself."

Scowarr scooted around the mage and halted in front of him. His smile was ingratiating. "How can I have a good time if my favorite wizard is angry with me?"

Kishpa stopped reluctantly. "I'm not angry with you," he said with considerable irritation as he watched Brandella turn yet again. It appeared as if she was taking a very roundabout route to Reehsha's shack. Why would she do that? he wondered. He sidestepped Scowarr and lengthened his stride, the funny man dogging him. The mage hadn't gone far, however, before a shrill cry brought him to yet another abrupt stop.

"It's Yeblidod," said Scowarr, looking back over his shoulder.

The dwarf's woman came to them on unsteady legs and with eyes swollen from crying.

"Kishpa, come back," she begged. "Come back to the beach and help my Mertwig."

"New trouble?" the mage asked.

"He needs you," Yeblidod said. She pulled at his robes, grabbed at his arms, wailing in her fear and pain. Although Kishpa was desperate to follow after Brandella, he did not have such a hard heart that he could refuse his old friend's wife. Casting a troubled glance in the direction in which Brandella had gone, he sighed deeply and retraced his steps with Yeblidod.

\* \* \* \* \*

"I can't just leave without saying good-bye," Brandella said mournfully, staring out into the glimmering sea. She and Tanis had been sitting so quietly that a small flock of gulls had come to rest on the sand at their feet, obviously hoping the two had brought food to share.

Tanis knew there might be little time left, but he also knew how hard it was to part from those you love without saying farewell. He thought about Kitiara's abrupt departure. The gulls' hard, black eyes reminded him of the angry gleam in Kit's eyes as she'd stormed away.

Brandella saw the sadness in his face and seemed to know him for a kindred spirit. "Is it the leaving that hurts the worst, or is it the lack of a good-bye?" she asked plaintively.

"Both." He laughed harshly, thinking of the good-bye slap he'd received from Kit. "But it's better, in the end," he added thoughtfully, "to tell someone how you feel and to be told the same. Without those words to hold onto—for good or ill—you're just adrift."

Brandella pulled her shawl tighter against the twilight chill. "Are you adrift?" she asked.

His silence appeared to be answer enough. Brandella made a sudden move to take his hand, then seemed to rethink the movement and merely sat quietly.

The weaver was like no woman he had ever known, Tanis thought, but she could not be his. It was driving him mad.

She broke the awkward silence, asking, "What should I do?"

Swallowing hard, he suggested, "Leave Kishpa a note. That way he'll always have your words. He'll have something to hold on to."

She thought about it for a moment and then slowly, sadly, said, "Yes, that may be best. Otherwise, I might not be able to part with him at all."

At that moment, Tanis remembered the enchanted writing instrument that Kishpa had given him. A band of sligs had been after it, the mage had said. He was right: they wouldn't find it here. He fished it out of the inside pocket of his tunic and handed it to her. "This was once Kishpa's," he said with feeling. "He gave it to me so that I might leave it in this time and place. From his hand to my hand to yours, I give it to you to write him his farewell."

She took it lovingly. It was wooden and plain, but that didn't seem to matter to Brandella. Her Kishpa once had possessed it.

"Thank you," she said, fighting her emotions.

Embarrassed, the half-elf said, "I ask but one thing. When you finish your note, leave the writing instrument behind. Don't take it with you."

"I will do as you ask," she said, throwing her arms around the half-elf in gratitude, the movement scaring off the half-dozen seagulls at their feet.

The smell of her hair, and the touch of her hands on his back, made Tanis light-headed.

A moment later she pulled away awkwardly. "Are you all right?" he asked in a whisper.

She nodded her head but did not meet his eyes. "I will go and write the note now."

He agreed too heartily, he thought. "Yes. Good. When it is done, meet me by the east gate of the village."

She had barely left his side when he called to her, "Please hurry!" He wasn't sure if he said it because he feared time was running out or because he simply needed to see her again as soon as possible.

\* \* \* \* \*

Scowarr didn't follow Kishpa and Yeblidod. He had watched Tanis, Kishpa, and Brandella, and had seen every move they had made. The funny man was a jester, but no fool; he sensed trouble was brewing, and he figured that as the savior of Ankatavaka, he had a duty to try to stop it. The arrival of Yeblidod had been his great good fortune. But Kishpa would not be put off for long. Scowarr figured to handle this himself, now, quickly, before the great victory of which he was so grand a part was marred by betrayal and murder.

Scowarr followed the path that Brandella had taken, hoping that his worst fears would not be realized. When he circled around Reehsha's shack, he discovered that they had.

# 23

# Farewell Notes

Tanis's defense of Mertwig had swayed many of the elves of Ankatavaka. But Canpho had seen that Kishpa was unmoved; the mage had so little concern for the dwarf that the red-robed wizard had left without saying so much as a kind word about his old friend. With the celebrants arguing among themselves, each taking sides, the healer decided to settle the issue of Mertwig's guilt or innocence once and for all.

"I am sending a runner after Piklaker, the artist," Canpho said. "When he is brought back, he will tell us all how he was paid for his work. If he was paid in stolen goods, Mertwig will be punished. If he took a promise of work for payment from the dwarf, then it will go hard with the dwarf's accuser. So shall it be."

Everyone seemed pleased with Canpho's decision. All, that is, except Mertwig. "Unthinkable!" he cried, sputtering in his rage. "My honor remains in question? Am I to be considered a criminal until I am proven innocent on the morrow? The insult is too great!"

Yeblidod had sensed that Mertwig was in more trouble than he could handle. With her world seemingly crumbling around her, she had slipped away and run after Kishpa. He had always been her husband's friend. Surely he would not let Mertwig down now when he was needed most.

When Yeblidod returned a short while later with Kishpa in tow, Mertwig still stood railing against the injustice of Canpho's decision. Many among the elves had turned against the dwarf, but Kishpa had it in his power to rally the people behind his friend. But only if he so chose . . .

Mertwig did not see the mage; he was too involved in his own defense. Kishpa heard his old friend declare, "I've lived here my whole life. You all know me, yet it seems that the only friend I have in all of Ankatavaka is a virtual stranger!" At those words, the mage felt a deep shame—and he finally found his voice.

Interrupting Mertwig, the mage thundered, "He has more than one friend in this village, and I count myself as one!"

All heads turned to Kishpa. But not for long.

The dwarf was too hurt and angry with the mage to let him speak—no matter what he had to say. In a shrill voice, Mertwig shouted, "You had your chance to speak, Kishpa. You had many chances to speak, but you did not. Do you think I need your help now? Now, when the whole village has turned against me?"

"We have not turned against you," Canpho assured him. The faces in the crowd didn't reflect that reassurance, though.

"I side with you," said Kishpa simply.

Mertwig stomped, gesticulating, from side to side. "Too late," declared the dwarf in a rage. "Too late. I've had enough of this place. If I were an elf, this would not be happening. You would not treat one of your own with this contempt. I will not have it! No more. Yeblidod and I are leaving. We shall find a new home where our word will be trusted."

"Mertwig, no!" cried Kishpa, his face a picture of horror.

"You call yourself friend?" the dwarf challenged the mage.

"Yes. Of course!" Kishpa took several hurried steps that brought him within arm's length of his one-time companion. The rest of the elves stepped back from the two.

"Then make sure my son is sent to me when the ship returns," Mertwig said. "That shall be your charge. Do you accept it? Or," he added sarcastically, "does it rankle against your lofty code of conduct to see to such matters?"

Kishpa went white. "I . . . I will look to your son," he said, chastened.

"Thank you. Now, make way for Yeblidod and me. We are leaving Ankatavaka with our honor and our dignity. Let no one say otherwise!"

Confused and unwilling to look at faces she had known for more than one hundred and forty years, the dwarf's wife took her husband's arm and walked with him past Canpho, past Kishpa, past everyone, into self-exile.

\* \* \* \* \*

The first thing Brandella did when she stepped through the door of her home was to rush to her loom. She lit one candle and feverishly went to work on the unfinished scarf she had planned to give Kishpa. It would be her farewell present. It had to be, for it was the very scarf that he had carried with him until his old age.

As she worked the loom, Brandella wept. Her tears ran down her cheeks and dripped onto the fabric below. When the scarf was finished, it bore not only her craftsmanship but her love.

Tenderly, she laid the scarf down on her bed, leaning it against his side of the long, down-filled pillow. With shaking hands, she took a piece of parchment from her table and sat down to write. The words did not come easily:

*Dearest to my heart—*

*I would never leave you if I had a choice. But Tanis has come for me, and I cannot refuse him. You see, he comes at your behest, through your own magic as an old man. This life that we live, he says, is not real. It is only as you remember it in your ancient days. In your old age, you think of me still. I love you for that—and for so much more. Just as you have not forgotten me, I promise that I will not forget you. And I will always love you. Believe that. Wear this scarf that I wove with my tears at our parting. But cry not for me because I will always be with you.*

*Forever,*
*Brandella*

She thought of so many other things she might have said, so many memories she might have included to warm his soul, but she didn't know where to begin or how to end. So she left it at that, hoping that her declaration of love, unfettered by other thoughts or remembrances, would tell him most clearly how she felt.

She left the note on top of the scarf and headed for the door—until a thought flew into her head. She looked up at the ceiling and stared at the picture she had drawn so long ago. There she saw the image of Tanis carrying her away. But the dream that she had painted did not tell her if Tanis succeeded in his quest. What if Tanis failed? What if he were unable to take her out of Kishpa's memory? What if he escaped, but she did not; what would Tanis remember of her?

She rushed back to her table and wrote another note, this one for the half-elf. She read it over when she was finished and then closed her eyes to keep her emotions in check. One thing was certain: she knew Kishpa would not understand; he must not see it. She folded the note, put it in a metal box, and then remembered that she was to leave behind the writing instrument with which she had written both her letters. She placed the pen in the box with the note to Tanis, covered it with its lid, and then took the box with her as she rushed outside into the deepening twilight.

On her way to Ankatavaka's east gate, Brandella stopped at the spot where Tanis slew the giant spider. A warrior remembers all his battlefields, she thought, so it was here that she buried the metal box. Later, she would speak of this to Tanis. If he survived and she did not, she wanted him to know that he should never feel adrift.

\* \* \* \* \*

The breach in his friendship with Mertwig was painful enough, but to find out that Brandella had deserted him was more than Kishpa could bear. He stood alone, sobbing quietly to himself, clutching the brightly colored scarf in one hand and her note to him in the other.

His mind raced with a thousand rancid thoughts of betrayal. She spoke of love in her note. What did she know of love if she could leave him feeling this way? What did she know of love if she could so casually disappear with a stranger? And this nonsense of being imagined and remembered in his own mind when he was old—how had the half-elf convinced her of that? Why did Tanis fabricate such lies?

"I should have let him drown," he shouted at the figures that Brandella had painted on the walls and ceiling.

"I should have killed him a hundred times over for this crime he has committed in stealing away my Brandella. My Brandella! Not his! She might have been fooled by his cleverness, but she will learn of his deceit and come back to me more loving than ever. I shall get her back!" he vowed. "I must!"

But he did not move.

It still didn't seem possible that she had gone. He stared once again at the scarf and the note in his hands. Suddenly, he screamed something unintelligible, crumpled the letter, and threw it and the scarf against the wall.

Even before they hit and fell to the floor below, he had scrambled after them, scooping them up quickly with the tenderness with which one might pick up a baby. They were all that he had of her. At least for the moment.

\* \* \* \* \*

They stood at the east gate. Bloodstains still marred the ground where the enemy had been routed only hours before.

"I thought you had changed your mind," Tanis admitted.

"I considered it many times," Brandella replied uneasily. "If I were not used to Kishpa's magic, I would have thought everything you said was the raving of a madman. Even now, I wonder if I'm putting my life in the hands of someone from whom I should flee."

"My words of reassurance will mean nothing. Only when you see that you have been set free will you know that I have spoken the truth."

She stood without pretension, her arms at her sides. In the battlefield beyond, a meadow bird called, then was silent. "I am waiting, then."

The sun had set, and the only light shining on them came from a pair of torches that illuminated the east gate. Tanis took one of them in hand. "Follow me. There is a place we must go," he announced with more confidence than he felt. "It is from there that Kishpa's magic will deliver us."

Tanis took her by the hand and led her out of Anka-tavaka through the darkening night. The air was sweet, and the half-elf imagined himself taking his woman for a walk underneath the stars.

Look at her, he thought, glancing over his shoulder. She comes so willingly, so lovingly, to be with her man. What a contrast with Kitiara! The swordswoman had done as she pleased; if anything, Tanis had followed her bidding. But Brandella . . . Tanis scowled. If only this night belonged to him and not to Kishpa. But what were these thoughts that the half-elf was thinking? He had come to do an old man's bidding and found himself contemplating ways to steal the mage's memories for himself. Tanis, not Mertwig, should be the one on trial, the half-elf thought. But Brandella smiled at him with such tenderness. Her hand fit his so perfectly—

Tanis stumbled into a tree stump, nearly losing his balance.

"Are you all right?" Brandella moved closer, carrying with her a scent of wildflowers and cloves. The darkness deepened her forest-green blouse to black. Her eyes shone in her porcelain face.

"Uh, I guess so," he said. To hide his embarrassment, Tanis waved his torch over the tree stump as if he were examining the cause of his misstep. A shadow crossed the top of the stump when the light passed near by. "Hollow," said the half-elf. "It seems we are close. This is where Scowarr saved my life. That means I was standing over there when I first appeared in this place." He pointed his torch toward the center of a grassy meadow.

For some reason—Tanis hoped it was Brandella's desire to prolong their time together—the two of them walked very slowly in the direction he had indicated. He still held her hand.

Finally, he said, "I think this is the spot where I appeared." He took a deep breath.

"Wait!"

There was no fear in her torchlit face. Something else stirred there, but he did not know what it meant. "What is it?" he asked.

Brandella spoke. "Should something go wrong—"

"Nothing will go wrong. Kishpa said—"

"Listen to me," she ordered, drawing him close. "If you should return to your world without me . . . if I cannot leave Kishpa's memory . . . if I should disappear . . . then go to the spot where you killed the giant spider. I left something for you there, at the foot of the barricade, buried in a box. It is only for you. For you, Tanis. Do you understand?"

"Yes," he said. His mind, caught by her nearness, seemed to go blank. "It's time," he finally added. "Are you ready?"

She closed her eyes and nodded.

Holding her hand in his, Tanis called out into the darkness, "Kishpa! Bring us back! Brandella is yours again. Free her!"

Nothing happened.

"Kishpa!"

"I am here." Kishpa's voice answered.

Tanis felt a wave of relief. They would not be left to die in the mage's memory, after all. But then Tanis's body went rigid with shock. The voice was that of a young man, not an old mage lying near death. And Tanis felt the point of a knife held tightly against his back.

## 24

# A Stitch in Time

"If you try to turn around," said Kishpa in a voice as sharp as his knife, "I will plunge this blade so deep into your back that the tip will come out your stomach."

Tanis did not move. Brandella whirled, however, and darted toward Kishpa. "You don't understand," she pleaded, reaching for her lover.

Kishpa pushed her away. "I understand enough," he snarled. "The half-elf has filled your head with clever lies, and you were foolish enough to listen to them."

"They're not lies," said Tanis, taking care not to move. "You're standing in the way of your own last wish."

"I think not," Kishpa spat out. "I think there is no such 'magic.' Rather, my strange friend, you're standing in the way of your own last breath!"

"No, Kishpa!" cried Brandella. She lunged for his arm.

Tanis immediately jumped away from the mage, and the blade jabbed into air. But Kishpa was quick on his feet, too. He pounced forward as Tanis spun around, and the half-elf saw the knife slash down at him.

Tanis's right hand shot up to grab the wrist of the knife-wielding arm, and the two were momentarily locked in a test of strength.

It did not last long. Tanis was, by far, the stronger of the two, and he not only pushed the knife away, he sent the mage flying backward off his feet.

"I could kill you with my magic," shouted Kishpa, scrambling upright, his face dark with rage, "but I would rather do it with my bare hands. You're a traitor and a thief. You betrayed my trust, and you have stolen my woman."

As Kishpa rushed Tanis with his knife outstretched, Brandella ran between the two of them, yelling, "Stop this!"

Kishpa did not stop. Tanis elbowed her out of the way, leaving himself wide open to the mage's attack. Before Tanis could move, though, a small figure leaped out of the darkness, smashing into Kishpa's shoulder, spinning him around, and sending him sprawling to the ground.

It was Scowarr.

The mage was more startled than stunned. He recovered quickly, scrambling back to his feet. Little Shoulders, however, did not fare so well. He hit the ground head-first and lay still, blood oozing from his nose.

Enraged, Kishpa lunged at Scowarr with the apparent intention of slicing Little Shoulders open like a melon.

Tanis drew his own blade, the broadsword gleaming red in the night. "Leave him be!" ordered the half-elf. "He is not your enemy. His only crime is that he is my friend."

"That is crime enough!" declared Kishpa.

"Then you must kill me, too!" Brandella said defiantly. "I am his friend, as well. Just as *you* should be." She stepped in front of Kishpa, blocking his path to the stalwart human who lay stunned on the forest clearing floor.

"This is madness," shouted the mage. He turned away from Scowarr and advanced upon Tanis, sword waving menacingly in his hand. "Who sent you here?" demanded Kishpa. "What evil wizardry is behind all of this?"

"I tell you, there is nothing evil here," insisted Tanis, keeping his enchanted sword at the ready. "It was *you* who sent me here!"

"Pah! I don't believe it!"

With that, Kishpa whipped his knife in an arc toward Tanis's head. The half-elf instinctively tried to lift his own sword to block the dagger. But he couldn't. The red glow had disappeared, and the sword was too heavy to lift. At the last possible instant, Tanis jumped out of the way, his leather tunic slashed by Kishpa's blade.

The mage laughed bitterly. "Your sword cannot be used against the one who enchanted it. You are going to die."

Tanis dropped his blade but stood his ground. He would not run.

"He is defenseless," shouted Brandella, darting before Kishpa. "You cannot kill an unarmed man. It is not your way. Can this be the Kishpa whom I have loved? Whom I *still* love?"

She reached for him, but he shook her off again. "Is this the Brandella who ran from me? Who betrayed me?" the mage cried.

With the grace of a cat, the weaver took long, purposeful strides to stand next to Tanis. She held the flaming torch in one hand, and with her other she took Tanis's arm. Then she lifted her eyes to the starry sky and called out, "Kishpa! Wizard of wisdom and love, hear me now in your mind's eye. Forgive yourself for your callow, jealous, youthful ways. I know you for the kind and generous man you have always been. And so shall I always remember you. Free me now to remember you as you have remembered me."

No one moved. Not even Kishpa. They waited for thunder. For lightning. For a puff of smoke.

Nothing happened.

The mage came forward. "Let go of him," he said quietly.

She began to loosen her grip, but Tanis would not let her hand go free. The air no longer carried the sweet scent of a woodland; it had no smell at all. The wind no longer caressed him; it had ceased to blow. The stars were no longer mysterious; they had vanished into a void of black. Something was happening . . .

Tanis started to speak, to warn them, but he didn't get the chance. The world vanished. There was no light, no dark; there were no shades of gray. No warmth, no chill, no feeling at all. Nothing existed except the void . . . and the slow, irregular beating of a heart . . . and Brandella. She floated in this netherworld with him, holding his arm, yet seemingly miles away. It looked as if she were trying to say something, but he couldn't understand her in the oppressive gloom. Despite his elvensight, he could barely see her. When he tried to pull her closer, he discovered that he couldn't move his limbs. When he tried to call to her, he found that the sound of his voice was drowned out by the dull pounding of the unseen heart.

Then, without any warning, the heart began to beat faster. And stronger. The gloom slowly lifted. Colors, sounds, and familiar sights returned. But not the familiar sight of Kishpa in a jealous rage. The old wizard's memory had shifted—perhaps intentionally, Tanis thought—and the half-elf now found himself walking with his head turned, looking at Brandella. She was about to speak to him when he stumbled into something and nearly lost his balance.

"Are you all right?"

"Uh . . . I guess so," he said, swinging his torch over the

object that had stood in his way. It was a tree stump.

"I didn't mean that. I meant what happened when everything went dark . . . when Kishpa nearly"—her voice caught in her throat—"when he nearly . . . nearly died."

"Were you frightened?" Tanis took her other hand.

"Not for myself," she said. "For Kishpa. I sensed him, his closeness, in a way I have never experienced before. I spoke to him. He knew it was me, and I felt his joy. Did you hear his heart begin to pound? He wants so much to live!"

Tanis countered, "And he wants so much to help *you* live. Look!" The half-elf indicated the stump. "Don't you see? He brought us back in time to where I tripped on this hollow tree trunk. He doesn't want us to get caught by his younger self again. He's given us a chance, and we've got to make the most of it." His mind swirled with ideas. "Give me three long strips of cloth," Tanis demanded.

"What for?"

"There's no time to explain. Just give me the cloth."

She ripped the bottom of her hip-length blouse three times and handed him the strips of woven green cloth. "Now what?" she asked, her face serious.

Tanis took the pieces and said, "Climb inside the tree trunk, and take the torch with you."

She looked uncertain. "What about you?"

"Just get down there!"

## 25

# A Second Chance

*A shaft of light shot up into the night sky from in-*side the hollow stump. Kishpa saw it and stealthily approached. He wondered if Tanis and Brandella had taken to the tunnels underneath the cliffs. That would explain the light. Clearly, he was not far behind them.

Kishpa's magic had helped him follow them. His anger would do the rest. The mage drew his knife and moved toward the beacon of his rage.

\* \* \* \* \*

Tanis crouched behind the tree stump, shrouded in the shadows thrown by Brandella's torch. He heard Kishpa before he saw him. With his keen elvensight, he soon saw the mage, as well. He also saw the knife.

He didn't want to hurt the mage, but he didn't wish to get hurt—or killed—himself either. And he certainly didn't want to kill the wizard, if for no other reason than that such an action might cause the mage to cease to exist in the future. In such an instance, killing the young Kishpa would be tantamount to killing himself and Brandella.

Why wouldn't the dying old man bring them out of his memory? He'd had the chance, but he didn't do it. Or maybe he couldn't do it. Tanis shook his head. He refused to believe that.

Kishpa was getting close, and Tanis cursed himself for letting his mind wander. He had to time his actions perfectly, or the mage's knife would be buried in his body right up to the hilt . . . and it was a long blade.

The half-elf changed his position ever so slightly, like an animal readying itself to spring at its prey. And Kishpa stopped. It was almost as if he sensed the danger. Tanis realized that the wizard's strong magic might have warned him. There was no way of knowing for sure, so the half-elf kept calm and waited for Kishpa to make his next move.

The mage studied the darkness, apparently saw nothing out of the ordinary, and then eased slowly toward the tree stump, seemingly mesmerized by the light that shone from within.

Tanis, watching him come closer, leaned farther back behind the cover of the stump to make sure he could not be seen. Even when the mage was illuminated by the light from inside the hollow tree, Tanis remained still, unmoving, waiting.

No longer in the darkness, the mage seemed emboldened to move more quickly. Three swift steps took him to the edge of the tree stump, where he leaned over to look down. Before Kishpa could focus his eyes on the flaming torch below, Tanis rose up from his hiding place, swinging his right fist at the mage's head.

His powerful right hand was just about to hit its mark when there was a blur of motion and a small figure hurtled out of the darkness, striking both Kishpa and Tanis. The impact sent them spinning away from each other.

The small figure that struck them was Scowarr.

Again.

Tanis had forgotten all about him. He swore softly.

Little Shoulders hit the ground hard, and he lay there momentarily stunned.

As Scowarr watched, Kishpa and Tanis circled the stump, each lit by the ghostly torchlight. The mage still held his knife, but Tanis wisely did not reach for his sword.

"I mean you no harm," said Tanis quietly.

"But I mean *you* harm," replied the mage angrily.

"Tanis!" cried Brandella.

There was a whoosh of bright, blinding light. Brandella threw her torch straight through the hollow opening of the tree stump. Apparently acting on instinct, the mage lunged for it.

With the wizard distracted by the torch, Tanis leaped across the opening, knocking the burning stick of wood toward Scowarr and smashing into Kishpa's chest with his head. The mage went down.

They grappled on the ground, Tanis desperately trying to avoid the wild swinging of Kishpa's knife. He had little success. The blade slashed the half-elf's upper right arm, leaving a gash that sent blood streaming down his wrist. Kishpa struggled to deliver a more penetrating blow while Tanis tried to pin down the mage's free-swinging hand. Kishpa was more successful than the half-elf; this time, the blade sliced into Tanis's upper back, cutting through his tunic and leaving a thin trail of blood oozing across his left shoulder in a jagged diagonal.

When Tanis felt the blade cutting his flesh for a second time, the pain finally drove him to smash his fist hard against Kishpa's left shoulder. The blow struck the mage like a hammer, and his hand spasmed, but he would not drop the knife.

Tanis had been so consumed with stripping Kishpa of his blade, however, that he did not pay enough attention to the mage's other hand. Kishpa scooped up a rock and bashed it against the back of Tanis's head. The half-elf instantly went limp.

Scowarr watched the entire fight with his jaw hanging halfway down his chest. Kishpa, trapped under the half-elf, tried to push his opponent off his body. Tanis may not have known where he was or who he was fighting, but in a fog of pain and confusion, he struggled to stay on top of Kishpa.

The mage hit him again with the rock, except this time the blow struck Tanis's back rather than his head. The fresh shock of the pain helped clear the half-elf's befuddled brain. Before the mage could hit him again, Tanis grabbed Kishpa by the hair, slamming his head against the ground until the mage's eyes glazed over and he stopped struggling.

"Help me," Tanis croaked to Scowarr.

Scowarr struggled to his feet. "Help you?" he squeaked. "What for? The fight's over."

Tanis groggily got to his knees. He swayed there for a moment before toppling over.

"Oh," said Scowarr, hurrying to the half-elf's side. "Come on now; I'll help you get up."

"No. Here," Tanis said weakly, offering the three strips of cloth from Brandella's shirt. "Tie his arms and legs. Then gag him."

Little Shoulders took the three pieces of cloth and immediately went to work as Tanis lay nearby, trying to shake off the pain and lethargy.

"How is this?" asked Scowarr, showing off the elaborate knot binding the mage's wrists.

"Good."

Kishpa began to stir.

"Hurry!" urged Tanis. "You've got to finish before he can cast a spell."

Scowarr quickly stuffed a strip of cloth in the mage's mouth and frantically began tying Kishpa's legs.

"What are you doing?" demanded Brandella, climbing out of the hollow tree stump. Fear vied with anger on her face.

"Making sure I don't get turned into a tree or a fish," said Scowarr.

"Is this necessary?" she demanded, turning toward Tanis.

The half-elf managed to rise to his feet, but his legs were wobbly. "If we're going to get a head start, it is," he said.

"A head start to where?" she asked, examining the fabric that held Kishpa helpless. Tanis gave her a warning look, but she gestured him away. "Perhaps we must bind him, but I will make sure his bonds aren't too tight. A head start to where?" she repeated.

"To the place where the old Kishpa is dying," he explained. "It's on the way toward Solace. I have been thinking; maybe we have to be close to that spot. Maybe that's why he couldn't bring us out of his memory: we're too far away."

She softened at the mention of the ancient mage and looked down into her Kishpa's face. "I'm so glad you grew old," she whispered.

"It's so much better than the alternative," agreed Scowarr, who obviously had no idea what she was talking about.

"Come," said Tanis. "We can't waste a moment. You know now, as well as I do, how close to death our old friend is. Our trip will take time, and he has precious little of that left."

"I'm coming," she replied. But she didn't get up, for Kishpa had opened his eyes.

With the gag in his mouth, all he could do was make unintelligible sounds.

She kissed him on the forehead. "I'm sorry," said Brandella. "I can't help you."

He tried to speak again, shaking his head and imploring her with his eyes.

"I love you," she said, "but Tanis is telling the truth. Listen to me: I heard your ancient, brave heart beating, and I spoke to you. I sensed your presence all around me. You're dying, remembering how we used to be. Except that I will be no more when you . . . when you die. You didn't want that, so you sent Tanis to get me. I know it sounds impossible, but it's true. I wish you could believe it."

Kishpa grew wild-eyed with frustration and made more sounds that she could not understand. He obviously wanted her to remove the gag. She shook her head and stroked his hair, as black as hers but straight.

"I'm going with Tanis to the place where you're dying, nearly a hundred years in the future," she whispered. "He hopes that the magic will work better there. No matter what happens—" She couldn't say anymore. She simply leaned over him, hugged him, and kissed his eyes.

He was choking on the gag, trying to talk to her, but Tanis pulled her away.

Kishpa began thrashing on the ground, trying to get free.

"Let's get going," Scowarr urged.

"You're not coming," Tanis replied.

"He's eventually going to work himself out of his bonds," said Little Shoulders. "When he does, what he'd do to me if I were here would not be funny. And funny is my life's work. So I'm going with the two of you."

## 26

# Goblins at Dawn

TRAVELING AT NIGHT WAS UNHEARD OF; THE ROADS could be deadly. A person could just as easily fall into a ditch and break a leg in the darkness as fall into a pack of thieves. Tanis, Brandella, and Scowarr had no choice, however. They had to brave the blackness.

With only one torch to light their way, they set out to the east. They hadn't gotten far, though, before Brandella ordered, "Stop!"

"What is it?" Scowarr asked anxiously. His light brown hair stood up in bunches all over his head. Tonight he looked more like a comedian than the savior of Ankatavaka.

Brandella gestured. "Lean the torch closer to Tanis."

The puzzled half-elf stood still as Little Shoulders dipped the torch in his direction.

"Just as I thought: blood," Brandella said reproachfully. "How come you didn't tell me?"

"I . . ."

She cut him off, saying, "Never mind. I know. You didn't want to worry me. Or the wounds don't hurt. Or some other silly excuse. Well, we're stopping right here and now and cleaning those wounds so that you don't die on us."

"There's no time—" Tanis attempted again.

"Quiet!" she ordered. This was no introspective weaver; Tanis saw the Brandella who had rained arrows on the attacking humans—was it less than a day before? "You risked your life for me; the least I can do is risk my future for you," she said briskly. "We're stopping!"

There was no use arguing. Tanis let her inspect the cuts and clean them with yet another piece of cloth—this one gleaned, under protest, from Scowarr's new suit.

"At least the cuts no longer bleed," Brandella said, working so close to the wound that Tanis felt her breath on his skin. "Still, I wish we had salve."

"It's all right," Tanis assured her. Her hands were warm, and her touch was gentle—that was medicine enough for the half-elf.

Finally, Brandella declared them able to continue on their way. They marched throughout much of the night, stopping only for the weaver to check occasionally on Tanis's wounds. Eventually, though, exhaustion began to overwhelm them.

"We'll make better time in the morning if we get some sleep before dawn," Scowarr suggested after he tripped and fell over a boulder on the side of the trail. He rubbed the shinbone he'd barked against the granite.

"He's right," conceded Brandella.

Reluctantly, Tanis agreed. They found a flat, grassy stretch of ground just off the trail and settled in for a short rest. Scowarr offered to take the first watch.

He promptly fell asleep.

\* \* \* \* \*

Tanis bolted awake. A sound had penetrated his slumber. Blinking his eyes in the gray, misty dawn, he saw that the torch had gone out. He sat up and listened again, wondering what had awakened him. Was it an animal in the brush? Could it simply have been a dream? Had Scowarr snored too loudly?

"Snored!" Tanis expostulated softly. "Scowarr!"

The slender human only shifted and murmured. The sound that had awakened him came again from farther down the trail, echoing in the cavernous forest. It was a scream, faint but unmistakable.

"Get up!" Tanis cried, leaping to his feet and grabbing his sword.

"Huh?" Scowarr mumbled. He stared with glassy eyes. "I wasn't asleep!"

Brandella rose cautiously to her feet. She could have been a deer, her feet moved so silently through the glade. She said nothing, but her eyes were questioning.

"Follow after me, but keep quiet," Tanis said. "Don't show yourselves if you can help it." And with that, Tanis took off at a dead run down the trail.

He left the scabbard behind; his exposed sword glowed red with anticipation. Trees flashed by as he raced down the path. The screaming was louder now. He was getting close, and he slowed. The cries seemed to be coming from just beyond the bend.

The trail turned, and so did he—right into a band of four goblins who were attacking the dwarf, Mertwig, and his wife, Yeblidod. She was screaming, and pelting the orange creatures with rocks. Mertwig was bleeding, but he continued to battle the beasts. However, there were simply too many of the creatures for the game dwarf. He swung his powerful battle-axe, yet it was not enough. He had been stabbed several times, and a long, broken goblin tooth protruded from his right leg. Nevertheless, he fought on.

Tanis charged into the goblins, shouting curses at them with every swing of his blade.

The creatures, who tended to enjoy a fight as long as the odds were heavily in their favor, didn't seem to mind a second opponent. Two to one weren't bad odds, after all, and the exhausted dwarf was ready to fall.

The tallest of the goblins, a dirty orange monster with lemon yellow eyes, stood closest to Tanis. It swiveled to face the half-elf, holding a broadsword in one hand and a club that looked suspiciously like a human thigh bone in the other. With a simple flick of his wrist, the tall goblin threw the club directly at Tanis's head. It flew end over end, and Tanis used his sword to split the bone in half—the long way!

The startled creature who had tossed the club snorted and muttered a word in goblin. Tanis, who spoke a few phrases of the goblin tongue, smiled humorlessly. The word had been "Luck!" The goblin swung his sword at the oncoming stranger, obviously expecting Tanis to foolishly run right into the cutting edge of his blade. Tanis kept coming. Luck, indeed.

Tanis did run into the arc of the swinging edge of the goblin's sword, but he deftly parried the blow. Stepping in close, he swung his balled fist into the creature's throat. The goblin fell to the ground, choking.

Seeing this, the three others abandoned their fight with Mertwig to take on the surprising new threat. Two of the goblins came at Tanis, one beast swinging a battle-axe in its long arms, the other goblin a bloody broadsword. The third began to circle around behind the half-elf, holding a hatchet.

It was soon close behind Tanis, hatchet raised and ready—when it fell over sideways, a large rock striking it hard in the side of the face, smashing cheekbone and nose.

Brandella had thrown the granite missile.

Scowarr ran to the downed goblin to make sure it didn't rise again. He kneeled over the dazed creature and asked, "Are you the kind of unlucky goblin who, if it rained soup, would only have a fork in your hand?"

The creature didn't laugh. It couldn't. Its throat was cut. The eyes, dull in death as in life, rolled back in their sockets.

The two remaining goblins bared their sharp fangs; the intruders had evened the odds. Tanis took advantage of the goblins' surprise to impale his sword in the belly of one of them, but the hideous being grabbed hold of the blade and wouldn't let go. As the dying creature twisted away from Tanis, it pulled the sword out of the half-elf's hand. At the same moment, the other goblin struck Tanis a glancing blow with his battle-axe, hitting him in the same spot on the shoulder that Kishpa had cut. Tanis winced in pain and backed away, nearly tripping over a tree root.

The goblin bandit pressed its advantage and swung again. Tanis jumped out of the way but this time lost his footing and fell. The final goblin grinned—until Mertwig's battle-axe struck him from behind, crushing his skull.

"A lot of nerve, ignoring me like that," the dwarf spat at the dead bandit at his feet. Then he sat heavily on the ground with a groan.

Yeblidod ran to him.

\*  \*  \*  \*  \*

Tanis pulled the tooth out of Mertwig's leg, and then Yeblidod used her healing powers on her husband. At least, she tried. The dwarf was badly hurt; that he had fought so nobly and for so long was a testament to his brave heart. That he lived at all as the sun rose over Krynn was due entirely to Yeblidod.

"You saved my life a second time," Tanis humbly told the dying dwarf.

Mertwig shook his head and coughed. Smears of

blood appeared on his lips. "You stood up for me . . . twice," he finally rasped. "You were there . . . when I needed . . . needed help most. I won't forget."

"Shhhh," soothed Yeblidod. "Rest." The trees, swathed in early morning mist, waved serenely overhead, contrasting with the anguished scene below.

"What are you doing out here on the path to Solace?" Brandella asked Mertwig's wife.

"Self-exile," the matronly dwarf replied as she bathed her husband's burning forehead with a wet cloth. "Canpho insisted on a trial, and Mertwig would not abide the insult. We left last night."

"Just like that?" she asked. "After so many years?"

"Yes," Yeblidod answered reservedly, green eyes soft above the slightly humped nose. "I didn't want to go, but it was Mertwig's wish. We packed what we owned, put it in a handcart, and left."

"But your cart . . ." Brandella asked, looking confused. She squinted into the mist at the gaily painted handcart. "That's not . . ."

Tanis interrupted. "*Their* cart went into the sea when they were trying to rescue Scowarr and me."

Yeblidod flushed slightly. "A neighbor and friend lent us her cart. We still have friends in Ankatavaka, whatever Mertwig may believe," she added sadly.

The three sat quietly for a moment, watching as Mertwig's eyes fluttered shut in apparent sleep.

"You can't continue on," Tanis suddenly told the dwarven woman. "Mertwig is too ill. You, yourself, have been through an ordeal. You must go back to Ankatavaka. His pride is less important now than his life."

Mertwig's eyes flew open again. "No!" he wailed. He grasped at Tanis's hand. "I won't go back."

"Why?" asked Brandella.

The dwarf looked away. "I have no friends . . . no friends . . . left in Ankatavaka," he said breathlessly.

"Of course you do," insisted Brandella. "What about Kishpa?"

He shook his head with an infinite sadness in his eyes. Brandella's eyes filled with tears. So did Yeblidod's.

"Kishpa and you have been so close for so long—and it has come to this," the weaver said in hushed tones. The two women rose and walked a short distance away, arms around each other's waist.

Mertwig watched them go. "Where is the human?" asked the dwarf, grasping at Tanis's hand.

"Scowarr's standing watch. Why? Do you want to speak with him?" Tanis made a move to rise.

"No," Mertwig objected hoarsely. "Just you. Alone. While I can."

Tanis leaned closer. "What is it?"

Mertwig pressed his lips together and scrutinized the half-elf. "I can't . . . can't tell Yeblidod . . . or Kishpa . . . not anyone," he wheezed. "But I . . . I have to."

"Tell what?" Tanis asked, keeping his voice soft.

"The truth. Before I die. I can't . . . can't carry it to my . . . my grave."

Tanis began to protest, then stopped. It was obvious that the dwarf wouldn't survive much longer. "I'm listening," said Tanis gently.

"I am guilty . . . guilty," Mertwig said, and shuddered. "I stole . . . stole to buy . . . to buy the glass ball. I lied. But I couldn't admit admit it. Not in front of . . . Yeblidod. Do you understand?"

Tanis was about to answer when Scowarr skidded to a stop right next to him. "Someone is coming!" he announced, nearly incoherent in his excitement. "I think it's Kishpa. We've got to go!"

Tanis held up his hand to stop Scowarr. He turned back to Mertwig to tell him that he understood.

But the old dwarf was dead.

## 27

# Return to Solace

*Quickly, the half-elf led Brandella and Scowarr* to a safe place behind a stand of nearby trees.

"He should be coming soon," said Little Shoulders.

The human was right. Kishpa came striding down the path, fluttering crimson robe nearly black in the uncertain dawn light, a determined look on his face.

Brandella instinctively started to go to him; she knew how Kishpa would feel when he turned into the clearing and found that Mertwig was dead. Tanis had to grab her arm to stop her.

"Yeblidod will be there with him," the half-elf told Brandella quietly. She nodded and silently began to sob.

"We'll make a wide circle around the camp," Tanis added, putting his arm around Brandella's shoulder. "We'd better go."

\* \* \* \* \*

They traveled at a relentless pace, never knowing how close behind them the young Kishpa might be and never knowing when the blackness of death might snuff out their hope of leaving the ancient wizard's memory.

In two days' time, they reached the woods in which Tanis would one day, many years hence, survive a terrible fire and befriend a dying mage. The trees were not as tall as Tanis remembered them from before the fire, nor was the pond as wide. Yet the place where Kishpa would one day sit and set his magic in motion was easily found. Tanis brought Brandella to the spot and said, "He is thinking of you right now from this very place."

Brandella knelt there and stroked the cool, damp grass.

"I . . ." she began, and swallowed. "I have tried to imagine what Kishpa might have looked like as an old man."

Tanis could not help her without describing the ravages of the flames. He cast about for an answer.

Scowarr rescued him. "Are you leaving now?" the human called from the edge of the pond. He was doing his best to hide his sadness.

"We're going to try," Tanis replied. "Let us say goodbye, my friend."

Scowarr, his new suit showing signs of wear but his tufted hair surprisingly tidy, tossed a last stone into the water and then walked to where the half-elf stood with Brandella. He hugged them both. "I hate farewells," he said. "They're never funny."

Tanis nodded. "I will think of you often," he said.

Brandella kissed Little Shoulders on the cheek. He blushed.

"You can think of me all you want," Scowarr told the

half-elf. "Me? I'll be thinking of her."

Despite—no, because of—the somber moment, they all laughed.

Scowarr's eyes dribbled tears—of laughter, he insisted. "Fine," he said, "*Now* you laugh. It took you long enough, Half-Elven."

And then it was time.

Scowarr stepped back to watch as Tanis and Brandella held hands and called out to Kishpa to take them out of his memory and deliver them to the present.

They chanted his name.

They sang to him.

They shouted to him.

They pleaded with him.

*Nothing happened.*

"Back so soon?" quipped Scowarr.

\* \* \* \* \*

Tanis wandered into the woods, away from the pond. His limbs ached with fatigue, and his head hurt from trying to devise some other way to reach the old Kishpa. In the end, he realized that he had to face up to the truth: He was never leaving this place. He had tried and failed. The best Tanis could hope for was that the old mage would live a little longer so that Tanis might have time for himself before the inevitable plunge into darkness.

Knowing now that this would be the last world that he would see, Tanis felt a terrible loneliness. He had promised that he would meet his old friends in five years at the Inn of the Last Home. It was a reunion that would never be. When he failed to appear, they would all wonder what had become of him. Kit would think he was avoiding her—if she herself showed up. Sturm might talk about going to look for him, and Caramon would jump at the chance for such an adventure. But Raistlin, smiling darkly, would never allow his brother to begin such a quest. Raistlin. Would the young mage suspect that it was magic that had kept Tanis from their reunion? Tas would be hurt that the half-elf had not come back, but then he'd likely forget all about it because that was the way of kender.

It was Flint whom Tanis felt worst about. The old dwarf had been brother, father, uncle, and friend to him. It would go hard with Flint if he never returned. The old dwarf was gruff and full of bluster, but he had a heart that was very capable of breaking. And break it would. Flint would guess what the others would not let themselves think: If Tanis didn't show up at the Inn of the Last Home, it meant that he was dead. He desperately wished to spare Flint some of the pain that would come on that distant day.

And then Tanis realized that he could.

The half-elf ran back through the woods, racing for the clearing where Brandella and Scowarr waited for him. He pushed through tree branches and hurtled over bushes, not because he knew how to leave the mage's memory, but because he was going home to see his dearest friend. Of all his companions, only Flint Fireforge existed in this time. Dwarves easily lived more than a hundred years. Flint would be young and dashing—or at least as dashing as Flint could ever be, Tanis amended.

If Tanis couldn't return for the reunion, he would do the next best thing and find Flint now.

Brandella and Scowarr sat wide-eyed with surprise as he ran toward them. He had just broken through the trees and was coming around the far side of the pond when it happened: *Everything changed.*

The pond, the trees, the rolling hills beyond—all disappeared, to be instantly replaced by a view of Solace! It would have taken days to walk it from the glade, yet he had arrived in Solace in the blink of an eye. It was as if his wish had come true. Or had it?

Sitting together at the foot of the massive vallenwood tree that housed the Inn of the Last Home, were Brandella and Scowarr. They looked as startled as he was.

"How did we get here?" asked Scowarr, confused.

"I don't know," Tanis replied. "Unless this, too, is part of Kishpa's memory."

He looked down, unable to meet Brandella's gaze any longer, as he said, "Whatever time is left, you should spend with your mage." He wanted to reach out and hold her, but instead he said, "Find him, Brandella. Let him know that you love him." And then he spoke his own feelings: "You should let the one you love know that you will always treasure her." His eyes shone. "Always."

Her face glowed. Tanis wondered what that meant, but he didn't stay to find out. He swallowed his good-bye in a whisper and rushed away.

*　*　*　*　*

Tanis knocked on the rounded door. Weeds waved around the flat stones that led to Flint's ground-level abode. The hill dwarf had been leery at first of the prospect of living in trees, Tanis remembered; the call of ale would be strong enough to lure Flint up the spiral stairway to the Inn of the Last Home, but the dwarf couldn't help preferring lower altitudes for his own lodgings. The oaken door showed the talents of the metalsmith within—hinges, bolts, door handle crafted with artistry.

"Who ish it?" demanded a familiar voice that the half-elf suspected was dulled by ale.

"A friend."

"Imposshible," called out the voice. "I don't"—hiccup—"like anybody."

"That's not true," countered Tanis.

"Are you calling me a liar?" Tanis heard the sound of a chair being shoved back.

"No," the half-elf hastened to reply. "Not at all. I'm simply saying that you have friends you don't even know about."

There was a pause; the dwarf must have been considering the possibility. Then—"Hmmph. Not likely!"—came the response.

Tanis leaned one tired arm against the side of the

dwelling. "Must we talk through the door, Flint?"

"You know my name?" Bootsteps ventured closer to the door. Tanis hoped the testy dwarf wasn't standing there, battle-axe in hand, only steps away.

He tried to make his voice agreeable. "More than that. I also know you're one of fourteen brothers and sisters."

Another pause. "Who told you that?"

"You did."

"Imposshible!"

"Will you *please* open the door?"

Tanis heard the latch give way. Then the door swung open, revealing a youthful, if drunken, Flint Fireforge. The half-elf could only marvel at the unlined face, the nose roundish but not yet bulbous, the body trim if a littly pudgy. Still, there were the ruddy cheeks, the bushy beard, the bright eyes. Tanis hadn't realized how lonely he was until he saw his old friend. Nearly washed away in a flood of emotions, Tanis blurted, "I found you!"

Flint looked unimpressed. "Congratulations. Now you can unfind me." The dwarf immediately started closing the door.

"Wait!"

Flint sighed but halted. "What ish it? What?"

"I just want to talk to you." Tanis knew that Flint wouldn't know him, but he somehow still hoped that there would be a spark of recognition. He could see nothing untoward in the dwarf's eyes.

The dwarf peered at the half-elf standing in the doorway. "You don't look familiar. You don't sound familiar. You don't even smell familiar," Flint said irascibly. "You look like you've been through too many battles in too little time."

Nonetheless, Flint felt a strange kinship with the half-elf, perhaps because of the need he could see in the stranger's face. He had known need like that himself. Or maybe, thought the dwarf, I'm just drunk.

Flint asked in an unfriendly tone, "Talk? What about?"

"Can I come in?"

"I'll come out. If it's business, I do my talking at the inn."

"I'll buy you a plate of Otik's spiced fried potatoes," Tanis offered.

The dwarf gazed up, his beard aquiver with suspicion. "Otik who?"

Tanis shook his head. Of course; Otik hadn't bought the Inn yet. "Never mind," he said. "I'll buy you the ale."

They made their way up to the Inn of the Last Home, perched high in its majestic vallenwood tree.

The two old friends who had yet to meet in the real world sat across from each other, one eating potatoes, the other drinking ale. Tanis took in the sight of the big main room of the inn. The walls were dirty with soot; the stained glass windows were so grimy that you couldn't tell if it was day or night. The floor looked as if it hadn't been washed in a month. And the odor defied description. Tanis had never appreciated Otik so much until that moment. As for the present innkeeper, he seemed a decent, if slovenly, sort. He was tall and skinny with a crooked nose and sad green eyes. Flint called him "Hey, You."

The inn and its owner didn't matter that much to Tanis. The important thing was that he was there with Flint Fireforge.

"So, do you want to buy one of the toys I've made?" questioned the dwarf between swallows of watered slop.

"No. I . . . I just want to know how you are," Tanis said, and immediately felt foolish.

Flint narrowed his eyes and tilted his head. He seemed to be thinking—work that came hard with all the bad ale he'd consumed.

"What I mean is," Tanis added awkwardly, "how are you managing your business without a helper?"

"What do I need a helper for? I'm in my prime!" The dwarf sat up defensively.

"Well, there may come a time," suggested Tanis, "when you'll want to have someone around to help keep your books, collect debts from those who owe you money, those sorts of things."

Flint downed the last of his mug of ale and called out over his shoulder, "Hey, You, give me another."

The innkeeper was right behind him, listening. "I don't know about the other things you mentioned, young fellow, but Flint here certainly does need someone to drag him out of this place when he's had too much to drink and gets into a fight." He wrinkled a crooked nose, grabbed Flint's tankard, and swabbed the table with a rag that seemed to leave the wooden surface greasier than before.

Tanis smiled. He had pulled the feisty dwarf out of nearly every tavern in Ansalon when they'd traveled the countryside together. But that wouldn't happen for decades yet. "Someday," he said softly to Flint, "you'll have a helper who will do all those things for you."

The dwarf's face folded into disbelief. "That will be the day I call a kender my friend," scoffed the dwarf.

Tanis choked on his potatoes.

Hey, You poured Tanis some ale to help him wash away the food caught in his throat. The half-elf gratefully drank and was just catching his breath when a hand came down hard on his right shoulder.

"I've been looking for you," said Kishpa.

## 28

# Help from a Friend

Tanis was tired of running from the mage. More than that, he was tired of hearing Kishpa's name on Brandella's lips. What had the mage sacrificed for the woman? What had the mage done to show his deep affection? As far as Tanis was concerned, Kishpa ran a poor second to him in devotion to Brandella. Yet the woman loved Kishpa above all else. And that rankled.

The hand that rested on his shoulder did not worry the half-elf. It was the other hand that concerned him. Once before, Kishpa had held a knife to his back, and he might again. The way Tanis was feeling just then, he was of a mind to break that hand in as many places as he could.

Tanis grabbed the hand on his shoulder and jerked forward with his whole body, throwing the mage over his head. Over the surprised Flint's head, as well.

Kishpa landed on his back on top of a wooden table, which crashed to the floor under his weight.

"And here I was suggesting that *you* stop *Flint* from fighting," complained Hey, You, quickly tabulating the cost of the table and adding it to Tanis's bill.

"He's good," Flint said approvingly to the innkeeper when Tanis got up and went after the mage. The dwarf protectively picked up his new tankard of ale.

"Yes, but can he afford the damages?" the innkeeper queried, his sad eyes growing more doleful. He'd obviously become resigned to bar fights in his acquaintance with the dwarf.

"I'll pay for anything he breaks," offered Flint. "I haven't seen a good fight since—"

"Since this morning," said Hey, You.

"Helps me digest my breakfast," explained the dwarf. "Did you just see that blow to the belly? That fellow I was drinking with sure knows how to throw a punch."

"Don't count that other one out," cautioned the innkeeper. "He seems to be able to absorb the punishment."

Tanis fought with a cold fury, his fists burying Kishpa under an avalanche of punches to the stomach and head. The mage rocked with each blow, yet he didn't break and he didn't bleed. Nor, strangely, did he fight back.

Breathing heavily, Tanis picked up Kishpa, held him over his head, and then threw him again, this time against the wall. The mage hit the wall with a thud and then slid to the floor in a heap.

"At least he didn't break anything this time," said the innkeeper.

"All this activity is making me thirsty," complained Flint, watching Tanis manhandle the mage. The dwarf tossed down a mouthful of ale.

Tanis walked toward the wall to pick up Kishpa. Before he got there, though, the mage calmly stood up on his own. The half-elf stopped, wary.

"Wise move," Kishpa snarled. "My magic protected me from your attack. But what is going to protect you from mine?"

"Magic?" protested Flint loudly, jumping to his feet, accidentally knocking the table askew. "Unfair! Nobody said anything about magic."

Tanis eased his way to the left, edging closer to an overturned chair while Kishpa strode toward the half-elf. When Kishpa was right in front of him, Tanis picked up one of the chair's upturned legs and smashed it over the mage's head. It shattered into a dozen pieces. But Kishpa just stood there, giving Tanis a malevolent smile.

The innkeeper scribbled again on the tally sheet. Flint handed him the half-full tankard, which the man took without a word.

Flint watched as Kishpa and Tanis faced off again. "Where's Brandella?" the mage demanded.

Tanis felt a curious satisfaction. "I don't know. You've missed her."

The half-elf didn't see the mage's hands move. Nobody saw them. Nonetheless, Tanis was struck in the eye by a punch that staggered him. An unseen fist hit him in the cheekbone, nearly knocking him senseless and snapping his head to one side so hard that he spun halfway around. A blow to the stomach left him on his knees. In all of this, Kishpa never moved. Nor did he continue the pummeling once Tanis was down. He merely took a deep breath as though he had labored hard and then quietly stood over the fallen half-elf.

"Reorx's beard!" Flint thundered and charged at Kishpa, butting his head into the mage's back. Caught off-guard, Kishpa fell forward, landing on top of Tanis.

"I wish I had my battle-axe!" the dwarf roared.

He was hardly helpless, though, without his favorite weapon; as Tanis sat up, Flint kneed Kishpa in the small of the back, eliciting a groan from the mage. "That will teach you to pick on folks with your magic!" the dwarf declared. Then he threw a punch meant to strike the side of the mage's head. He missed, hitting Tanis in the chest, instead.

"Oh. Sorry," said the dwarf as Tanis fell backward.

Meanwhile, Kishpa muttered several words under his breath, words that neither Tanis nor Flint had ever heard before. Without warning, Flint was lifted off the mage's back as if he were a puppet on a set of strings. He hovered in the air near the ceiling.

"Hey, you, get me down from here!" insisted the dwarf.

The innkeeper shrugged thin shoulders. "Don't know how."

"I meant *him!*" Flint said with exasperation, flailing his arms and legs. The dwarf pointed at the mage. "Let me down, and fight fair!"

"Is two against one 'fair'?" Kishpa asked calmly, blue eyes mild.

"The boy was already down," Flint countered. "It was one against one when I hit you." He aimed an unsuccessful kick at the mage's head.

Tanis began another attempt to get to his feet. The mage took a handful of the half-elf's tunic with one hand, seemingly holding him steady in order to strike him with the other.

"Kishpa!" a new voice sang from the doorway. "Don't!"

The mage twisted to face the door. His eyes sparkled with joy, and a huge grin lit his face. He let go of Tanis and ran to his Brandella. When he did so, Tanis stayed on his feet, but Flint suddenly fell to the floor, hitting the wooden planks with a thud.

"Thanks," the dwarf muttered under his breath, pulling splinters out of his beard.

"I've been looking all over for you," Kishpa declared, taking Brandella into his arms. Scowarr peeked around from behind the woman and skittered into the room, staying out of the mage's sight.

Meanwhile, Brandella fought free of Kishpa. The mage's expression instantly turned somber. "What's wrong?" he asked, following her into the Inn.

She pushed Kishpa aside and hurried to Tanis, studying his bruised face with a gentle hand. "Why did you do this?" she demanded of the mage.

"Because he deserved it," Kishpa answered defiantly. "I could have killed him, but I didn't. After all, he has a journey to make. And," he added with infinite sadness, "so do you."

Her hand fell from Tanis's jaw. Curly hair framed a suddenly joyful face. "Kishpa . . . you haven't come to stop us?"

He shook his head. She threw her arms around him and kissed him on the neck, the cheek, and then the lips. Tanis, teetering on weak legs, turned away and sank into a chair.

"I tried to tell you when that gag was in my mouth," Kishpa explained, "but none of you would take it out and listen to me. What you said to me . . . made sense. I believe you. I've been trying to catch up to you to tell you."

"Then why'd you fight me?" Tanis demanded.

"You started it," the mage grumbled.

"Men!" exhorted Brandella. Then she kissed Kishpa again and straightened his robes. "It was all for nothing," she said pensively. "There will be no good-byes between us because we can't leave. It seems—"

"You're wrong," he said gently. "You can go. At least you can if my magic is strong enough."

Tanis heard the wizard and blinked several times, trying to remember what Clotnik had told him so long ago. He'd said it was Kishpa who would bring them back to the present. But he hadn't said *which* Kishpa. Tanis laughed harshly. All along, he had been trying to get the wrong Kishpa to help them while running away from the right one!

"I'm sorry about Mertwig," Brandella said tenderly,

stroking her lover's face.

The mage lowered his head. "That's the other reason I've come to help," he said. "I was wrong about Mertwig, and he died. I can't take the risk of doing that to you, too."

Brandella hugged him.

"I wish I knew what was going on," said Flint.

"This kind of thing happens all the time in the inn-keeper business," Hey, You confided to the dwarf. "You learn to ignore it." He passed Flint another ale.

With the help of Scowarr, Tanis hobbled over to where Kishpa and Brandella were lost in each others' arms. He cleared his throat to get their attention, and then said, "It would be better not to wait. If you can free us from the ancient Kishpa's memory, you should do it soon."

The mage reluctantly pulled away from Brandella and nodded. "I don't know if my magic will work. I've re-thought all of my spells, trying to find a new combina-tion of conjurings that will have the desired effect. I don't know if I can do it."

"But you can try," countered Tanis.

"And so I shall. But I would like a moment alone with Brandella first."

Tanis limped toward the dwarf and innkeeper near the bar. Flint was appraising the half-elf with an approving eye.

"You did well," Flint said. "A rule of thumb, though." He leaned closely. Tanis winced at the odor of stale ale on the dwarf's breath. *"Don't ever fight wizards."*

Tanis looked Flint straight in his slightly bloodshot eyes. "Then why did you jump in to help me?"

Flint shrugged. "You looked like you could use a hand. Who are you, anyway?"

"His name is Tanis," said Scowarr, who had quietly joined the trio. "But he is rarely funny."

"And you are?" the dwarf asked Little Shoulders. "Tell me something amusing." Scowarr sat down next to Flint and began quietly telling him a story . . .

As Scowarr spoke in low tones, Tanis drifted toward Brandella and Kishpa. The mage saw him coming and regretfully led the woman to the doorway of the Inn of the Last Home. Tanis joined her there, taking her hand.

Kishpa kissed her one last time. And then he surprised Tanis by saying, "Half-Elven, there is no one I would entrust her with but you. I thank you for coming to get her. I know you risked not only your life but your world to do this thing for me. Don't think it escapes me."

Tanis touched Kishpa's arm. "Have a good life between now and then."

Kishpa put his hand over Tanis's but said nothing.

The mage stepped back, gave Brandella a last, loving look, and then closed his eyes. Kishpa's lips began to move. At first, Tanis didn't hear him say anything. Soon, though, he could make out the faint sound of odd words spoken in a peculiar rhythm. The chanting became louder.

At that moment, Tanis also heard the sound of Flint roaring with laughter. Scowarr had found a willing audience.

Kishpa's chanting grew even louder.

Tanis felt the pull of the magic. Soon his mind swirled with images. He saw the burnt glade next to the pond. He saw ashes floating in the water. He heard the ragged breathing of the ancient Kishpa. But it was a blur—unreal, untouchable, yet somehow tangible. He and Brandella floated there, looking down from on high as if they were seeing a picture in a cloud that kept changing with the wind.

They were getting closer. He could smell the aftermath of the fire. He could even feel the heat of the sun. Soon the ground below seemed almost real enough to step down upon.

Suddenly, he noticed a change. Something that he had noted was no longer there. Then he realized: The breathing had stopped. The ground beneath his feet vanished. The glade disappeared. The sights, the smells, all were no more. Everything was gone except for an impenetrable darkness and the familiar sound of a beating heart. Except it was beating too slowly, irregularly. Tanis was still holding Brandella's hand, but he could not see her in the blackness.

Kishpa, ancient in years and ravaged by fire, was losing his final battle.

Although neither could hear the other, Tanis and Brandella called out to Kishpa, urging him, begging him, to fight death just a little longer, to live, to bring them home.

Their cries fell on ears that could no longer hear.

Kishpa was dead.

The beating heart stilled.

Tanis realized that they might exist in this netherworld forever, sailing on a sea of black in a mind that no longer could think or feel.

The darkness loomed empty, bleak, and seemingly never-ending . . . until they saw a spot of light far in the distance. It was tiny but bright. And it was getting ever closer. Was it a sun? A moon? A fire that would consume them? All Tanis knew was that they were hurtling straight toward it.

# PART III

## 29

# Life After Death

*The bright light was not a star, a moon, or a fire.*
It was merely an opening at the end of an almost infinite
corridor, much like the bright light one sees when looking at the opening of a mine from deep inside the shaft.

When Tanis and Brandella finally came tumbling out
of the darkness, they were dumped onto a flower bed
awash with vivid colors. Above them stood trees with
bright purple leaves.

Blinded by the light, neither could see anything but
flashes of brilliant color for several minutes. As they
groped about the flower bed, Tanis called out, "Are you
all right? Are you hurt?"

Brandella's voice floated shakily to him through the blotches of red, orange, purple, and magenta. "Nothing broken. What about you?"

He made another attempt to focus on what appeared to be a chrysanthemum—although he'd never seen one in that particular shade of chartreuse. "Fine. I'm fine. At least I think so."

"I wonder where we are," Brandella said, rubbing her eyes.

"You're in my garden!" boomed an angry male voice. "And you're ruining it!"

Tanis tried to crawl toward the voice, squashing a splotch of pink under one knee.

The voice grew more strident. "Don't move! You're making it worse. Wait until your eyes adjust."

They did as they were instructed. As they sat, though, Tanis asked, "Other than your garden, what is this place?"

There was a pause. "You don't know?"

Tanis shook his head.

A short, baritone chuckle broke the silence. "Why, this place is Death. Everyone who comes here knows that."

Flower gardens in Death? Tanis wondered. A white and black tulip slowly came into focus before him, then drifted out again.

"That can't be," explained Brandella. "We're not dead. At least I don't think we are. Are we dead, Tanis?"

Tanis studied the tulip. When it came back into focus again, it was lavender and black. He shook his head, hoping to clear it, and a cloud of unfocused multicolored snow drifted down past his eyes. "I have no idea. I certainly hope not."

Their eyes slowly stopped tearing, and they were able to see their surroundings. They saw the flowers and the trees. And they saw the man who glared at them. He was a middle-aged human of stature, with a full beard, elegantly sweeping mustache, and sinewy arms. He obviously had been a well-built, powerful man in his youth.

He was dressed simply, in loose white pants and a flowing, white shirt.

Dozens of petals clung to Brandella's mane of curly hair. She looked at Tanis and giggled, and Tanis knew his own red-brown locks were similarly adorned.

"Ah, you two can see now?" the man demanded. "Then please leave my garden."

They gingerly stepped out of the flowers. The man stood half a head taller than Tanis. Brandella made an attempt to assuage the man's irritation.

"I've never seen flowers like that," she said. "They're beautiful." She knelt to smell a blossoming yellow and green flower with splotches of pink and red on its petals. The man, seemingly mollified, smiled indulgently down on her.

"They're from the Age of Dreams," the man said, hands on his hips. "They don't grow on Krynn anymore. The same is true of the trees."

She sniffed at the blossom, and a look of surprise crossed her face. "It has no scent," she said, perplexed, rocking back on her heels.

"That's the shame of it," admitted their guide. "They look good, but they're dead. Like everything else here."

"Everything except us," corrected Brandella in a hopeful voice.

Flashing them an odd look, the gardener turned and said, as he walked away, "If that's so, then you'll regret it soon enough."

"Why?" asked Tanis, following the broad, white-shirted back along a red-tiled path that clashed with the profusion of purples and pinks in the vegetation.

"Why, you'll starve," said the man over his shoulder in a matter-of-fact voice. "There's nothing to eat here. Nothing. It's all dead: the animals, the fruits, even the trees. All dead. Just like you will be if you don't get out of here."

They hurried after the gardener until they found themselves at the foot of a small hill nearly covered with white trees, bushes, and flowers. There were a few dark spots but not very many.

"If this is Death, how do we leave it?" Tanis questioned. "Is there a way?"

The man ignored Tanis and pointed to the hill of white. "That's mine," he said proudly. "I wish it were smaller and whiter but," he humbly added, "it was the best I could do when I was alive."

"That's very nice," the half-elf said perfunctorily, sweeping more petals off his shoulders, "but how do we get out of this place? You've got to help us!"

The man calmly changed direction and advanced on Tanis. He didn't seem threatening in the least, so Tanis didn't deign to protect himself. He should have. Like a bolt of lightning, the man's hand shot across and his fingers encircled Tanis's throat.

He squeezed.

Tanis tried to pry his attacker's bony fingers away from his wind pipe, but the grip was like that of death itself. Blue spots began to dance before the half-elf's eyes.

"Tanis!" Brandella cried. "I . . . can't move." She stood a few feet away, frozen in the act of reaching to help him.

The half-elf was on the verge of passing out when the man let go of him. Tanis staggered and fell to the smooth tile path, gasping for air. Tanis sensed, rather than saw, Brandella's body relax from its rigid stance, and he looked up at the gardener, who enunciated angrily, "My hill is more than 'very nice.' Look, you, at the hills and mountains all around. What do you see?"

Tanis looked, but he could not speak. It was Brandella who answered. "Hundreds, maybe thousands, of tall, dark mountains in every direction," she said tentatively.

"Very good," the man said, face pallid and eyes terrible. Tanis realized how formidable he must have been in life. The man's lips were thin and tight with anger. Nearby, in vivid contrast to the gardener's mood, pink petals drifted from a small bush to the ground.

"Very good," the man said again, gesturing at the hills.

"And *my* mountain is small and white. Those other peaks there, and there, and there"—and he stressed each word with a stab of a bony finger—"are the lies and terrible crimes of my neighbors. My hill represents my failings when I lived on Krynn. I'm not perfect. I had my faults."

Tanis felt his eyes narrow. "Pride? Maybe a bad temper?" he rasped from his seat on the path.

The gardener shot Tanis a surprised look. Reluctant respect grew in his eyes, and the hint of a smile crinkled the edges of his mouth.

"Good guesses," replied the man, who continued blandly. "As for your demand that I 'have' to help you leave Death, let me tell you that your fate is of no matter to me. Besides, everyone comes here eventually."

Brandella stepped carefully before the man. "With all due respect," she said, obviously hoping not to anger the garden's caretaker, "everyone may come here, but some may come before their time. I don't mean that they die young, but that they don't belong here at all. Not yet. And if that is so, there must be a way to go back. Could you not tell us how we might return?"

The man watched the weaver fixedly. "Nicely said," he finally offered, bowing with a flair that matched his white suit. "Spoken with respect and grace. Perhaps I shall tell you what I know, after all."

"You're very kind," Brandella said sweetly, mustering all of her considerable charm. By the gods, she's going to curtsy, Tanis thought, still seated, and started to speak, but the woman silenced him with a look. She remained standing, however.

The man pointed toward the horizon at the tallest of the forbidding mountains. "It is said that on the other side of Fistandantilus's mountain there lies a portal that leads back to Life. Of course, to my knowledge, no one has ever scaled the wizard's monument to evil. Not even Fistandantilus himself. He lives on this side of it, always in its shadow, never seeing the light of day."

"If you know that that is the way back to Life," Tanis recklessly questioned, "why don't you attempt to go back yourself?"

Their guide gave him a long, hard look. "Half-elf, your human side occasionally oversteps the elven," he commented. Tanis swallowed nervously but kept his expression blank. He started to rise, in case the man attacked him again.

"I lived my life," the man finally answered. "I lived it well. There is little more I could do except grow older and more doddering. I am also told by those who have come after me that I left behind something of a reputation. Why spoil it? Besides, I have my flowers here—and the peace, usually," he added with a pointed look at Tanis, "to tend to them. Is that answer enough for you, my inquisitive young despoiler of gardens?"

"Yes," Tanis replied, chewing nervously on his lip, "but one more question, if I may?"

The man paused, considered, then nodded his head.

Tanis stared into the eyes of the man and asked, "Who are you?"

The gardener spoke off-handedly. "I am called Dragonbane. Huma Dragonbane. I was a Knight of Solamnia."

## 30

# A Small Sacrifice

Tanis stopped breathing and grew dizzy; the shock was so great. In a whisper, he finally managed to croak, "Huma of the Lance . . ."

The man in white, backed by the variegated tones of vegetation seemingly gone mad, cocked a quizzical eyebrow at the half-elf. "They called me that, too. Then you've heard of me?"

"Yes. Oh, yes," said Tanis, awestruck at the sight of the hero who, myth had it, had driven the evil dragons from Krynn during the Age of Dreams.

"It's nice to be remembered," the dead Knight said simply. "But you must go now to find your way back to Life.

If you fail, do come back again and see my flowers. I have the best garden in all of Death!" He caught Tanis's eye and then cocked his head back and laughed. "Or is that my *pride* talking?"

\* \* \* \* \*

They marched for hours upon end, yet the sun never moved from its position directly overhead, the clouds did not sweep across the sky, and the dead who populated this world seemed not to stir. Finally they chanced upon an old, haggard woman with scraggly gray hair and a cherubic-looking little blond boy, who were fixing a wagon wheel. The wagon leaned at a precarious angle at a crossroad that sat hard upon a hill, down which streamed a fast-running brook.

"Can you help me and my grandson?" pleaded the woman in an aged, cracking voice. Dressed in a ragged, dark-blue dress that Tanis was sure hadn't been in fashion for centuries, the hag leaned wearily against the wagon. The little boy, wearing a similarly outdated tight-fitting shirt and breeches the color of dried blood, appeared subdued.

"If we can," agreed Tanis pleasantly. "That wheel doesn't look too badly broken."

The woman's skin was mottled with age spots and her hair was faded. She straightened and moved away from the wagon. "Not the wheel," she said sharply, eyes glinting over a thin nose. "The wagon can never be fixed. It's something else that we need."

"Oh?" Tanis found his hand drifting toward his broadsword, although he wasn't sure why.

"Come here," the woman insisted, pointing at the half-elf.

Brandella took Tanis's arm and held him back. "I don't trust her," she whispered in Tanis's ear. "Look how she hides something behind her back."

Tanis nodded. "Just tell me what you 'need' and I will do what I can," he called out, holding his ground.

The woman scowled. "Nothing much," she said weakly. Her voice broke and an expression of infinite melancholy spread over her features. "Only a little kindness." Tanis felt guilt wash over him like the petals of Huma's flowers. "A small sacrifice," she continued pathetically. "Perhaps your lives."

The little boy who was with her giggled, nodding his head appreciatively.

"Tanis, look at their eyes," Brandella warned.

Even from a distance, the half-elf could see the pair's eyes turn to fire, burning in their sockets with bright blue flame. The boy laughed again. "I see you!" he cried happily at Tanis and Brandella. "I see you live and that your hearts still beat." He turned to the old woman and excitedly cried, "They still beat. They beat!"

"Demons?" Brandella whispered.

Tanis took hold of the handle of his sword but did not remove the blade from its scabbard. "I will not fight an old woman and a boy," he said.

The hag laughed along with the child as they jumped off the wagon and, slowly, confidently, advanced toward Tanis and Brandella. The crone slowly pulled her hand out from behind her back, revealing a small shovel with razor-sharp edges. It looked like a macabre version of one of Flint's children's toys, something to use to dig a modest hole in a very hard surface. She held the trowel in front of her body as if it were a weapon, while she and the boy began to circle to the right.

"Nice people," Brandella said under her breath. She and Tanis backed up, stepping off the trail and into the high grass in the direction of the nearby stream.

"It beats!" sang the boy.

"It beats!" echoed the old woman.

The sun poured over Tanis and the weaver, who repeatedly wiped their sleeves across their eyes. Brandella faltered. "We can't just keep on walking backward," she said.

With their next footfall, Tanis and Brandella left the

tall grass and stepped on a thin layer of leaves and sticks. In that moment, the ground beneath their feet broke apart with a splintering crack. They scrambled to keep their footing, kicking over a pile of small stones, but their momentum sent them falling into a fifteen-foot-deep pit in the earth.

Neither was badly hurt; the soft, damp soil had cushioned the worst of their fall. They scrambled to a crouch as two bloodless faces with blue-flame eyes appeared at the edge above them. "It worked, grandma!" the lad said to the harridan.

"But why?" Tanis asked Brandella quietly. And then he stood up and asked that same question of those above. "What do you want of us?"

"Your beating hearts!" cried the old woman, shaking the trowel. "To hold the beating heart of a living person in your hands is to leave Death and return to Life. We've waited at this crossroads three thousand eight hundred and eighty one years, hoping this day would come." She clapped her hands. "Our patience has been rewarded."

"Not yet, it hasn't," Tanis challenged. "You don't know for certain that that tale is true. We were told that the path out of Death is to be found on the other side of Fistandantilus's mountain. And we were told this by none other than Huma of the Lance!"

"Who?" asked the old woman.

Tanis cast the hag a stunned look. "Why, the most famous hero in all of Krynn," he shouted.

She appeared to consider, then shook her head. "Must have been after my time. Never heard of him," she said with a shrug.

Tanis was beside himself with frustration. "Even if our beating hearts *were* your way out of Death, you can't get at them from where you stand, anymore than we can escape you from inside this pit."

"Wrong!" the little blond boy chirped. "You'll grow weak from hunger. You need to eat." He nodded wisely. "I used to eat. Food was good. I liked soup. Didn't I,

Grandma?" he asked, tugging at the woman's blue skirts.

"Yes," she said, patting the boy on the head. "He was fond of my fish soup," she told her victims proudly.

"You will go to sleep before you die," the little boy continued. "Then we'll climb down and cut you open with grandma's shovel. Hold your hearts in our hands, go back to Life, and eat soup. Right, Grandma?"

She smiled and nodded, the movement loosening the knot of gray hair at the nape of her neck. "You can see why I'm so proud of him, can't you?"

Tanis sat on the soft earth, ignoring the gloating dead ones above, and tried to think.

Brandella plopped down with a sigh. "I know this isn't the time to mention it," she said, "but I'm getting hungry. And I'm awfully thirsty, too." She sighed again and picked at a thread hanging from her soft leather slippers.

"It'll pass," said Tanis.

"Yes, and so will we, and we're already in our grave."

They sat silently for a few moments, contemplating the truth of her words, until Brandella angrily banged her fist against the side of the pit. A large clump of dirt fell to the ground. Looking at the small hole she had made in the wall of their tomb, she lifted her head, saying, "That's it!"

Tanis just peered at her. "What?"

She scrabbled toward the half-elf, ignoring the dirt she was grinding into the knees of her woven trousers. "The stream bends right behind this pit. That's probably why the ground is so soft and damp. Don't you see?" she exclaimed, her voice rising, "I think I know how we can get—"

Tanis clamped his hand over her mouth. "Softly," he said in her ear. "They're listening."

Chastened, she nodded her head, and Tanis removed his hand from her mouth, leaving a dirty smudge on her cheek. She leaned close to the half-elf and in a low voice said, "The ground is so soft that we can dig our way out of here. The two up there won't have any idea where we're coming up."

"It could take more time than we have left to live," he warned her.

"How long will we live if we don't try it?" she asked, a crease between her exasperated eyes. "Do you have a better idea, Half-Elven?"

Tanis pursed his lips and thought. Then he said, "Let's start digging."

Tanis dug at the earth with his sword, which no longer glowed red, and Brandella used both hands to pull the loose dirt he broke from the wall out of their way.

"What are you doing down there?" demanded the old woman, peering into the pit.

Tanis and Brandella paid her no mind; they kept on digging at a ferocious pace.

"What are they doing?" the old woman asked her grandson.

"Digging a tunnel," guessed the little boy.

With a self-satisfied grin, the boy's grandmother said, "They'll be dead long before they ever dig their way to the top. Foolish creatures."

Sweat poured from their bodies as Tanis and Brandella clawed and scraped at the earth, flinging big clumps of wet dirt through their legs like dogs digging a hole for a bone. The harder they worked, the more they sweated, and the more they sweated, the drier became their throats.

"How far are we from the pit?" panted Brandella after several hours of hard labor. A layer of soil had been added to the smudge Tanis had left on her cheek.

"About six feet, I'd say." The damp walls of the tunnel made his voice seem dead, and the weaver shivered.

She paused, a handful of dirt dropping from suddenly listless fingers. "We aren't going to make it, are we?" she asked.

"Don't know," Tanis said. "Just keep digging."

Every muscle in Tanis's body cried out from the work he was doing in such cramped quarters. Brandella fared no better with fingernails that were broken and bloody. Dirt caked their clothes, inside and out, and generous helpings of earth crept into their eyes, ears, and mouths.

"I don't know how much longer I can keep this up," she said wearily.

"Do you have a better idea?" Tanis gently mocked, echoing her earlier question.

He couldn't tell if she gave a short laugh or a sob, but she kept on digging.

31

# Cave-In!

"*There's water trickling in!*" Brandella cried fearfully. "I can hear it dripping!"

From inside the pit, they couldn't tell in which direction they were digging. Obviously, they'd headed toward the stream.

A mud puddle quickly formed at the base of the tunnel, and a short while later the water flow grew from a trickle into a thin but steady stream. Soon, the whole bottom of the gently sloping tunnel turned into a muddy mess, making it difficult for the two to work; they kept slipping and sliding as they tried to dig.

Tanis was in front, stretched out with his head and

arms at the location where the water was coming into the tunnel. Brandella was behind him, reaching forward to get at the dirt that Tanis pushed back in her direction. It was her job to take that dirt and move it still farther back into the tunnel.

The last thing she expected at that moment was to feel something tickling her ankle and feet; she'd long since lost her shoes. She screamed, kicking her feet.

Tanis squirmed to one side; she could barely see his mud-striped face in the gloom. "What is it?" he asked.

"I . . . don't know," she said, fearing that the little blond boy had climbed down after them. In the positions they were in, barely able to move, even a child could easily get at them from behind.

The tickling continued despite her thrashing. Then it stopped. Started. Stopped.

Tanis, frantic to try to help her, turned on his side, making a desperate attempt to slide backward and squeeze next to her.

But the tickling feeling had come from dirt beginning to fall on her legs from the roof of their tunnel. She knew what it was when the entire tunnel began collapsing on her feet . . .

"Cave-in!" she screamed.

Tanis hadn't gotten far when he heard her cry. He reached back and grabbed her by the shoulders, pulling her out of harm's way. At least for the moment.

When the dust and dirt that nearly choked them finally began to settle, Brandella rested her head on Tanis's stomach and said in despair, "We're trapped. We can't get out now; we can't get back to the pit. When the water gets higher, we'll drown."

Tanis was thinking the same thing; there would be no more digging in this lifetime. The only consolation he could think of was that those two ghouls waiting at the top of the pit would not be able to get at them while the half-elf and weaver still lived.

Stroking Brandella's mud-encrusted hair, Tanis did not

speak. He leaned his head back against the wall from where the water was seeping and thought, not about his coming death, but about the living. Kitiara. And Laurana, the elven princess he'd grown up with, who'd had a crush on him for years and who'd given him the ring of golden ivy leaves that he still wore. His companions . . .

"I'm sorry you didn't get to know Flint," he finally said, closing his eyes against the gloom. He continued to stroke the weaver's hair.

She shifted to try to peer at him. "Who's Flint?"

"The dwarf in the inn. He was my closest friend."

"You'll miss him," she said simply. "And he'll miss you. I'm so sorry that I'm the cause of your loss."

He traced one finger around the curve of her ear. "No," he said. "Don't ever think that. I did what Kishpa asked of my own free will. It was my choice. You have no blame."

"Still—" she persisted.

His hand moved to the nape of her neck. She had been Kishpa's while the mage lived. Perhaps in the little time that remained to them, she could now be his.

"Tell me, Tanis," she asked sleepily, almost resigned to death, "did wars finally end in your time?"

He laughed bitterly. "What would all the generals do? How would they survive?"

She pushed herself to her elbows and reached forward through the gloom. Her fingers found his chin, his cheek, his pointed ear. "You don't think much of people, do you, Tanis?" she asked gently.

"I like *certain* people a very great deal," he countered meaningfully. He wished he could see her expression.

"So do I," she whispered. Now, more than ever, he wished there was at least a little light shining on her face. Even his elvensight was of little use to him here; the angle wasn't right. What was she trying to say to him? Or, rather, what was he trying to hear?

He wondered why he was being so diffident. Why couldn't he be more direct with her? After all, there wasn't much time left. The water rose ever faster; the tunnel was nearly half-filled with cold, suffocating slime, all of it running downhill toward their feet.

"How long do we have?" Brandella asked quietly.

"Not long," he said gently. "Another hour. Maybe less."

Tanis's mind drifted. He remembered a time when he was young. He and Laurana had gone off together to take a swim. The water had been cold, and they'd huddled close on the shore for warmth. Even the memory kept the chill away.

"Do you hear something?" Brandella asked.

Reluctantly pulled from his reverie, Tanis could only focus on the sound of the water spilling into the tunnel. "No," he said, listening for voices and hearing none. An instant later, though, he knew what she meant. There was a low thumping sound, and the water seemed to be making far more noise as it gushed into the deepening pond in which they were sprawled.

The earth behind Tanis, where the water came into the tunnel, began to break away from the wall in big clumps. The chunks of muddy earth slid and fell down the wall, and with each new piece of the tunnel that fell, more water shot inside.

The water level began to rise very fast. Death, Tanis realized, would come much sooner than he had figured. The water was rising to their shoulders and would soon reach their heads. It would be only a matter of minutes after that before the water would cover their mouths and noses.

They hugged each other, savoring the warmth.

Suddenly, the clumping sound exploded into a roar. The wall that they'd been digging at broke wide open, and a tide of cold water smashed into the tunnel.

## 32

# DROWNING

The water exploded through the tunnel wall with
so much force that it threw Tanis and Brandella against
the far side of their tomb as if they were pieces of driftwood in a pounding surf.

They thrashed in the rushing water, trying desperately
to get above the surface of the flood to draw a breath.
But there was no surface. The water had almost instantly
filled the tunnel to the very top.

The enormous pressure of the water and the slope of
their tunnel kept them virtually pinned against the area
that had caved in. Yet the very force of the water made
Tanis realize that there was, in fact, a possible way out—

if only they could swim against the tide and make their way through the broken tunnel wall through which the water was flooding in.

Tanis's lungs were on fire, and he felt the panic of imminent death rising inside his brain like a bubble that would soon burst. He couldn't hold his breath too much longer.

The muddy water obscured his elvensight. Nonetheless, he had to find Brandella. He groped in the murky, swirling sludge until he grabbed hold of one of her arms. With Brandella in tow, he pushed off the caved-in portion of the tunnel and then thrust himself against the fiercely flowing tide. Kicking his legs as hard as he could, and stroking madly with his one free arm, he almost made it to the opening.

But the current was too strong. It threw him and Brandella back with tremendous force, turning their bodies into battering rams. They slammed against the far end of the tunnel with such a jarring impact that Tanis could no longer hold his breath. His mouth opened.

But so did the tunnel.

The debris that had blocked their path from the cave-in gave way. It turned to loose mud that became the crest of a fast-moving wave. Tanis and Brandella were swept along with it, sputtering for air as they were washed back through the tunnel they had dug.

In mere seconds, they were deposited back at the bottom of the pit. Coughing until they felt their insides would split, Tanis and Brandella crawled away from the opening, where muddy water gushed in.

The leathery old woman and her grandson leaned over to study this new development. They watched as the bottom of the pit quickly filled with water.

The boy smiled. "They're alive, Grandma!"

"So they are, child," she replied. "And they're still our prisoners."

He raised two fingers. "Two of them and two of us," he said gravely.

As the depth of the water in the pit increased, Tanis and Brandella were forced to stand, their muscles protesting after the unwonted battering of the past few days. Then, when the pit became a deep lake, the pair had to tread water. Soon they found themselves rising with the water level toward the top of the pit!

"What will those two . . . up there . . . do when we get . . . close to them?" Brandella asked between gasps.

"Anything they can," Tanis replied, watching the two above as carefully as he could while still coughing up dirty water.

The old woman said something to the little boy, who nodded and smiled. They hurried together to the corner of the pit and bent over, each picking something off the ground.

Neither Tanis nor Brandella could see what was in the ghouls' hands. "They're up . . . to something," Tanis wheezed. "Be careful."

The pit continued to fill from the tunnel down below, the water running downhill from the underbelly of the stream on the high ground above. Tanis and Brandella were just five feet from the lip of the pit. Two more feet and Tanis felt he could reach up to dry land and pull himself out of the water.

"Now!" screamed the crone, rearing back and throwing a rock right at Tanis; it splashed next to his head. The boy threw his rock at Brandella. It struck her a glancing blow in the arm; she winced in pain.

"More!" cried the old woman. "Aim for their heads!"

Now it was clear why the ghouls had waited so long to act. The two would stun them, then pull them from the water when they were near the top.

"Dive!" Tanis ordered.

Brandella took as deep a breath as she could manage and dove beneath the surface. A rock hit her in the back as she went head-first into the murky depths.

Tanis followed right behind, a stone grazing his ear just as his face hit the water. He knew one thing: He planned to be as far away as possible from the old woman and the boy when he came up for air.

Swimming a foot below the surface, he blindly stroked his way to the far side of the pit. When he felt the muddy wall, he shot straight up, hoping his momentum would help him reach the edge so he could climb out. Instead, he found himself right underneath the two who wanted his heart. They'd anticipated his move and run to the far side of the pit. Both heaved rocks the size of their fists from a distance of a mere few feet. One struck Tanis in the shoulder. The other narrowly missed his temple; he deflected it with an outstretched arm.

Falling back into the water, Tanis barely had the time to take another breath before diving under again. He swam in no particular direction, and that turned out to be a wise decision. When he came up for air, the hag and her grandson were more than fifteen feet away and the rocks they threw at him sailed wide of their mark.

Tanis didn't see Brandella. He hoped she'd since come up for air and gone down below again. Waiting for her to surface, however, was out of the question. He took three quick breaths, then one deep lungful of air, and dove, even as more rocks came hurtling in his direction.

Once again, Tanis chose a random direction. Swimming deep enough under water to hide his movement, he made his way to another side of the pit. With his lungs afire, he kicked down hard and fought his way to the top, reaching for the dry ground. The two ghouls were not there.

This was his chance. With palms flat on the outside of the pit, he began pulling himself up out of the water. A rock splashed next to his hip. Another rock bounced past his hand. With a grunt, he swung one leg up out of the pit, and then the other. He rolled away from the edge and came up on his feet. The old woman and the boy were dashing toward him, the boy hurling a rock that flew over Tanis's head. The old woman waved her trowel as if it were a dagger. It was sharp enough to be one.

Even now, Tanis would not draw his sword against them. But he had no qualms about defending himself. The boy stopped short of attacking him, but the old woman came at the half-elf with hate in her eyes. "I need your heart!" she wailed.

Tanis grabbed her by the wrist and wrestled the razor-edged trowel out of her hands. The boy lunged for it, but Tanis was faster. He kicked it into the pit; it immediately sank out of sight.

While Tanis restrained the old woman by pinning her arms against her body with a bear hug, Brandella scrambled out of the pit and hurried to his side. She grabbed the boy from behind, swinging his legs off the ground. He flailed and kicked, but she held him tight, her arms strong from years of archery practice.

"What are we going to do with them?" she asked, keeping one arm locked across the boy's chest. His eyes flashed flame at Tanis. "We need time to get away."

Tanis looked at Brandella, and she looked at him, and the same idea struck them simultaneously. With gigantic muddy splashes, the two ghouls landed in the water of the pit.

"I can't swim!" the crone gurgled. The little boy flung both arms around her neck. She struggled in vain to loosen his hold.

"You can't die, either," Tanis called back.

*　*　*　*　*

"I've never been so filthy in my life," Brandella said after they'd walked about a mile.

"Is this what they mean when they say, 'Here's mud in your eye'?" Tanis said, a crooked grin creasing his worn face.

She gazed at him, eyebrows raised. She'd tried to wipe away the vestiges of their stint in the tunnel but had succeeded only in spreading the mud more evenly around her face. Some of it had dried to a thin film. "Scowarr would be proud of you, Half-Elven. You've almost developed a funny bone."

He snorted.

"You're certainly amusing-looking, too," she taunted, "with those streaks of mud in your hair."

Tanis countered, "You've changed a bit, as well, since I first saw you that evening in Reehsha's shack."

She giggled. "Reehsha's cabin. Wasn't that a palace?"

He joined her laughter. "It looked like it hadn't been scrubbed since the Cataclysm."

"Well, so do we," she rejoined. They laughed again. Then they sobered as both realized that their companions back at Ankatavaka had vanished with Kishpa's death. They trudged on for some time through the unvarying glare of the sun. The landscape was flat, dry, and dull. Only a few weeds broke through the crust of the ground. After a while, they didn't bother to look up, merely plodding along in silence, heads down.

"Maybe we'll find a pond or stream we can wash up in," Tanis finally said.

She nodded, scuffing her wet shoes, which she'd fished from the pit with a stick as Tanis warded off the two ghouls with a board from the old woman's wagon. "I wouldn't mind drinking some nice clean water for a change, either. I still have the taste of mud in my mouth."

"At least it was something to eat," joked Tanis, his stomach grumbling.

The woman met his quip with a smile. Then she looked up and stood stock-still. Tanis took a few extra steps and looked back at her, eyes questioning.

"Tanis . . ." she whispered, indicating the route ahead.

He looked up. The mountain of Fistandantilus loomed ahead of them. Suddenly, it was as if the sunshine gave no warmth. He shivered despite the glare.

"What's that at the base?" Brandella asked, her voice still quiet.

He looked.

It was a village.

## 33

# Welcome to Yagorn

*"I wonder who lives there," Tanis marveled,* looking down upon a small village nestled in a shaft of light below Fistandantilus's towering, dark mountain.

"Let's hope they're friendly," ventured Brandella.

They trudged, hungry and thirsty, down the path to the outskirts of a brightly colored, bustling little town. Tanis took note of the humans, dwarves, elves, and gnomes, all of whom were dashing into and out of warm and inviting-looking buildings that lined the main road through the village. He smiled suddenly and laughed.

Brandella gave him a questioning look. A flake of dried mud dropped from her chin to the soiled shirt that used to be green. She said, "You seem to be in surprisingly good spirits, considering where we are."

He had to admit he was. "I always thought of dying as some sort of eternal sleep. But here the sun is always at high noon. It's never dark—except around the bleak, evil mountains—it doesn't rain, the wind doesn't blow . . . it's like a perfect summer day, every day."

Brandella made a wry face. "Monotonous, isn't it?"

"I hope that we're here just long enough that it doesn't become so," he said.

"STOP!" The new voice came from behind a fence. They stopped and watched in amazement as the owner of the voice, quivering with fear, slid out in front of them. "STOP!"

"We've stopped," Tanis explained patiently.

The creature, which barely came up to Tanis's waist, cringed. "Not hurt me!" It fairly imploded with fear.

"A gully dwarf!" Brandella exclaimed. "What do you suppose it wants?"

In reply, the pudgy little creature pulled a leather pouch from over its shoulder and thrust its hand into the bag. It drew out a squashed piece of fried dough. "Magic!" the gully dwarf squeaked. "Stop!"

Tanis sighed. Brandella kneeled and stretched out one hand, palm up. "What's your name?" she asked softly. "May I see what you have?" She half-turned to Tanis and said, "Look. He's found food around here!"

Tanis cleared his throat. "Brandella, I think . . ."

The gully dwarf curled into a quivering ball on the hard-packed dirt street. Only one arm remained free, waving the moldy dough in a semicircle. An algae-green eye peered over a filthy sleeve. Brandella took it as an invitation. "Look," she said. "He's offering . . ."

Tanis shook his head. "I don't think . . ."

Suddenly, the dwarf leaped into the air, shrieked, "MAGIC!" at the top of its lungs, flung the fried dough onto the ground, and dove for the shelter of a nearby stairway. The dough hit the ground with a crack—and split open. Its insides had turned to dust. Brandella poked at it with a tentative finger and grimaced.

The half-elf tried to look sympathetic. "My guess is that the gully dwarf died with that in its pack," Tanis said.

The gully dwarf had reappeared and was venturing back into the street. "Strong magic, you!" it proclaimed, and pointed at the weaver and Tanis. "You still here!" Its dull eyes were wide.

"Magic?" Brandella asked. "Who is he, anyway?"

Her question was answered, not by the half-elf, but by a creature slightly shorter than the gully dwarf. This one resembled a muscular human child, except for the pointed ears, olive eyes, and orange-red hair swept into a long braid at the top of her head.

"That's the town guardian. Isn't that interesting? Where are you two from? You're alive, aren't you? I used to be alive. I'm dead now, though. That's pretty interesting, too, but not as interesting as being alive," the creature rattled on.

"A kender," Tanis said with a groan. "I'm trapped in Death with a kender and a gully dwarf."

Brandella remained kneeling, but she kept a wary eye on the newest creature. Kender are notorious for their curiosity, which usually involves "finding" numerous shiny, often expensive objects that "just happen" to fall out of strangers' pouches, purses, and packs. All Brandella had left that could be easily filched were her muddy shoes, but the shoes had shiny buckles and the kender had been giving them appreciative glances.

"Where are we?" the weaver asked the kender.

"Yagorn. It's just packed with dead people," the Kender said, reaching over and dragging the filthy gully dwarf toward her. The kender seemed used to the dwarf's odor, but Brandella winced.

"He smells like a dead rat," she complained.

"Thanks for the compliment," the kender observed.

The gully dwarf beamed, picked up the fragment of

dough, and reached around the Kender to present it to Brandella. "Strong magic. You take," it said.

She put out a reluctant hand. "Thank you," she said.

Tanis shifted impatiently beside the trio. "An odd town, with a gully dwarf as its main guard. What does he guard against?"

The kender, who had shifted his gaze to Tanis's scabbard, gave the half-elf a bright-eyed look. "Nobody grubbier than Clym here gets inside the village. Of course, until now we haven't seen anybody filthier than Jard. But the town council says we must keep up the image, living in the shadow of Fistandantilus's mountain, and all."

"Do many people come to climb it?" Brandella asked.

The kender looked surprised and interested, which was typical for one of her race. "Why would someone want to do that? Not that it's not a good idea, of course. In fact, I'd like to try it. What do you think might be up there?" The kender stopped to examine a silver buckle that had suddenly materialized in her hand.

Brandella exclaimed and snatched the bauble away from the creature. She refastened it to her shoe. Tanis squelched a smile.

"Say! Is that yours?" the kender asked innocently. "Lucky thing I found it, huh? Are you here to climb the mountain?"

"We're looking for the portal to Life on the other side, of course," Tanis explained.

The kender laughed. So did the gully dwarf.

"You seem to be funnier than you realize," Brandella said darkly to the half-elf.

"Portal?" the gully dwarf queried.

The kender patted him on the shoulder, then faced Tanis and Brandella. "Who told you about a portal?"

"Huma of the Lance," Tanis said.

The gully dwarf laughed again. "The man with the flower garden?" the kender asked.

"That's him," Brandella replied.

"He tells everyone he's Huma. Which is pretty incredible because . . ."

"You mean he isn't?" Tanis demanded.

The kender, for once, said nothing. The gully dwarf gave Tanis a condescending look that seemed to say, "Are you *that* stupid?" Which was quite a statement from a gully dwarf, Tanis thought.

The half-elf got the message. Then, in a low voice, he asked, "Does that mean that there's no portal?"

"If there is, nobody's ever found it. Although I'd like to look," the kender chimed. "But no one would go with me, I guess. Would you?" Correctly interpreting Tanis's malignant glare, the kender hurried on, her orange-red braid quivering in her haste. "No, I guess not."

Tanis pulled Brandella aside and softly suggested, "If we're going to find out about Fistandantilus's mountain, we've got to find someone to talk to besides a gully dwarf and a kender." He tugged at his leather tunic; it had gone from slightly slimy when wet, to stiff and tight when dry.

"Is there anyplace nearby where we can wash this mud off ourselves?" Tanis asked the kender.

"Oh, yes," she replied enthusiastically. "A lovely place!"

"Where?"

"The Baths of Behobiphi. It's the white building on the left side. The one with the soapy bushes on the far side. That's where Behobiphi dumps the water after it's used," the kender confided. "Sometimes I help Behobiphi look after people's clothes while they bathe."

Brandella looked dubious. "He hires a kender to guard valuables?"

The kender looked away. "Well, not exactly *hires*. I just help out on my own. To be nice, you understand. In fact, Behobiphi sometimes doesn't even know I'm there."

"Most of the time, I'll wager," Tanis muttered.

Brandella swallowed a smile and addressed the kender. "Can you take us there?" she asked sweetly, deftly retrieving her other buckle from the creature's pouch.

The olive eyes widened again.

"Wow! You lost the other one, too? Good thing I was around to keep you from losing them permanently. I mean, that would've . . ."

The kender's chatter rattling on ahead and the smell of the gully dwarf following behind, Brandella and Tanis marched down Yagorn's main street, attracting very little attention until the gully dwarf suddenly pointed at them and shouted, "Alive! Alive! Magic!" Soon a crowd of the curious pressed about them; the kender had a field day finding "lost" objects as humans, gnomes, and others scrutinized the two strangers. Luckily, they'd reached the Baths. The gully dwarf beat on the nine-foot door and then dashed, terrified, down the street and into an alley.

The door opened, and they were greeted by an eight-foot minotaur with a sheet wrapped around his body. The half-man, half-bull looked out at the crowd that had followed Tanis and Brandella, and, nostrils flaring, asked dubiously, "You all want baths?"

"Just us," Tanis answered. Brandella stared, wordless, at the beast. "The, ah, living ones," the half-elf explained.

The beast turned gentle, liquid eyes toward the pair. "Living?" the minotaur asked. "Haven't seen one of them here in more than three thousand years. And now, two at once!" He took Tanis and Brandella by their hands and ushered them inside. The Kender waved good-bye.

"I am honored that you wish to partake of my baths," said Behobiphi in reverent tones. "By the gods," he added, "you certainly do need them, too. I dare say you are rather dirty. Are living beings this dirty all the time? Is this how it is on Krynn now, all mud and dirt?"

Tanis smiled and shook his head. "A recent accident. We'd like to get cleaned up and then find our way back to Life. We heard that there is a portal on the other side of Fistandantilus's mountain that will take us there."

"That's the story Huma tells, isn't it?" The minotaur seemed sympathetic for a creature known on Krynn for its bloodthirsty nature. Tanis and Brandella glanced at each other, both sinking into despair.

"Not too many believe that one," the minotaur went on while he showed them two tubs full of hot, soapy water. His voice was so deep, it was difficult to decipher. "After all, the whole idea of a portal is kind of old-fashioned, don't you think?" He shook his horned head. "I don't know how these rumors get started."

Behobiphi pulled a sheet across a rope to separate the two tubs. "When you're through washing," he said, pointing to a pile of towels, "take one of those and go out in the back. Softfire will help dry you off."

The minotaur was about to leave when Tanis called out, "If there is no portal, then is there some other way to get out of Death? Any way at all?"

The creature paused and scratched one leg with a sharp hoof. "Hundreds of theories. Maybe thousands. For instance, the gnomes of Yagorn have been working on a machine for a couple of thousand years that's supposed to get us all back to Life. It ought to work, too. Have you noticed that the sun here doesn't go down?"

Tanis nodded doubtfully.

"Well, the gnomes figure that if night ever comes to Death, then a new day of Life will have to dawn for all of us who dwell here," Behobiphi said, and wrapped his sheet more tightly. "So they're trying to build a machine that will pull the sun out of the sky. They think they may have the problem licked in another three or four thousand years. Now, that, you have to admit, is every bit as plausible as Huma's portal, right?" He favored Tanis with a guileless glance.

Sadly, Tanis had to agree. He began to undress; on the other side of the divider, he could hear Brandella doing the same. A shoe clunked to the floor, and a low wail sounded through the thin curtain.

"My buckles!" Brandella mourned.

# 34

# SOFTFIRE

DRIPPING WET, WITH A TOWEL WRAPPED AROUND HIS body, Tanis led the way out a rear door into the yard behind the minotaur's baths—and stopped short. "Back!" ordered Tanis. "Get back inside! Hurry!"

Brandella, caught off-guard, tripped and fell on the slippery, tiled floor in the doorway. Tanis, his eyes glued on the terrifying sight in the yard and feeling a fear beyond his understanding, didn't look where he was going. He stumbled over her feet and crashed, arms flailing, on top of her. "Dragon!" he shouted.

"Don't be frightened," boomed a loud, deep, but not unfriendly voice. "I see Behobiphi didn't warn you; he sometimes forgets."

Tanis rolled off Brandella, and the two sat up in the doorway and stared. An old silver dragon sat quietly in the shade of a grove of trees, a thin line of smoke trailing from its nostrils.

"I am Softfire," said the dragon with what may have been the dragon equivalent of a smile. "The heat of my fire breath will help dry you. Please step forward. I won't burn you."

The dragonfear faded. Tanis stood and tried to hold himself with some dignity—difficult when clad only in a towel. "Stay here," he whispered to Brandella.

"If he wanted to kill us, he could have done it already," she argued. "I'm coming with you."

That made some grudging sense to Tanis, so he didn't protest. They stepped forward into the chilly yard.

"That's a good spot," said Softfire. "Stand there." The dragon breathed a clear blue flame that shot out near them. They both flinched but managed to keep from bolting. The air near them grew hot, but not unbearably so, and soon, with each breath of fire, the water that dripped from their bodies began to rapidly evaporate. Even their hair dried.

"The minotaur will bring you your clothes, all cleaned," said Softfire. "In the meantime, come and scratch under my chin. I like the way it feels."

Tanis hung back, but Brandella walked fearlessly up to the beast. "Were you this friendly when you were alive?" she asked, running her fingernails under the beast's jaw.

"Oooohhhh, that's good," sighed Softfire, lifting his chin higher. He licked his dragon lips with a forked tongue and chuckled deep in his throat. "No," he finally answered. "I was a terror when I was young and alive. You should have seen me during what you call the Second Dragon Wars. There was one battle—"

Behobiphi interrupted from the bathhouse doorway. "You're not going to tell them your old war stories, are you?" the minotaur asked.

"Why not?" Softfire asked indignantly, condensation from the steamy bath surrounding him with a hazy silver aura. "My tales may be old to you, but they're new to them."

"That may be," Behobiphi said briskly, "but there are more customers waiting. Please be quick with your tale, as well as with all of your embellishments."

The dragon snorted, the heat from his fiery exhalation scorching a stone wall. Tanis realized how tame the beast was, and what it would be like if riled. He resolved not to rile it.

"Embellishments?" the dragon complained. "I ought to snuff out your entire establishment for that insult!"

Tanis got the impression that the minotaur and the dragon had had this conversation regularly during the past few centuries.

"Do what you will," sighed the minotaur. "Just do it quickly." Behobiphi handed Tanis and Brandella their freshly cleaned clothes and went back into the house.

"We really would love to hear your stories," said Tanis, "but we happen to be in a hurry. We need to find out how to get back to the living world—and quickly."

"That seems to be a preoccupation of so many here," observed the dragon. "I wonder why?"

"We can't speak for the others, but we're not supposed to be here. We're still alive," said Brandella, scratching Softfire under his left ear.

"Aaahhhhh . . . Oooohhh. You do that well." The dragon stretched like a huge tabby.

Tanis joined in, scratching the dragon under his right ear.

"Eeehhhhh . . . Aahhhhhh. You're too wonderful for words. What nice creatures you are to do this for me. I almost hate to help you leave." He closed his eyes.

"Then there is a way?" Tanis asked excitedly. He and Brandella exchanged glances; the weaver kept rubbing the silver dragon, scratching his scaly neck in quick, deft strokes. The creature thumped the ground several times with a huge, taloned hind leg; several branches broke from trees and fell to the earth.

"I don't know," Softfire said. "But I do know this: The only way out of Death for you is with magic; it won't work on anyone else here." The creature opened eyes that were more knowing than sleepy. "I heard a story from a brass dragon friend about a strange new spell being offered among all the mages; it might be exactly what you need." Softfire's gaze flicked from Tanis to Brandella and back again. Then the deep voice continued. "According to my friend, a wizard who recently died had quite a collection of bizarre and unusual spells—"

"*Kishpa*," breathed Brandella, squeezing Tanis's arm.

The dragon's eyes drifted shut again, but his voice continued to reverberate. "All the wizards like to trade spells, bartering a fire spell for a darkness spell—that sort of thing. Of course," the dragon continued, twisting his neck so Brandella could reach an out-of-the-way spot, "there is little they can do with their magic here, but they enjoy the collecting; it adds to their status among their peers. Anyway, this new mage arrived and promptly gave away—didn't want anything in return— one of his spells to every mage he could find."

"Where is this new wizard?" begged Brandella.

"I wish I could tell you," said Softfire with a massive, scaly shrug, "but he could be anywhere. Death is a large place that stretches beyond imagining. He would be impossible to find."

Brandella sighed.

"This spell that he gave away, the one that you said might help us, do you know what it is?" Tanis asked.

"That's the peculiar part. It's a totally useless spell to the Dead in our world. The spell allows the Living to leave the Dead; it's the kind of spell—"

"—that Kishpa would have loved when he was alive," exulted Brandella. "It is *exactly* the kind of useless spell he collected, something that would be just as useless in the world of the Living as it is in the world of the Dead."

"Except to us," Tanis added.

"And he must have known that," she cried, tears joyfully running down her face.

"You keep on like that," warned Softfire, "and I'm going to have to dry you all over again."

Brandella kissed the dragon's heavily scaled cheek while happily crying out to Tanis, "Don't you see?"

"Yes," Tanis admitted, surprised by the jealousy he felt. Even after Kishpa's death, it seemed, the half-elf could not compete with the mage. "We must find someone who has the spell—and quickly, because we will grow weaker with no food or water. And it must be someone who will share it with us."

"Softfire!" Brandella demanded. "I've heard that certain dragons were magic-users. Do you know the spell?"

The old silver dragon shook his head. "I can't help you with that. The only magic I know is keeping my lips from burning when I breathe fire."

"Where can we find a magic-user who will know the spell?" Brandella insisted.

Softfire pointed his nose toward the dark mountain. "As I said, Death is a far-flung place; there's quite a lot of room for new arrivals. The closest mage is him. Fistandantilus will surely know the spell and know how to invoke it."

Tanis felt a chill of fear encircle his spine. Softfire fixed him with a wise gaze, seeming to know how he felt about the evil wizard. "But beware," warned the dragon. "If he helps you, he will exact a price—and it may not be one you want to pay."

*　*　*　*　*

"I can hardly swallow," Brandella said painfully.

Tanis had been daydreaming about ale and spiced potatoes at the Inn of the Last Home. "The water Behobiphi gave us before we left didn't help at all. And neither did the food," he complained. "My throat has never been so dry."

They had no choice but to trudge on.

Told by Softfire that Fistandantilus lived in a hut at the top of the foothills, they had already climbed for several hours without finding the wizard's home.

Dark clouds hovered at the peak of Fistandantilus's towering mountain. A cold drizzle fell upon them as they climbed still higher, the water offering no pleasure to their tongues. Nothing grew on the huge slag heap of evil above them; it ran with sulphurous mud, and sharp, dark stones stood out from the sides like monstrous daggers.

A short while later, they stumbled upon a ramshackle hut partially hidden by a mudslide. Its roof was falling down and, from inside, they heard pitiful moans and groans. Brandella went white, and Tanis felt his insides tighten in fear.

"Something terrible is happening in there," he said in a low voice.

"Maybe the wizard is hurt or ill," Brandella countered without much conviction.

"Fistandantilus isn't like Kishpa. Fistandantilus was one of the most evil mages who ever lived. Most likely, he's torturing someone." Tanis could see by the flash of her brown eyes that he'd said exactly what she was really thinking and that she didn't appreciate his putting her thoughts into words.

The moans grew louder and more insistent, almost as if whoever was in pain knew they were out there and was entreating them to come to his rescue.

"Fistandantilus?" Tanis called out.

The wails stopped.

"Show yourself," Tanis insisted.

"I choose not to," the voice rasped. A dead plant exploded into flame only feet away. Tanis leaped between Brandella and the threat, and the voice laughed. "Don't bother, Half-Elven. Fistandantilus is everywhere."

Tanis took Brandella's hand.

"You do not show yourself because you can't," Tanis

proclaimed with a show of bravado.

Brandella looked at the half-elf with warning. "Careful," she mouthed.

"Why are you here?" the deadly voice demanded.

"If you are so powerful, then show yourself," Tanis repeated.

There was a tension-filled pause before Fistandantilus spoke again. "Half-elf, I tire of this. I have been in this state of invisibility since long before I died, when I traded my corporal being for extra years of life. That meant I also agreed to give up my body in this world, as well."

"If you have no body," asked Brandella, shivering as much from fear as from the raw, damp wind, "then what are you?"

"I am magic," came the reply.

Tanis felt Brandella's hand grow moist in his own. Or perhaps it was he who was sweating; he could not tell for certain.

Although they saw no one, they sensed Fistandantilus eyeing them and felt naked before him. Finally, with an edge of menace to his voice, the dead mage asked, "What brings Tanis and Brandella to my mountain?"

"If you know our names, than you know our reason," Tanis said, surprising himself with his own boldness. After all, Fistandantilus had used his magic to destroy two massive armies, including his own troops, during the Dwarfgate War. What was to stop the wizard, even on a whim, from destroying one human woman and a half-elf?

Laughter cascaded around them. "True," the menacing voice sibilated. "I've been walking with you in these foothills for quite some time now. Too bad about your thirst. Nothing I can do about it as long as you're alive. When you die of thirst tomorrow, though, come back and I'll conjure you a whole sea of cold, clean water.

"You are magic," Tanis said bitterly, "but you are powerless to help us. You are even powerless to help yourself."

This time the sound that surrounded them bore no resemblance to laughter. Like a thousand voices crying out in pain, a scream shivered through the rocks and made their skin crawl. Then they heard the words: "I did not create this mountain of darkness, of gloom, of horror, by *helping* anyone . . . except myself." The wind blew up hard and cold, a burning, wet spray lashing their faces as the rain whipped down from a gray and tumultuous sky. "If I help you," he said harshly, "it is because you will help *me* in return. Or you will die."

"What do you want?" Tanis asked warily.

"To return to Life with you."

## 35

# The Bargain

"There are many risks I would take to return to the Living," Tanis said slowly, knowing that he might be consigning himself and Brandella to death, "but I would not want it on my conscience that I was the one who returned Fistandantilus to Krynn."

"So noble," the wizard said, voice dripping with sarcasm. "You won't soil your hands, but what about the woman? Are you so cavalier with her life that you condemn her without asking if she feels as you do?"

"He need not ask," Brandella resolutely sang out. "You give us the chance to die heroes by refusing your bargain. We thank you for it."

Tanis squeezed her hand, but he dared not look at the brave woman who stood by his side. She warmly returned the caress. The half-elf found himself strangely unafraid of his fate. The only thing he wanted in life, he felt, was to wrap his arms around the weaver and hold her close. The presence of the unseen Fistandantilus, however, kept him rooted in place.

"You care so much for the living, but what do you care for the dead?" the wizard said ominously. A lifeless tree behind them cracked and fell, sparks flying as it struck the dead ground.

"You speak in riddles," said Tanis coolly, glad he was able to resist the instinct to flinch at the mage's explosive spells. "Say what you mean."

"There are many here whom you have known," the mage replied, his voice in harmony with the whining cold wind that shivered through the gnarled dead trees behind his dilapidated cabin. "I can look inside your minds to see those whom you have loved and lost. They exist here in *my* world." The wizard paused, and more rocks quaked and tumbled as if the mage had imbued them with life. If there was any doubt about Fistandantilus's meaning, he dispelled it when he finally said, "I cannot kill again those you once knew, but I can make their existence in Death as painful as the worst moments of their lives."

Tanis felt something cold and slimy against his scalp. It lasted only a moment, but he knew without any question that it was Fistandantilus's touch. A moment later, Brandella shivered and Tanis knew she'd experienced the same sensation.

"What are you doing?" demanded Tanis.

"Learning," came the sibilant answer. "For example, Brandella had a sister, a darling little girl. Her name was Cadaloopee."

Brandella wrenched her hand free from Tanis and covered her eyes. She quivered and whispered, "Caddie was washed away in a flood."

"The little girl plays here, running in a sun-dappled wood," the mage continued as lightning flashed out of nowhere, striking the cabin but seemingly inflicting no damage. "But I can make the rains come. I can make the fear of drowning well up in her little girl's mind." The voice was a banshee's shriek. "I can make Cadaloopee relive her worst fears. I can—"

"Stop!" shouted Brandella. Tanis put his arm around her shoulder. Convulsions of shivers passed through her slender frame. He longed to challenge the mage. To defeat him. But Tanis was no magic-user.

The wizard chuckled, his low laughter like a buzzing in their ears. "As for the half-elf, I wonder if he thinks of his poor mother, who died so soon after he was born?"

Tanis stiffened. His eyes flashed with anger, but he held his tongue. He felt Brandella's arm curl around his waist, offering him what help she could.

"She was a pretty elfmaid, full of life," came the voice. "But fragile. Very fragile. Both in body and mind. Here, in Death, she leads an idyllic existence, caring and cared for by her loved ones. I wonder what she would feel if I arranged for your brutish father to arrive on her doorstep?"

Tanis's heart pounding in his chest, he now knew the depth of his hatred for the wizard. The mage deserved his dark mountain of horrors. And Tanis wished he could bury the wizard at the bottom of it.

"What? No response?" Fistandantilus asked with a caustic edge.

"You will not harm my mother in any way," Tanis said through clenched teeth.

"Of course I won't." The voice crawled with false reassurance. "Just as long as you do as I ask."

Tanis swallowed hard. The mage had had devastating power in life; his bleak, windswept mountain of evil was testament to that. The half-elf pondered the legacy that Fistandantilus had left on Krynn . . . and he shuddered. It was in that moment, though, that the half-elf saw a glimmer of hope. The mage had performed his magic on Krynn; here, in Death, he was a prisoner of his own creation, existing in the shadow of his horrible deeds. And Tanis remembered something Softfire had said.

The half-elf stopped, consciously willing the disappearance of the half-formed idea. If the mage could read his thoughts, Tanis didn't want Fistandantilus to follow what he had been thinking.

Turning to Brandella, he gently said, "We should consider his offer."

She stared at him, shocked. Her dark eyes with their dark lashes glowed against her porcelain skin.

"What difference does it make where evil dwells, here or on Krynn?" he argued, seeing her reaction. "Life is short compared to the time one spends in this place. Better Fistandantilus should walk among the living than to terrorize the dead for all eternity."

"Do you mean what you're saying?" she asked coldly, "or are you just trying to convince yourself?"

"I'm trying to tell you that this is our only way." Hating to play Fistandantilus's game, yet knowing there was no other choice, he fixed his face into a sneer and harshly demanded, "How could you possibly live with yourself, knowing that your sister would exist in perpetual terror?"

Her lips trembled; she was unable to speak.

Acting as though he were trying to speak with her privately, he leaned close to Brandella and whispered, "He was defeated in Life before; he can be defeated again." Tanis knew, of course, that the mage had heard every word. Fistandantilus remained silent.

Brandella seemed to be slightly swayed, to think, for a moment, that their actions, should the pair agree to the mage's terms, would not be irreversible.

"Let me talk to him," he said coaxingly.

With enormous reluctance, she nodded.

"You say you will make a bargain with us," Tanis said tentatively to the mage. "How are we to know that you will keep your end of the deal?"

"You cannot know," said the wizard. "You must trust me because there is no one else who can help you before you die. The real question is, can I trust you to keep *your* end of our arrangement?"

Tanis looked up at the towering mountain, then at the sorry excuse for a cabin, and finally at the open, gray land in front of him, imagining the wizard hovering there. "It would seem," said the half-elf, "that we must trust each other equally."

The voice laughed with a sound of stones rattling on metal. "Trust each other? Hardly," Fistandantilus crooned. "You forget whom you are talking to. I tell you now that if you cross me, you will regret it for as long as you live—which won't be very long—and for as long as you are dead. Which will be much, much longer. You have my promise on that."

# 36

# The Flickering Candle

*"I thought I knew you,"* Brandella breathed in Tanis's ear.

"You do," he replied cryptically.

The woman, her lips set in a thin line, gave him a suspicious glance as she wiped rain from her face. What did he mean by that? she wondered.

They trudged into the wizard's cabin, soaked to the bone; the never-ending wind and rain had slashed mercilessly at them. Fistandantilus, Brandella thought, was lucky to lack a body that could ache with cold and hunger. Suddenly, it occurred to her that she might be hallucinating all of this. After all, she was weak from lack of food and sleep, and the unrelenting weather had taken its toll.

"It's just a nightmare. I'll wake up soon," she whispered to herself.

Tanis watched Brandella worriedly. She seemed pale and ill. They had been busy for several hours doing the wizard's bidding. While storm clouds roiled overheard, they had fixed the roof of the cabin, covering it with tree branches. Next, they swept the mud and water out of the cabin, making it as dry as possible. Of course, it was still thoroughly damp, the air nearly unbreathable in its closeness despite the open door. But Fistandantilus seemed pleased.

The spell, said the mage, had to be performed in a lighted, dry place so that he was fully separated from his endlessly bleak, rain-drenched world. Clearly, thought Tanis, the wizard is afraid that the pull of Death will be too strong to escape. Tanis hoped that was so . . . just in case.

"Don't light the candle until I begin the spell," Fistandantilus ordered. His sibilant whisper seemed to have grown stronger. Tanis felt a ripple of fear shiver up his neck. Brandella looked increasingly strained, purple smudges darkening the nearly translucent skin beneath her eyes.

A single candle stood in its holder on a bare wooden table. The wax looked ancient yet unused, the wick charred from untold attempts to set it ablaze, standing up in seeming defiance of any flame. Next to the candle, two small black stones lay on a small pile of torn parchment.

"Look behind you on the wall," said the mage.

The dim light reflected off a small mirror in a gold frame.

"Half-elf," Fistandantilus ordered, "take the mirror and hold it in your hands—carefully." The storm increased its tempo outside. Yet despite the sound of the wind, Tanis could hear the sighing voice of the mage as though it buzzed inside his head.

Tanis went to the mirror. It was hanging at eye-level. He reached up to take it off the wall—and froze. Then he waved his hand before the shimmering piece of glass; his face was not reflected. Even when he held it at the correct angle to catch the gray light from the doorway, the mirror showed nothing. Tanis looked back at the weaver. She was shivering, holding herself erect by sheer stubbornness.

"Stop that," the mage ordered Tanis. "I told you to hold it carefully."

"Why is this mirror so important?" Tanis asked as he came to the table that held the candle.

The chill in the room deepened. "When I use the spell to send you back to Life, you will take the mirror with you," the voice explained. "It holds, by a spell, my image, the way I looked when I was alive. When it is brought back to your plane, the image will be freed and I will walk once more on Krynn."

Tanis regarded the thick, strange glass. Despite himself, he couldn't help staring into it, trying to see the face of the mage who was hidden somewhere inside.

Fistandantilus laughed without humor. "That isn't the only spell that is going to Krynn with you from this place beyond the grave. I have put a spell upon you both." Tanis noticed that Brandella was wringing her hands again; her eyes were glassy, her face blank. The mage's next words only increased the tension. "Remember: If you betray me, death will come from those who love you most. You have been warned."

Suddenly, the door slammed shut, and the room turned dark. Tanis jumped, but Brandella seemed oblivious to anything but her fear.

"It is time," said Fistandantilus, excitement turning his voice painfully dissonant. "Get ready to light the candle, human."

Tanis held the mirror in one hand and groped for Brandella's hand with the other. When he found it, she pulled away. Her hand was cold as death.

The chant began so low it was almost inaudible. Slowly, the sound grew louder, the words unknown and unknowable.

Brandella fumbled next to the candle until her fingers settled on the two stones. She struck them together several times until a spark struck the torn parchment below, setting it aflame. She picked up one end of a paper fragment and, hands shaking, used it to light the candle.

The chanting grew still louder. The cabin began to quiver as if the wind outside were trying to pick the little shack off the ground and hurl it off the foothills, down to the valley below. Water and mud dripped between growing cracks in the ceiling. The dead branches crisscrossed over one section of the roof began to break apart and tumble into the room. A moan escaped the terrified weaver, but Tanis dared not comfort her.

Fistandantilus continued his chant, his own voice howling even louder than the wind.

Tanis didn't know what was breaking the cabin apart—the spell or Death trying to hold on to its victim. The forces of magic and nature were clearly at war.

No matter that the roof was collapsing, that the wind whipped through the splintering walls; the candle remained lit, the point of fire standing straight and unmoving, without so much as a flicker.

The magic was strong. Tanis felt a change coming. There was little time left, yet every move he made from this point on was critical. By the light of the candle, Tanis reached out and snatched Brandella by the arm. Again, she tried to pull away. But this time the half-elf would not allow it. In his heart, he knew that she might very well sacrifice herself to keep Fistandantilus from returning to Life. He did not want her to do anything that might interfere with his plans.

He was right. She fought for her freedom, kicking at him, while trying to get at the candle to snuff it out.

"Traitor!" she screamed, her face a distorted mask of

hatred.

If something didn't happen soon, they might be injured by the debris falling all around them. So far, the main beams of the cabin were holding, but the land itself seemed to be shaking. From somewhere on high, a roar grew louder with every instant. Through the broken rooftop, Tanis saw, with a terrible certainty, what had caused the shattering sound. The entire top of Fistandantilus's dark mountain, the pinnacle that loomed high above them, had broken off and an avalanche of sulphurous blackness was crashing down right toward the cabin.

Timing was all. Tanis knew that if he made his move too soon, Fistandantilus would stop Kishpa's spell and allow them to be crushed by the avalanche. But if Tanis waited too long, if he didn't act in the instant before the spell took effect, he risked the worst of all, bringing the infamous wizard back into Life.

Tanis had to wager that Fistandantilus was fully occupied. The half-elf let himself recall what the old dragon, Softfire, had said: *The wizards in Death had little use of their magic.* Tanis gambled that the wizard had been bluffing, that he had no power over Brandella's sister or Tanis's mother, that his power in Death extended mainly to pyrotechnics designed to impress visitors. After all, the mage was doomed to stay in the shadows of his horrid mountain; the half-elf hoped Fistandantilus's power was far more limited than the mage had let on.

Soon Tanis would no longer have to pretend to go along with the wizard. As far as the half-elf was concerned, Fistandantilus's threat was empty and the half-elf did not fear him; he just wanted the mage to cast Kishpa's spell.

But when was the right time to act?

*"Kyvorek blastene tyvvelekk winderfall!"* the voice of Fistandantilus thundered. *"Tylvvanus! Tylvvanus!"* The voice was greater than the din of the fast-approaching avalanche, greater even than the crumbling foothills

above the cabin that gave way with huge mudslides, threatening to bury them before the avalanche sealed their doom. Brandella and Tanis saw it all through the porous roof and the splintering walls. The weaver screamed and tried, again unsuccessfully, to pull away from the half-elf.

They had seconds to live. Yet Tanis waited. He sensed that Kishpa's spell was not complete. There had to be a sign, a moment—*something*—that would tell him that they were about to be transported back to the world of the living. But there was nothing. And Death was nearly upon them.

Brandella screamed again. The mudslide loomed like a tidal wave, poised on its crest and about to break over them. At the same moment, the avalanche smashed through the mud. There was no time left. Tanis raised his hand—the hand that held the mirror—over his head.

Out of the corner of his eye, he saw something—the candle flickered for the very first time. It must be the sign! He threw the mirror with all of his might against the candle. The light was snuffed, and the mirror fell to the rock floor, shattering it into a thousand slivers of useless glass.

*"No!"* screamed the mage.

# PART IV

## 37

# Brandella in His Eyes

They heard the rushing wind, the roar of the massive wave of mud, and the crashing of the avalanche. The sounds filled their ears like the echo of the surf in a sea shell. Before them, however, they saw the sun shining in a bright blue sky, felt a cool breeze upon their skin, and heard the flapping of wings as several birds flew away in fear upon the astonishing arrival of a human and a half-elf in their charred thicket of bushes.

Tanis tried to get his bearings. It didn't take him long. He saw the burnt glade and the ash-covered pond. The air was redolent with the scent of fire. But when he looked at the tree trunk upon which Kishpa had rested, the mage was nowhere in sight. Neither was Clotnik.

"Where are we?" Brandella asked in a small voice, gratefully gripping the half-elf's hand, the hand she had so recently disdained. "It looks familiar."

"You were here with me before, when it was a younger wood, before the fire that destroyed it. Brandella," Tanis said quietly, reverently, "We are home. It was from this place that I came for you. And it is to this place that we have been returned."

"And without Fistandantilus," she added, shame-facedly. "I'm sorry. I didn't trust you."

Tanis kept his voice steady and looked straight at her. She didn't meet his eyes, however. "You had no way of knowing what I planned," he said, squeezing her hand, "and I couldn't risk telling you. Besides, the important thing is that we're here."

She finally smiled at him and took his other hand. Her voice was soft. "Yes. Somehow we have managed . . . thanks to you."

Tanis gently pulled her closer. She did not resist. When their bodies touched, he let go of her hands, encircling her with his arms. Brandella slipped her own arms under Tanis's and joined him willingly in an embrace. Her head rested on his shoulder.

In that moment, Tanis was at peace.

He lifted her head and they looked at each other with searching eyes. And just as quickly as he had found peace, he lost it. The half-elf had done his duty for Kishpa; now he wanted to do something for himself. Yet he paused. What if she were merely grateful? What if her hug was meant as one given by a sister to a brother? What if she flatly rejected him? And really, was it that different from a romance with Kitiara? It was still love between a human and one of elven blood. Even with only half-elven blood, he would be doomed to watching his beloved grow old and die—decades, and possibly centuries, before him.

He thought of all those things and much more as he

looked down upon her parted lips and deep, engulfing eyes. He had to know how the beautiful human weaver, the courageous archer, felt about Tanis Half-Elven. Yet he did not know if he had the right to find out.

Despite himself, he slowly, tentatively lowered his head toward hers. She shifted in his arms. He couldn't tell if she was snuggling in closer or getting a grip so that she could push him away. A voice startled them, calling out, "Who's there?"

As if they had been caught doing something forbidden, Tanis and Brandella quickly parted, carelessly stepping on blackened tree branches. The brittle wood cracked, tossing up little clouds of ash.

"Throw down your weapons and show yourselves," ordered the voice, "or I'll have my men shower that thicket with arrows!"

"Clotnik, is that you?"

"Tanis?"

The half-elf threw back his head and laughed. "'Tell your *men* to disappear," he said as he pulled Brandella with him out of the bushes.

When they emerged into a clearing near the pond, Clotnik stood there alone, brown hair and beard as rumpled as ever, eyes bright green beneath a sloped forehead. "My men are all gone," he said with an impish grin. "They're very good at following orders."

Tanis and Clotnik clasped hands with the warmth of old friends. The juggler was clearly glad to see him, and Tanis felt the same way.

"I thought you were gone forever," admitted the juggler. "I had given up on your ever returning. You must tell me everything that happened. Everything!"

"I will," Tanis agreed. "Later. First, though, we must drink and eat. We are," he said, glancing at Brandella with a playful grin, "so thirsty and hungry that we're close to Death."

She smiled back at him, and the dwarf's gaze drifted toward the woman who stood behind Tanis. He looked up at her with fascination and not a little awe.

Tanis gathered his wits about him. "Brandella, the weaver, may I introduce Clotnik, the juggler. Brandella, Clotnik is a friend of Kishpa's.

The homely dwarf with the drooping ears nodded his head. "I know you," Clotnik finally said.

Brandella studied the dwarf's face. She walked past Tanis, stepping closer to the dwarf, whose eyes seemed to beg for a spark of recognition.

She reached out and touched his face, then ran her fingers over his matted brown hair. Clotnik looked up at her with a childlike expression . . . and she threw her arms around him. "It's you," she cried. "You stayed with Kishpa all these years!"

Tanis stared at both of them, bewildered. He'd been in Ankatavaka, too, but he hadn't recognized Clotnik during his short stay. And he would have remembered. There were few dwarves in the elven village. In fact, the only ones he remembered were Mertwig and Yeblidod.

Suddenly, Tanis's eyes opened wide. Was it possible? Clotnik had Mertwig's weak chin and high, slanting forehead. He had Yeblidod's bright green eyes and slightly humped nose. But the half-elf didn't remember seeing a younger Clotnik in the village.

"Did you see my father?" the juggler asked before Tanis had uttered a word.

"Mertwig?"

"Yes," said Clotnik, his eyes misting. "Then you met him?"

"I did, indeed," Tanis replied happily, glad to be able to draw the past and the present so closely together for the dwarf.

"You're so grown up!" Brandella interrupted. "By the gods, I haven't seen you since you were a little boy and your mother and father sent you away on the ship before the humans attacked Ankatavaka." She laughed. "That was either almost one hundred years ago or just last week," she said merrily.

So, thought the half-elf, that's why I didn't know him. "It was the last time I saw you, too," said Clotnik. "But I always remembered the most beautiful woman I'd ever seen. Not that Kishpa would let me forget. But come," he said, "we'll talk more after you've had food and water."

\* \* \* \* \*

"How long since I left?" Tanis asked after swallowing the last of Clotnik's jerked beef. Brandella had finished eating and sat off to one side, braiding her long hair into a thick plait that hung over one shoulder.

"Three days," replied the juggler, unconsciously gazing at the tree where Kishpa had lain. Tanis and Brandella followed his eyes to the spot.

"When did he die?" asked the half-elf gently.

Clotnik didn't answer at once. Nor did he look at his two companions. Instead, he poked at the ash-strewn ground at the pond's edge as his lips quivered and his hands shook. Brandella leaned over and touched his shoulder, rubbing it tenderly, her own eyes red-rimmed and liquid. She had changed from her filthy woven top into one of Clotnik's longest white shirts; now she used the puffy sleeve to wipe a tear from the little dwarf's cheek. Clotnik shivered but let her minister to him.

"He . . . He . . . lived throughout the whole first day," stammered the dwarf. He steadied himself but would not look up. "I didn't think he'd live an hour," said the juggler, shaking his head. "His eyes were closed the whole time. He never spoke to me or even acknowledged that I was there." Finally, Clotnik lifted his head and spoke directly to Tanis. "It seemed that he was reliving something that was part nightmare and part the sweetest of idylls. When it was bad for him, he thrashed and moaned—and cried. When it was good, I believe, he smiled and even laughed somewhere deep inside. Was that what you saw, Tanis? Was that how it was for him in the past: part nightmare and part idyll?"

"I suppose it was," the half-elf reflected, suddenly suffering deep pangs of guilt about his feelings for Brandella.

Clotnik stared at the ground again. "He nearly died twice during that first day," he said. "The first time, he sat straight up and screamed at someone, 'Not yet! Not yet!' Then he blinked several times as if he were lost or confused. Soon, though, he smiled again, as if it were all right. The second time, I really thought I'd lost him. It had just gotten dark. Lunitari was low in the sky, casting a dim red light on him, when he began to choke and cough up blood. His eyes opened wide as if Death had caught him by surprise. He stopped breathing. I listened for a heartbeat and couldn't hear one. He was absolutely still. I went to close his eyes, but I stopped."

Clotnik bit his lip and glanced wonderingly at Brandella. "When I looked into his eyes," he said, "I saw you."

She took his hand as tears flowed freely down her cheeks. "Kishpa came back to life," Clotnik told her in a whisper. His eyes glittered like emeralds. "For you."

"Where did you bury him?" she asked in a voice racked with emotion.

Clotnik rose and pulled her to her feet. "I'll take you to him."

Tanis chose to stay behind. The grave was at the top of a hill beyond the glade. Clotnik left her there and returned to sit quietly next to Tanis.

Her grief was private. Her words to Kishpa were carried away on the wind, but who was to say they were not heard?

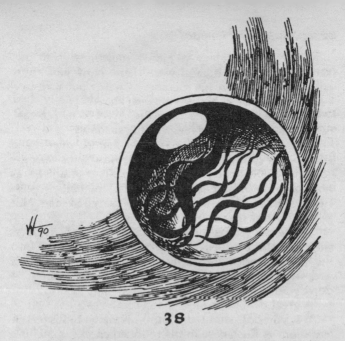

## 38

# Fathers and Sons

---

"Tell me about my father," Clotnik insisted while they awaited Brandella's return from the grave site. The dwarf and the half-elf sat on a log near the water's edge.

"Is that why you found me in Solace and brought me to Kishpa?" asked the half-elf. "Was it so I would meet your father?"

Clotnik squinted into the harsh afternoon light from the lowering sun. Long shadows splayed out behind them, and Tanis pondered the shadow that a father could throw over the life of his child. How well he knew it.

"I told you before you entered Kishpa's memory that I wanted to go myself," the dwarf reminded him. "Kishpa wouldn't let me. He was hiding something from me, Tanis. I'm sure of it. You were there. Now you know what Kishpa knew; his memory is now your memory. What was it he did not want me to know?"

Tanis averted his eyes from the dwarf to let his gaze fall, once again, on the lengthening shadows.

"Was my father an evil man? Was that it?" questioned Clotnik nervously, seeing that Tanis wasn't answering.

Tanis shook his head vehemently. "Not at all! I was only pausing to gather my thoughts," the half-elf reassured Clotnik. "He was, in fact, a rather good man. Not perfect. Better than most, I would say."

"You're not telling me anything," scowled the juggler, slinging a sharp-edged, fire-scarred chunk of granite into the lake. It landed with a plunk, scattering sodden ashes and sending floating wood bobbing on the ripples. "I don't want generalities. Tell me what happened!"

"A great deal happened. I don't know—"

"Yes, you do!" shouted Clotnik, jumping to his feet in agitation. A flush rose in his rounded cheeks, matching the glow cast by the setting sun. "Was Mertwig a thief? Did he steal? Tell me! I've heard the talk from villagers. Some said he ran away before the issue could be settled. Others said he was so offended by the accusation that he left Ankatavaka in a huff. With no help from Kishpa, I learned that it was right after that time that my father died." He wrung his stubby hands, his eyes brilliant with anguish. "My mother went back to the village and met me when the ship brought me home, but I was very young then and I don't remember much. All I know was that she was always very sad after I returned. For a very long time, I thought I was the cause of her sadness."

Clotnik stared at his hands as if he might have done something with them to spare Yeblidod her agony.

Finally, he said, "My mother died within a year of my father's death."

Tanis shook his head sadly. "I didn't know. I'm sorry," he offered. "I liked her very much." He remembered her warm alto, the kindness of her touch.

"I've heard all about my mother," Clotnik said with a world-weary sigh. His voice was leaden. "I'm proud of her and think of her often. She left me that glass ball that I juggle. The one you caught in the Inn."

Tanis held his breath. "I remember," the half-elf said softly. "Please. Sit down. I'll tell you what I can."

Clotnik sat, his attention squarely on Tanis. The half-elf touched his fingertips to his lips, contemplating his words, and the dwarf leaned forward.

"If you want to know what kind of person your father was," spoke Tanis, "I can tell you this: He twice saved my life. Both times, Clotnik, he was in great peril or great pain—or both. The first time, he attacked a giant spider that was about to devour me. I would have perished if he hadn't diverted the monster's attention to himself."

Clotnik beamed with incipient pride. But he said nothing, seeming to want to avoid interrupting the narrative.

"The second time," Tanis continued, "he was mortally wounded, yet he dragged himself to my rescue, slaying a goblin who was about to strike me from behind." Tanis looked directly in Clotnik's eyes. "Do these sound like the actions of a bad man?"

The slanting amber light from the setting sun bathed Clotnik's face, his eyes sparkling with a pleasure that went far beyond the reflected glory of the bright orb in the western sky. No, Tanis thought, the reflected glory came from Mertwig. Clotnik seemed to sit straighter, hold his head more erect—even his ears seemed to droop less. He was seeing himself in a different way, Tanis realized; Clotnik had become the son of a hero. Tanis found himself envying the dwarf.

"He did all that?" the dwarf said in awe.

"That and more," Tanis replied, wishing he were describing his own father. "He was also protective of you and generous to your mother. His first impulse was to send you out of harm's way when there was fear of a human invasion. And he wanted only the best for your mother—even," he said without thinking, "when he couldn't afford it." He caught his breath, hoping Clotnik had missed the slip.

Borne up on this proud image of his father, Clotnik shook his head. "Then why wouldn't Kishpa tell me? Why, when I asked him about the rumors, did he say he didn't know? He'd always change the subject."

"For a simple reason," Tanis said with a benevolent smile. "Kishpa really didn't know." Tanis did not add, however, that *he* was the only person to whom the dwarf told the truth, just moments before he died.

"I still don't understand," Clotnik said.

"What?"

The dwarf swung and faced Tanis again. The setting sun left him a silhouette to the half-elf. "If there were rumors about my father in Ankatavaka," Clotnik asked, "why didn't Kishpa stand up for him?"

Tanis bent over to peel a piece of wood from the log. He busied himself with pulling little chips of charred wood from the piece, then wiped his sooty hands on the sandy ground. "He stood up for you, didn't he?" Tanis answered, deflecting the question. "He took care of you all these years. Isn't that what Brandella said?"

"It's just strange," insisted the dwarf. "Kishpa took me in very soon after my mother died. Brandella had already disappeared, and I've always wondered if it was her loss that caused him to take me in. It seemed he needed someone to talk to. And me . . . I needed someone to listen to. He treated me as if I were his own. But when I grew and the stories persisted about my father, he took me away from Ankatavaka. We traveled all across Ansalon. We had no friends except each other and, to amuse myself and Kishpa, I learned to juggle."

"And you learned it well. No magic involved?"

"None at all," the dwarf said proudly. "I would not allow Kishpa to enchant the balls. Not even the glass one, though he begged me to let him."

Tanis found that he couldn't speak.

"Kishpa was a good father to me. I just wish he would have let me enter his past; I would have loved to have seen my father, talked to him." The droopy-eared dwarf turned to Tanis in sudden contrition. "Forgive me! I never asked if you found your own father. Here I am, so concerned only with myself. I should have—"

Tanis stemmed the rush of words with a wave of one tanned hand. "Don't apologize. Except for meeting Brandella—and that's a very large exception—I would much rather that you had gone to meet your father, too."

"He was not what you'd hoped?"

"He was not what anyone would have hoped," said Tanis dryly. "Sometimes it's better to imagine the truth."

"But not in my case?" asked Clotnik.

"No," said Tanis with a smile. "Not in your case."

The dwarf leaned back, contented.

The sun was nearly down, and dusk had settled over the land. "Brandella should be back soon," said Tanis. "Before she returns, tell me something."

"Anything."

"Why did Kishpa and Brandella part? You said something about her disappearing."

"That's what he called it. He never spoke of it much. It seemed too painful to him. All he said was she had painted a picture of some kind that foretold a time when she would be taken away from him. And someone did, indeed, come and fetch her. He never saw her again."

Tanis sat in stunned silence, the mystified expression on his face hidden by the enveloping darkness of night.

It was that same darkness, however, that eventually began to trouble the half-elf. "Brandella should have been back by now," he said, rising to his feet. "Maybe I should make sure she's all right."

"I'll show you the way," said Clotnik.

They walked quietly through the night, making their way out of the glade and up the hill. When they reached the grave site, Brandella was gone.

## 39

# At the Camp of the Sligs

"Sligs," whispered Clotnik, sniffing the air. "I can smell their stinking odor. They must have taken her," he said with disgust. He kicked at the ground. "Kishpa's fire didn't stop them. They're still after that enchanted quill." Suddenly, he whirled in the dark to face Tanis. "You did get rid of the quill, didn't you?"

"Yes," said Tanis distractedly, looking for some sign that would tell him in what direction the cousins of the hobgoblins had gone. "I left it in Kishpa's memory, just as he instructed." His elven eyesight helped him see slig footprints all over the grave site, but they told him nothing he didn't already know. Meanwhile his mind spun with recriminations. He berated himself for letting Brandella wander off alone. To have come this far with her only to lose her to a band of sligs filled him with rage. He would have exploded in frustration if he had not spotted a faint point of light on a distant hill. He gestured. "Over there! It looks like a campfire."

They headed indirectly toward the light. Tanis led the way, making sure they did not leave themselves silhouetted against the horizon. Hugging lower ground, they were fast-moving shadows intent upon their destination. When they got close enough to smell the smoke from the campfire, Tanis ducked behind a burned stump and said, "We'll circle around behind. They'll be less likely to expect anyone from the direction they came from."

Breathing hard, Clotnik nodded in agreement. When they neared the rear of the camp, the dwarf managed to ask between gasps, "I wonder where they got the wood for a fire? Everything out here burned up three days ago."

Tanis's answer was to clap his hand over Clotnik's mouth and drag him, face down, to the ground.

A nearby slig guard paused as though it had heard voices. Sounds drifted down from the raucous slig camp above; the creature quirked its pointed ears down below, obviously trying to discern whether these new sounds came from below or from the camp. Its sword at the ready, the slig tromped down the hill to investigate.

"Don't move," Tanis whispered in Clotnik's ear. "And whatever happens, don't let its spittle touch your skin; it's poisonous."

Clotnik nodded, and Tanis removed his hand.

Flickering light from the fire at the top of the hill illuminated the slig guard in yellow flashes. More than six feet in height, the slig wore no clothes, although its back was daubed with broad stripes of black and brown. Its body was a mass of tough, horny hide that seemed more like flexible stone than skin. A tail dragged along the ground. When the slig looked their way, Tanis saw its long, thin mouth open to reveal rows of thick, sharp teeth. Its almost hornlike ears were huge and pointed.

Clotnik turned to whisper to Tanis, but the half-elf had disappeared without making a sound. Alone, not knowing what he should do, the dwarf froze. All Clotnik could do was watch the slig in silent terror as the guard made its way closer to where he hid in the brush.

The slig's jaws moved up and down as it filled its mouth with spittle. It was moving lower on the hill, the heavy metal trinket that dangled from its massive left ear swinging back and forth with each step.

The slig loomed closer. The dwarf tried to sink into the ground, to disappear, but it didn't seem to do any good. The creature kept coming in his direction.

Off to one side, Tanis watched as the slig came abreast of him, moving toward Clotnik, who was fidgeting in the brush below. As soon as the creature passed him, Tanis leaped up and unsheathed his sword.

The slig heard the familiar sound and turned with surprising speed—right into Tanis's blade. The half-elf speared the creature in the throat, just above the armorlike hide that protected its chest. As it fell, it tried to call out a warning, but all it could do was gurgle.

Tanis did not wait for the slig to die. He took the creature's sword and gathered up Clotnik. "Here, take this," he said, handing the weapon to the dwarf. "I hope you won't need it."

"I won't need it for long," he said in a shaking voice. Even his brown beard quivered. "I'm not a fighter."

Tanis took the young dwarf by the shoulders and looked directly into his green eyes. "I once knew a man who was much more terrified than you when he went into battle for the first time. When it was over, he was not only still alive, he was a hero. You'll do all right. Just stay behind me. And don't move around so much; you draw too much attention."

Tanis moved carefully up the hill until he could see the slig camp. And Brandella.

She was tied to a stake in the ground, lying next to the

fire. One of the sligs, obviously the leader by its size, stood over her, spitting its poisoned saliva just inches from her face. It splattered on the ground next to the long braid of black hair that coiled over one shoulder. She didn't cry out. She didn't even move. She simply stared up at the slig with defiance on her face.

The sligs seemed impressed, but not enough to stop. Tanis tried to make out what the slig leader was saying. It sounded like Common tongue, but all the half-elf could hear was the shouted warning, "Tell or die!"

Clotnik crawled up next to Tanis and saw the remnants of a water wagon, empty barrels lying on their sides all around it. The wagon obviously had been on its way to the glade to fill up at the pond. The dwarf wondered where the driver was. His attention was arrested by something black turning above the blaze, juices dripping down and causing the wood to sizzle and the flames to jump. Clotnik leaned close and whispered, "Where'd they get the venison? I thought all the animals had left with the fire."

Tanis looked at him, expressionless, and Clotnik realized the chunk of meat above the blaze was no deer. He swallowed hard and looked away.

Tanis continued to scan the camp. If there had been a wagon, something must have pulled it. On the far side of the camp, he saw what he was looking for: two brawny bullboggs. The six-legged draft animals, crosses between horse, bull and buffalo, weren't fast, but they were steady and dependable.

"How fast can you run?" Tanis whispered.

"How fast do I need to run?" the dwarf replied nervously.

"Faster than the sligs."

"If they're behind me, I'll run like the wind."

"You'd better," said Tanis, "because you're going to attack their camp—you and your 'men'—and then you're going to run like you've never run before."

Clotnik swallowed again. Hard.

* * * * *

Brandella had fought the sligs after they surprised her at Kishpa's grave site. It wasn't her own life that she was defending, though: it was the peace of Kishpa and the lives of Tanis and Clotnik. At all cost, she did not want the sligs to disturb her mage's grave, digging it up for the enchanted quill that they so ruthlessly demanded of her. She told them she knew where it was—although she had no intention of ever telling them. Nor did she want the sligs to know that she had two companions just a short distance away. Far preferable, she thought, to die for those who had done so much to try to save her.

Her fight with the sligs was decidedly short. One of the creatures knocked her down with a swipe of its gargantuan right hand, hitting her so hard that she thought for a moment that it had broken her jaw. Two of the wilder sligs grabbed each of her arms, intending, she guessed in terror, to eat her limbs raw. They were stopped by their leader, who kicked them away from the woman.

It was getting dark. Although sligs often lived in caves, they did not like to be out in the open in the dark. The leader, who towered above the other creatures and had a long scar that ran down its snout, ordered the band to take Brandella back to their camp. They would learn there, with torture, what they wanted to know.

They cooked the wagon driver right in front of her, making her watch the man burn on the spit. She refused to talk. But she listened.

"We could trade her for weapons."

"Only if she's in perfect condition."

"If she doesn't talk soon, though . . ."

"Broken bones and burns will lower her value."

The leader cut them short with a snarl. "If we get the quill, it will be well worth the loss of her life. Besides," it added, "if we can't trade her, we can always eat her."

Brandella lay quietly by the campfire, thinking of Kishpa and Tanis and Scowarr and the brave acts she'd witnessed the past several days. She was determined, despite a tremor in her abdomen that she couldn't quite control, to live up to those examples. But she blanched as the leader of the sligs took a slat from a broken water barrel and put one end of it in the fire; after the end began to smolder, the slig walked to the weaver and held the burning wood near her face. In Common, the slig said, "I am going to set your hair on fire. Loose hair burns in a flash, but a tight braid should burn slowly—satisfactory for our purposes. If you don't tell me where the magic quill is, I will let the flames continue, to burn your head and face until there is nothing left. Do you understand?"

She looked away.

Its thin lips drew back from sharp teeth. "Yes, you understand."

Brandella clenched her teeth and decided she would not cry out, even when the pain became unbearable.

The slig lowered the burning piece of wood. Brandella could hear the crackle of the wood and feel the heat.

A shout suddenly went up at the camp's western perimeter, and Brandella closed her eyes. "Attack!" cried one slig. A rush of heavy slig feet ran past her body, toward the commotion.

Brandella knew it was Tanis and Clotnik, and her heart sank. They were throwing their lives away for nothing. They couldn't possibly attack a band this large and survive—there were at least twenty of the creatures!

"A small disturbance," said the leader, who did not run with the others. "My troops are taking care of it. And I will take care of you."

It touched the burning stick to her hair.

## 40

# A Fading Memory

The slig heard the noise before it saw the source.
There was a pounding that made the earth shake. The
creature was slow, however, in taking its eyes off Brandella's burning hair. When it looked up, Tanis, riding one
of the bullboggs, was only feet away.

The half-elf kicked the slig in the chest, knocking it
backward into the fire. It screamed and rolled. In the
same motion, Tanis leaped off the bullbogg and, wielding his sword, hacked at Brandella's hair, cutting off the
long braid at the base of her neck. With the next well-
aimed stroke, he slashed her bonds. He sheathed the
sword, leaped back on the bullbogg, and held out his

arm to her. She sprang up and took it, swinging behind him onto the broad back of the bullbogg. Behind them, the slig leader continued to shriek from the blaze.

Tanis dug his heels into the animal's generous flanks, and it took off at a dead run, all six legs churning. Behind him thundered the second bullbogg, tied to the first.

Tanis rode the lumbering beast down the hill, in the same direction in which the band of sligs had run. He came up behind them and cut one down after another with the gray metal sword that Flint had forged for him. It wasn't as light and easy in his hands as when it had been enchanted by Kishpa, but it still did its work.

Plunging through the front ranks of the enemy, Tanis thought he saw movement ahead that contrasted with the herky-jerky running style of the lizardlike sligs. "Clotnik!" he bellowed.

"It's me!" came a relieved tenor.

Tanis slowed his bullbogg long enough for Clotnik to climb on the second animal. And then they galloped away, leaving the sligs cursing after them.

\* \* \* \* \*

They watered the bullboggs at the pond in the glade, gathered their meager belongings, then quickly set out to the west, putting as much distance between themselves and the sligs as they could before exhaustion overtook them.

When they finally stopped to rest, Tanis took the first watch. Brandella had insisted on the second watch, and he went to wake her two hours later, just before the dawning. He kneeled next to her and watched her sleep, as peaceful as the nearly soundless forest night. He was thinking of the future; she would fit in fine with his small group of friends. Flint, Sturm, Caramon, and Tas would instantly see that she was one of them—although she'd have to keep an eye on her valuables around the kender. Even Raistlin might welcome her in order to learn about Kishpa's magic. Of course, Kit would hate her, but Brandella could hold her own with the swordswoman. Together, they would make quite a group. And maybe, over time, Brandella would come to see him in a new light. He could wait. And he would.

Tanis reached down to touch her shoulder and wake her.

His hand passed through her.

"Brandella!" he cried.

Startled out of a deep sleep, she sat straight up, her newly shortened curls dancing around her shoulders. "What's wrong? What's happened?" she demanded, looking all about for any sign of danger. "Sligs?"

Shocked awake, Clotnik had run to the bullboggs before he realized he was the only one moving. He stopped and looked back at Tanis and Brandella. And he listened . . .

"I wanted to wake you," Tanis said, confused. "Except there was nothing there to touch. My hand went right through you!"

She touched her own hand and felt flesh and bone. "You must have fallen asleep and dreamed it," she said soothingly. "I'm still here. See?" She held out her hand to him. He reached out to take it, but although he could see it, he could not touch it or hold it.

Brandella gasped. It was true.

"Do you feel anything?" Tanis asked, trying to comfort her and to fathom what was happening.

Her eyes flashed with terror. "I don't feel any different than I felt before. Tanis! I don't understand it!"

The early morning fog seemed to flow right through her. It was as if she was becoming one with the fog, thin and airy.

"Did the sligs do anything to you?" Tanis asked, his mind racing. "Did they give you anything to eat or drink?"

She shook her head, bewildered. "No. Nothing."

Tanis strained to think. "Wait!" he cried, putting out one hand but stopping just short of trying to touch her.

"When you were at Kishpa's grave, did anything happen? Anything unusual?"

She brushed a dead leaf off the sleeve of Clotnik's borrowed white shirt. The leaf fell to the ground, and Tanis picked it up and crumpled it. That, at least, was real. Then she spoke quietly. "There was no magic. Nothing like that. It must be something else." Despair began to tinge her husky voice.

"It *is* something else," said Clotnik. "It's something you cannot fight with a sword, Tanis. I'm sorry."

Tanis turned to face Clotnik, danger etched on the half-elf's face. He advanced upon the dwarf, saying, "You speak as if you know all about it."

Clotnik gave a half-smile filled with weariness. He didn't back up. "It will do you no good to take your anger out on me," he said softly, his eyes large and sad. "I didn't know. Kishpa only suggested that it might happen. Even he didn't know for sure."

"Didn't know what?" Brandella pleaded. "What's happening to me, Clotnik?"

"You're as real as life to Tanis," the dwarf said tenderly. "For him, your heart beats, your skin feels warm to the touch, your voice is like music played by an inspired musician."

Brandella blushed. Embarrassed that his secret was so obvious, Tanis studied the nearby trees.

"It's because he sees you as real that you are real," Clotnik said. "The way it was supposed to work was that Tanis would return from Kishpa's memory alone, remembering you in his own mind. Instead, he went one step further, *physically* bringing you out of Kishpa's memory to exist in his own world. Kishpa said it could happen. But he also said that if it did, it wouldn't last."

"*Why?*" demanded Tanis. "Why can't it last? Why can't she stay here with me?" There. Now she knew. When he looked at her, her eyes were moist with tears. Yet even now, he didn't know if they were tears of regret or tears of pity.

With infinite sadness, Clotnik said, "She cannot stay because she is a memory. And like all memories, she must fade."

"If she didn't fade from Kishpa's memory," Tanis challenged, "she won't fade from mine."

"That was Kishpa's wish," the dwarf said. "But you will have to remember her only in your mind's eye. There is nothing we can do. She is fading."

Tanis ached to hold her in his arms, but now it was impossible. "Walk with me," he whispered to Brandella. He wanted to be alone with her.

Clotnik bowed his head as they passed him on their way to a nearby deer path. "Good-bye," he said in a low voice.

She stopped. Although trembling with her own fear, not quite knowing her fate, she kissed Mertwig's son on the cheek. There was no sense of touch between them, yet there was no doubt in Clotnik's mind that he had just been blessed.

\* \* \* \* \*

Streaks of sunlight slanted low across the land as day was born. The light seemed to cut through Brandella as if she weren't there. She cried out and stumbled off the trail, searching for shadows.

Tanis hurried after her, calling out, "Don't be afraid."

"Afraid!" she bitterly replied. "After I fade, I will be just a memory, something that happened in your past. You will go on, but I will not."

"Brandella, oh, my Brandella," he said. Fallen leaves crunched under his knees as he dropped down beside her. "Think of it this way. My memory is a world by itself, like Kishpa's. You'll be *alive* there. And not a single day will pass when you won't find something new and fresh to discover."

She cocked her head to one side, her slender body seemingly afloat in the shadows.

"Listen," he persisted, "memory and imagination are

like colors on a painter's palette, constantly being mixed to create something new. And that's what you'll find inside me, Brandella: a whole new world that's yours to explore." He struggled to find words to reassure her. "Everything I remember about you will be changing. Some days, when I wonder what you were like as a little girl, I'll picture you as a child. And you'll be young again. Some nights I'll be walking along a city street—a place you've never been—but I'll be thinking of you, talking to you. You'll answer in my mind. You'll be anywhere and everywhere."

She clasped her hands, edging farther out of the light. "I hope what you're saying is true."

"I'll never forget you," he promised as she faded away, blending into the shadows.

"And I'll always be with you," she said in a voice so soft that Tanis wasn't sure if he'd heard it. And perhaps he hadn't. It may have come from somewhere inside him.

# 41

# A New Thought, An Old Place

Zarjephwu, the leader of the sligs, bathed his burned body in the pond that they'd found in the glade. They had followed the tracks of the bullboggs in the moonlight, but, fearing the night, decided to go no farther. They had not, however, given up the chase. As far as Zarjephwu was concerned, the woman who had escaped certainly knew where the enchanted quill was; otherwise why would those two have risked their lives to save her?

When dawn broke, Zarjephwu roused himself from the same water that had so recently soothed Kishpa's burned flesh. The slig summoned his warriors.

"We have come a long way in search of the enchanted quill," said the slig. "We will not stop now."

"But the others have bullboggs to ride. How could you let this happen?" complained Ghuchaz, a young, ambitious warrior who chafed under Zarjephwu's leadership.

The entire band seemed to hold its breath. To question Zarjephwu was tantamount to a death sentence. Silently, they backed away from young Ghuchaz, who quickly sensed that he had gone too far. Meanwhile, Zarjephwu licked the top of his snout while he considered the upstart's challenge. His tiny eyes flickered.

Sligs don't apologize, nor do they make excuses. Ghuchaz, however, was smarter than the others. Before Zarjephwu made his move, the young warrior hurriedly made his own, piping up to say, "I think I know how we can overtake the bullboggs and catch our prey."

Startled, the leader of the sligs held back from his intended attack, asking, "How?"

Ghuchaz smiled knowingly. Zarjephwu was bigger and stronger, but the younger slig was far more cunning. In a short while, he would be the head of the band . . . and he would soon possess the enchanted quill.

In order to lull Zarjephwu into thinking he was cowed, Ghuchaz put on a meek face and eased up next to his leader to whisper the plan in his ear. "The bullboggs' tracks lead due west, and they're easy to follow," he said softly, tiny eyes flickering at his mates, who avoided the gaze of the young upstart. "We should head northwest; there's a settlement of humans there. We can raid them and get horses and bullboggs of our own. If the weather holds and there are no rain or dust storms, we can easily pick up the tracks of our prey again. We'll catch them in a matter of days."

Zarjephwu listened impassively. He knew the young one was right. It would be good to have someone this clever at his right hand. Or it might be dangerous.

The latter thought was on Zarjephwu's mind when Ghuchaz suddenly lowered his head and bit deep with his long, sharp teeth into his leader's unprotected throat. But he did not rip. Zarjephwu had been caught off-guard, yet was able to strike back with such speed and force that Ghuchaz's head was crushed before he even knew he'd been hit with two rocklike fists. The young slig's body slid to the ground.

Blood ran down Zarjephwu's neck, covering his hard, scaled body. The importance of the enchanted quill was never more apparent. Such a deceit would not have been possible if Zarjephwu had had possession of the writing instrument. It would protect his band—and, especially, protect him—by foretelling the future. His bite wound, his burns, they were just pains he had to endure. They were not important. The only thing that mattered was getting that quill.

\* \* \* \* \*

Clotnik paced in front of the bullboggs, the tethered animals watching the dwarf in stolid, buffalolike contentment. The dwarf kept looking down the shadowed deer trail, waiting to learn of Brandella's fate.

After the morning fog had burned off, Clotnik spied Tanis walking slowly up the trail, back to their camp. He was alone, his expression unreadable.

The dwarf's question was clear in Clotnik's face. Looking up at the sky, gazing anywhere but at Clotnik, trying to keep his emotions under control, Tanis answered, "She was afraid at first."

"And then?" Clotnik moved closer.

"I think she found hope."

The dwarf nodded even though he didn't understand what Tanis was talking about. Mostly, he just wanted to console the half-elf. "If there's anything I can do . . ."

Tanis thought for a moment. "Yes," he finally said. "There is something. Tell me everything you know about Brandella. I want to hear it, and remember it all."

\* \* \* \* \*

Clotnik talked, and Tanis listened. They sat on a hillock, catching cool breezes, as the dwarf told him the stories that Kishpa had passed down to him about Brandella. It helped, but even now the jealousy still gnawed at Tanis; he resented that everything he was learning was based on Kishpa's recollections. He wanted so much for her to speak to him directly.

Then he remembered that she had written him a note.

She'd told him that it was just for him, and that it was buried in Ankatavaka. He jumped to his feet.

"What is it?" asked Clotnik.

Tanis didn't answer at first. Doubt shot through him like an arrow. She had written the note to him when they were in Kishpa's memory. As far as he knew, it had happened only in the old mage's mind; in reality, Tanis had never been to the village. If he went to Ankatavaka, would the note actually be there? It didn't seem possible, but he had to find out.

"Come. We're going," he said, putting his hand out to the dwarf.

"Where?" asked Clotnik, taking the offered hand and hoisting himself up off the ground.

"To Ankatavaka."

\*　　\*　　\*　　\*　　\*

Tanis thought of Brandella, picturing her writing the note. Each time he imagined it differently. Once he saw her weeping upon the parchment as she wrote a letter of farewell. A second time he conjured up the image of her writing it with painstaking care, crumbling one sheet of parchment after another, unable to find the words to convey her feelings. The third time, she wrote a letter that told him how to find her if ever she were lost. He imagined that she wrote, "Look for me in your dreams." He promised himself that he would.

Clotnik, seeing the half-elf deep in thought, did not bother him. They rode side by side, heading west toward Ankatavaka, just one more day's journey away. When the dwarf told Tanis that the village was in ruins, abandoned decades ago after a damaging flood, it hadn't deterred him. He still wanted to go, telling the dwarf there was something there that he hoped to find.

To amuse himself, Clotnik reached for his traveling bag and took out several of his juggling balls: the brass, gold, and the glass. He hadn't practiced in more than a week, and he didn't want to get rusty. As the bullbogg beneath him lumbered along the trail, Clotnik began tossing the balls into the air in a lazy, steady circle.

A flash of movement caught Tanis's attention and he glanced over at Clotnik. It amazed the half-elf that the dwarf could so comfortably juggle while being carried aloft by a moving creature. He watched in fascination—until he realized that Clotnik was juggling the exquisite clear glass ball with the blue and green markings.

Tanis's lips went dry. He wanted to tell Clotnik to stop, but he feared his voice would startle the dwarf and cause an accident.

Seeing that he had an audience, Clotnik's exercise turned into an elaborate act. The brass ball flew high in the air, followed by the gold, then the glass. What had been a small, tight circle became a breathtakingly large ellipse, at the apex of which the ball almost disappeared.

Tanis couldn't stand it anymore. In as calm a voice as he could muster, hoping it wouldn't break Clotnik's concentration, he said, "That's very good. But I wonder—"

Suddenly, the bullbogg beneath the dwarf stumbled in a rut just as he threw the glass ball high into the sky. It went up at a crazy angle, far over to his right.

Tanis judged the trajectory and spurred his bullbogg into a gallop. The animal ran faster than the half-elf expected. He overran the glass ball; it was coming down behind him. Letting go of the tether around the animal's neck, Tanis leaped off the creature's back and tried to catch the quickly falling glass ball.

Twisting in the air so that he was looking up into the sky, Tanis hit the ground hard, back first. The glass ball was falling from the sky above him. He lifted his hands to catch it . . . and Clotnik plucked it out of the air just above the half-elf's outstretched fingers, the dwarf's bullbogg nearly trampling Tanis as he trotted by.

The dwarf circled around and rode up to Tanis, asking, "Are you all right?"

The half-elf didn't answer. In a silent fury, he picked himself up, dusted himself off, and then reached up and grabbed the glass ball out of Clotnik's hand. "Don't you *ever* juggle with that ball again! Not ever!"

Clotnik tried to take the ball back. Tanis wouldn't give it to him. "Why is it so important to you?" questioned the dwarf. "Why should you care?"

"Because I know what that glass ball cost your father."

"It's pretty, but it's old. It can't be worth that much," protested Clotnik.

"It was worth his life," said Tanis.

The dwarf didn't move. He just stared at the beautifully detailed glass ball in Tanis's hand. The orb's delicate swirls carried memories of blue summer skies and green forests.

"It was the last gift he bought your mother," the half-elf explained, softening. "He wanted her to have it even though he could not afford the cost."

"Then he *did* steal?" Clotnik demanded coldly.

Tanis paused. What good would the truth do Clotnik? For his part, Tanis wished he had been told that his father had been a good and generous man instead of being left to search out the bitter truth. In the end, it wasn't the truth that mattered, anyway, but what you believed to be true. The half-elf was the only one who knew for certain that Mertwig had once made a terrible error in judgment. That secret, he decided, would die with him.

"Your father," said Tanis, "was someone to admire and respect." Thinking fast, he explained, "Mertwig paid for that glass ball with his life because he and your mother were attacked by goblins who tried to steal it. He wouldn't let them take it. And he died fighting them, saving my life in the bargain. So, my friend, please don't juggle this glass ball anymore. Keep it safe, and when you look upon it, think of the love your father had for your mother."

Tanis offered the trinket to Clotnik, who took it reverently in hand. "On the soul of my father, you have my word," said the dwarf.

\* \* \* \* \*

The raid on the human settlement had gone well, Zarjephwu thought. Not a single human survived, and only one slig had been killed. The bold midday raid netted the remaining fifteen sligs a small herd of bullboggs and several horses, enough animals for each slig to have an extra mount.

They rode their animals hard, not caring if the beasts dropped dead along the way. When that happened, a slig would jump on another steed and keep on riding. By nightfall, they had caught the trail of the woman and her rescuers. Sometime during the following day, they would catch them.

That night, in their camp, the band praised Zarjephwu for his clever strategy and wise leadership. He wondered how many of them suspected that the idea of heading northwest to raid the humans had been Ghuchaz's. Not that it mattered. After what he had done to the young slig, he was safe from challenge. And once he had the enchanted quill, none of them would ever succeed if they dared to try.

Zarjephwu, lying on the hard ground, felt the pain of his burns. As he drifted off to sleep, his jaw opened and sharp teeth glistened in the light of the three-quarter moon. He remembered the man—or was it a half-elf?—who had kicked him into the cookfire and run off with the woman. His reptilian face settled into a smile. Sligs despised elves. He would see that one again tomorrow.

42

# The Ruins of Ankatavaka

The smell of salt air came wafting to Tanis on a gentle sea breeze. He knew they were getting close to the Straits of Algoni. And Ankatavaka. Unconsciously, the half-elf leaned forward on his bullbogg, straining to see some sign of the village beyond the wood in which they rode. He wondered if this was the same forest in which the human soldiers had gathered before making their charge upon the elven barricades. His father had been among those men.

Tanis pushed the memory out of his mind. He didn't want to remember his father. Rubbing the bullbogg's sweaty neck, Tanis led them, plodding, through the trees, finding only the barest semblance of a trail; what had been there before had long since been reclaimed by nature.

"When were you here last?" Tanis called back to Clotnik, who had fallen behind.

The dwarf muttered an oath; Tanis heard him swat back a branch that had blocked his path. "It's been at least sixty years. The floods came thirty-eight years ago. Maybe you remember that winter when it rained almost every day?"

"Of course. I was with my friend Flint." Tanis laughed. "We were making our way across a desert in Taladas when the rains started. Almost overnight, the desert was flooded. We had to save ourselves by grabbing hold of a drowned skrit. Have you ever spent three days holding on to the back of a dead, six-foot beetle?"

"I'm pleased to say that I haven't." Clotnik batted back another branch.

Their voices trailed off. Through the trees, Tanis saw an open field; beyond that meadow stood the crumbling walls of Ankatavaka. He pointed, about to call out, but Clotnik said, "I see it." Then, in a mournful voice, he added, "It looks so sad."

Even from a distance, the village had an air of death. They rode on, crossing the open field. It was flat, punctuated by no landmark except a lonely tree trunk. Tanis detoured to pass the stump, remembering. When he reached it, he looked down and saw with satisfaction that it was hollow.

The main gate loomed ahead of them. It was open, admitting anyone or anything to the streets of the village. But entering by way of the gate was unnecessary. What had once been a well-protected village was now a shambles of dilapidated walls that looked like ancient ruins.

As they rode through the gate, a gust of wind flew in with them, blowing dust and, it seemed to Tanis, carrying them on its wings to another time. Everywhere he looked, he imagined the village as he remembered it. He could see the elves on the barricades, east, south, and north. He could hear the cheers of the villagers when Kishpa's rain spell stopped the human army on the first day of the siege. And when he looked to the south, he re-fought the battle on the top of the barricade.

He remembered the arrow that had come out of no-where to save his life. Gazing across the open village square, he saw the building from which that arrow had been loosed. Brandella had lived there once, long ago. He had been in her room on the second floor, but only in Kishpa's mind. He wanted to see it again.

The two-story house listed to one side, one wall hav-ing collapsed. It looked as if the entire structure was on the verge of falling. He rode to it anyway, dismounted, and walked to the doorway.

"Where are you going?" asked Clotnik from atop his bullbogg.

"Inside."

"Too dangerous," cautioned the juggler.

"Don't worry," he replied airily. "I'll be careful." But, in fact, he bounded up a rickety staircase that had no busi-ness holding his weight. When he reached the top, he found the door to Brandella's home hanging by a single hinge. He pushed through and entered, finding the place stripped bare of furniture, one wall gone, the roof parti-ally torn away. The vast mural that had covered her home was so faded by wind, rain, and sun that it was nearly impossible to make out any of the images—save one. In a far corner, low on the wall, he saw a surpris-ingly fresh drawing. It depicted a man, seen from be-hind, his face unshown. Inside his body there hovered the figure of a woman, her face also unshown. He reached out to touch it. When he withdrew his hand, there was paint on his fingertips. His eyes opened wide. Was it still wet? Or had some of the color come off sim-ply because the painting was exposed to the damp sea air? And why was this visible when all the others had faded? If memory served him, her bed had been against this wall. Maybe whoever lived here after her also kept the bed against the wall, protecting it. Or maybe it had been painted, somehow, expressly for him. For this moment. By her.

A cracking sound caught his attention. A moment later, there was a loud crash and a cloud of dust drifted up to the second floor.

"Tanis!" Clotnik shouted from the street. "Are you all right?"

He went to the window. "Couldn't be better!" he sang out.

"The building is falling apart," warned the juggler. "Get out of there—fast!"

"I'm coming." With that, Tanis hurried to the door and made for the stairs—except that several steps in the center of the staircase were gone. It had been that portion of the steps that had given way, breaking apart and crashing to the floor below. The half-elf grimaced. Getting out was not going to be easy. But there was no other way.

Going slowly, putting all of his weight on each of the stairs, was the worst thing he could do. He had to take the stairs at a run, leap over the missing section, and hope that when he landed on the lower half of the staircase, it wouldn't collapse.

The half-elf took a deep breath, then plunged down the staircase at breakneck speed, his feet flying, taking three steps at a time. When he reached the chasm between the stairs, he jumped, soaring over the empty space and coming down on the lower section with his right foot. The stair broke.

Tanis bounced off the wall on his right. His momentum carried him down the staircase while he scrambled to keep his balance. Neither Tanis nor the stairs stayed upright. Tanis hit the last few steps hard and rolled out the doorway, into the street. The staircase crashed behind him, a cloud of dust following him out into the air.

Clotnik jumped down from his bullbogg and ran to Tanis, who waved him off. "I'm all right," said the half-elf. "I just need to catch my breath."

The dwarf's face reflected vying emotions: worry, fear, annoyance. His voice snapped like dry wood. "Just because this is a ghost village is no reason for you to end up dead. Be careful!"

"I'll do my best," promised Tanis, gasping for air.

While Tanis huffed and puffed, the dwarf wandered away alone to rediscover his own memories; after all, he had grown up in Ankatavaka. Clotnik had gone only as far as the center of the village square, however, when he stopped, looked up, and smiled.

A short while later, Tanis approached on foot, asking, "What are you looking at?"

"This statue," the dwarf answered with nostalgia. "I remember when it was dedicated. I had just come back by ship and had learned that my father was dead. Everything in my life had changed. I didn't even know who this person was," he said, pointing up at the weathered stone sculpture.

Tanis glanced up, and his face filled with a look of wonder. It was Scowarr! He stood there, a sword jutting from one hand, his head wrapped in bandages that were on the verge of coming undone. Underneath, on the base, the inscription read: "Let us not forget the Great Scowarr. He came as a stranger. He left as a hero."

## 43

# The Metal Box

While Tanis was telling the dwarf about Sco-warr, a movement down the street caught the dwarf's eye. "There's someone there," said Clotnik.

Tanis hadn't seen the figure.

"It looked like an old man who ducked out of the way when he saw us," Clotnik explained. "I'm going after him. If some of the elves stayed on after the others left, I might find someone who remembers my father."

Tanis hoped not, but he held his tongue. "Go ahead," he said. "I have something to do here, anyway." Correctly interpreting Clotnik's look, the half-elf promised, "Nothing dangerous."

Clotnik hurried down the street, heading toward the beach. The once-tidy cobblestones lay in disarray, with gaps that now bobbed with weeds. Tanis watched the dwarf until Clotnik rounded a corner and was gone. The half-elf was grateful to be alone. He didn't want Clotnik around to see his disappointment if he couldn't find the message Brandella had buried for him. Nor did he want the dwarf reading over his shoulder if he did find the letter.

Brandella had said the note was buried at the foot of the barricade where he had slain the giant spider. Judging the distance from the main gate and the street from which Mertwig had arrived to save him, Tanis easily reconstructed the spot. A bright orange wildflower grew there, vivid contrast to the pale green weeds that dotted the littered area. Tanis dug it up by its roots, considered tossing it aside, then—not quite knowing why—spent several minutes replanting it a short distance away.

Then he began in earnest. He took out his sword and dug it deep into the earth to soften the hard clay. Kneeling, he began digging with his hands, scooping out the dirt and tossing it next to him.

It was hot, hard work. The ground was unyielding, and there was no telling how deep the box might be after nearly a hundred years—especially if flood waters had deposited layers of mud over the land. And then, of course, there was always the chance that the box wasn't there at all. Tanis shook his head, refusing to consider that possibility, and kept digging.

He pushed deeper and deeper, until he had dug a hole a hand's span deep. Then twice that. Still, he dug . . . hoping . . . dreaming . . . wishing that his own experience in Kishpa's memory were as real as the mage's. After all, reasoned Tanis, didn't Clotnik say that Brandella disappeared at about the same time the half-elf took her away? And would Scowarr have been a hero had Tanis not been there beside him? Wasn't it possible that he, Tanis, had actually been there in the past, living and breathing, if only for a short while, somehow bridging the gap between memory and reality? "You're fooling yourself, Half-Elven," he chided.

Yet he continued to dig.

\* \* \* \* \*

Zarjephwu crept among the ruins of the village walls. The sligs had left their steeds in the wood and cautiously covered the ground between the forest and the village, not knowing if their prey was keeping watch. Zarjephwu's command had spread out behind him, using tumbled walls and piles of weathered debris as cover.

Soon Zarjephwu saw Tanis hard at work, trying to dig something out of the ground. He signaled his warriors to keep their heads down and wait while he studied the half-elf. When Tanis raised his head to wipe the sweat from his brow, the slig leader knew the man in the village square was the one he sought, the one who had kicked him into the fire. The half-elf looked worn and battle-scarred, but a light shone in his face, a light that the warrior slig interpreted as the euphoria of nearing a yearned-for goal. Zarjephwu gave the grimace that passed as a smile with sligs. He figured he knew just what Tanis sought.

The slig unconsciously rubbed his burnt, hard-scaled skin. Half of his back and one of his arms was discolored from his roll in the flames. Zarjephwu had spent the better part of two days thinking about what he would do to the person who had caused him this pain. He'd lingered lovingly over the goriest details.

It was clear to the slig leader that the half-elf was looking for something. And if it was buried so deeply underground, then it had to be something very valuable—like the enchanted quill. Zarjephwu grinned, choosing to wait and let the half-elf do all the work before the slig snatched the prize.

\* \* \* \* \*

Consumed by the task at hand, Tanis was unaware of the eyes that watched him from the ruins. The hole he had dug was nearly an arm's length deep, and he was finally ready to give up. There was nothing to be found. All he had to show for his clawing at the hard, rock-strewn dirt were bloody fingers and aching arms. In disgust, he threw his sword into the hole.

A strange sound greeted his ears: The blade clanged against something metallic!

Tanis instantly dove down on his stomach, sticking his head and shoulders into the hole. He pulled his sword up and tossed it behind him, scrabbling at yet another layer of dirt. There were more stones, more roots, and more crusted clay. And something entirely different.

It felt like the lid of a box.

\* \* \* \* \*

Zarjephwu had wedged himself partly underneath a large slab of stone that once had anchored Ankatavaka's main gate; lying under a rock where it was cool and damp came naturally to the lizardlike slig. With deceptively sleepy eyes, he watched and waited. He was beginning to worry that he'd seen no sign of anyone else. Where was the woman? Where was the half-elf's accomplice in her rescue? Had they gone to the shore and sailed away? If that was so, reasoned the slig, then what was the half-elf digging up?

When Tanis suddenly leaped into the hole, Zarjephwu sensed that his wait had finally ended. He gave a signal as he rose to his feet. Fourteen other sligs immediately appeared as if by magic, rising from their hiding places. Silently, they advanced upon Tanis.

\* \* \* \* \*

Tanis's heart was pounding harder than when he'd fought the giant spider on this same spot. He frantically worked his fingers in every direction, probing the edges of his find.

It was a small, square box, still brightly painted in reds and blues in the same distinctly feminine style as the paintings in Brandella's room, but dotted with specks of rust. His soul soared with hope. Hurriedly digging around all four sides of it, Tanis freed the box from its resting place of nearly one hundred years.

With the box finally in his hands, Tanis pulled himself out of the hole with a triumphant cry.

Had he looked toward the outer edges of the village, he would have seen the sligs coming toward him. But when he came out of the hole, his back was to them and he had no eyes for anything except his prize.

The sligs were spread out over a wide area, the nearest, Zarjephwu, a mere thirty feet away and closing in fast.

Tanis tried to open the box; it was rusted shut. He pulled his knife from his belt to try to pry it open.

Twenty feet away, the sligs began to come together as a pack. They moved with a deadly stealth, their spears, bardiches, and battle-axes already in their sharp-nailed fingers.

The knife seemed to help. Tanis managed to wedge it under a corner of the lid and edge it upward. The top was bending a bit, coming off, but slowly.

The sligs crept just fifteen feet away. Zarjephwu signaled to the others that he wanted to take the half-elf prisoner. The torture would be exquisite.

Then Tanis heard something . . . inside the box. It was impossible that an animal could have been in it; the box had been sealed thoroughly. Nonetheless, he held it a little farther away from his body as he popped the top off. Inside, he saw two things: the quill he'd given Brandella and a folded piece of ancient parchment. In large letters across the parchment, written in Common, was the emphatic warning, *Sligs Behind You!*

## 44

# To the Death

Tanis spun around to see long, reptilian arms stretched out to drag him down.

Knife still in his hand, he slashed at the hand of the closest slig, eliciting a scream. Two others hit him with their heads, butting him in the shoulder and chest. He went down from the impact, the metal box flying out of his hand. The quill tumbled free and fell to the ground. The note—Brandella's note—with the warning scrawled across it fluttered out of the box and down into the hole from which it had been dug.

Rolling sharply to his left, drawing a sharp breath as he tumbled over shards of broken cobblestone, the half-elf avoided a spear that clattered to the ground, narrowly missing one of his legs. His sword lay somewhere behind him. He was dead if he couldn't get to it—and probably dead even if he did. But he had to try.

The sligs swarmed after him, but the biggest one, the one with ugly burns on his body, shouted, "Get the quill!"

The sligs fell into confusion, momentarily breaking off their attack to follow Zarjephwu's orders. Tanis also saw the quill, but grabbing it and dying with it in his hand wasn't going to do him any good. Instead, he lunged backward for his sword, grabbed it by the handle, and rolled over and up unto his knees.

A tall, skinny slig scooped the quill off the ground. It didn't have the writing instrument long. Tanis swung his sword, lopping off the creature's arm and slashing into its chest with one sweep. The quill dribbled from lifeless fingers.

The closest sligs scrambled for the quill again. Tanis jumped to his feet, slashing at one of the creatures, but found his sword blocked by a spear held up at both ends by Zarjephwu. Black eyes with points of silver stared at the half-elf with palpable hatred; the powerful creature's muscles barely bulged with his effort. "The quill is ours," he said in guttural Common. "And so is your life." With that, he let out a stream of poisonous spittle, aimed at Tanis's face, trying to blind him.

The half-elf ducked out of the way, falling backward, trying desperately to keep his footing. Two arms caught him and tried to crush him: another slig. Tanis felt the air whoosh out of his chest as the creature used all its strength to squeeze the life from him. The half-elf tried to fight back, but his arms were pinned to his sides and he couldn't do anything to free himself.

Just as Tanis was about to black out, the slig suddenly let go. Tanis did not know what had saved him; he simply sagged to the ground. This time, however, another set of hands grabbed him and pulled him back up.

"Clotnik!" the half-elf gasped.

The dwarf had used his sword to stab the slig, running it through from back to front. The blade was still stuck in the slig, and Clotnik was unable to get it out.

Tanis couldn't help remembering that Mertwig had saved Tanis's life in this same place. Plucking from the ground the spear that had recently missed his leg, he tossed it to the dwarf. As he did so, Tanis, breathing heavily, managed to call out, "You remind me of your father."

Clotnik beamed.

"I'll thank you properly later," the half-elf added. "First, let's get Kishpa's enchanted quill back from these creatures."

The dwarf's face broke into a horrified grimace. "The quill?" he squeaked. "*They've* got it?"

There were thirteen sligs to fight, all bigger and stronger than the half-elf and the dwarf. There was no use in running; the pair would never get away. But that was only one reason for fighting. The other reason was that letting the enchanted quill, with its future-foretelling magic, fall into the hands of the sligs was purely unthinkable.

However, a very tall slig warrior held the quill high and was proudly passing it to Zarjephwu. Tanis didn't even think; he immediately forged in among the sligs. Clotnik plowed right behind him, his eyes a dangerous green and his weak chin nearly firm.

The half-elf blocked a blow from a bardiche with his sword, hammered another slig in the gut with a closed fist, but staggered under the might of an elbow that caught him in the side of the head. Meanwhile, Clotnik jabbed a slig in the thigh with his spear, and the creature fell to its knees. Tanis saw his chance. He jumped on the back of the fallen slig, gaining enough height to swing his blade at the enchanted quill held aloft by the tall slig.

Tanis's blade sang, cutting through the air, and then it sliced the quill into neat halves.

The bellow of rage from the snarling mouth of Zarjephwu made his fellow sligs cower in fear. He was so maddened by the loss of the quill that he broke the neck of one of his own warriors, who had stood between him and Tanis.

Clotnik tried to cover Tanis's retreat, stabbing the point of his spear into the shoulder of one slig and then smashing the other end of his spear into the snout of another. But there were too many of them, coming from too many directions.

Several massive hands clawed at Clotnik's legs, tearing at his skin with their long, sharp-nailed fingertips. More hands grabbed him about the waist, dragging him down.

Tanis tried to protect the fallen dwarf, but two sligs locked their massive hands on his sword arm, easily holding it immobile. As Zarjephwu charged at him, the two began bending his arm back. The half-elf knew they were waiting to hear the crack of a bone.

A shrill, otherworldly scream suddenly erupted from somewhere behind Tanis. In the midst of their murdering, all the sligs stopped cold. The two who were trying to snap Tanis's arm were so startled they turned to look. Even Zarjephwu stopped, shock sweeping over his features.

Though Tanis could not twist to see what had so surprised the sligs, there was something faintly familiar about the high-pitched scream. In the next instant, the two sligs holding Tanis let go and began to run. One was just a bit too slow. A sword slashed its back, and it fell, writhing, to the ground.

Tanis turned to face this scourge of the sligs—and faced Scowarr! The granite statue had come to life. The flapping head bandages, the impossibly high-pitched cry of combined fear and courage, the wildly swinging sword . . . it was the Hero of Ankatakava, in all his glory!

Tanis was so startled by the sight of his old friend that

he almost fell victim to the sharp edge of a slig broadsword. He dodged the blade at the last possible moment, even as he called out an exultant greeting to the magically awakened statue.

But Scowarr did not answer. His lips, gray granite, only screamed. He fell upon the warriors holding Clotnik down, slaughtering them as if he were an avenging god. The slender human's short hair, bursting in tufts from gaps in the bandages, bristled with vengeance.

Scowarr then turned and, shouting incoherently in his shrill voice, ran after a half-dozen fleeing sligs.

Another slig, however, did not run.

Zarjephwu was fearful of the strange, screaming creature with the flapping bandages, but he held no terror of Tanis, and it was the half-elf who had brought his band low. There would be no opportunity to torture the half-elf, but at least he would have the satisfaction of killing him.

The slig leader threw away his spear and bent into a crouch. His jaw opened wide and venomous spittle dripped from his tongue. He eyed Tanis with a lean and hungry look. The half-elf knew that the sligs often ate their victims, sometimes alive.

The slig moved on all fours, slowly closing the distance between them. Even in his crouch, the slig was nearly as tall as Tanis. Behind him, Clotnik moaned, his blood soaking the ground of the long-abandoned village of his birth. Tanis had to draw his enemy away, and so he backed up, keeping his eye on the slig with every step.

Zarjephwu enjoyed the pursuit. The half-elf seemed unnerved to him; the creature both hated and reveled in the weakness of his prey. Carefully, the slig maneuvered toward Tanis, forcing him in a certain direction, waiting for the right moment to pounce and sink his teeth into the half-elf's throat.

As far as Tanis could figure, he had retreated nearly halfway across the open village square. He cast a quick glance away from the slig to see Clotnik trying to drag himself toward his tethered bullbogg. If he was lucky, the dwarf might be able to get away.

Then Tanis backed up against something hard. He was trapped in the center of the square, his back against the base of Scowarr's statue. A moment of panic struck Tanis. He'd made a terrible mistake.

Zarjephwu sprang.

Tanis did the only thing he could think of; he let his back slide down the base of the statue while he kicked up with his legs. His feet caught the slig in the stomach, sending the creature still higher. Zarjephwu flew over the base. An instant later, he cried out and then went silent.

Blood dripped down on Tanis from above.

The half-elf looked up and, astonished, saw that the statue of Scowarr was back in place! Impaled upon the statue's sword was the slig.

Tanis rose shakily, looking up at his old friend, expecting a word, a handshake. The statue, aged and weathered, was as impassive as the stone that formed it. Had he dreamed that Scowarr had come to his aid and scattered the sligs? But then Tanis's eyes fell on the inscription below the statue. It had changed! Magically altered from the original, the new inscription read, *Now, is that funny, or what?*

Tanis roared with laughter.

## 45

# The Letter

"I've stopped the bleeding," Tanis said, looking down with deep concern at the pale, pained face of Clotnik. "You've been torn up badly, especially your back. Except for some very theatrical scars, though, you should be all right." He tried to muster a reassuring expression.

"I've got to be able to juggle," the dwarf said worriedly. "Will my arms be able to move naturally?"

"I don't know for sure," Tanis replied. "But I think so."

Clotnik seemed satisfied with the half-elf's answer and closed his eyes to rest.

Rising from the shade of Scowarr's statue, where Tanis

had carried the dwarf, Tanis let out a deep breath and felt his neck and shoulder muscles loosen.

Now that Clotnik was taken care of, he was anxious to retrieve Brandella's letter. He hurried back to the hole he had dug and found the folded parchment at the bottom. It was old, yellowed, and crumbling at the edges. He lifted it tenderly, lovingly, from its temporary grave and slowly walked back toward Clotnik as he read the words Brandella had written to him so long ago. . . .

*Tanis—Who Risked Everything for Me,*

*I write this now, just moments before leaving with you on what may be a hopeless journey. I know you are convinced that we both will leave Kishpa's memory, but I have my doubts. Should you make your way back to your own world without me, I want you to know how much I thought of you. And what I felt for you. But then you know that, don't you? You asked me once what binds two people together through time. I imagined that you wanted to know how Kishpa and I could love each other so deeply through all these years, so that you, yourself, could somehow learn the secret of finding such a love. How do I answer?*

*I must look to my weaving and tell you that the kind of love you seek is like one of my scarves. Just as a scarf covers the vulnerable throat from the cold, so does a deep and generous love protect what is vulnerable about you from the world. Love, like a scarf, wraps itself around you on the coldest of days, one more time around you when the winds of evil fortune blow their worst. And, like a scarf, a great love covers your heart. But also like a scarf, love can be easily lost or left behind if one is not careful to remember it.*

*Now you wait for me while I write a letter that you may never read. So I'll stop now, except to say that should you leave this world while I remain here, I will hold you dear in my memory. After all, what is memory except a way of keeping the things you never want to lose?*

*Farewell but Never Good-bye,*
*Brandella*

Tanis reached the gently snoring Clotnik and sat next to him on a weathered block from the village wall, re-reading the letter even as it crumbled in his hands. He tried to read between the lines, under the lines, around the lines—he wanted to understand exactly what she meant. Why hadn't she come right out and said what she felt for him? She'd expected that he somehow knew. Then, again, maybe it was better that he could imagine how she felt.

\* \* \* \* \*

As Tanis sat immersed in Brandella's letter, six of the seven dead sligs that littered the ruins began to stir. Although they continued to lie as they had fallen, something profound was happening to their bodies. Regardless of their size, shape, or the wounds that had felled them, they started to transform. Slowly at first, the huge hands became smaller, and the fingers lost their long, sharp nails. The transformation picking up speed, their skin lost its scaly hardness. Snouts shrank, jaws and teeth lost their carnivorous appearance. Ears got smaller. Each of the bodies began to change shape, clothing suddenly appeared to cover their nakedness, and weapons evolved in their hands. Soon the eyes fluttered open, though no breath passed their lips.

\* \* \* \* \*

"Kind of a slow reader, aren't you, half-elf?"

The cracked voice came from directly behind him, and Tanis instantly reached for his knife.

"Now, now. None of that, young fellow."

Tanis looked over his shoulder. An old elf, looking

none too steady on his feet, stood a few feet away. Faded tunic and woven slacks, many times patched but scrupulously clean, covered the wiry body. The half-elf put his knife back in its sheath. "You shouldn't sneak up on people like that," he said.

"Didn't sneak," the old man said with a sniff, amber eyes defensive. "Made plenty of noise, but you didn't hear me. I'm not surprised, what with you having your nose glued to that piece of paper."

Tanis refolded Brandella's note.

The old elf pointed at Clotnik and said, "He was trying to find me before, but I wouldn't let him. Don't like people looking for me."

Tanis could think of nothing to say.

The old elf grinned, his wrinkled face seeming a little younger. "It's funny," he said after a bit, "but that dwarf looks a little familiar."

"He's the son of Mertwig and Yeblidod," Tanis offered.

"Ah," said the elf, nodding his head. "I remember them. The dwarf was a—"

"Old one," Tanis cut in sharply, "keep your opinions to yourself." He glanced down at Clotnik to make sure the juggler had not awakened. He lay there peacefully, and Tanis was satisfied.

The elf made a sour face but said no more about Mertwig.

"Tell me, old one," Tanis asked intently, leaning close to the elf. "Do you remember a woman—a human—who lived in this village? Her name was Brandella."

The elf put a leathery finger to his lower lip. "Brandella? Let me see . . . she was Kishpa's friend, wasn't she?"

Tanis smiled happily. "Tell me about her."

"I've got to go," the elf suddenly announced, backing away.

"What's wrong?" Tanis asked in alarm.

"Don't like crowds. That's why I live here alone. Good-bye, now."

"Crowds?" Tanis asked. "A half-elf and one sleeping dwarf?" At that moment, though, he looked up and saw a sight that filled him with joy. Walking toward him were Flint, Sturm, Camaron, Raistlin, Tas, and—his heart shivered—even Kitiara. Even as the old elf backed away, Tanis shoved Brandella's note in his tunic and shouted a greeting, leaping up and running happily toward his good and true companions.

# 46

# Fistandantilus's Revenge

*Flint Fireforge was in the lead, long beard* swinging with his step and strong, short arms carrying his battle-axe over one shoulder. The others followed close behind. Tanis didn't notice, at first, that they were not smiling. In fact, had he looked closely, he would have seen that their faces showed precious little expression at all.

"I thought you were all spread to the four winds," Tanis called out as he narrowed the gap between them. None spoke a reply, but he didn't wait for one. He immediately shouted, "How did you find me?"

Again, he received no answer.

It struck Tanis that they must be bringing bad news or they wouldn't be so quiet. Even Tasslehoff Burrfoot seemed subdued—odd in a kender. Tas and Flint hadn't stopped once to bicker.

Tanis tried again. "I didn't expect to see you for five years!" he cried.

As the half-elf drew near, he looked his friends over with approval. They might have been bringing bad news, but he had to marvel at how fine they all looked on this particular day. Even with the memory of Brandella echoing in his mind, he realized that Kit had never been more beautiful. She looked exactly as he pictured her in his mind, both regal and wild, her bright brown eyes flashing with adventure, curls of close-cropped black hair creeping from under her helm. He was particularly pleased that Kit had come with the others, because that meant she'd forgiven him for ending their affair that last night at the Inn. Perhaps they could still be friends.

His eyes quickly scanned the others.

Sturm stood straight and proud, his armor gleaming, Caramon walked with his usual swagger, yet he seemed unusually independent of Raistlin—a change that Tanis viewed with approval. The young mage, himself, never looked healthier; in fact, he looked a bit younger. Tanis often remembered those days, when he and Raistlin were closer friends, with great fondness.

With arms spread wide to greet Flint and the others with claps on the back, Tanis cheerfully charged among them. He was met, in return, by Flint's battle-axe swinging at his head!

Tanis saw it coming and thought it was a joke. He didn't react—at least not right away. It was only when he saw that the weapon was coming at him too fast and too hard to be stopped in time, that he demanded, "What's the matter with you?" and tried to duck out of the way. But it was too late. If he hadn't already had his arm up high to slap Flint on the back, he never would have been able to block the descent of Flint's arm with his own. A blunt edge of the battle-axe hit Tanis in the shoulder, numbing him for a moment.

"Are you crazy?" Tanis demanded.

Flint didn't answer. His normally bright eyes were dull. He merely raised his battle-axe for another try at the half-elf's head.

Tanis turned to the others for help. Instead, Kitiara's blade nearly disemboweled him. Barely twisting out of the way, he demanded, "Why are you doing this?" Shaken and confused, he scrambled backward as the companions, eerily silent, advanced upon him, their weapons held high. The sun beat starkly on the scene. The weeds twisted in a slight breeze that did nothing to abate the heat.

The half-elf looked around wildly. "Why won't any of you speak to me? What's happened to you?"

When none answered, Tanis found himself instinctively reaching for the handle of his sword. But he would not draw the blade from his scabbard. *These were his closest friends.*

Then he realized what was happening.

"Fistandantilus!" he breathed.

The evil wizard had promised him death at the hands of those whom he loved most, if the half-elf and Brandella tricked him. From beyond Life, Fistandantilus had somehow brought his threatened spell to bear. And now Tanis's closest companions had come to slay him. Yet he could not possibly consider fighting them when they were mere pawns of the mage's magic.

He continued to retreat, frantically trying to think of some way to break the spell. Then it came to him: Scowarr! Perhaps more magic remained in the statue; perhaps it could be used to break the spell that held his friends entrapped.

He turned and ran toward the granite sculpture.

His six companions continued their slow and steady pace, following him with an inexorable certainty more unnerving than an all-out charge.

"End the spell!" begged Tanis of Scowarr. "Use your magic to save my friends. Whatever power was given to the stone of your statue, please use it now!"

The half-elf turned toward his old friends. They had not stopped their advance. They had spread out with the obvious intention of circling the statue and trapping him there.

Clotnik, roused by Tanis's pleading to the statue, opened his eyes and tried, blearily, to see what the danger was. The dwarf wondered if his mind was playing tricks on him. Perhaps he was delirious, he considered. Not trusting his own senses, he did not speak. Instead, he tried to rise and help Tanis fight this new enemy, not understanding that they were the half-elf's friends.

The dwarf got as far as his knees before he toppled over. A cry escaped his lips, and Tanis rushed to his side.

"Stay still," Tanis said, looking back at Sturm and the others. "You'll open your wounds." He would have thrown the dwarf over his shoulder and run, but he knew he wouldn't get far before his friends caught up to them. And with Clotnik in his arms, Tanis wouldn't be free to fight back. Yet even as he thought it through, the half-elf couldn't imagine battling Flint and the others.

The sharp stab of pain that brought Tanis to Clotnik's aid also brought crystal clarity to the dwarf's mind. While the half-elf hovered over him, Clotnik glanced back at what had so troubled him before.

"Tanis!" he cried, grabbing him by the front of his tunic. "Am I crazy? Where are the dead sligs?"

The half-elf looked back. Clotnik was right; the bodies were gone, all except the one that had impaled itself on Scowarr's sword. They had killed seven of the sligs. . . .

Tanis finally understood. These weren't his friends who had surrounded him and were coming in for the kill. They were the images of his six companions, gleaned from his own mind. The evil wizard's spell worked through the dead, his only conduit to the living plane. The magic was not as powerful as that which Fistandantilus had once possessed, but it was strong enough to destroy Tanis. At least the half-elf knew he could fight these spell creatures. But could he win?

The Caramon image broke from the circle and, with his head held low, ran deliberately at Tanis, trying to smash him against the base of the statue.

The half-elf neatly sidestepped the charge, tripping Caramon as he passed. The big man went down hard but quickly jumped back to his feet. Tanis no longer paid any attention to him, though; the Tas image was already on the attack with his hoopak. At the same time, the images of Sturm and Kit came at him from either side, their blades flashing silver in the sunlight. The Flint image was on the other side of the statue, creeping up behind him. Only the image of Raistlin held back.

Tanis finally reached for his sword, unsheathing it with a flourish. To his amazement, the blade glowed red!

The magic flowed once again from his sword, through his arm, and into his heart. With a lightning flick of his wrist, he cut Tas's hoopak off just above the would-be kender's hand. In the same motion, he parried Kit's lunge at his stomach and kicked Sturm's blade to one side.

Because Tanis was off balance from the kick, Caramon easily grabbed him by the hair and threw him into a crushing headlock. The half-elf countered by jabbing the point of his sword into Caramon's foot. The Caramon image immediately let go and tumbled over in pain, falling right next to Clotnik. The dwarf used the only weapon handy. He raised his brass juggling ball over Caramon's head . . .

"Don't!" shouted Tanis, unable to separate, even now, that this was not really Caramon.

Clotnik had no such confusion. He ignored Tanis, smashing Caramon's skull wide open with the brass ball. The image of Raistlin's brother twitched several times in death, then slowly turned back into a slig in front of Clotnik's disbelieving eyes.

Except for Tanis's words to Clotnik, it was a peculiar

battle, indeed, for there were no commands, shouts, oaths, or cries of pain from the remaining companions. Their images did not speak a single word or make a single sound. There were only the clash of weapons and a deathly, otherworldly silence. Even the breeze in the sun-bathed village square had stilled. It was as if the village of Ankatavaka—the dead stones, the weeds, the crumbled buildings—held its breath.

Clotnik battered Flint's right knee with an expertly thrown gold juggling ball; Mertwig's son was actually doing more damage than the half-elf. Tanis could easily have finished Flint off after Clotnik crippled him, but he looked at the face of his friend and could not bring himself to do it. He let him slip away, only to counter Flint's ferocious attack again a few moments later.

It was the image of Kit who drew first blood, her blade piercing Tanis in the thigh. It was a minor wound, but it brought home to the half-elf that he could not count on his defensive swordsmanship forever. Even with his enchanted blade, he was not invincible.

Sturm, Kit, and Tas regrouped as Flint was driven back, then came at Tanis all at once. The half-elf steeled himself, driving their faces from his mind, concentrating on their weapons and their bodies.

Sturm and Kit made their thrusts at the same moment. Tanis parried them both with one motion, then slashed at Kit's waist. She didn't scream. But he did. He had to turn away as her image crumpled over sideways.

His reaction left him wide open to Tas, who held a short, curved knife blade in his little hands.

Clotnik shouted a warning, and Tanis saw the kender image, its brown topknot swinging just like the original, but it was too late. The blade ripped at Tanis's sword arm. The pain nearly caused Tanis to drop the glowing blade. Grimacing, he flailed with the sword. To his horror, he ran through Tasslehoff Burrfoot. He watched in shock as the kender fell to his knees. Tanis wanted to throw his sword away in shame and self-loathing, but even as he watched, the little kender began changing into the lifeless form of a slig, four times Tas's size.

The sword of Sturm Brightblade was upon the half-elf before he'd recovered. Even with the help of his enchanted blade, Tanis was at the Knight's mercy. But a silver juggling ball, tossed by Clotnik, struck Sturm's blade, knocking it askew. Tanis brought his own blade to bear on the Knight's throat, just above the breastplate of his armor. Sturm—at least the image of him—was no more. Tanis felt bile rise in his throat.

Flint and Raistlin were the only ones left.

"Fistandantilus!" screamed Tanis, not wanting to kill them, too. "Give it up!"

"No need to shout," said Raistlin, his face expressionless, his voice the whispery, dead-leaf speech of the long-deceased wizard. "You have an odd assortment of friends, all of them good fighters except for this sickly mage. I easily could have had you killed and brought back to my world, but it seems you have had some magical help. I'll see to that interloper, you can be sure."

Tanis smiled. "If I were you, I'd stay clear of Kishpa. He just might be too much for you to handle. Besides, he'll have some help of his own."

"Who?"

"A great warrior named Scowarr."

Fistandantilus made no reply; Flint and Raistlin simply slumped to the ground, their bodies slowly returning to slig form.

In that same instant, Tanis's sword stopped glowing red. He raised it to the heavens and said, "Kishpa, I'm in your debt."

He sheathed the sword and wearily made his way to Clotnik, who sat propped against the base of the statue. "I'm glad that's over," said the dwarf, using one hand to stanch the bleeding from a reopened wound. "I was running out of juggling balls."

# Epilogue

*At the far end of the village square, the ancient* elf showed himself again, staying at a distance but calling out, "Do you treat all your old friends like that?"

Tanis laughed and shouted, "Be glad you're just an acquaintance." Then he waved for him to approach. Tentatively, the old elf made his way in their direction.

"This is the villager you chased earlier," Tanis explained to Clotnik, who nodded exhaustedly.

When the elf sat next to Tanis, he patted him on the back, saying, "You remind me of another young fellow who was here about a hundred years ago. Fought alongside *him*," he said, pointing at the statue of Scowarr.

Tanis narrowed his eyes and opened his mouth to speak, but the old elf, amber eyes nostalgic, continued, "That human, Brandella, that you asked me about?"

"Yes?" said Tanis anxiously.

The elf's creased face assumed a wise expression. "I remember her. She was a beautiful weaver. My wife had several of her scarves."

Tanis leaned close to the elf. "Do you remember anything personal about her?"

The elf paused to think, resting one elbow on a patched trouser leg. "A pleasant girl. Well-liked in the village, even though she was human. Actually," he confided, "I thought she was rather plain-looking, myself. Kishpa thought she was the most beautiful woman he had ever seen." The elf paused to consider, then added, "But of course, he had some human blood."

"What became of her?" Tanis pressed while Clotnik just looked on.

The elf, apparently tiring of the conversation, stood and brushed off his trousers. "She just disappeared one day," he said, leaving the impression that he, too, was about to take his leave. "Went off with a stranger. Kishpa went after her, but came back alone." The elf pursed his lips. "He never did say what happened."

*　*　*　*　*

When Clotnik was well enough to travel, he and Tanis left Ankatavaka together, heading east. They did not stay together long. When they reached a crossroads, Clotnik veered off for the closest town to show off his juggling skills. Tanis, however, craved solitude.

"Farewell," the dwarf said from atop a bullbogg. "We may never meet again." His sad expression deepened.

Tanis scrutinized his friend, memorizing the emerald eyes, slanted forehead, rounded body, forest-colored clothes. "You can be sure that you will live in my memory," the half-elf said.

Clotnik rewarded him with a quick smile so like

Mertwig's that the half-elf caught his breath. "And you in mine, my friend." Then the dwarf, sitting as straight as one can on a six-legged creature with an impossibly broad back, guided his steed up the path.

Tanis headed into the mountains near Solace. As he rode, he often read the letter Brandella had written him. It wasn't long, though, before the ancient parchment fell apart in his hands. It didn't matter. He had long since committed it to memory.

Cool, crisp days and chilly nights stretched out before him as the autumn season broke early in the high country. It was on one of these nights, as he drifted somewhere near sleep, that he thought once again of Kishpa and Brandella, the two of them sharing their great love. And then it hit him, and he sat bolt upright.

"It wasn't just Brandella whom I saved from Kishpa's memory," he whispered, "but Kishpa himself!"

He lay back down, smiling. What a master stroke, he thought. What a brilliant conceit. The old mage had contrived not only to save the woman he loved, but to save himself. For in Tanis's memory, Brandella and Kishpa lived together again, at the height of their youthful love, sacrificing what they wanted most in life—each other. What greater gesture of love could there be?

Tanis recalled their love as Kishpa remembered it. The half-elf knew he could change it all if he chose to. He could imagine that it was he whom Brandella really loved, and over time he could convince himself that this was so. The truth, he knew, was that memories not only fade; they change, become embellished, and are sometimes created out of whole cloth.

Maybe it never happened the way Kishpa remembered it. But it was a beautiful memory nonetheless. No matter how much he might despair, Tanis would know that a great love could exist—and might, therefore, someday exist for him.

* * * * *

319

As fall gave way to winter, Tanis began to brood that eventually, when he died, the story of Kishpa and Brandella would die with him. But there was another way that they might live on.

Tanis had planned to try his hand at sculpting upon leaving the Inn of the Last Home. Flint's metalsmithing had first sparked his interest, but it was the statue of Scowarr in Ankatavaka that truly inspired him. There was magic in that stone, and somehow it had come alive. He didn't know if he could fashion such a work, but he felt the passion to try. And he would do it in a way that was bigger than life.

He began in the winter, in the ice, snow, and freezing cold. He chose a granite mountain peak, painstakingly chiseling away the stone to suggest a face of ineffable beauty, intelligence, and warmth. With longing eyes, she looked across a narrow pass at the second of Tanis's creations: her desperate, headstrong, loving mage.

He worked on his masterpiece every day for more than fourteen months. By the spring of the following year, he didn't merely tell their story in stone, he told it in mountains—so that it would last.

He never left a signature in the stone or told anyone that he'd created it. It was his monument to memory. And imagination.

Tanis never picked up a chisel again. He left the mountains near Solace and disappeared. His adventures between the finishing of his creation and his rendezvous with the companions at the Inn of the Last Home will, it seems, have to await their own timely telling.

As for his sculpture, the mountain figures never came to life like the statue of Scowarr, but they did something even grander: They came to life in the minds of the untold thousands who saw them. People trekked from all over Krynn to be inspired by the images.

In time, a legend grew up about the man and the woman, and about the sculptor who had fashioned them. And this is that legend.